re rea Bolter has the In fact she's vice heir love-live geles ier husband a roll, at cafés, and watching romantic ready hundred times. Say "hi" at andreabolter.com

New York Billionaire is Andrea Bolter's debut title for Mills on. Visit her Author Profile page at millsandboon.co.uk

ner au pair, bookseller, marketing manager and seafront , **Jessica Gilmore** now works for an environmental y in York, England. Married with one daughter, one dog and two dog-loathing cats, she spends her time ng housework and can usually be found with her nose in k. Jessica writes emotional romance with a hint of ır, a splash of sunshine and a great deal of delicious and equally delicious heroes!

Wylie worked on a long career of careers to get to the e'd wanted from her late teens. She flicked her blonde ver her shoulder while playing the promotions game, her manicured hands on the backs of musicians in the business, smiled sweetly at awkward customers during ail nightmare known as the run-up to Christmas, and npletely lost in her car in every single town in Ireland vorking as a sales rep.

all that character-building and a healthy sense of to get her dream job, she feels—where she spends her reindeer slippers, with her hair in whatever band she to keep it out of the way, make-up as vague and distant y as manicured nails, while she gets to create the kind man she'd still like to believe is out there somewhere. rns out he is, she promises she'll let you know…after een out for a new wardrobe, a manicure and a make-

Andrea [illegible] has always been fascinated by matters of the heart. [illegible] the [illegible] girlfriends turn to for advice with their [illegible]. A city mouse, she lives in Los Angeles with her [illegible] and daughter. She loves travel, rock 'n' roll, sitting [illegible] romantic comedies she's always seen a hundred [illegible]

Her New York [illegible] Andrea [illegible]
A Book [illegible]

A fortunate [illegible] under, [illegible] charity [illegible] fluff [illegible] avoiding [illegible] a book [illegible] humour, [illegible] of [illegible] and a great deal of delicious food—and [illegible]

Trish W[illegible] one shelf [illegible] hair over [illegible] pared [illegible] music [illegible] the [illegible] got co[illegible] while [illegible]

It took all that [illegible] humour to [illegible] days in [illegible] can find [illegible] a memory [illegible] of dream [illegible] If it [illegible] she's [illegible] over...

One Summer in New York

ANDREA BOLTER
JESSICA GILMORE
TRISH WYLIE

MILLS & BOON

First Published in Great Britain 2019
by Mills & Boon, an imprint of HarperCollins*Publishers*
1 London Bridge Street, London, SE1 9GF

ISBN: 978-0-263-27661-9

0719

HER NEW YORK BILLIONAIRE

ANDREA BOLTER

For Alex

CHAPTER ONE

"WHY IS YOUR face blue?"

Holly froze in shock. She had just opened the door to the apartment she'd expected to find empty. But instead of flicking on the lights in a vacant living room she'd walked in on lamps already blazing. And a shirtless man sitting in the center of the sofa. Reading a newspaper. A gorgeous brown-haired shirtless man was reading a newspaper.

"Why is your face blue?" he repeated. Broad shoulders peeked out over the newspaper he was holding.

Why is your face blue? Holly heard the individual words but couldn't put them together to understand them as a question. She could hardly get over the fact that there was a man in the apartment, let alone make sense of the sounds coming from his mouth.

She checked the keys in her hand. Perhaps she was somehow in the wrong place.

And then she saw.

Her hands were blue. Cobalt Blue Two Eleven, to be exact. She'd know that color anywhere. It was one of her favorites.

It suddenly made sense. Just a few minutes ago she'd ducked out of the rain and under the front awning of the building to rifle through her duffel bag for the piece of paper that confirmed the address. The duffel held paint tubes and brushes, paperwork, clothes and heaven knew what else. The cap must have come off her Cobalt Two Eleven.

And she must have touched her face with paint-covered hands.

"What are you doing here?" Holly asked the shirtless man.

"This apartment belongs to my company."

He lowered his newspaper, folded it matter-of-factly and laid it beside him. Giving Holly a full view of his long, lean torso that led down to the plaid pajama bottoms covering the lower half of his body.

"What is it that *you* are doing here?"

The lump that had balled in Holly's throat delayed her response. She hadn't seen a half-naked man in a very long time. And she hadn't seen a man who looked like he did while he was busy being half-naked in…well, possibly ever.

"I'm staying here," she answered.

It had been a grueling journey, and the last thing she'd expected was to have to reckon with someone once she got here.

She blinked her eyes hard to pull herself together and tried not to panic. "I was told I could use this apartment."

"That must have been a mistake."

Mistake? What was this man talking about?

"I've just arrived from Florida. My brother, Vince, works in the Miami office of Benton Worldwide Properties. This is one of the apartments they keep for visitors to New York."

"That is correct."

"Vince arranged for me to stay here. He confirmed it last week. And he called again yesterday to Benton Boston headquarters."

"I am Ethan Benton, Vice President of Benton Worldwide. As you can see from my…" he gestured down his chest "…state of undress, *I* am staying here at the moment."

"Okay, well, I'm Holly Motta and I was counting on using this apartment. See?" She shook the blue-painted keys. "The Boston office left the keys in my name with the doorman downstairs."

"I apologize for the mistake. I have just arrived tonight myself. In the morning I will look into who is responsible for this egregious error and have their head lopped off."

The left corner of his mouth hitched up a bit.

Ethan Benton and his bare chest sat on a black leather sofa. Matching armchairs faced opposite, separated by a modern glass coffee table. The furnishings were spare. Two large framed photos were the only adornments on the wall. Both black and white, one was of a potted orchid and the other a maple tree.

Bland as a plain piece of toast. A typical corporate apartment, Holly guessed, having never been in one before. Elegant, yet all business. With no personal touches.

It was hardly the type of place where a beautiful shirtless man should be reading a newspaper. Not at all the kind of place where one brown curl of hair would fall in front of that man's forehead as if it were no big deal. As if that wasn't the most charming thing that a wet and exhausted young woman from Fort Pierce, Florida could imagine.

"Again, so sorry for the miscommunication," said the man that curl belonged to, "but you are going to have to leave. I will have the doorman hail you a taxi."

"Not so fast."

Holly snapped out of her fascination with his hair. She stomped over to one of the chairs opposite the sofa. Keeping her blue hands in the air, so as not to get paint anywhere, she lowered herself down.

"If your corporate office didn't have you scheduled to stay here, maybe it's *you* who should leave."

The corner of his mouth ticked up again—which was either cute or annoying. Holly wasn't sure yet.

"Obviously I am not going to leave my company's apartment."

Holly couldn't believe this was happening. This morning she had taken a bus from Fort Pierce to West Palm Beach airport. Then her flight to Newark, New Jersey had been delayed. When it had finally landed she'd taken another bus to the Port Authority terminal in Manhattan. It had been raining and dark by then, and there had hardly been a taxi to be had. She'd got drenched flagging one down. The cab brought her to this address on the Upper East Side.

And now—same as always, just when she was trying to do something for herself—someone else's need was somehow one-upping hers.

"What am I supposed to do?"

"I would suggest you go to a hotel."

Hotels in New York were expensive. Holly had been saving money for months to make a go of it when she got here. She couldn't use up any of her funds on a hotel stay.

"I can't afford it."

Ethan fixed a strangely searching stare on her.

While he assessed her Holly's eyes followed his long fingers as they casually traced the taut muscles of his chest down and then back up again. Down. And up. Down. And up.

After seemingly giving it some thought, he reasoned, "You must know people in New York that you can stay with?"

"No. I don't know anyone here. I came here to…"

Holly stopped herself. This man was a total stranger. She shouldn't be telling him anything about her life. He didn't need to know about her ex-husband, Ricky the Rat, her crazy mom, or any of it.

Maybe all that chaos was behind her now. Maybe the whole world was at her feet. Or maybe there were more hard times ahead.

Holly didn't know. But she was going to find out.

Hard rain continued to pelt against the window.

An unwelcome tear dropped its way out of her eye. When she instinctively reached up to brush it away before Ethan noticed she found Cobalt Two Eleven was smeared on the back of her hand as well.

"Are you *crying*?" Ethan asked, as if he were observing a revolutionary scientific function.

"I'm not crying," Holly denied. "It's been a long day."

"Perhaps you would like use the bathroom to wash up," Ethan offered. He pointed behind him. "It is the door on the right."

"Thank you." Holly hoisted herself up without touching anything, and made her way past Ethan and his curl of hair. "By the way—I'm not leaving."

Behind the sofa was a small dining table made of glass and steel like the coffee table. Four orange leather dining chairs provided a much-needed pop of color. Beyond that was a teeny kitchen.

Her brother had told her it was a very compact one-bedroom apartment. It would do quite fine. This was to be a temporary stepping stone for Holly. Either she was in New York to stay or it was merely a transition to somewhere else. Only time would tell.

She found her way into the marble-appointed bathroom and tapped the door closed with her boot. Made a mental commitment to also slam the door shut on her intense immediate attraction to Ethan Benton…astoundingly handsome, half-naked. Although it took her a stubborn minute to stop wondering what it might be like to lay her cheek against the firmness of one of those brawny shoulders.

Oh, no! She caught her reflection in the mirror above

the sink. It was so much worse than she could have envisioned. She had Cobalt Two Eleven streaked across her face in horizontal stripes. Like a tribal warrior. Her black bangs were plastered to her forehead in sweaty points. She was a scary mess. What must this man think of her?

Not wanting to get anything dirty, she used her elbow to start the faucet. With both hands under the running water, she saw color begin swirling down the drain. She rubbed her hands together until enough paint was removed that she could adjust the tap to make the water hotter and pick up the pristine bar of white soap.

Eventually her hands were scoured clean—save for a little residual blue around the cuticles and under the nails. As usual. She reached for the fluffy towel hanging on the rack.

Next, Holly wanted to get her jacket off before she tackled washing her face. She unzipped the sleek and stylish black leather jacket she had bought at the shopping mall in Fort Pierce yesterday. With Florida's mild climate, there hadn't been a lot of selection, but she'd needed something warm for New York. When she'd seen it, she'd known it was the one for her.

Ricky the Rat would have hated it. He'd have said it was highfalutin'. Yeah, well, falute *this*! Decisions were going to be made *by* her, *for* her from now on. Not based on what other people wanted or thought.

After her face was scrubbed she towel-dried her bangs and peeled off her ponytail band. Fluffed out the dark hair that had grown far past her shoulders. With the longer hair, she realized she already had a new look. New hair. New jacket. New city. She was ready for a new life.

Giving a yank on her tee shirt and a tug on her jeans, she was more than a little concerned about how she'd look to Ethan when she went back into the living room. Which was, of course, completely ridiculous because she didn't even know him.

* * *

My, my, but Holly Motta cleaned up well. Distracted by the blue paint on her face, Ethan hadn't noticed the other blue. The crystal color of her eyes. How they played against her lush jet-black hair.

As soon as she returned from the bathroom a rush of energy swept through the living room. He didn't know what kind of magic she held, but it wasn't like anything he had been in the same space with before.

All he could mutter was, "Better?"

It wasn't really a question.

He was glad he had nabbed a tee shirt from the bedroom, although he was still barefoot.

"Yes, thanks." She slid past him to her luggage, still at the front door.

He reached for his computer tablet and tapped the screen. Best to get Holly out of the apartment right now. For starters, he had no idea who she was. Ethan knew firsthand that there were all sorts of liars and scammers in this world, no matter how innocent they might look. He had his family's company to protect. The company that he was to run.

As soon as he could get his aunt Louise to retire.

As if a heart attack hadn't been enough, his beloved aunt was now losing her balance and mobility due to a rare neurological disorder that caused lack of feeling in her feet. Benton Worldwide's annual shareholders' gala was this Saturday. Ethan hoped Aunt Louise didn't have any bruises on her face from the fall he'd heard she'd taken last week.

Ethan owed everything to Aunt Louise and to Uncle Melvin, who had passed away five years ago. Without them he would just have been an abandoned child with no one to guide him toward a future.

His aunt had only one final request before she retired from the company that she, Uncle Mel and Ethan's late father had spent fifty years growing into an empire. She wanted to be sure that Ethan was settled in all areas of his life. Then she'd feel that everything was in its right place before she stepped down and let him take over. One last component to the family plan.

Ethan had lied to his aunt by claiming that he'd found what she wanted him to have. But he hadn't. So he had a lot to take care of in the next few days.

His temples pulsed as he thought about it all. Commotion was not an option. This exhilarating woman who had blown into the apartment needed to leave immediately. Not to mention the fact that there was something far too alluring about her that he had to get away from. Fast.

On top of it all he had a conference call in a few minutes that he still had to prepare for.

But with a few swipes across the tablet's screen he confirmed that all the Benton properties in New York were occupied.

Holly slung her jacket on the coat rack by the door and sat down on the floor. After pulling off one, then the other, she tossed her boots to the side. Ethan was mesmerized by her arms as they rummaged through her bag. She seemed to be made up only of elongated loose limbs that bent freely in every direction. Lanky. Gangly, even.

Downright adorable.

Nothing about Holly was at all like the rigid, hoity-toity blondes he usually kept company with. Women who were all wrong for him. Since he wasn't looking for someone right, that didn't matter. It kept his aunt happy to see him dating. But, of course, now he had told Aunt Louise that was all coming to an end. And he had a plan as to how to cover that lie.

Under her boots, Holly was wearing one red sock and one striped. She rolled those off and wiggled her toes. "That feels good..." She sighed, as if to herself.

Ethan's mouth quirked. "Miss Motta, please do not make yourself at home."

"I have nowhere else to go."

Holly death-stared him right in the face, putting on her best tough guy act. In reality she looked terrified that he was going to throw her out. She'd already been in tears before she washed up.

"Can't *you* be the one to leave?"

His stern expression melted a bit. What was he going to do? Toss her out into the cold rain?

She said she didn't know anyone in New York that she could stay with. Funny, but he didn't either. There were dozens—hundreds—of colleagues and workers in the city, connected with various Benton projects. Yet no one he'd call late on a rainy night to see if they had a sofa or guest room he could use.

Ridiculous. He'd sooner go back to the airport and sleep on his private jet.

He could pay for Holly's hotel room. Or he supposed he himself could go to a hotel. But—good heavens. He'd been in flight all day, had already unpacked and undressed here. Why on earth should he leave his own property?

"I do not suppose it will do for either of us to try to find other accommodation at this late hour."

"What's your plan, then?"

Ethan always had a plan. His life was structured around plans. He was about to embark on his biggest yet—moving Aunt Louise into retirement and taking the CEO seat.

"We will both spend the night here."

"Oh, no, I couldn't. I'm sure you're a very nice per—"

"I assure you, Miss Motta, I have no motive other than getting a peaceful night's rest. You will sleep in the bedroom and I will make do out here." He gestured toward the sofa.

"I need to think about that. That doesn't seem right.

Maybe I should call my brother. Let me just get my things straightened out." Holly returned to her task of sorting out her duffel bag, quarantining paint-stained items in a plastic bag.

She didn't look up at him until she lifted out a pair of white socks. They were splattered with the same blue that had been disguising her lovely face. "Occupational hazard."

"You are a painter, I take it?"

"Yup."

"And you have come to New York to pursue fame and fortune?"

"Ha! That would be nice. Who wouldn't want their work to hang in a museum or a gallery here…?"

"I sense there is a *but* at the end of that."

"I've been making money doing large pieces and collections for corporate properties."

"Office art, lobby art, art for furnished apartments?"

Ethan was well aware of that kind of work. He'd spent many hours with interior designers making decisions about the art at Benton developments all over the world.

"Indeed, the right pieces are vitally important to a unified decor. They announce a mood."

"A point of view," Holly chimed in.

"It sets the tone." He pointed at the two black and white nature photos on the wall. "Those, for example."

"Dull."

"Safe."

"Yawn."

They both laughed in agreement. A sizzle passed between them. It was so real Ethan was sure he saw smoke.

How alive Holly was. The type of person who said exactly what she thought. A bit like Aunt Louise. And nothing at all like most of the women he knew.

He flashed on a possibility.

Then quickly thought better of it.

"My aunt's new husband selected this apartment. He frequently comes down from Boston."

Ethan rolled his eyes. Fernando Layne was no favorite of his. Definitely no substitute for Uncle Mel. Fernando was a plaything for Aunt Louise. Ethan tolerated him.

"I will remodel this property while I am in New York. Perhaps you can advise me?"

What a stupid thing to say. He was never going see Holly again past this awkward evening interlude. An unfamiliar sense of disappointment came over him.

He generally steered clear of his feelings. When they did arrive they were usually of the painful variety and proved too confusing.

"Do you want to look at my website?" Holly gestured to the tablet he still had in his hand.

"I am sorry to be rude but I have a phone meeting in five minutes. I need to prepare."

"At this time of night?"

"I am expecting a call from Tokyo, if you must know." He also wasn't used to explaining himself to anyone. "I will take it in the bedroom," he declared.

Then he picked up a roll of architectural blueprints from the desk and marched down the hall, perturbed in twenty different ways.

Ten o'clock on a rainy New York night.

Holly had left Fort Pierce at eight that morning.

Hungry and tired, she absentmindedly ran her hand along the sofa where Ethan had been sitting when she came in. The leather still held his warmth.

She probably should have been afraid when she'd opened the door to find a total stranger in the apartment. Yet she hadn't felt the slightest inkling of fear. She'd felt ticked off, maybe. Or something else entirely.

It might have something to do with the fact that Ethan Benton looked less like a serial killer than he did the lord of a countryside manor. With his imposing height and lean muscles and that stunning wavy brown hair that had a touch of red flecked in it.

His tone was bossy, but she supposed it must have been quite a shock for him that a woman with a blue face, a tattered duffel bag and a squeaky-wheeled suitcase had just barged into the apartment he'd thought he had to himself.

Now she was trapped here with him unless she was willing to face the stormy night. The man—who may or may not have a British accent—definitely had the most soulful eyes she had ever seen. The man who was now in the next room, conducting business halfway around the world.

New York was getting off to a rollicking start.

Would he be angry with her if she checked to see if there was anything to eat? Should she care, given that this apartment was supposed to be *hers*?

A rumbling stomach propelled her to the kitchen. She'd picked at snacks all day, but had not had a proper meal. On the counter lay one basket of fruit, and another of breads and bagels. The refrigerator held beer, milk, eggs and cheese.

Had this food been purchased for her arrival as a hospitality custom? Or was it Ethan's? Or did it belong to his aunt's husband, who Ethan had said used this apartment frequently?

The sight of the food rendered Holly too hungry to care. Being hungry was a unique ache that she had experience with. Surely Ethan wouldn't mind if she took one shiny red apple.

She hoisted herself up to sit on the countertop. Let her legs and bare feet dangle. Smiled remembering the apple's symbolism here in New York. Like so many others, she was here to take her bite. With one satisfying chomp after the next, her mind wandered about what might be.

"Miss Motta!" Ethan looked startled to find her sitting on the kitchen counter after he finished his call. "Must you always make yourself so…so *comfortable*?"

Holly shrugged her shoulders and slid off the countertop. *Whatever*. If her sitting on the counter was a big deal to him, she wouldn't do it.

She jutted out her chin. "I bet you haven't eaten."

"Not since early this afternoon on the flight," he confessed. "Is there food?"

"Looks like there's eggs and some things for breakfast."

"We will have something delivered."

"Sounds good to me."

"What would you like?"

"You know what? I haven't been to New York in years. Want to get some famous New York pizza?"

"Pizza it is." He swiped on his tablet. "Yes, Giuseppe's. I ordered from there quite a bit when I was last in New York, working on a project. What type of pizza do you like?"

It was nice of him to let her choose. This man was a bundle of contradictions. Scolding one minute, courteous in the next.

"Everything," she answered, without having to think twice.

"Everything?"

"You know—pepperoni, sausage, salami, mushrooms, onions, peppers, olives. The whole shebang."

"Everything…" he repeated. "Why not?"

"I'll pay for my half."

His mouth twitched.

"Twenty minutes," he read out the online confirmation.

She eyed the kitchen clock.

"I guess I'm staying tonight." She crunched on her big apple.

A bolt of lightning struck, flashing bright light through the window.

CHAPTER TWO

ETHAN HAD A peculiar urge. The minute he'd said he'd sleep on the sofa tonight he'd wanted to lie down on the bed with Holly. Not to get under the covers. Just to lie on the bed with her. He wanted to relax. To hold her body against his. Caress her hair. Find out if those ebony locks were as silky as they looked.

Huh. A woman he had never met before, who had charged into his apartment and refused to leave. He had no idea who she really was or what she was doing here.

Yet he wanted to hold her.

The thought had interrupted his phone call several times.

He wasn't going mad. He'd just been working too hard. That was it. It had already been a long evening.

From the moment his flight had landed it had been one thing or another. He'd managed to sort out some of the details for the shareholders' gala. Many more remained. He'd heard there were construction delays on the low-income housing development in the Bronx that was so dear to his heart. He'd talked to a few people at the Boston headquarters to see how Aunt Louise was doing after the fall she'd taken. The news was not good. Then he'd worked on trying to resolve problems with a building permit in Detroit.

It had only been about an hour ago that Ethan had

changed into pajama bottoms and quieted down to read the newspaper. Before Holly had arrived, with the sparkling blue eyes and the creamy skin he now couldn't take his gaze off.

"While we're waiting for the pizza would it be okay if I took a shower?" she asked.

It would be okay if I took it with you.

Ethan surprised himself with the thought he didn't voice. He settled for, "Go right ahead."

Ethan did not like the way warmth resonated from Holly's body when she passed by him en route to the shower. Did not like it a bit because it stirred sensations low within him. Fierce sensations. *Urgent.*

The bathroom door shut with the quick smack that only happened when you closed it with a foot. Did she *always* shut doors with her feet?

His tongue flicked at his upper lip when he heard the sound of the shower. He couldn't help but imagine which article of clothing Holly was removing first. What each long limb might look like uncovered. Her torso was straight, rather than especially curvy, and he envisioned the smooth plain of her back. When he started to imagine what her… Well, he begged his brain to move to a different topic. No easy task.

Normally Ethan maintained a controlled world, without surprises. A world that allowed him to keep the upper hand. Maneuver as he saw fit. Because he was usually right.

Mushroom pizza, for heaven's sake.

A thirty-four-year-old man knew his own ways. Protected his orbit. Holly seemed to tip the universe off-kilter. Made the earth spin off its axis.

He preferred his pizza with only mushrooms on it!

She had to be stopped.

Yet he hadn't the heart to force her out on the street—

especially given the time of night. He didn't doubt that she was capable of fending for herself. But he didn't want her to.

That insane idea glimmered again. He needed to get it out of his head.

Ethan had too much to think about already. He was in a bind. Aunt Louise needed to retire. She'd had a distinguished career, and Ethan wanted her to go out on top. Concern was growing that she would sustain a fall in public. That word would spread. That people might remember her as a woman who had stayed on past her prime. That she was doddering, weak, bruised… All things that Louise Benton was most certainly not.

His aunt and his Uncle Melvin—his father's brother—had taken Ethan in as their own when he was nine years old. Now the time had come for the roles to be reversed. Ethan needed to make sure his decisions were in his aunt's best interests. His father would have told him to. Uncle Mel would have counted on him. It was the very least he could do.

But Aunt Louise had that one condition before she stepped down and moved from frigid Boston to the sunny compound in Barbados they'd had built for just that purpose. She wanted to know that Ethan would run their global business with a stable home life as a foundation.

Even though she and Uncle Mel hadn't been able to have children of their own, they'd experienced the joys and the heartaches of parenting through Ethan. In turn, his aunt wanted *him* to know the profound love of a parent for a child. And the united love and partnership that only came with decades of a shared life.

Aunt Louise would retire once Ethan was engaged to be married.

And because he'd become so alarmed about his aunt's

escalating health problems, and his responsibility to guard her reputation, Ethan had lied to her.

"You always say that deep down in your gut you know when something is right," Ethan had said, twisting his aunt's advice when he'd given her the news that he had met the soul mate he would wed.

Trouble was, Ethan had no such fiancée. Nor would he ever.

That was why he'd come to back to the States a few days ahead of the shareholders' gala. Tomorrow he was having lunch with the woman he planned to marry. In name only, of course.

He'd found a beautiful actress who'd be a suitable bride-to-be. This was New York, after all. There was hardly a better place to find a performer capable of pulling off this charade. He clicked on his tablet to the talent agency website where he'd located Penelope Perkins, an educated and sophisticated blonde with a stately neck.

It was a simple matter, really, in Ethan's mind. He'd chosen the actress and scheduled a meeting with her under the guise of hiring her for a promotional campaign for his company. If he found her to be acceptable and unencumbered he'd have her thoroughly investigated by Benton Worldwide's Head of Security, Chip Foley.

While Chip was completing a background check and every other kind of probe there was, Ethan and his stand-in fiancée would get to know each other and create a history for their relationship. Their engagement would be announced at the gala.

Penelope would also sign numerous non-disclosure and confidentiality agreements. She'd understand that if she were ever to reveal the arrangement she would be sued. Benton lawyers played hardball. They never lost their cases.

For her services, this performer would be paid generously.

It was a solid plan.

"Clean at last." Holly emerged from the bathroom while towel-drying her hair. A fresh tee shirt and sweatpants made her feel cozy after the day's journey. "Traveling makes you so grimy, you know?"

"Yes. I showered on the plane before arrival," Ethan agreed.

"You showered on the plane? How does someone shower on a plane?"

"I have a corporate jet. It does have a number of creature comforts."

Holly whistled. Highfalutin'. "I haven't flown that many times in my life. I'm still excited to get free soda and peanuts."

"Yes, well…perhaps you would enjoy all the amenities on private planes."

She tilted her head to one side and squeezed a little more moisture from the tips of her hair onto the plush towel. Sure, she'd like to be on a private plane, with a shower and enough room for her legs not to feel cramped into a ninety-degree position the entire flight. But that wasn't something that was ever going to happen, so she didn't see any point in discussing it.

"You have a little bit of an accent. And a kind of formal way of talking." Holly had a sometimes bad habit of blurting aloud everything that came into her mind. She called 'em as she saw 'em. "Are you American, or what?"

That left side of his mouth quivered up again in the start of a smile. "Boston-born. Oxford-educated. I would be the complete cliché of an entitled rich boy save for the fact that my father died when I was nine and I was raised by my aunt and uncle."

"What about your mother?"

The landline phone on the desk rang. Ethan turned to answer it. "Thank you. Please send him up." He headed toward the door. "Our pizza is here."

With his back to her, Holly was able to take in the full height of his slim, hard build. Probably about six foot three. Much taller than she was, and she always felt like a giant rag doll.

Ethan moved with effortless authority and confidence. Of course this was a man who showered on planes. This was a man who had been born to shower on planes.

Speaking of showers…it had been weird to shower in the apartment with him there. She knew there was no way he was an axe murderer who was going to hack her to bits. But she couldn't be a hundred percent sure that he was a gentleman who wasn't going to come into the bathroom while she was undressed.

A devilish thrill shot through her at the thought that he might have.

Attraction to a man during her first evening in New York was not on her itinerary. Especially not a man who had put all her plans in jeopardy.

She'd just have to make it through the night. In the morning her brother would help straighten things out about the apartment.

Staying here for a few weeks was meant to be the leg-up that she desperately needed. It would buy her time to find work and decide whether New York was where she should be. It had been two years since she'd kicked out Ricky the Rat. Two years was enough time to move on and move forward.

It was her brother, Vince, who had finally convinced her to take a chance. To take a risk. To take something for her own.

Maybe someday a man would fit into the picture. Not any time soon. She needed to concentrate on herself.

"Join me." Ethan gestured for her to come sit on the sofa after the delivery. He laid the pizza down on the coffee table, then dashed into the kitchen, returning with two plates, a stack of napkins and two bottles. "Will you have a beer?"

She took one from him and popped the cap with a satisfying twist.

As they sat down beside each other Holly winced involuntarily and moved away a bit. Being close to him felt scary. Strange. Strangely great…

He noticed her sudden stiffness. "I do not bite."

Pity. She held back a laugh. It wasn't fear that he'd bite that was bothering her. It might have been fear that he wouldn't.

Ethan flipped open the box and a meaty, cheesy, tomatoey aroma wafted up to their noses.

"I do not believe I have ever seen a pizza with this many ingredients on it."

As if performing a delicate procedure, he used two hands to lift one hefty slice onto a plate and handed it to Holly. Then he served himself.

"Ah…"

They groaned in unison as the first bites slid down their tongues. Unable even to speak, they each quickly devoured their slices.

Holly was the first to reach for a second. Then she sat back on the sofa and put her bare feet up on the coffee table.

"'Everything' is now officially my favorite pizza topping," Ethan confirmed, after taking another slice.

Observing Holly stretched out and seemingly comfortable, he did the same. His leaned back against the sofa.

Tentatively he extended one leg and then the other onto the coffee table, and crossed them just as Holly had hers.

And there they sat, both barefoot, eating pizza, as if they had known each other for eons rather than minutes.

She thought of something to ask. "Where did you fly in from?"

"Dubai. Before that I was in Stockholm. I have been out of the country for a month."

"Where do you live?"

"I keep a small apartment in Boston, near our headquarters. Although I travel most of the time."

"Your company has properties all over the world?"

He nodded and washed down his pizza with a sip of beer. "Yes. Some we build. Some we buy and refurbish. In the last couple of years I have been spending a lot of my time on affordable housing for low-income buyers."

"Vince told me about the development you built in Overtown. He said he was so proud to have been part of a project helping people in one of Miami's neediest areas."

That left side of Ethan's mouth rose up again, but this time it continued until the right side lifted to join it in one full-on heart-melting smile.

Holly almost choked on her pizza. She thought a person might enjoy looking at that smile for the rest of her life.

"After my aunt retires I plan to turn most of Benton's focus toward housing for homeless or low-income families."

"When will she retire?"

Ethan sized Holly up in a gaze that went from the tip of her head down to her toes. As if he were taking her all in. Measuring her for something.

When she couldn't stand the moment any longer she reached for another piece of pizza and pressed, "Does your aunt *want* to retire?"

Holly watched his concentration return to the conversation at hand.

"I think she must, whether she wants to or not. She has peripheral neuropathy. It is a rare inherited condition. She's starting to lose some of her faculties."

"I'm sorry."

"I am, too. She is a wonderful woman."

"She's lucky to have you looking out for her wellbeing." Holly didn't think anyone would ever care about *her* that much.

"I would like to see her relaxing in Barbados. Swimming in warm waters and enjoying her silly trophy husband."

"But she doesn't see it that way?"

"She has a stipulation that she is insistent on before she retires, the details of which have not been worked out yet." Ethan reached for his beer. "So, tell me, Miss Holly Motta, you have come to New York completely on your own?"

What did his aunt want? Was there a family secret?

Holly was dying to know. In fact she wanted to know about all of Ethan's joys and triumphs and struggles and defeats. Wanted to tell him all of hers. Though she couldn't fathom why.

Even if she had been open to meeting the right man—a man with whom she would share the deepest, darkest nooks and crannies of her life—it wouldn't be a man who showered on airplanes.

A man like Ethan Benton had no business with a girl who had grown up in a trailer park in Fort Pierce. *Never going to happen.* And she wasn't looking for someone, anyway. This was *her* time.

She chewed her pizza, suddenly agitated by the way Ethan continued to examine her, as if she was an object he was considering purchasing.

"I have to say I cannot remember the last time I was with a woman who ate half a pizza in one sitting."

"Of course not. You probably only keep company with women who eat one green bean and then tell you how full they are."

That crooked grin broke into a hearty belly laugh. "You are absolutely right. If they eat anything at all. You are definitely not like the women I tend to meet."

"Should I consider that a compliment?"

"Please tell me why you have come to New York alone."

"Who would I have come with if not alone? I haven't seen my mother in years. My brother, Vince, is doing well in Miami. I have no other ties."

She'd grown up strategizing and compensating for her unreliable mother. Looking out for Vince. Then working around Ricky's bad behavior. Juggling two or three jobs. Keeping the house clean. Making sure people were fed. Paying bills. Always being the responsible one. Day after day. Year after year.

"I'm through with being cautious." She couldn't believe she was blathering this out to a man she'd only just met. "Yes, I came to New York alone. No job. No permanent place to live. I don't even know if here's where I belong. That's why I was going to stay in this apartment for a while—to figure it out. I'm sure it all sounds insane to you."

"How it sounds is brave."

Ethan furrowed his brow. A minute ago Holly had confided that she wasn't in contact with her mother. No mention of a father. He sensed there was plenty more that she hadn't said. That she'd been through more than her share of trouble and strife. Although it might be a made-up story meant to evoke sympathy from him to let her stay in the apartment.

Every previous experience he'd had with women other than Aunt Louise had led him to believe that they were never what they seemed.

Starting with his own mother.

Do not trust *trust*. It was a lesson he'd learned decades ago.

That was why he'd devised this scheme to set up a fake relationship, so that Aunt Louise would think she had gotten her wish. She would retire with her mind at ease and her attention on her health.

An imitation fiancée would suit him perfectly. The women he'd known before had always wanted something from him. With this arrangement he'd dreamt up everyone would get what they were after. Clean and upfront, with clear expectations and no disappointment.

After he and Holly had finished eating she retrieved a pad and pencils from her luggage and sat herself in the window, with its second-floor view out onto the street. She turned sideways, somehow wedging her long legs into the windowsill, and propped her sketchpad on her knees.

"You are welcome to pull a chair over," Ethan tossed out, not in the habit of contorting himself to fit into small spaces.

"I'm fine, thanks."

Unsure what to do with himself, he picked up his tablet to check emails. If he'd been there alone, as planned, he would have gone to bed. It was going to be a busy week.

He could ask Holly to take her things into the bedroom. Then he could turn off the lights, try to get comfortable on the sofa and hope to fall asleep.

Yet it was so unusual for him to be in an apartment with someone he craved her company and wanted to prolong it. He wasn't ready for her to retreat to separate quarters.

How crazy was the idea that kept popping into his mind?

As Holly drew, he began telling her more about Aunt

Louise. About the cruel medical condition that was taking away pieces of her.

"How did your family's company get started?" she asked, while working on her drawing.

"With nothing. When my father and Uncle Mel were in their twenties they saved their money from doing carpentry work until they had enough to buy the South Boston apartment they grew up in. Then they bought the whole building. And then the one next to it."

"That takes focus and determination. Hmm..." She shook her head.

"Hmm—what?"

She kept her eyes on her pad. "It's just that nobody I've ever known has done anything like that."

"After my uncle married Louise, she helped them grow the business. My father died twenty-five years ago. Then Aunt Louise took over as CEO when Uncle Mel died five years ago."

Ethan had only vague memories of his father. But he so missed the uncle who had become a second father to him. Melvin Benton had been a smart leader. A just and fair man.

"Uncle Mel would have agreed that it is time for Aunt Louise to step down. Before industry gossip sullies her reputation as the competent successor to his legacy that she was."

"What is it that your aunt wants you to do before she'll agree to retire?"

Oh, so Holly had been paying close attention earlier, when he'd started to tell her about Aunt Louise's request and then stopped himself.

"She wants to see me established in my personal life. For me to have what she and Uncle Mel had. She is waiting for me to be engaged to be married."

"And now you are?"

"So to speak…"

"There's no 'so to speak.' You're either engaged or you're not."

"Not necessarily."

Why had he started this? He'd revealed more than he should have.

"Tell me," she persisted, without looking up.

"I would rather talk about you. You have come to New York with no work here at all? This city can be a very tough place."

"I know. But I do have some people to contact. You're probably thinking my coming to New York was a really reckless bet. But if I didn't do it now I never would have."

When Ethan glanced down to the inbox on his tablet his eyes opened wide at the latest email. It was the talent agency, apologizing for contacting him so late in the evening and asking for the duration of his booking for Penelope Perkins, his soon-to-be "fiancée." Because, the representative explained, Mrs. Perkins had just informed them of her pregnancy. She expected to be available for a few months but, after that her altered appearance might be an issue for any long-term acting assignment.

Good heavens. *Yes*, Mrs. Perkins's blossoming pregnancy was going to be an issue! That would be too much to disguise from Aunt Louise. First an engagement and then a pregnancy right away? Not to mention the fact that Penelope was apparently *Mrs.* Perkins. And a certain *Mr.* Perkins was be unlikely to be agreeable to such an arrangement.

The veins in Ethan's neck pulsed with frustration. As if he didn't have enough to do! Now the engagement plan he'd worked so hard to devise was in jeopardy. Could he choose someone else and get an appointment with her in time? He quickly tabbed through the photos of the other actresses on the website. They were all of a suitable age. Any one of them might do.

Then he glanced up to lovely Holly, sketching in the windowsill.

What if…?

He'd been exchanging pleasant conversation with Holly all evening. Why *not* her? It might work out quite nicely. Perhaps they could have an easy, friendly business partnership based on mutual need. He had a lot he could offer her.

Of course the fact that he found her so interesting was probably *not* a plus. It might add complication. But who was to say that he wouldn't have been attracted to Penelope Perkins, or some other actress he'd chosen?

A sense of chemistry would be palpable to Aunt Louise and anyone else they would encounter. It would make them believable as a couple. And he certainly wouldn't be acting on any impulses. It wasn't as if he was open to a genuine relationship.

A fake fiancée was all he was looking for. Holly was as good a bet as any.

He gazed at her unnoticed for a moment. She turned to a new page on her sketchpad. Then, when she asked him again about whether or not he was engaged, he finally told her the truth.

He picked up the beer he had been drinking with the pizza. Carefully peeling off the label that circled the neck of the bottle, he rolled it into a ring. And then stepped over to Holly in front of the window. Where anyone in New York could be walking by and might look up to see them.

"I was intending to hire an actress," he explained. "But I think Aunt Louise would like you. You remind me of her. There is something very…real about you."

He got down on one knee. Held up the beer label ring in the palm of his hand.

She gasped.

"Holly, I do not suppose you would… If you might consider… Would you, please? Can you pretend to marry me?"

CHAPTER THREE

"HEAR ME OUT," Ethan said, still on one knee.

Holly had been so stunned by his proposal that moments stood still in time. It was as if she watched the scene from outside her body.

In an Upper East Side apartment in New York an elegant man with wavy brown hair waited on bended knee after proposing to his dark-haired intended. Would she say yes?

Holly couldn't remember if she had dreamt of a moment like this when she was a little girl. A dashing prince, the romantic gesture of kneeling, white horse at the ready. She'd probably had those fantasies at some point but she couldn't recall them. They were buried under everything else.

Most of Holly's memories were of hard times.

Growing up, it had been her alarm clock that had snapped her out of any dreams she might have had. The clock had made her spring her up quickly to check if her mother had woken up and was getting dressed for work. Or if she wasn't going to get out of bed. Or hadn't made it home at all during the night. Leaving Holly to scrounge together breakfast and a sack lunch for her and Vince.

No, Holly hadn't had much time for fairy-tale dreams. She'd been proposed to before. After all, she'd been married. But Ricky's offer had been about as heartfelt as their marriage had been. It had been on a sweaty, humid day in his beat-up old truck and it had gone something like, "I guess you want to get married..."

At the time, she'd thought that was about as good as it was going to get.

"It would be strictly business, of course." Ethan continued with his proposition. "An engagement in name only."

So Holly's second marriage proposal was to be just as unromantic as her first.

A twinge of despair pinged through her.

Ethan was suggesting a fake engagement to appease his aunt and get her to retire before poor health tarnished her standing. She understood why he was asking, but she didn't see what would be in it for her.

He anticipated her immediate trepidation and added, "We can negotiate a contract that is mutually beneficial."

"That certainly sounds cut and dried, Mr. Benton."

Even having this discussion was making her uncomfortable. Because it brought up notions like a little girl's dreams and happily-ever-afters. Thoughts she couldn't afford to linger on. Not then and not now.

She squinted at him. "Could you please get up?"

"I can."

He rose, yet still held out the beer bottle label. Looking down at it he assured her, "We would purchase a proper engagement ring."

"Let's put the paper ring down for a minute, okay?"

He laid it gently onto the coffee table as if it was a thing of great value. "I have a scenario..." He gestured toward the sofa.

She followed him, but this time didn't sit next to him as she had when they were eating pizza. She chose one of the black chairs opposite him. Best to keep her distance.

"May I be frank?"

"Oh...okay," Holly answered with apprehension.

"You are new to New York. You mentioned that you do

not yet have work. You mentioned that you could not afford to stay in a hotel. I am offering you very easy temporary employment. Pose as my fiancée. What I would pay you will help you establish yourself here. Shall we bring it to the bargaining table? Name your price."

"Name my *price*!" Such a ruthless businessman! Everything was a deal to him. "Are you used to getting everything you want simply by demanding it?"

"Oh, I always get what I want." His stare drilled into her.

Wow, what a predator. And why did that excite her rather than repel her?

Just for entertainment's sake, she took a minute to fantasize what being his pretend fiancée might be like. She'd probably be physically near him quite a bit. He'd have his arm around her shoulder. Sometimes around her waist. They'd hold hands. He'd probably even place a kiss on her cheek in front of other people, just to put on a convincing show.

Holly snuck a glance at his mouth. Ripe lips that looked to be endlessly kissable. No way would a plan that involved her standing close to his lips ever, *ever* be a good idea.

But it didn't matter, because she was just playing along hypothetically. "I'm not for hire by the hour!" She feigned indignation.

"There need not be anything sordid about it, Miss Motta." Ethan eyed the paper ring on the table. "I assure you I am only proposing a trade agreement."

She didn't doubt that. This was a man who'd already said he kept company with stunning, glamorous women who ate one green bean. He'd never be interested in her romantically. She'd have nothing to worry about there.

But she couldn't resist throwing in for fun, "My brother, Vince, is up for a promotion in your Miami office. Let's say this deal included helping him along in his career…"

"Done," Ethan answered quickly. "I would have to look at his human resources file and speak with the people who work with him. But if he is deserving, I would certainly look to promote my future brother-in-law."

He leaned forward. Even though there was the coffee table between them, she could feel him zeroing in on her. Coming in for the kill. Determined to make the sale.

"What else, Miss Motta?"

He was so maddeningly sure of himself. Holly hadn't met many people who were like that.

She sat dumbfounded, way out of her league.

Ethan raised a finger in the air with a thought. "Shall we consider it another way? You need somewhere to live. How about if I give you this apartment? I will put it in your name."

Holly tried to keep her eyes from bugging out. *How about if I give you this apartment?* Who even *said* that?

"As you can imagine, real estate is something I have as a bartering tool. Regardless of what happens, you will have a home in New York."

A home in New York. He really did know how to persuade a deal.

"What is it that might happen?" She had no intention of taking him up on his offer, but she was curious. "How is it that you see this working?"

He'd obviously thought this through well. Today was Monday. His aunt Louise and her boy-toy husband, Fernando, would be coming down from Boston this week in preparation for their Saturday shareholders' gala. He'd present Holly to them on Wednesday night.

"Dinner. Le Cirque. Or one of the new Asian-Spanish fusion restaurants in Tribeca. Something flashy that shows us as a hip New York couple on top of the trends."

"How about instead I throw a pot roast in the slow cooker?" Holly countered, batting him the idea.

His mouth tipped. "A home-cooked meal? Like she and Uncle Mel used to make on Sundays? Brilliant!"

Holly was no gourmet cook, but she knew how to work with the basics. She'd had to learn if she and her brother were ever going to eat. When they were kids she'd search through the pockets of pants left on the floor. Between the couch cushions. Under the seats in the car. Somehow she'd find enough money to buy a few groceries and put a meal together for her and Vince. Restaurant visits had been few and far between.

"Mashed potatoes. Roasted carrots. Apple pie..." She completed the menu.

"Perfect. I will try to be of assistance."

"Continue," she requested.

It was amusing to hear Ethan's outline for the masquerade that she wasn't actually going to be any part of.

Their next appearance would be at the shareholders' gala on Saturday, where Holly would be formally introduced as Ethan's fiancée.

"So I'd look amazing that night? Dress? Jewels? Hair and makeup? The whole nine yards?"

He sat silent for a minute, as if lost in his own memories. But then he snapped back with, "Of course. A couture gown would be chosen for you. My tuxedo tie will match your attire."

"It'd be a crime if it didn't."

Then there would be an engagement party in Boston. A month or so later would come the announcement that Aunt Louise was stepping down. A grand retirement luncheon would send her off in style.

"In between those dates," Ethan explained, "I would travel, so that you and I should not have to attend many events together. I will devise reasons that I have to spend prolonged periods in Florence or Sydney or the like."

Ethan went on. After those appearances Aunt Louise

and Fernando would move to Barbados as planned. Ethan and Holly—the happy couple—would fly to the island for long weekends three or four times during the first year. In between those visits Holly would be free to live the life she chose, as long as there was nothing criminal or anything that attracted attention.

Then they'd evaluate. They could continue to visit Aunt Louise and make excuses as to why they hadn't yet married. Or they could tell fibs about a lavish wedding that would take an entire year to plan.

"Or," he continued, "especially if you were to meet someone else and need to be free, we could call off the engagement. Aunt Louise would be settled into her island life of leisure. By that point there would not be any danger of her wanting to return to frigid Boston and the working grind."

"And what if *you* were the one to meet someone?" she clipped, pretending to advocate a deal for herself.

"Impossible!" he spat immediately. "I will never marry."

His harshness hit her like a slap in the face.

Or perhaps it was a warning.

"I see," she assured him, and knew she'd understood his underlying message.

"Therefore, when we split up, you will own this apartment outright—which you can either keep, lease or sell. And the engagement ring. And whatever clothing and jewels have been purchased. Your brother's position will be secure. We can also agree on a monetary settlement. In exchange for very little labor on your part, I can provide you with a lifetime of comfort and luxury."

Game over.

Enough was enough.

Even if it could be as simple as he made it sound she had come to New York to get her own life straightened out. Not to get tangled up in someone else's.

"Ethan, I appreciate the offer. And I think it's great that you've done so much planning on this. It shows how much you care about your aunt. But this is not for me."

He swallowed hard. His Adam's apple bobbed in his throat. His jaw tightened.

Was he upset?

Of course. This was a man who was used to getting everything he wanted. It wasn't personal. She was a mere obstacle for him to overcome in order to reach his goal.

Ethan tapped his tablet. "Holly Motta dot com—is that it?"

She nodded, yes. What was he up to?

He typed.

"Huh…" His thumb slid through what she assumed to be her website's gallery. "Huh…"

What was he thinking? She took great pride in her work. Suddenly it mattered to her what he thought of it. Which was silly, because his opinion was of no concern to her at all. Yet she sat on the edge of the chair, spine held stiff as she waited for a comment.

His thumb continued to swipe the tablet.

"Hmm…" His next sound was at a higher pitch than the one before. It sounded like approval.

"Why are you looking at my website?"

Ethan ignored the question and continued. His finger slid less frequently. He was spending more time on each piece of work.

Holly imagined what it might feel like to have that thumb slide across her cheek instead of the tablet screen. Or slowly down the center of her chest. That thumb and its nine partners on those two big hands looked as if they'd always know exactly what to do.

More fantasy. She hadn't been touched in a long, long time.

Finally Ethan looked from the screen to her. "These are extraordinary."

"Thank you," she breathed with gratification—and relief.

He raised a finger in the air again. "Perhaps we can negotiate a merger that would be satisfying to both of us."

She squished her eyebrows.

"In exchange for you posing as my fiancée, as I have outlined, you will be financially compensated and you will become legal owner of this apartment and any items such as clothes and jewels that have been purchased for this position. Your brother's career will not be impacted negatively should our work together come to an end. *And...*" He paused for emphasis.

Holly leaned forward in her chair, her back still board-straight.

"I have a five-building development under construction in Chelsea. There will be furnished apartments, office lofts and common space lobbies—all in need of artwork. I will commission you for the project."

Holly's lungs emptied. A commission for a big corporate project. That was exactly what she'd hoped she'd find in New York. A chance to have her work seen by thousands of people. The kind of exposure that could lead from one job to the next and to a sustained and successful career.

This was all too much. Fantastic, frightening, impossible… Obviously getting involved in any way with Ethan Benton was a terrible idea. She'd be beholden to him. Serving another person's agenda again. Just what she'd come to New York to get away from.

But this could be a once-in-a-lifetime opportunity. An apartment. A job. It sounded as if he was open to most any demand she could come up with. She really did owe it to herself to contemplate this opportunity.

Her brain was no longer operating normally. The clock on Ethan's desk reminded her that it was after midnight. She'd left Fort Pierce early that morning.

"That really is an incredible offer…" She exhaled. "But I'm too tired to think straight. I'm going to need to sleep on it."

"As you wish."

Holly moved to collect the luggage she'd arrived with. Ethan beat her to it and hoisted the duffel bag over his shoulder. He wrenched the handle of the suitcase. Its wheels tottered as fast as her mind whirled as she followed him to the bedroom.

"Good night, then." He placed the bags just inside the doorway and couldn't get out of the room fast enough.

Before closing the door she poked her head out and called, "Ethan Benton, you don't play fair."

Over his shoulder, he turned his face back toward her. "I told you. I always get what I want."

Holly shut the door with her bare foot and leaned back against it. She pursed her lips together to keep from screaming. Her heart thumped so loud she was sure Ethan would hear it in the other room. *Goodness gracious.*

Ethan Benton and his proposition were quite simply the most exciting things that had ever happened to her!

A rush went through her as she recalled that devilish grin creeping slowly up his mouth. Those deep brown eyes that had stayed glued on her, assuring her he was listening to her when she spoke.

Holly hadn't talked and listened as much as she had tonight in a long time. She hadn't dated anyone since leaving Ricky the Rat two years ago. With her in Fort Pierce and Vince a two-hour drive away in Miami, she usually saw her brother twice a month. There was a girls' night here and there with friends. That was about it.

She hadn't really thought about it, but now when she did she realized she led a fairly solitary existence. Hopefully New York would jostle that, along with everything else.

But the change *wasn't* going to come by stepping into Ethan Benton's life. Although it might be the most fun she'd ever have. A jet-set world she'd only read about in magazines… Who wouldn't want to dash off to Barbados for long weekends? To walk on pink sand with her toes in sparkling blue water. Attend glitzy parties…throw some of her own. Buy clothes without looking at the price tag. Never worry about where the rent or her next meal was coming from. Have the best of everything.

It would be amazing—even if it was only for a short time—to be completely taken care of. After all those years of putting other people ahead of her.

Which reminded her of how this deal could benefit her brother. Becoming part of the Benton family, even in name only, might help him further his career in a way he'd never have the chance to otherwise. He'd get to spend more time with Ethan and Louise. They'd see up close how capable and special he was.

No. This wasn't about Vince. He'd be fine on his own. He was a grown man and his career was underway.

It was time for *her* future to begin. Period. In the morning she would tell Ethan no.

Besides, once he heard that she had already been married and divorced he wouldn't think she was an appropriate choice for his game.

Right now, she needed to get some sleep.

She stopped short at the sight of the room's king-size bed. This was where Ethan Benton had been planning to lay that tall, sturdy frame of his tonight. A wiggle shot up her spine at the mental image of him stretched out on this bed. Perhaps only wearing the plaid pajama bottoms as when she'd first seen him on the sofa.

On the bed she counted one, two…eight plush pillows, overlapped in a tidy row against the brown leather headboard. She imagined Ethan's head against those pillows, with that curl of hair tousled on his forehead.

The luxury pillowcases alternated in color, tan then black. Which coordinated with the tightly fitted tan sheets. She ran a finger along the black duvet, tracing it down the right side of the bed. Then across the bottom. Then up the left. It was all too matchy-matchy for her tastes, but clearly made of expensive fabrics.

She eyed the wall-to-wall closet. If she took Ethan up on his proposal it would become filled with designer gowns for glamorous black tie dinners. Trendy separates for groundbreaking ceremonies. Classic sportswear for sailing jaunts and tennis tournaments. The finest shoes and purses and jewels.

None of that was her. She couldn't picture it. Not even for make-believe.

Back on earth, Holly didn't know whether she should unpack her suitcase full of jeans, comfortable skirts and tee shirts. She slid the blond wood closet door open to see if anything was inside.

Four men's suits hung neatly on wooden hangers, with breathing room in between each. Dark gray, light gray, navy pinstripe and a beautiful maroon. They looked to be Ethan's size. He'd probably look especially handsome in that maroon. It would go well with his brown eyes and that brown hair with its speckles of red.

There were freshly laundered shirts. Complementary ties. Polished shoes. A tuxedo and its accessories. Two pairs of pressed jeans. A pair of casual boots. She resisted the temptation to open any drawers. She had seen an overcoat and a leather jacket on the coat rack by the front door.

It wasn't a large wardrobe. Ethan had said he traveled a lot, but hadn't mentioned how long he was staying in New York.

She fingered the lapel of the maroon suit jacket. Ricky

the Rat had only owned one wrinkly black suit. She could count on one hand the times he'd worn it. He was the jeans and workboots type. There were times she'd thought he was sexy.

One of the times he hadn't been sexy was when she'd come home from work early one day and the workboots were all he'd had on. While he was in bed with their neighbor Kiki.

The rain was heavier outside now. Holly watched the bedroom window being pounded with sheets of the downpour. A rumble of thunder emphasized the storm's strength. *Good.* Let it wash away her past.

Deciding to leave her suitcase on the floor for the night, she pulled back the duvet on the bed and climbed into the king-size reminder of the man who was already making her feel as if she were spiraling away from her old life. Even though her encounter with him would come to an end in the morning, her transition to something new had begun.

The bed was divine. The mattress firm. The sheets crisp. She pulled the thick cover over her. Beyond comfortable, she nestled in the oasis, away from cares and plans. It was a peaceful heaven on earth after such a long day. Time to rest her body and mind. She was going to sleep like a log…

Two hours later Holly tossed and turned with exasperation. She hadn't kept her eyes shut for more than a minute before her brain had assaulted her with more and more opinions.

What Ethan was proposing could be her lucky break. A commission to do the artwork for his big development in Chelsea… A chance to really get started in New York…

She'd come to the city armed with work references, but the life of an artist could be tricky. Maybe nothing would pan out from the names and phone numbers she'd collected. Or she'd get small jobs here and there but they might not lead to anything else.

Ethan's proposition was a multi-phase project that would probably be six months of work at least. In that time she could really put down roots here.

She was determined to make her entire living as an artist. Not to have to work anymore as a maid or a nanny during the lean times. Her goals were clear. New York was the place where dreams were made or broken. If it didn't work out here, so be it—but she was certainly going to take her shot.

Imagine how much easier it would be without any astronomical rent to pay. New York apartment prices were notoriously high. Holly knew that she would probably have to live with a roommate. Maybe several of them. Some might have come to New York for the twenty-four-hour-a-day lifestyle, for the party that never ended. The household might be full of noise and people and activity at all hours of the day and night. It might prevent Holly from getting her work done or resting when she needed to.

Or she might end up with people who were slobs. Not able to tolerate a dirty mess, she would end up cleaning up after them. Cleaning up after people—how much of her life had she already spent doing that? She'd never minded taking care of her brother, but her ex-husband hadn't ever seemed even to know where the trash can or the washing machine were. Nor had her mother.

Maybe these roommate slobs wouldn't pay their share of their rent and she'd get evicted. She might end up having to move from place to place through no fault of her own. That would be maddening.

Ethan was offering work and a place to live. This tasteful apartment all to herself. It was one thing to be allowed to stay here while she looked for a place. It was quite another to have it *belong* to her. She could paint here. Reposition the furniture in the living room to make the most of the natural light.

Wait a minute.

Part of Ethan's bargain was that he would pay her. She would be able to afford to rent studio space. A New York artist with her own studio… If *that* wasn't a dream come true!

But on the other hand…

And she needed to consider…

She couldn't really…

And then what…?

When Holly opened her eyes, a drizzly morning sky crept in through the window. At some point she had finally dozed off, her mind twirling about the past and what the future could hold. Now, with morning's dawn in Ethan Benton's bedroom, certainty hit her like a ton of bricks.

If something seemed too good to be true, it was.

Not cut out to be anyone's pretend anything, Holly was only who she was. Ethan was kidding himself. It could only end in disaster. She would do him a favor by acknowledging the impossibility of his proposal, even though he wasn't able to see it for himself.

His judgment was clouded by his deep love for his aunt Louise. How touching was his concern for her welfare, for her reputation and her happiness. Blood ran thick. A good man took his family responsibilities seriously…

She had to call her brother. She wouldn't tell him about Ethan's offer. But she *did* need his help sorting out this confusion about her staying in the apartment. It would be good to hear his voice. In the end, he was the only one she really had in her corner.

He'd be working out in the garage of the little house he rented in Miami. Lifting weights. Bench pressing and hoisting dumbbells before showering and getting to work at Benton.

"Vinz." She pictured him, no doubt in a muscle shirt drenched in sweat. His close-cropped blond hair so unlike her black. The round blue eyes marking him as her kin.

"Holz! How's the Big Apple so far?"

She explained the mix-up with the apartment.

Vince promised to make some calls as soon as he got into the office. "I'll get it fixed," he assured her.

"I don't know if you can."

"Listen to me, big sis. We're going to sniff out opportunities for you and you're going take them. You'll grab everything that's thrown your way."

"Yeah."

"Remember—straight up or fall down!" He chanted their lifelong rally call—the desperate bravado of two kids with no one but each other to root for them.

After hanging up, Holly held the phone in her hand and stared absently out the window for a while. Thick clouds in the sky moved horizontally across her vision.

There had always been rainy days. No one knew how many more were ahead. It would be such a gift to have an umbrella.

Finally she tossed the phone onto the bed and opened the door.

Ethan was in the kitchen. She watched him start a pot of coffee before he noticed she was there. When he did, she leaned against the doorway. Her hair was probably a mess. Surely she had bags under her eyes from her fitful night. She lifted her hand and looked at her fingers with their perpetual paint around the cuticles and under the nails. She was who she was.

"Okay, Ethan. I'll marry you."

CHAPTER FOUR

She said yes! Ethan wanted to shout it from the rooftops. *She said yes!*

His blood coursed. His muscles tingled.

She said yes!

And then he caught himself. *Good heavens.* There was no cause for fireworks to be launched from his heart. There was no reason to announce his undying devotion in front of the citizens of Manhattan. He was not a giddy groom filled with bliss and anticipation.

A woman he'd met yesterday had agreed to a jointly beneficial contract. He signed deals every day. This was just another one.

With a flick on the switch of the coffeepot he shook his head, trying to dislodge the obvious cobwebs in his skull.

He'd gotten a bit carried away.

Truthfully, he hadn't been alone with a woman in a long time—and certainly not in the close quarters of a small apartment. Perhaps that had stirred up a primal reaction in him. While the mating ritual wasn't part of his daily life, it *was* a natural phenomenon.

Although Ethan employed thousands of women in all aspects of his business, he shunned intimate social situations with them as much as possible. Keeping a clear and level head was what he did best. Women were distracting. Distractions were to be avoided. Problem—solution.

This was the first lesson he needed in order to carry off his plan. He was going to be spending a lot of time with an attractive woman. He'd need to guard and defend himself against her feminine charms. It wasn't personal. It didn't matter whether it was Holly, pregnant Penelope Perkins or another actress he'd picked from a photograph.

In three measured breaths, with his face toward the coffeepot, he set his focus. *Guard and defend.*

Then he turned to Holly, still standing in the doorway. Dark cascades of hair fell around her pretty face, which had a just-woken flush in her cheeks. Her tee shirt was definitely not concealing a bra.

Involuntarily, his body began to lean toward hers. A kiss pushed forward from his lips.

Guard and defend!

In the nick of time, he pulled himself back. Her allure was something he'd need to get accustomed to. His body's involuntary response to her worried him…told him that might be difficult.

But he would be triumphant. For the sake of Aunt Louise he could conquer anything.

Ethan directed himself to talk, since he couldn't kiss. "How did you sleep?"

"Great," she lied.

Her eyes looked tired. He hadn't got much sleep, either. He was far too tall to stretch out comfortably on that sofa. Plus, his mind had taunted him with replays of the evening.

"That coffee smells good," she said as she massaged the back of her neck.

"It does. How do you take it?"

"Lots of milk or cream. No sugar."

Ethan opened one of the cabinets to look for cups. It held only drinking glasses. He hadn't spent enough time in this apartment to know where everything was kept. His second try yielded large white mugs. Setting them on the black granite countertop, he poured the steaming coffee.

The kitchen was Manhattan Minimal. Pint-size efficiency. Cabinets, sink and dishwasher on one side. Stove and refrigerator on the other. A one-person kitchen. Too cramped for two people to work in.

Which was why when Holly stepped in to open the fridge he felt her hips brush past him. In turn, his hips reacted of their own volition—which, fortunately, she didn't notice.

"What are we eating for breakfast?' she asked as she peered into the refrigerator.

"What do we have?" He'd only had bottles of water when he'd got in yesterday, and beer last night with the pizza.

"Eggs, butter and cheese. And the bread and fruit." She pointed to the baskets on the counter. "We can work with this."

The way she said *we* made Ethan's ears prick up. He wasn't used to *we*. He'd worked very hard at avoiding *we*. This was no time to start. Although for the first time he was curious about *we*. He reasoned that this fake engagement was a perfect way of safely pretending to experience *we*, with both parties knowing fully well that the truth was *me* and *me* achieving individual goals.

Right. However, now it felt somewhat confusing.

Holly pulled the carton of milk out of the fridge and handed it to him. Ethan was keenly aware of their fingertips touching during the exchange.

She laid ingredients on the counter. "How does cheese omelets, toasted bagels and sliced fruit sound?"

"What do you generally eat for breakfast?"

Holly giggled. A bit of blush rose in her cheeks. *How adorable*. "Was that a get-to-know-each-other question?"

"It was. If we are going to be convincing as an engaged couple, we have to know those sorts of things about each other."

He handed her a mug. She took a slow sip and exhaled her satisfaction.

"You put the perfect amount of milk in my cup, so we must be off to a good start."

Ethan felt ridiculously proud that she liked her coffee.

"How do you take yours?" she went up.

"Also without sugar. But not as much milk."

"I'll eat anything…" She went back to his question. "If we hadn't polished off that pizza, that's great cold in the morning."

"Cold pizza? Noted."

"Do you know how to cook?"

"I could probably manage to broil a steak without ruining it."

"Eggs?"

"Not really," he confessed.

"Today you learn, then."

"Is that so?"

"I'll put on a show for your aunt Louise, but surely you don't think I'm going to be cooking and cleaning for you." Her face stilled in a moment of earnest uncertainty. "*Do* you?"

"Of course not, phony fiancée."

"It's just that I've done plenty of taking care of people in my life. I just want to take care of myself."

Holly had been through a lot. He'd been able to tell that about her from the start—had seen it right through her spunky attitude. She was no fresh-faced hopeful, arriving in New York full of delusions and fantasies. There was a past. A past that he suspected included hardship and pain.

Another one of those innate urges told him to wrap his arms around her and promise that he'd make up for all her hurts. That now she would be the one taken care of. That he'd quite like to make it his life's mission to take care of her in every possible way.

Once again he had to chastise himself sternly. He had merely hired her to perform a service. For which she would be paid very well. With that opportunity she would be able to find whatever she'd come to New York to get. She didn't need him.

The agony of that shocked him. A reminder to guard and defend.

Holly handed him the carton of eggs. She gave him a bowl. "Four."

Finding a cutting board and a knife, Holly sliced cheese while Ethan cracked eggs. They stood side by side at their tasks, each dependent on the other in order to get the job done. Ethan appreciated teamwork. That was what made Benton Worldwide, and every other successful venture work. It must be the same in a marriage.

Two bagels were halved and popped into the toaster.

"Frying pan?" she mused to herself, and quickly moved to his other side to find one.

His mind flipped back to the past. To Aunt Louise and Uncle Melvin. It had been almost ten years since they'd done the normal things that married couples did. Mel had died over five years ago. Before that recurrences of his cancer had often had him bedridden. But they'd had moments like these. Hundreds, even thousands of cozy day-to-day moments like preparing breakfast.

Those moments strung together added up to a life shared between two people.

In reality, with their success and privilege it was not as if Aunt Louise and Uncle Mel had often been in the kitchen frying up eggs. But they had always cooked Sunday supper together whenever they could. It had been one of their signatures.

Ethan had potent memories of the two of them together as a couple. The way they'd been with each other. Even if it they had just been at the front door on the way out, helping each other layer on coats, scarves and hats to brave the Boston winter. How they'd maneuvered around each other. With effortless choreography. Totally at ease with each other, aware of each other's moves, each other's needs, each other's comforts.

He understood why Aunt Louise so wanted that same security for him. Why she was concerned with the way he jetted around the globe, working all the time, never stopping, never settling. The wisdom of age had shown her what might happen to a man who didn't balance power and labor with the other things that made life worth living. Family. Love.

But his aunt should accept that after all Ethan had been through love wasn't an option for him. He would never open his heart. Her destiny wasn't his. Yet he couldn't blame her for wishing things were different. That his past hadn't defined his future.

In reflection, Aunt Louise had valued her relationship with Uncle Mel above everything else in her life. She'd had a love so true it had never let her down.

Unlike him.

This ruse was the best solution. If the knowledge that Ethan was engaged to be married made Aunt Louise happy, and put her mind at ease, then he'd have taken good care of her. Ethan was in charge of all decisions now, and he wanted them to be in his aunt's best interests.

He and Holly sat down at the table with their breakfast. Just as she had with the pizza last night, she dug in like a hungry animal. She took big bites and didn't try to disguise her obvious pleasure.

Ethan asked if maybe she had gone hungry as a child.

"My mother was…unpredictable."

Something he himself knew more than a little about. Anger burned his throat.

A bittersweet smile crossed her mouth as she cut circular slices of an orange and handed one to him. "Vince and I used to call these rings of sunshine. There were always oranges in Florida."

He wanted to know how she'd been wronged. But he wasn't going to walk on that common ground.

"Aunt Louise and Fernando are coming for dinner on Wednesday." He cut to the matter at hand. "We need to prepare. Our first order of business is making this apartment look like we truly live here. We will start with…"

"The artwork!" they chimed in unison.

"We will visit my favorite galleries in Soho. You can make the final selection."

Outside, stormy skies had given way to more hard rain.

"Dress accordingly."

He plucked his phone from his pocket and began tapping.

Half an hour later, a stocky man in a suit and chauffeur's cap held a car door open for Holly.

"This is my driver, Leonard," Ethan introduced.

"Ma'am."

Holly darted into the black car without getting too wet from the downpour. Sliding across the tan leather backseat, she made room for Ethan beside her. Leonard shut the passenger door and hurried around to the driver's seat.

As they pulled away from the apartment building, Ethan activated the privacy glass that separated the front seat from the back.

Holly didn't know what she'd gotten herself into. Fear and excitement rattled her at the same time.

Soho galleries and shareholders' galas… She didn't really know how she was going to fake her way through a life so different from hers. Being ferried around New York in a town car with a privacy glass.

Ethan had clearly noticed her discomfort at his shielding his driver from any conversation they were going to have. "Obviously we need complete discretion to pull off our little enterprise, do we not?"

"Yup."

"Off we go, then. Yes?"

As crazy as it was, she'd already said yes to this wild ride with him. "Yes."

She watched New York though the car window. The city was gorgeous in the rain. Buildings seemed even taller and grander beneath the turbulent skies. People in dark clothes with umbrellas hurried along the sidewalks. To her eyes, they looked as if they were from a bygone era. Her mind snapped mental pictures. She wanted to paint all of it.

While Ethan checked messages on his phone Holly was aware of every breath he took. Her lungs couldn't help synchronizing each of his inhales and exhales with her own. They were so near each other on the seat her leg rested along his. She detected a faint smell of his woodsy shampoo.

You'll get used to him, she told herself. *Soon enough, he won't be so enchanting.*

Ethan touched his phone and brought the device to his ear.

"Nathan. Did you receive my text? Have you made all of the appointments for today?"

He nodded once as he listened.

"Diane—got it. Jeremy—got it. Thank you. Set me up for meetings next week with Con East and the Jersey City contractors."

He looked toward Holly and licked his top lip, although she was sure he didn't realize he had.

"I will be in New York for a while this time. As a matter of fact I have quite the announcement to make at the shareholders' gala."

A squiggle shot up Holly's back. No one had ever looked at her the way he did.

Ethan sent a sincere laugh into the phone. "All right, Nathan. I suppose I can spare you your beheading. *This* time."

He clicked off the call. "That explains the mystery about the apartment. Nathan had me booked in for the same dates but next month. You were right—it was meant to be yours. But now, to everyone concerned, the apartment is *ours*."

Holly pulled up the collar on her leather jacket as Leonard shuttled them downtown.

Curbside at the first gallery, Leonard helped them out of the car. And then back in as they made their way to the second. And then to the third.

Naturally the staff at each were overjoyed to see Ethan. They reminisced about art openings and museum dedications. Holly felt completely out of place, with nothing to add to the conversations. But she held her own, making intelligent comments about the art on display.

Ethan didn't mention anything about their upcoming nuptials. That announcement was for the gala. Instead he introduced Holly as a friend and painter from Florida whom he had been lucky enough to enlist for an upcoming commission.

Back in the town car again, they munched on the fancy sandwiches Ethan had had Leonard pick up from a gourmet shop. They discussed the paintings they had seen. Holly wanted two, and explained why she'd chosen them.

"If we had more time I'd have my brother send up some canvases that he's storing for me," she said. "If it was really our apartment I'd like to have my own work on the walls."

"I would like that, too," Ethan agreed, with such unexpected warmth it stretched at her heart.

He was masterful at throwing her off-kilter. When

they'd been making breakfast that morning she'd had the feeling several times that he was going to kiss her. At one moment she had desperately hoped he would, while in the next she'd known she must turn away.

Ethan Benton was a bundle of inconsistencies.

Such a precise way he used a paper napkin to brush away imagined crumbs from the corners of his mouth. He was so definite about everything he did. Hobnobbing with gallery people or eating take-out lunch in the car—he did everything with finesse.

It wasn't as if any crumb would dare stick to those glorious lips. Men who showered on planes didn't get food on their faces.

Yet Holly knew there was something damaged underneath all Ethan's confidence and class…

"Can I paint you?"

He contemplated the question as he slowly popped the seal on his bottle of artisan soda.

"You know those drab black and whites of the tree and the flower on the wall?" she went on.

Last night when they'd been critiquing those photographs, flickers had flown between them.

"Flat, corporate…"

"Impersonal," she finished. "That's where I'd hang a painting of you. It would bring personality to the whole room and really make it ours."

"Yes…" he concurred with reluctance. "I suppose it would."

In a flash, Holly understood his hesitation. People were often uncomfortable at the prospect of her painting them. It involved trust. They had to be reassured that she wasn't going to accentuate their pointy nose or, worse still, the loneliness in their eyes.

A good portrait exposed someone's secrets. What was it that Ethan was worried she would reveal to the world?

"Can I?"

"I doubt we could get a painting done in two days' time."

"Let me show you."

Once people had seen Holly's work, she was able to put them at ease. She pulled out her phone and thumbed to her website. "I don't know if you saw these when you were on my site last night. But look. I don't do a typical portrait."

She showed him the screen. "I call them painted sketches. See how they're a bit abstract? And not all that detailed? I would just catch the essence of you."

He whipped his head sideways to face her. "What makes you think you know the essence of me?" he challenged.

Holly's throat jammed at the confrontation. He was right. She *didn't* know him. They'd met yesterday.

But she knew she could get something. Those big and expressive eyes. And, yes, there was some kind of longing behind them.

She might not know him, but she wanted to. This morning at breakfast he had been visibly shaken when she'd hinted at the hardships she'd endured. She had sensed some kind of connection there—a fierce similarity.

She hadn't explicitly told him about the mother who had never consistently provided food for her children. She hadn't mentioned the father who'd come around every couple of years with promises he'd never kept. How Holly had often had to fend for her younger brother and herself.

Yet the damage that dwelled behind Ethan's eyes had made her want to lay her pain bare to him. And for him to lay all his beside hers. As if in that rawness their wounds could be healed.

But none of that was ever to be. They were business partners. Nothing more. Besides, she wasn't going to make herself vulnerable to anyone ever again.

"Never mind." She called his bluff. "I guess we won't

ever find out how much of the real you I could get on a canvas."

One side of his mouth hiked. "I did not say no."

"So you'll let me paint you?"

"I will have you know right now that I have very little patience for sitting still."

"You probably had to sit for family portraits with Aunt Louise and Uncle Mel, right? Dressed up in uncomfortable Christmas clothes by the fireplace? The dutiful family dog by your side? It was torture. You had to sit without moving for what seemed like an eternity."

"I absolutely hated having to hold one position while a greasy bald man who smelled like pipe tobacco painted us."

Flirty words tumbled out of her mouth before she could sensor them. "I promise I'll smell a lot better than the bald man did."

"No doubt."

"And it won't take long."

"I think it might."

Were they still talking about painting?

He lowered the glass separating them from the driver. "Leonard, we are going to change our next stop to Wooster and Broome."

Leonard let them out in front of a painting supplies store the likes of which Holly had never been in before.

She ordered a lot of her materials online, because there were no shops in Fort Pierce that carried fine products like these. When she was low on money she'd make do with what was available at the local brand-name craft store, that also sold knitting yarn and foam balls for school projects.

She cowered at another memory of her ex-husband. As usual, Ricky hadn't wanted to go shopping with her because he thought painting was silly and that she should spend more time going to motorcycle races with him.

Yelling at her to hurry up while she picked out some tubes of paint, Ricky had lost his patience. With a flick of his hand he'd knocked down a display of Valentine's Day supplies. Heart-shaped cardboard boxes, Cupid cutouts and red and pink pompoms had crashed to the floor as Ricky stormed out of the store.

Humiliated, Holly had been left to make apologies and pay for his outburst.

It had been a few months later that she'd caught Ricky in bed with their neighbor. But she'd known that day in the craft store that she couldn't stay married to him.

Now here she was, a million miles away in Soho, the mecca of the American art world, with another man who would never be right for her. Although in completely opposite ways.

Life had a sense of humor.

She chose an easel, stretched canvases in several sizes, new paint and brushes, and palettes and sketchpads, pastels and charcoals. All top-notch. This was the Holly equivalent of a kid in a candy shop.

At the checkout, Ethan opened up an account for her. "That way you can pick up whatever tools and materials you need for Benton projects."

"My goodness…" Her eyes bugged out. "Thank you."

"Of course, my dearest." He winked. "And the next item on the agenda is buying my pretty fiancée some proper clothes."

CHAPTER FIVE

"WHAT'S WRONG WITH my clothes?" Holly demanded as Leonard helped them out of the car in front of a Fifth Avenue shopping mecca.

"Not a thing. You do the artist with paint on her hands bit quite well. All you need is a French cigarette in your mouth and a beret on your head," Ethan answered.

"Very funny."

He laid his hand on the center of her back to guide her through the store's revolving entrance door. Holly's shoulders perked up at his touch.

"However," he continued as they bustled through the busy sales floor, "there is the shareholders' gala, and then there'll be charity dinners and social occasions we will be attending. As we discussed, this arrangement necessitates an appropriate wardrobe."

When they reached the Personal Styling department, an older blonde woman in a sleeveless black dress and pearls was awaiting their arrival.

"Are you Diane?" Ethan extended his right hand. "My assistant, Nathan, spoke with you earlier."

"It's a pleasure to meet you, Mr. Benton." Diane took his outstretched hand with both of hers.

"This is my friend Holly Motta."

"Oh…" Diane gave her a limp handshake, taking notice of the paint under Holly's fingernails.

"Hi!" Holly chirped.

She was going to have to get used to the surprise in people's voices when they met her. Everyone probably knew Ethan as a wealthy playboy who dated fashion models and princesses of small countries. He'd have no reason to be with a mere mortal like her.

Ethan raised his eyebrows at Holly, which made her giggle and feel more at ease.

He peered straight into Holly's eyes while he spoke to the other woman. "Diane, my friend will be accompanying me to numerous events. She is an artist, with little need for formal clothes. Can you help us outfit her in a way that stays true to her creative and unique self?"

Holly's mouth dropped open. Could anyone have said anything more perfect? He wanted to buy her clothes but he didn't want to change her.

Diane was stunned as well. "Cer…certainly," she stuttered. "Can I offer you a glass of champagne?"

And thus began her trip to Fantasyland. While Ethan sipped bubbly on a purple velvet settee, Diane showed Holly into a private dressing room that was larger than all the fitting rooms in the discount shops she usually went to put together.

Six full-length mirrors were positioned to allow for a three-hundred-and-sixty-degree view. The carpet was cream-colored, as was the furniture—no doubt chosen so as not to compete with the clothes. A vanity table with padded chair was ready for any primping needs. Hats, gloves, scarves and purses had been pre-selected and lay waiting in a glass display case. A collection of shoes stood neatly on a shoe rack. Jackets and coats hung from pegs.

Diane ducked away behind one of the mirrors.

Holly whistled out loud as she took it all in. And then

laughed at her predicament. She'd overheard Ethan talking on the phone in the car about a Diane. And a Jeremy. He had prearranged the gallery visits and now this, too. And Holly had thought *herself* to be the taking-care-of-business type! She could take a lesson from him.

"We'll start with daywear," Diane announced as she wheeled in a rack of clothes.

Besides the fact that there hadn't been any money when she was growing up, Holly had never been especially interested in clothes. She dressed functionally and comfortably, and ended up staining most everything with paint anyway. But if she had ever dreamt of wearing stylish garments made of luxurious materials these would be them.

The first ensemble Holly tried on was a white pantsuit. The slim line of the trousers made her legs look eight feet long. And the coordinating blazer with its thin satin lapels was both distinguished and chic. Worn with a navy silk shirt unbuttoned one notch past prim, the outfit delivered "sexy" as well.

Diane moved in quickly to pin the jacket's waist for a trimmer fit.

She suggested Holly try a brown slingback shoe, then plucked the proper size from a stack of boxes waiting at the ready. Diane might be a bit snobby, but she sure as heck knew what she was doing.

"Perhaps you'd like to add a touch of lipstick?" Diane inquired—a polite way of reminding Holly that she'd need to attend to her makeup and hair.

Diane opened a drawer in the vanity table that contained a palette of options. Holly dabbed on some lip gloss, undid her ponytail and brushed her hair. Surveying herself in the mirror, she knew this was without question the best she had ever looked.

"Shall we show Mr. Benton?" Diane suggested.

When Holly stepped into the waiting lounge that

seemed destined for wealthy boyfriends and mothers of brides, Ethan was busy typing into his phone.

He leaned comfortably back on the settee with one leg crossed over the other knee. Effortless elegance. Although the wavy reddish-brown hair that always had a bit of a tousle to it made sure hints of his untamed side came through.

Ethan glanced up. His eyes went through her and then right back down to his phone.

Holly was delighted as recognition gradually took hold. His jaw slackened. Eyebrows bunched. Nostrils flared.

Only then did his eyes rise up again for the double-take.

And take her in he did, indeed. Ever so slowly. From the tip of her head to the pointy toes of her designer shoes. His gaze was wicked. As if she was standing in front of him naked rather than dressed in this finery. The feeling thrilled and aroused her down to her core.

That smile made its way millimeter by millimeter across Ethan's face. "My, my…"

"So you approve?" she flirted.

"To say the least."

"Do you want to see more?"

Focused on the opening of her shirt, where perhaps that questionable button should have been closed but wasn't, he sighed. "I would most *definitely* like to see more."

She pivoted, and when her face was out of view from him let a satisfied grin explode. This was so much fun. She was long overdue for some harmless fun. *Harmless*, right?

Diane helped her into the next outfit and pinned it for alterations. Another silk blouse—this one black, with a square neckline and a gold zipper down the back—tucked into a tan pencil skirt. The look was dressy, but edgy.

Ethan's reaction was all she could have hoped for as he lingered over the snug fit of the skirt across her hips.

Next, dark wash jeans tucked into boots and a flowing

white blouse were complemented by Holly's own black leather jacket.

"More," Ethan demanded.

A crisp red dress with a pleated skirt, short sleeves and matching belt provided a timeless silhouette.

A silver satin cocktail dress draped her curves without being tight. At the sight of her in that one, Ethan shifted in his seat.

As a kid, Holly had sprouted up early and had always been the tallest girl in her class. She remembered feeling big and awkward. It had taken her years to train herself out of slouching her shoulders forward. Slim, but with hips wider than was proportionate to her small bustline, she'd never thought she wore clothes well.

Until today.

With Diane's wizardry to pinch here and fold there, these clothes looked as if they'd been custom-made to flatter her perfectly.

In all, ten outfits were put together, ranging from casual to semi-formal. Extra pieces would be added to mix and match.

Ethan had promised that no matter what happened with their phony engagement the clothes would be hers to keep. That had meant nothing to Holly when he'd said it, but now she understood how important an offer that was.

In these outfits she was *distinctive*. They made a statement. The woman who wore them was someone to take seriously. These were clothes that were the epitome of good taste, that she could—and would—care for and wear for years to come.

But the *pièce de resistance* came when Diane brought out an evening gown for the black-tie shareholders' gala. Tears unexpectedly sprang in Holly's eyes at the artistry of it. She couldn't fathom *ever* needing a dress so fancy.

It was a pearly sky-blue completely covered in hand-sewn crystals. Holly was surprised at how much the gown weighed. Sleeveless with a deep-scooped neck, it skimmed the floor until Diane had her step into coordinating high-heeled sandals.

Whether the dress complemented Holly's icy blue eyes or her eyes enhanced the dress, it didn't matter. There couldn't be a more perfect gown.

She hoped Ethan liked it.

As she stepped into the lounge to model it for him, she wanted to be sure that she was wearing the gown rather than the gown wearing *her*. Standing up straight, with her shoulders back, Holly reminded herself of what she had learned from the posture correction videos that had helped her rid herself of her slump. Stand tall. Ribs over hips. Hips over heels.

She smiled demurely at Ethan as she approached.

He hiccupped as he almost choked on his sip of champagne.

Holly giggled. She high-fived herself in her mind. *Mission accomplished.*

She cooed, high on a unique rush of power she'd never known she had, "Do you still want to marry me?"

Ethan set his champagne flute down on the side table and cleared his throat. "You have no idea…"

"One more stop and then we will go to dinner," Ethan said as he ushered Holly back into the car.

Leonard shut the passenger door, then went around to slide into his place behind the wheel. He deftly maneuvered them away from the curb to join the Fifth Avenue traffic.

Ethan was thinking ahead. "What else do you need for the gala? I assume you would like to have your hair and makeup done?"

"Please."

"I will have Nathan book that."

Holly held her hands up in front of her. There was often a rainbow of colors staining her fingers and nails, but today it was just the Cobalt Two Eleven leftover from last night's spill. "And I think I need a manicure, don't you agree?"

"The way you look in that gown, I doubt anyone would notice."

No fair for him to say things like that. Things that made her want to lean over and cover his luscious lips with an hour-long kiss. Not fair at all for him to speak words that made her contemplate what it would be like to be with someone who made her feel good about herself. Who was on her side.

Not just for business purposes.

Gridlocked traffic was only allowing them to inch forward. The rain had ceased for the moment but the sky was a thick grey. Throngs of pedestrians rushed to and fro. Some darted across the streets, jaywalking quickly in between cars. Horns honked. Drivers yelled at each other. Music blared from taxicab radios. A siren screamed.

Together, it sounded like a riotous symphony. New York was alive and kicking.

One minute she had been crammed into an economy seat on a packed airplane, headed for the Big Apple and who knew what. And then a minute later she was modeling a jewel-encrusted evening gown for a young billionaire.

A smokin' hot young billionaire who had ogled her as if he not only wanted to see those clothes on her, but also wanted to see them in a heap on the floor beside his bed.

By the end of her fashion show Holly had been imagining it as well. How it might feel to have Ethan's big and no doubt able hands unzipping the zippers and unbuttoning the buttons of those finely crafted garments.

How far would it be safe to go with this charade they had embarked on? Surely not as far as clothes being strewn at the bedside.

Holly was going to have to learn to regally accept a peck on the cheek in front of other people without melting into a puddle of desire. She might have to place a reciprocal smooch on Ethan's face at some point. If push came to shove she might even have to receive a kiss on the lips at, say, the shareholders' gala when their engagement was announced.

She had no idea how she'd handle that, but she would cross that bridge when she came to it. However, under no circumstances would her make-believe fiancé's tuxedo—or anything else of his—end up crumpled at the foot of her bed.

No one would ever see them behind closed doors. And she'd do well to remember that to a man like Ethan Benton this was all just a deal. A game. A con. He'd only go as far as was absolutely necessary to do what he deemed right for his aunt Louise's future.

Holly would keep her eye on the prize. A great place to live, steady work, a leg-up for Vince. That was more than she could have ever hoped for. Let alone on her first day here. That was enough. That was astounding.

"Out." Ethan opened the car door in the middle of the street. "This traffic is unbearable. We will go on foot."

"What?"

He firmly grasped Holly's hand and slid them out of the backseat. "Leonard, meet us in front," he instructed, before thumping the door shut. He tugged Holly. "Come on."

"Where are we going?" she asked as he ushered her to the sidewalk.

"I told you. One more stop."

They joined the masses of legs charging north on Fifth Avenue. New Yorkers during rush hour. Always in a hurry. Always somewhere to go. The air was cold. The pace was exhilarating.

Maybe this would become home. Maybe this enthralling city itself would fill up the emptiness she'd always had inside.

Two blocks later she stopped dead in her tracks. They had arrived at their destination. She looked up to take in the majesty of the Art Deco architecture. The bronze sculpture of Atlas holding up the building's clock. The elaborate window displays.

People were moving in and out of the store's entry doors. Many of those leaving held the light blue shopping bags that were known the world over.

"I do not suppose it would do for my fiancée to wear an engagement ring made from a beer bottle wrapper," he said, and winked.

So he hadn't brought her to a jewelry store to get a ring. He'd brought her to *THE* jewelry store.

Ricky had never given her an engagement ring. They'd waited for a sale at the jewelry store in their local mall and bought the two cheapest gold bands there. It had only been last month that she'd gotten around to selling hers for bulk weight to help pay for her plane ticket to New York.

Now she was standing in front of the most well-known jewelry store in the world! Little blue bags!

Inside, Ethan gave his name and they were immediately escorted to the private salon. A man in a pinstriped suit introduced himself as Jeremy Markham.

Again Holly remembered hearing Ethan on the phone that morning with his assistant, Nathan, mentioning a Diane and a Jeremy. Diane was clothes…obviously Jeremy was jewels. Ethan had everything figured out.

"Jeremy, we will need some help with a wardrobe of jewelry in the weeks to come, but today we would like to choose a diamond ring."

"Of course, sir. May I present a selection?"

Ethan nodded.

A private appointment to pick out an engagement ring? Ho-hum, just an ordinary day.

"Please, sit down." Jeremy, chin up high, held a chair out for Holly after giving her a once-over. Like Diane with the clothes, had this salesman who clearly only dealt with VIPs already figured out that Holly was just one big fake? Another opportunist going after a rich man's money.

Using a key extracted from his jacket pocket, Jeremy let himself into a back room.

Ethan pulled a chair next to Holly's.

"Check these out!" she exclaimed at the glass case to the left of them.

A heritage collection of gemstone jewelry was on display. Elaborate necklaces and bracelets made from pounds of gold and carat upon carat of colorful stones. The pieces were too ornate for her taste, but she was attracted to the hues.

What had really caught her eye was a simple ring of blue topaz. The stone was a large oval cut, bordered on each side by two small diamonds.

"Look at how stunning that ring is. That blue is so brilliant it's blinding. Light is bouncing off it in twenty different directions."

Holly's eyes were light blue, like the stone. It had always been her favorite color from as far back as she could remember. Maybe that was why she'd instantly fallen in love with the sky-blue evening gown Ethan had bought for her.

While it had always been pink for girls and blue for boys Holly, as usual, had swum against the stream. It wasn't as if the trailer she'd lived in with her mom and brother had had any décor to it. The walls had been covered in flowery peeling wallpaper. Sheets and blankets had always been chosen by what was on clearance sale, which had usually translated to scratchy fabrics with dark prints. But Holly could remember a few occasions when her father had been in town for a day or so with some money and bought her new clothes. She'd always chosen items in shades of blue.

"It's just dazzling," she continued, pointing to the ring. "I've never seen anything like it."

Ethan glanced over to it and shrugged his shoulders, indifferent.

Jeremy returned with two velvet trays that held a wide variety of ring styles, all with humongous diamonds.

Ethan whispered to Holly, "We ought to be able to find something perfect amongst these."

She shot one final glance at the astounding blue topaz. "Whatever you say. You're the boss..."

"Feng, we will start with hot and sour soup. Follow that with the chef's special duck, beef with broccoli, shrimp chow mein. And oolong tea."

"Thank you, Mr. Ethan." The waiter bowed and hurried away.

After the jewelry store, Ethan had instructed Leonard to drive them to Chinatown. Now he and Holly were comfortably ensconced in a booth at a casual restaurant his family often frequented when they were in New York.

"I am famished," Ethan proclaimed. "Shopping is exhausting."

With a suitably enormous diamond engagement ring now on Holly's finger, the day's checklist was complete. They had been downtown, midtown, and now back downtown, but he was craving familiar food.

"Do you do a lot of shopping?" Holly questioned.

"I suppose I do my fair share, but it is not an activity I have a feeling for one way or another," he lied.

Watching Holly model one comely outfit after another would rank pretty darn high on his list of pleasurable pastimes. Although a lot of his other work had been accomplished today as well, thanks to the convenience of technology. Securing a fiancée had been at the top of his to-do list.

"Do you..." Holly twirled a lock of her raven hair "...shop for women on a regular basis?"

Hmm...fishing, was she?

"Women have dragged me to find gold in China, the finest silks in India, the best leather in Buenos Aires, if that is what you are asking."

She brushed her bangs out of her eyes and sat up straight. "Oh."

The previous women in his life were a sore point with him. In fact Ethan and women had never been a good combination, period. Going all the way back to his mother. Other than Aunt Louise, every woman Ethan had encountered seemed to him to be one hundred percent selfish. Only out for what they could get. Gifts, money, travel, status—you name it.

Which was why he was resolute that he'd never fall in love. To love you had to trust. And that was something he was never going to be tricked into again.

So it was a logical step for him to dream up this scheme that would allow Aunt Louise to think Ethan had found lifelong love as she had with Uncle Mel. Ethan would never have to marry a woman whose motivation he'd question. Intention, compensation and expectation were all upfront with this plan. It might be the brainiest partnership deal he'd ever conceived.

"Hot and sour soup." Feng placed the steaming bowl on the table. While he ladled out two servings he questioned, "May I ask if Mrs. Louise is feeling better?"

His aunt Louise had been in New York several times in the past few months. Feng had probably seen her more recently than Ethan had.

"Was she unwell when she was last here?"

The waiter pursed his lips and bowed his head, which said more than any words could.

Ethan's heart sank. This validated the fact that he was on the right track. Doing whatever it took to get Aunt Louise to retire and relax in Barbados before worse things than stumbles and bruises stole her dignity.

It was all going to work out.

As long as Ethan continued to stare past but not into Holly Motta's face. Because when he did steal a glance she didn't look like a business proposition. Or a gold-digger out to get what she deemed hers. With that slouch she kept correcting, and that milky skin, and the hint of ache in her eyes…

No, she was a living, breathing, kindred spirit who could shred his master plan into a million slices if he wasn't careful.

"Why are you looking at me like that?" she asked with her spoon in the air.

"Like what?" Ethan threw back his head with an exaggerated nonchalance.

She gave him a mock frown.

"Eat your soup," he told her.

One very ungenteel slurp later… *"Yummo!"*

"We should learn more about each other if we are to be convincing as a couple. You clearly like food."

He mocked her slurp until they were both laughing.

"My turn," she said. "You're an only child."

"You have one brother."

"You studied at Oxford."

"What is your favorite movie?"

Holly dismissed him with a wave of her hand. "Are you kidding me? If we're going to get to know each other we have to get real. What is the one thing that has hurt you the most in your life?"

His mother. Of course it was his mother. Nothing could

devastate a nine-year-old boy more than being left behind by his mother. It was horrible enough that his father had died instantly when a drunk driver had plowed into his car at racing speed, killing him instantly. But then shortly after that to lose his mother in the way he had… It was unthinkable.

"Beef with snow peas. Shrimp chow mein. Chef's special duck," Feng announced as he and another waiter positioned the platters in the center of the table. "Please enjoy."

Saved by the duck.

Ethan wasn't going to expose his darkness and despair to someone he'd met only yesterday. As a matter of fact he wasn't in the habit of talking about his feelings with *anyone*. It was better that way.

He scooped a portion of each dish onto his and Holly's plates.

But wasn't it rather amazing that this woman was so genuine she didn't want to discuss trivial matters?

As she lifted her chopsticks to grab at her chow mein he admired the diamond ring he had put on her finger. It was staggering in its size and clarity, and he knew any woman would be filled with pride to wear something so timeless and flawless.

Yet he could kick himself because he hadn't bought her the blue topaz ring she had admired at the store!

Quick thinking had told him to buy the type of ring that was expected of him. Anything other than a traditional diamond engagement ring would invite inquiry. Such as where and why and what sentiments had inspired him to buy such an unusual ring. Those were extra questions they didn't need. It would just add to the risk of them flubbing up as a believable couple.

But now he thought blue ring, purple ring, green ring—what would it matter if that was what she wanted?

Pulsing and vibrant, Holly Motta had careened into his apartment with blue paint on her face and, he feared, had changed his life forever. Forcing him to think about women differently than he ever had. Making him for the first time vaguely envision a role in which he cared if someone was happy. Edging him into speculation about what it would be like if someone cared about his happiness, too.

And now she was making it hard to concentrate on anything other than leaping across the table and planting a kiss on that sweet mouth that was busy with noodles.

After a bite of food to steady himself, Ethan resumed their interview. "Tell me something about yourself that I would not have guessed."

"I used to be—" she blurted, and then abruptly stopped herself. She put her chopsticks down and took a slow sip of her tea. Trying to recover, she finished with, "A pretty good softball player."

Aha, so it wasn't as easy for her to be as open and candid as she wanted him to believe it was. What had she been about to say that had proved too difficult to reveal? And what had she avoided telling him at breakfast that morning about the mother she'd characterized as *unpredictable*?

He'd gone along with her easy sincerity, but Ethan really didn't know the first thing about her. He'd garnered that she'd had a difficult childhood, but it wasn't like him to take anyone at face value. Not after what he'd seen of life.

Guard and defend.

He had his family's empire to protect.

"Excuse me," he said as he put his chopsticks down and pulled out his phone. "I have just remembered one more bit of business for the day."

He texted Chip Foley, Benton Worldwide's Head of Security. Just as he'd intended to do if he'd hired an actress for the fiancée job.

Chip, please run everything you can on a Holly Motta from Fort Pierce, Florida. Claims her occupation is artist. I would place her age at about thirty. Tall, slim, blue eyes, black hair. She says her brother Vince works for us in Miami. I do not know if it is the same last name. Do an across-the-board check on her for me.

After hitting the "send" button, his eyes returned to Holly.

She pointed her chopsticks at him and taunted, "Hey, you never told me what it was in your life that hurt you the most."

CHAPTER SIX

It was the dead of night, but Holly could still hear New York outside the bedroom window. Cars drove by. A dog barked. People laughed boisterously on the street.

The city that never slept.

Lying in Ethan's bed, with her head sinking into his soft pillows, she could hardly make sense of the day. Visiting Soho galleries, buying all those art supplies, a new wardrobe, a diamond ring… Then that dinner in Chinatown.

She'd lived a lifetime in the last twenty-four hours.

Ethan was just beyond the door in the living room. Was he sleeping? Was he working? Or was he lying awake thinking about her as she was of him?

Of course not, Holly reminded herself. Ethan Benton had more important things on his mind then his wife for hire. She'd better remember that.

But when they'd watched each other's faces at the restaurant it had seemed as if maybe she would, in fact, linger in his thoughts and keep him up at night. He'd looked at her as if there was nowhere else he'd rather be. The restaurant might have been crowded and clamoring, but he'd never taken his eyes off her.

Through most of the evening they would have convinced anyone they were an engaged couple. Finishing each other's sentences… Digging their chopsticks into each other's plates…

And then there had been those awkward moments when they'd asked each other questions neither was ready to answer.

Holly hadn't been able to bring herself to tell Ethan that she had been married. She feared he would think of her as a used product and not want to go through with their agreement. He didn't need to know about her mistake in marrying someone who hadn't loved her for who she was. Who hadn't supported the person she wanted to become. Ricky Dowd wasn't a name that *ever* needed to come up in conversation.

They would go through with their pretend engagement so that Ethan could protect his aunt as her health declined. And, as he'd said, either they would continue to meet for official occasions or eventually call off their deal. Whatever happened, Ethan would never have to know about Holly's wasted time on wrong decisions that tonight seemed like a million years ago.

Just as she might not find out what he was hiding because he didn't want to tell her what had caused him the most hurt in his life. It had to be something terrible, because both times when he'd avoided the topic his eyes had turned to coal.

But the rest of the evening was a dream she never wanted to wake from. When they had got to unimportant questions, like favorite movies and television shows, they'd laughed themselves dizzy remembering jokes from silly comedies. Laughed some more about bad childhood haircuts and mean teachers they'd hated in school.

They had stayed long after the restaurant had emptied, until the staff had been ready to leave. Feng had walked them out to the street and waved them goodbye as they'd tucked themselves into the car so Leonard could deposit them home.

Holly drifted off to sleep, replaying over and over again how Ethan had gently kissed the back of her hand and thanked her for an unforgettable day before he closed the bedroom door.

In the morning, Ethan scrutinized his unshaven face in the bathroom mirror. He hadn't laughed as much as he had last night in a long time. Truth be told, he couldn't remember ever laughing that much. Everything was full power with Holly. Near her, he felt alive with a liquid fire.

That might burn down his life as he knew it.

After showering and dressing, he charted a direct route into the kitchen toward the coffeepot.

"Morning," she greeted him.

"Yes."

He was careful not to touch her as he crossed behind her in the tiny kitchen to pour a cup. It took stupendous will not to reach for her, to put his arms around her waist and find out what her hair might smell like if his face was buried in it.

Instead, more guarding and defending.

He gained distance by busying himself with checking the morning's urgencies on his tablet. His approval was needed on important architectural specifications for the Jersey City project. An email chain between several of the interested parties provided updates. Thank heavens for work. He needed the interruption from his growing and wholly off-track desires for more than what he'd signed up for with Holly.

Despite his efforts, his eyes of their own volition kept darting upward from the screen as he watched her lay out a light breakfast of toast and juice.

"Right, then, we have an important day," he directed

as soon as they'd sat down with their food. "Aunt Louise and Fernando will arrive at six o'clock. She does not like to stay out late in the evening. We should have dinner on the table by seven."

"I made a shopping list," Holly reported. "I'll go to the store, then get the pot roast into the slow cooker."

"I have several meetings today. Can you manage the shopping on your own?"

She snickered. "I've been doing the grocery shopping since I was seven years old. I think I can handle a New York City supermarket."

"I am the one who would have trouble."

"But after that I'll need you for the painting. I have the canvas size I want. And I'll use acrylic so it will dry quickly. We'll hang it later this afternoon, and no one will be any the wiser that I only painted it today."

With a busy day ahead, he'd selectively forgotten that he had agreed to her doing a painting of him. He had no time for posing. Although a painting by her would be a very eye-catching and convincing symbol that they were really a couple.

Plus, it would put him in proximity with her from midday. Which he had to admit he'd be looking forward to.

He mentally reprimanded himself for that thought.

In front of the building, Ethan watched Holly walk down the block while Leonard held the car door open for him. Her glossy hair swung to and fro. It was another gloomy day, but dry at the moment. Her jeans and that black leather jacket she seemed to favor would be sufficient for her shopping trip. Why he was concerned with how she was dressed for the weather was baffling. And disturbing.

But what would a Florida girl know about winter? She might catch cold…

Leonard ferried him from one appointment to the next. The low-income housing project in the Bronx was behind schedule and over budget. He pored over blueprints with the architect until they found a way to enlarge the kitchens for the exterior-facing units. The architect was feuding with the contractor over the selection of materials, but that always seemed to be the case. Ethan was able to smooth some ruffled feathers.

He stopped at the hotel where the shareholders' gala would be held on Saturday. Gave his authorization for the layout of the ballroom. Visualizing the room full of formally dressed people, he could picture them raising their champagne glasses as Aunt Louise offered a toast to him and Holly. His bride-to-be would charm the crowd with her engaging smile and shimmering gown…

In the silence of the empty ballroom, Ethan's heart pleaded for something he couldn't fully grasp. A dull ache thudded in the center of his chest.

Swiftly shoving those confusing feelings aside, he hurried out through the hotel doors to Leonard's car and his next meeting.

The multi-use development in Chelsea had come a long way since he'd last seen it. As he strode through he offered dozens of hellos to the many workers laboring on the project's five buildings. It was for this large venture that he'd offered Holly the commission to do the artwork. The opportunity that had sealed the negotiations for her to agree to pose as his fiancée.

Ethan's interior designer had been intrigued to hear about the up-and-coming artist from Florida he had brought onto the job. He had provided Stella with Holly's website address.

Midday, he returned to the apartment. Holly must not have had any trouble with the slow cooker, because the aroma of cooking meat practically had him salivating.

"My, my…" he said as he removed his coat and hung it on the rack.

The open area by the living room window had been turned into a temporary artist's studio.

"I've been working."

"I can see."

The easel they had bought yesterday was unpacked and in use. A side table with a tarp thrown over it for protection had become a paint station. Another tarp covered the area's floor.

"What have you done with my apartment?"

"Hey, I thought it was *my* apartment."

"Tonight it will be *our* apartment."

"Don't worry. I'll clean it all up after I do the painting of you."

"What do we have here?"

Three pastel drawings on paper lay on the floor. Moving vehicles was their theme. One was a bright yellow taxi done in abstracted horizontal lines that made it look as if it was in motion. Ditto for a blue city bus motoring along. And likewise for a silver train car that appeared to be whizzing by.

"I was working out some ideas. Will there be a valet and transportation station at the Chelsea development?"

Of course. He nodded with immediate understanding. Paintings like this would be stylish and hip, and convey the movement of the city. They'd be perfect. Even if their marriage arrangement proved to be the wrong move, Ethan was at least sure he'd hired an artist who would produce what he needed for the multi-million-dollar project.

"Excellent."

"We'd better not waste any time. When can you be ready to sit for me?"

A grin tried to crack at his mouth. "Let me just wash up. Dinner smells delicious."

Minutes later, he stepped onto the tarp of her studio area.

"I am ready for you," he said bravely, with arms outstretched.

In reality, he didn't know what to expect. Was not at all comfortable with how Holly might portray him. He reminded himself that this was ultimately for the good of Aunt Louise. He could put up with a little uneasiness for the sake of her wellbeing.

"I'll have you sitting on the stool." Holly, all business, gestured for him to take his place.

She studied him intently. Backed away to get one perspective. Inched to the side for another. Then came in close. So close he could feel the heat of her body, which made him want to do anything *but* sit still.

"What are you deciding on?"

"The perspective. I think I'll do it at an angle that's a partial profile."

"Will it be only my face?"

She ran a finger across his upper chest from shoulder to shoulder to illustrate the cut-off point. Blood pumped double-time to every inch of him she touched. He instinctively leaned away.

"Don't worry. I won't bite."

His voice came out a jagged growl. "It was not you I was worried about."

She smiled quizzically for several beats. His chest muscles continued to vibrate from her touch.

It occurred to him that for all the questions they'd asked each other about favorite things and childhood memories, they hadn't talked about past relationships.

Had a man broken her heart? Had she broken someone's? Was she looking for love?

Did she wonder about him?

Love wasn't on the bargaining table in their business deal. He'd never loved. Didn't love. Wouldn't love. That was a contract signed a long time ago.

Holly programmed some upbeat music into her phone and began. She wanted to do a preliminary pencil drawing on paper, and when she was satisfied with that move on to paint and canvas.

With a last adjustment to his angle, she requested, "Try not to move."

"Do I need to be silent?"

"I'll let you know when I'm sketching your mouth. Just keep your head still when you talk."

With his face turned toward the window, it was odd to feel her eyes on him when he couldn't see her face. Odd, but spine-tingling. And erotic. He wished he could rip off his clothes and have her paint him in the nude.

Holly made him want to let go of the well-bred and well-mannered businessman he was. With her, he wanted to howl naked under the moonlight. And to ravage her with the savage passion he kept tightly caged inside him.

"Can you soften your facial expression?" she asked, making him realize that he was not masking his arousal.

He neutralized his jaw.

"Tell me about your morning," she coaxed.

He appreciated her trying to help him relax. "There are ongoing issues with my housing development in the Bronx. I want to build the maximum number of comfortable units on the property to give as many families as possible a home of their own."

"What are the problems?"

"Materials are costly. I have shareholders to answer to. And Aunt Louise. I promised this as a break-even project—not one on which the company would lose a lot of money. I may have to move it into the category of charitable endeavor. I will have to present it accordingly. Tricky."

"Here, take a look." Holly unclipped from the easel the large piece of paper she'd been using for her sketch and held it up in front of her for him to see.

After preparing himself to hate it, he saw that it wasn't bad at all. She'd used those same short lines she had on the transportation drawings. Together, the strokes formed the likeness of a pensive man looking into the distance.

Holly's face was flushed. She was nervously waiting for his reaction.

With a voice tight and caught, she squeaked, "What do you think?"

"Is this how I look?"

"Well, obviously you're handsome. I hoped I could convey your seriousness, too."

She'd said "handsome" as matter-of-factly as it would have been to say he was wearing a white shirt. He liked it that she thought he was handsome.

"I suppose I am serious."

"That feels like your core. You're formal. You're measured."

"Whereas *you* just say or do anything that comes into your mind."

"And you don't seem like someone who ever loses control."

Oh, if she only knew the thoughts he was having about grabbing her and showing her exactly how out of control he could be.

She was uncovering wild ideas in him. Holly, with her mesmerizing black hair and sinewy limbs. He'd stripped open more of his true self to her in the last two days than he had with anyone in his life. Not all his secrets, but he'd revealed a lot.

And he must rein that in right now. She only needed to know what was relevant to their phony engagement. Nothing more.

He stood up from his stool to stretch and take a break. Checked messages on his phone. Fired off a couple of texts.

Using a sketchpad, Holly quickly drew more versions

of his mouth until she was satisfied. Then showed him the one that she liked.

"Interesting… It looks as if it is easy enough for you to make a small correction here and there and come out with a quite different result."

She shrugged her shoulders. "I guess so. Trial and error."

"I would not have a clue how to do that."

"I'll show you sometime."

"I would like that."

How absurd this was—letting someone sketch his mouth. In the middle of a workday. When he had a thousand other things on his mind.

But he didn't care. Inexplicably, he wanted to be near Holly. She'd definitely cast a spell on him.

She lifted a large canvas onto her easel and adjusted the height. Then picked out her first brush.

"I'm ready to paint. Let's begin."

"Holly Motta, this is my aunt, Louise Benton." Ethan made the introduction as soon as he'd ushered in the visitors.

With a welcoming smile Holly shook the older lady's hand. "I'm happy to finally meet you. I've heard so much about you."

"And I so little about you…" Louise assessed her. "How pretty you are, dear."

"I'd say the same about you. Let Ethan take your coat."

Holly reminded herself to stay focused in spite of her nerves. At this moment her end of the contract had come due. Louise had to be convinced beyond a shadow of a doubt that not only was she Ethan's true love, but that he had made the right choice in her.

As Ethan helped his aunt to remove her coat Louise almost lost her balance. A telltale sign of her medical condition. How difficult living with a chronic problem like that must be. Still, Louise had style despite her petite and frail frame. A sheet of thin white hair curled under at her shoulders…her simple dark green dress was the picture of good taste.

She was the type of accomplished woman Holly looked up to. Holly was glad she had chosen to wear the black trousers and gray blouse from the new clothes Ethan had bought her. Even though it was dinner at home, these were not people who dined in jeans.

"Such an unusual silver necklace…" Holly initiated conversation.

Louise looked to Ethan. "Yes, my dear nephew brought it back from…remind me where it was from?"

"Turkey."

"Yes, Istanbul. Ethan always brings me unique trinkets from his travels."

With Louise's head turned toward Ethan, Holly noticed the large bruise across her cheekbone. That must have been from the fall Ethan had said she'd taken last week. Holly understood his wish to shield his aunt from the public eye, with her decline so visible.

"Huh…low…oh…" Louise's husband, Fernando, finally insisted on being acknowledged. Ethan hadn't yet taken his coat, and nor had an introduction been made.

"Yes, Fernando Layne—meet my fiancée, Holly Motta."

"Charmed," Fernando replied, without extending his hand.

"Nice to meet you." Holly rocked back on her heels, unsure how to move on if they weren't going to shake hands.

"Are we having cocktails?" Fernando flung his coat to Ethan.

"Let me mix you something," Ethan offered.

"I know where the drinks are." Fernando rebuffed him and headed to the liquor cabinet.

Ethan had told Holly it was Fernando who had bought

this apartment. On behalf of Benton Worldwide and with the company's money, of course. And that he made frequent shopping trips to New York.

Forty-five years old trying to look twenty-five, judging from his slicked-back hair and skinny pants. No doubt Fernando preferred chic New York to less flashy Boston, although Holly couldn't say for sure having never been there. But in an instant she knew that she wouldn't trust Fernando if her life depended on it.

"Louise." Fernando presented his wife with a glass of brown liquor.

She refused. "You know I'm not drinking with the new medications," she said.

"A sparkling water, then." He took the glass and drank it in one tip, then scurried back to the bar to pour Louise some water. Not asking if Holly and Ethan wanted anything.

Fernando's eye caught the painting of Ethan, now on the wall where those impersonal black and white photos had been. "You two have certainly settled in."

Holly bit her lip. *If he only knew.* About her barging in on Ethan just two days ago… That this apartment Fernando thought was his had become part of Ethan and Holly's agreement… How no one in this room knew that her feelings for Ethan were becoming closer to real rather than the masquerade they were meant to be…

"Did you do this, my dear?" Louise moved toward the painting to take a closer look.

It had turned out well, especially for only an afternoon's work. It was all done in blue—a tribute to the paint color she'd had on her face and hands when she had first rushed into this apartment, expecting it to be empty.

She'd probably had more fun than she should have painting Ethan. What an impressive subject he was. With his upright posture. Finely chiseled jaw. The deep, deep eyes with just a hint of crinkle at the outer corners. And his mouth! That mouth! No wonder it had taken her a few sketches until she got it right. Lips not so full as to be feminine. Lips she longed to explore with her own, not with her paintbrush…

"The first of many to come, I hope." Holly slipped her arm through Ethan's in a way she thought a fiancée in love might. His muscles jumped, but at least he didn't bristle and pull away. "Ethan's not keen on sitting for me."

"He never was," Louise agreed. "Didn't we have to bribe you with sweets in order to get you to stay still for those Christmas portraits every year?"

"I told Holly about that crotchety old painter who smelled of pipe tobacco. She is lucky I was not scarred for life."

Conversational banter. *Check.* This couldn't be going better.

"I see you captured that distinctive curl of hair over Ethan's forehead," Louise noted.

That curl had captured Holly—not the other way around. The magnificent way his wavy hair spilled over in front. Just a little bit. Just enough…

It was the one thing that wasn't completely tamed and restrained about Ethan. Somehow that curl hinted at the fiery, emotional man she knew lay beneath the custom-made suits and the multi-million-dollar deals.

"I certainly never learned how to paint or draw," Ethan said, with a convincingly proud smile of approval at his fiancée's handiwork.

While they chatted about the painting Fernando moseyed over to Ethan's desk. Out of the corner of her eye, Holly saw him snooping at the papers on top of it.

Fernando was making himself a bit too much at home. Funny that Holly felt territorial after only two days. She knew that Fernando used this apartment frequently. But he didn't keep any of his personal possessions here because other employees and associates of Benton Worldwide also used it when they were in New York.

Still, she didn't think Fernando had the right to be looking at anything Ethan might have put down on the desk. But it wasn't her place to say anything.

"Louise, would you like to sit down at the table?" Holly suggested.

She took Louise's elbow and guided her toward the dining area. Ethan and Fernando followed suit behind them.

Holly overheard Fernando hiss to Ethan, "I know what you're up to. You've found a wife so that Louise will retire and you can take over. If you think I'm going to spend the rest of her life getting sunburned on a boring island, you've got another think coming."

CHAPTER SEVEN

"SO FAR SO GOOD," Holly said as she placed four plates on the kitchen counter so that she and Ethan could begin to serve dinner.

"Except that I had forgotten how much I detest that little Fernando," he retorted.

Holly was only playing the role of soon-to-be member of this unusual family. She shouldn't be privy to the disagreements and resentments that might lie beneath the surface. So it wouldn't be proper for her to ask Ethan what Fernando had meant about not wanting to move to Barbados when Louise retired. Obviously the comment had made Ethan mad.

She removed the lid of the slow cooker. "Where did they meet?"

Speaking in a hushed voice, because Aunt Louise and her man-toy weren't far away at the dining table, Ethan explained. "Our office manager at Headquarters hired him. His title is 'Client Relations Coordinator,' or some such nonsense. He does scarcely more than order fancy coffees for meetings and come here to New York or go to Europe to spend the company's money. Of course I cannot fire him." Ethan gritted his teeth. "As much as I would like to."

With serving utensils, Holly lifted hearty chunks of the pot roast onto each plate. Ethan reached in with a fork to assist her. They worked seamlessly as a team, anticipating each other's moves. Now pros at navigating the square footage of the small kitchen.

"What does she see in him?"

"Companionship. I suppose he makes her feel younger. She was devastated after Uncle Mel died."

"She must miss Mel horribly."

"They were a partnership in more ways than I can count. Not being able to have children brought them even closer. Taking me in was another thing they did together."

With Ethan having witnessed such a solid marriage between his aunt and uncle, Holly wondered why he was so adamant that he himself would never marry for love. What had happened to close him off to the possibility?

Ethan ladled mashed potatoes while Holly spooned gravy on top. "So Fernando has been able to fill the hole left by your uncle's death?"

"Hardly. He could *never* step into my uncle's shoes. But I will grant that he provides a diversion. Within a year of Uncle Mel's death Aunt Louise began having symptoms of this hereditary neuropathy that she remembers her mother suffering from."

"Losing your husband and developing an illness, one after the other. That's awful."

"She could have sunk into a depression. Fernando at least gives her something to do. He keeps her busy with Boston society dinners and parties on Cape Cod. He will do the same in Barbados. I will remind him that *I* am the boss as often as I need to. We know a lot of people there. He can develop a social calendar for her."

"Give her things to look forward to?"

"Yes. Without children, there are no grandchildren on the horizon. Although I suppose she assumes you and I will have..." He trailed off.

Children. With Ethan.

The mere thought halted Holly in place. A home of her own. Filled with noise and food and laughter and love. Beautiful toddlers running around with reddish-brown tufts of hair falling onto their foreheads. Tall Ethan reaching down to hold little hands.

Did he ever think about having children?

He'd frozen too, holding a spoon in his hand, also lost in contemplation. Was he picturing the same thing?

He'd be a good father. The way he put so much care and thought into his aunt and what was best for her was like the devotion and concern she had for Vince, having practically raised her brother single-handedly because her mother had proved incapable. She had more of that kind of love to give.

Someday.

It wasn't going to be now.

That was much further far down the line. If ever.

No, this current arrangement was ideal. A new life for herself in New York. Not being pulled down by other people. Putting herself first. Free at last.

Everything was upfront with Ethan. There was zero chance of her being hurt. Zero love. Zero disappointment. So he was intelligent and intense? And gorgeous? That was ultimately irrelevant to the duties at hand. They were two professionals, doing their jobs.

Holly used tongs to crown each dinner plate with roasted carrots. Forging ahead. Although she wished her fingernails weren't spotted with paint.

"We did it. Dinner is served."

As she carried two plates to the dining table, she saw Fernando's hand atop of Louise's. The older woman's face did seem to have a livelier blush with his attention on her. Even if Fernando's intentions were less than honorable, Holly could understand the purpose he filled. Life was all about compromises.

Ethan brought the other two plates. While he poured water she ducked back into the kitchen for rolls and butter before sitting to eat.

"Holly, this is delicious," Louise proclaimed.

"I'm glad you like it. You sound surprised?"

"Indeed. I don't know that Ethan has ever dated a woman before who would know how to make an old-fashioned pot roast."

Ethan leaned to pat Holly's arm. She smiled at the unspoken compliment, as a fiancée should. "Aunt Louise, I have never dated a woman who has likely ever eaten pot roast, let alone prepared it."

"Where did you learn to cook like this?"

"I took a course in cooking classic American comfort food," Holly fibbed, without missing a beat. Louise didn't need to know that if she hadn't taught herself to cook she and Vince wouldn't have eaten. "I'll have to make cheeseburgers for you next time."

"Now, Ethan, dear," Louise said, "you have been keeping your delightful lady a secret. You must tell us everything about where and how you met," she insisted.

Fernando buttered a roll and gobbled it down.

Holly and Ethan, the happy couple, gazed lovingly at each other as if to signal that they were off and running. They'd been rehearsing. Now they'd be put to the test.

"Aunt Louise, I wanted to be absolutely sure of myself before I said anything to you," Ethan began. "Holly's brother is Vince Motta. He works for us in the Miami office."

Aunt Louise listened attentively as she continued eating. Fernando chomped on chunks of meat that he yanked off his fork with his lower teeth.

"It was at the groundbreaking ceremony for the Coconut Grove project," Holly continued. For accuracy, Ethan had filled her in on the details of that luncheon. "We were both reaching for the same shrimp on the buffet table. Our hands touched."

"And it was magic."

Ethan fluttered his eyelashes, which made Holly giggle.

She'd visualized this fairy tale over and over—to the point that now she would have sworn it had actually happened. The elegant outdoor celebration… Her in a pink dress, talking to her brother, Vince, and a couple of his coworkers… After excusing herself she left them to explore the lavish seafood table. And just as she reached for the plumpest, juiciest-looking shrimp on the tray a hand from the opposite direction nabbed the same one.

She tugged on her end of the shrimp, the other hand on the other end, until their fingers intertwined.

They turned to look at each other.

He surrendered the crustacean.

The skies parted.

The angels cascaded down from heaven playing trumpets.

"It was love at first shrimp…" They sighed in unison.

"How romantic." Louise was sufficiently charmed.

"We talked for hours that afternoon." Ethan laid it on thick. "But then I had to board a plane for Bangkok."

"We didn't see each other again for months."

Caught up in their "reminiscing," they moved their faces toward each other. Involuntarily. As if pulled together by a magnet.

Ethan bent in and brought his mouth to Holly's. Only it wasn't a feather-soft fake dinner kiss, meant to convince his aunt. No, his unexpected lips were bold. And hot. And they smashed against hers.

Their insistence didn't let her pull away. She swirled inside. Got lost in the moment. Let it go on several beats too many.

Until she could finally separate herself from him.

Holly feared that everyone at the table could hear her heart pounding outside her chest.

Ethan looked as shocked as she felt. But after a moment he picked up his fork and resumed eating. Following his lead, she did the same.

Fortunately neither Louise nor Fernando had noticed anything strange. Holly and Ethan were engaged, after all. Why *wouldn't* they spontaneously kiss?

But he wasn't helping her any with a kiss like that. Let that be a warning to her.

Louise inquired, "Are your people from Miami, dear?"

Holly barely had a moment to catch her breath—nowhere near enough time to recover from that inebriating kiss before there came the next flaming hoop she had to jump through. She didn't have "people." And the people she did have she needed to keep a secret. Her people were not Benton kind of people.

"No. Fort Pierce."

"Fort *Pierce*?" Fernando tossed back.

Certainly not the kind of stylish metropolis full of chic hotels, South Beach beauties and all-night parties that would interest him.

"We met again last year here in New York, when Holly was exhibiting paintings at a Soho gallery," Ethan fibbed to move their story forward.

"Then wasn't the next time when you came down and we visited Key West?"

He leaned over to brush the side of her cheek with the back of his hand. "It was then that I knew for sure."

His tender touch across Holly's face made it a struggle to keep her eyes open. Especially after that not so gentle kiss had rocked her to the bone.

Ethan sensed he had made her uncomfortable. "More water, anyone?" he said quickly, refilling glasses without waiting for an answer.

Thankfully giving her a moment to regroup.

After a couple of quiet sips Holly ventured, “I’m so happy we’re finally together in New York. I haven’t been here in five years.”

Ethan, Louise and Fernando all looked at her.

Oh, no! Oh! No!

Fernando’s eyes narrowed. “I thought you said you had a painting exhibition here last year?”

Gulp. Ethan’s soft stroke to her face had thrown her off course. Let her talk before she thought.

Dead silence. Which was finally broken by the sound of a fax coming in on Ethan’s desk.

“I meant that I haven’t explored the city in years.” Holly took a shot. “That was a work trip. I hardly left the gallery.”

“Shall we have dessert?” Ethan did his best to defuse the moment.

“Let me help you, dear.” Louise slowly rose and followed Ethan into the kitchen.

Fernando kept his glare on Holly one uncomfortable moment longer before he shot up to strut to the liquor cabinet.

Left at the table, Holly stood and began clearing the dishes. Not knowing how badly she had messed things up. Whether Ethan would be furious with her or sympathetic over her flub. Unsure if anyone had bought her quick cover-up.

Louise, even with her reduced ability, had offered to help Ethan with dessert in the kitchen. She must want to say something to him that she didn’t want Holly to hear.

Careful not to interrupt Ethan and his aunt’s private conversation, she stacked the dirty plates and brushed crumbs off the table. The dessert dishes and silverware were on a side shelf, so she set those out.

The evening had been going so nicely. Louise seemed

to like her. Hopefully Holly hadn't unraveled everything with one slip of the tongue.

With each passing minute Holly had come to like the idea of being Ethan's pretend fiancée more and more. She wanted to make this work. To have the art commission and a place to live. It was a peculiar arrangement, for sure, but a better starting point for a new life than she could ever have imagined. At almost thirty, it was time for her to rewind and reboot. Put the bad choices—Ricky—and the bad luck—her mother—behind her.

When Ethan had sweetened the deal by agreeing to use his influence to help her brother, Vince, get a promotion, Holly had had to roll the dice and give it a try. Ethan had said he couldn't make any promises, but Holly knew Vince was a hard and devoted worker who could easily manage additional responsibilities. She'd never forgive herself if her mistake tonight had done anything to endanger his chances of success.

And, *wow*, she was going to have to lay down some ground rules about her physical interactions with Ethan. She was shocked at how she was drawn to him almost hypnotically, easily touching his arm and lightly laying a hand on the small of his back as if it was no big deal. Like a fiancée would.

But that kiss had shown her how quickly things could go too far. His mouth on hers had dizzied her, made her lose track of her thoughts, forget the company she was in. Ethan's lips were dangerous weapons. They could completely daze her, leave her woozy and unable to do the job he had hired her for.

What she needed was to figure out a system whereby his touch had no effect on her. She'd work that out. This *was* playacting, after all.

The dessert and coffee dishes set, an odd sight greeted Holly when she turned around from the table. Fernando was again in front of Ethan's desk. This time he was peering at the fax they had just heard come through. His eyes widened and he snatched the piece of paper from the machine, folded it and slid it into his pocket. Not noticing that Holly was watching.

Because Fernando supposedly spent a lot of time in this apartment, the fax might be something he was expecting. But it irked her that he was again hovering around the paperwork and personal items that Ethan had spread out on the desk. However, she didn't know all the facts. He was Louise's husband. She couldn't question him even though she wanted to. She was a hired hand who didn't know what went on in this family.

She had already screwed up. Her job right now was to keep her nose down. And do her best to salvage the rest of the evening.

Ethan's arm around Holly's shoulder, they said goodbye to Louise and Fernando as the elevator door closed.

Back in the apartment, Ethan clenched his fist in victory. "Success!"

"Do you think everything went all right? I was so worried. And then I bungled up about not having spent time in New York."

"You recovered. Aunt Louise adored you instantly."

"She did?"

"In the kitchen she told me she could tell right away that you had good character and were not out for our money or the family name."

"If she only knew…"

Ethan mused on that truth.

Together they cleared the remains of the apple crisp and cinnamon-flavored coffee. The kitchen looked as if they had just fed a hundred people. Dirty pots and pans were strewn on every available surface. The sink was stacked with plates. Spills puddled on the countertops.

"I will pay the housekeeper triple to clean this tomorrow!" Ethan said.

"Do you want to go out?" Holly asked.

"Out? Right now?"

"Yes. It's not that late. And I'm full of nervous energy."

Ethan contemplated the idea. Aunt Louise had started to tire so easily the dinner had been over even earlier than expected. "Where would you like to go?"

"Show me some of the Benton buildings in New York."

He whipped out his phone.

Ten minutes later they were curbside as Leonard pulled up in the town car. It was a dry but very cold evening. Holly wore that favorite black leather jacket, and looked utterly lovable with a red beanie, scarf and gloves. Ethan didn't bring a hat, but dressed warmly with his own brown leather jacket and wool scarf.

Once they'd pulled away from the building Ethan recited to Leonard a quick list of addresses and the tour commenced. As usual, his driver maneuvered the car deftly through the always-present Manhattan traffic.

Holly had had the right idea. The crisp night was invigorating.

Or maybe *she* was the cause of the vigor he felt.

She had played her part to a tee at dinner, and he was sure Aunt Louise suspected nothing of his ruse. How fragile his dearly loved aunt had looked tonight. With those bruises on her face from the tumble she'd taken—in front of employees, no less—at Benton headquarters.

He plugged a reminder into his phone to hire an expert makeup artist for the gala.

But a nagging complication had plagued him throughout dinner. Nothing about the evening had felt fake. Everything had come naturally. From their comfortable banter to the way he and Holly had served the food together and the electrifying kiss they'd shared while telling the story of how they met.

Moment after moment had passed when he had almost forgotten this was a charade. Worse still, the feeling had filled him with a jarring elation and contentment.

This was new territory and it petrified him. He'd never given serious thought to a real-life real wife, and now was not the time to start. Concentrating on moving Aunt Louise into retirement and moving the company into a more charitable direction was plenty for the foreseeable future. Plus, he had vowed long ago never to be swayed into forgetting one critical fact.

Women were not to be trusted.

Aunt Louise was the only exception in his life. Didn't he know that well enough?

All—and that meant *all*—the women he had ever dated had betrayed him. Society girls, daughters of noblemen and businesswomen alike. They might have approached him as a colleague. Or cozied up to him as the wholesome girl-next-door. Others had come on stronger and seduced him with sexual wiles.

Not that he hadn't gone along with them.

He'd satisfied his urges. Indulged in temptations.

Several of them quite memorable.

Yes, maybe a few of them had made him imagine going past three dates or three weeks. But in the end they had always showed their true colors. They hadn't been who they'd said they were. Even some of their body parts hadn't been real. They had all been something other than what they had seemed. Out for something. A piece of *him*.

And his mother—his own mother—had been the worst offender of them all. That a woman could turn her back on her own son for personal gain was a hurt he'd do well to remember for the rest of his life. Apparently women were capable of the unthinkable.

So, even though his aunt sensed that Holly's intentions were good, he mustn't forget that they were performing in a play. All he could really know was that Holly was a competent actress. Instinct told him that this enchanting woman had a kind heart and honorable aims. But he'd only known her for a couple of days. She might prove herself to be just like the others. And there was plenty she could be hiding. Ethan hadn't received the background probe from his security chief yet.

"This is the Seventy-Fourth Street development we did about a decade ago." He pointed out the window when they reached their first destination. "Leonard, can you pull over to the curb?"

Lit from within, the gleaming glass tower shot upward into the night sky. Ethan leaned close to Holly, beside him in the backseat, to show off some details.

"We did the first story with a wider base, and then the remaining twenty-nine floors in a slender tower coming up in the middle. The larger platform of the first level allows for greenery to encircle building."

"Is the first-story garden accessible?" Holly asked, wide-eyed.

"Yes. It was designed so that employees in the offices can go outside into green space whenever they want."

Their next destination was Forty-First Street.

"This one is over twenty-five years old. It was the last project my father worked on before he died. Here they had the issue of erecting new construction in between two buildings from the nineteen-thirties," he explained.

"New York is amazing like that, isn't it?" Holly seemed to understand him.

"You can see that we did not build right up against the buildings on either side. We created those cement walkways and benches." He pointed. "We built our structure thinner than we might have, so that occupants in the buildings on either side could still see out of their windows."

Ethan was enjoying this tremendously. He was so proud of what his father, Uncle Mel and Aunt Louise had produced. He loved to visit the Benton properties that his father had helped construct. They were all he had left of his dad. Steel, glass and concrete. But they were monuments that would endure for years to come.

They rode downtown to look at a low-rise housing development near the East River. Holly asked a million questions about why a door was placed where it was and what materials had been used for what.

Next was a refurbishment in Greenwich Village from the eighteen-nineties. "We spent a fortune on those windows!"

"They look original." Holly nodded in appreciation.

"That was the idea."

Then Ethan had Leonard park curbside in front of the massive Chelsea construction zone. The steel skeleton columns were up for all five buildings. Architectural renderings of what the finished project would look like were hung on fences and announced it to be "Benton Chelsea Plaza."

"This is all one property?" Holly was surprised by the size of the site.

"Five buildings of living, working and retail space. And I have commissioned a talented and, I might add, beautiful painter to do the artwork for the public spaces."

"The Chelsea project! This is it!"

Despite the cold, she lowered the car window and jutted out half of her torso to get a better view. Ethan bent forward to get an arm in front of her and pointed out some features.

Although he'd make sure Aunt Louise received the accolades, this venture was really all his. He'd made the difficult decisions and agonized over the setbacks. He knew this endeavor would have made Uncle Mel and his father proud if they had been alive to see it. And it would allow Aunt Louise to go into retirement on a high note.

His chest pressed into Holly's back as he pointed through the window. Impulse ordered him to move her scarf aside, so that he could kiss the back of her neck. Sheer will kept him from doing so. But it was being sorely tested in this close proximity.

It wasn't difficult to envision losing power over himself in an instant and laying her down on the car seat, climbing on top of her and delving into her softness. A softness he might not ever be able to return from.

Which was not at all part of their deal.

In fact, that kiss at dinner had been much too much. He himself had been startled by the force of it. He could sense it had unbalanced Holly as well.

He'd only meant to enhance their charade with some harmless and sanctioned affection. Prior to that his "guard and defend" strategy had helped him withstand her casual pats on his arm and his back all evening. Yet his own lips had barely touched hers when they'd begun to demand more, and he hadn't restrained himself in time. That kiss had been out of the scope of what was necessary in both intensity and duration.

His actions had overpowered him—a phenomenon he wasn't accustomed to. Lesson learned.

He forced himself back to describing the project. "For Building One we have leases for three fine dining restaurants and a food court of six casual establishments."

"So all that open space will be outdoor seating?"

"Exactly. And we will have a retractable awning with heating units for the colder months."

"I can imagine it."

He continued telling her about the plaza's features. As

with everything Benton Worldwide built, Ethan hoped to live up to architecture's fundamental principle of providing a building with both form and function for its users.

"I just thought of one other building I would like to take you to see. It is not a Benton property, but I think you will agree it has merit."

"You've brought me to the Empire State Building?" As she and Ethan got out of the car Holly craned her neck up at the monolith.

"As long as we were looking at New York architecture," he said, nodding, "I thought we ought to give this grand dame her due."

Taking her hand, Ethan led her into the Art Deco lobby, with its twenty-four-karat gold ceiling murals and marble walls. "Whew!" she whistled.

"Do you want to go up to the top?" he asked.

"Heck, *yes*."

But as they rode the escalator up one floor to the ticketing level memory slapped Holly hard.

She didn't mention to Ethan that she had been here once before. With Ricky. They'd come to New York for a long summer weekend. Stayed in a cheap hotel room in New Jersey.

The Empire State Building had been one of the sights Holly had most wanted to see on their trip. The weather had been hot and humid and the ticket lines crowded with tourists. Unlike tonight—late on a winter Wednesday.

Ricky had got impatient. He'd wanted a beer. He'd tugged her back down to street level, found a bar and that had been the last Holly had seen of the Empire State Building.

"Are you nervous about the elevator ride up?" Ethan asked, reacting to what must be showing on her face.

"No! I was just…um…let's go!"

Rocketing into the sky, Holly felt excitement pump through her veins. She was happy to leave old memories as far behind as she was leaving the asphalt of Thirty-Fourth Street and Fifth Avenue.

When they reached the top Ethan guided her quickly through the indoor viewpoints and exhibits to the outside observation deck.

And there it was.

Three hundred and sixty degrees of New York in the dazzling clear night.

It was utterly freezing. Two sorts of chills ran through her—one from the cold and the other sheer awe.

"Oh. My. Gosh." That was all she could say.

The city was so glorious, with the grid of its streets, the grandeur of its buildings and the galaxies of its lights.

They passed a few other visitors as they circled the deck. Holly gawked at Times Square. At Central Park. The Chrysler Building. The Statue of Liberty. The Hudson River.

She begged for a second lap around. "Let's take selfies!" She grinned as she pulled out her phone.

"You look very beautiful," Ethan said in a husky voice. "Your cheeks are pink from the cold."

She sensed him watching her more than he was looking at the views. He'd seen the sight of Manhattan before. It was probably all ho-hum to a global traveler like him. He had seen all the wonders of the world. And was probably amused at Holly's enthusiasm.

But he gamely put his arm around her and they posed to get photos with the skyline behind them, the Brooklyn Bridge in the distance. Holly surrendered the phone to him, to lift it higher than she could. He clicked several shots.

As he handed the phone back to her he kissed her on the cheek.

"I am *so* sorry." He backed away. "I did not mean to do that. I have no idea why I did."

"Maybe because a million romantic movie scenes have taken place right here?"

"Yes, that must be it. My apologies. It will not happen again."

She braved it and said what she wanted to say. "Actually, I'm glad you did. At dinner in front of your aunt and Fernando I got so flustered when you kissed me. I think I'll need to practice physical contact with you until it feels more expected."

She wasn't sure if she had really said that out loud or merely thought it. Rehearse kissing Ethan? That was insane.

"You might be right."

He moved in front of her so they were face to face. With her back to the observation deck's railing. The glistening city behind her.

Her breath sputtered. "In order to be convincing…"

Ethan arched down and brushed his mouth ever so slightly against hers. A wisp of his breath warmed her lips when he asked, "So, for example, you need to practice doing that?"

"Uh-huh," she squeaked out.

Why did he have to be so attractive? This would be much easier if she had become the fake fiancée of an unappealing man who didn't ignite her inside.

Clearly practice was all that was needed. Practice would make perfect. Eventually she'd become numb to him. Kissing would be a choreographed action they'd perform like trained seals.

She was sure of it.

"What about this?" he taunted, and more strength applied a firmer kiss to her lips.

A jolt shot up her back. Her hips rocked forward uncontrollably.

"I... I..." She struggled to take in a complete breath. "I think I need to work on that one."

She tilted her head back for mercy.

Giving her none, he took both sides of her face in his two hands and drew her to him. He kissed her yet again. Harder. Longer.

"Do we need to rehearse this?"

Now he'd opened his mouth. And he didn't stop there. The tip of his tongue parted her lips. Forced her tongue to meet his. Drove her to take. Give. Insist on more.

A dark moan rumbled from low in his gut.

A group of tourists strode past, ignoring them and pointing out landmarks in spirited voices. Holly couldn't see them. Ethan was all she could see.

His hands slid from the sides of her face slowly down her arms to the tips of her fingers. His lips traced across her jaw and then he murmured into her neck, "Do you think an engaged couple might need to kiss like that on occasion?"

"I do," she whispered.

He took hold of her hips and crushed himself into her. Pinned her back against the railing. She stretched her arms up around his neck, going pliant and yielding against the steel of his body.

With New York as her witness, he kissed her again and again and again. Until they had only one heartbeat. Until there could be no doubt in anyone's mind that this was a couple who were deeply in love.

CHAPTER EIGHT

FLOATING ON A CLOUD. Ethan had heard that saying before but this was the first time he'd experienced what it meant. Yes, his physical body lay on the uncomfortable leather sofa that was too small to stretch out on. But his heart and soul wafted above him in a silken, curvy vision he never wanted to wake from.

Of course, real sleep eluded him. It seemed an utter waste of time when Holly Motta was in the world. Sleep would just be hours and minutes spent away from thinking about her. What if, during sleep, his subconscious drifted away from the cocoon of her embrace? No, sleep was not time well spent. Not when instead he could linger in this half-daze, filled with the memory of her velvety lips on his and her long arms wrapped around him.

Though reality nagged at him.

After that mind-bending interlude of kissing at the Empire State Building they both knew that something unintentional, inappropriate and very dangerous had passed between them. Something they were going to need to backtrack from. To run from. And to return themselves to the "strictly business" contract they had made.

During the car ride afterward they'd chit-chatted about the architecture of a couple of noteworthy buildings along the way. Once they'd got home Holly hadn't been able to get away from him fast enough. She'd emerged from the bathroom in a tee shirt and pajama shorts, poured herself a glass of water, voiced a quick good-night and then rapped the bedroom door closed with her foot.

Ethan hoped that she was in his bed, resting in peaceful sleep. At least one of them ought to be. If he was being honest, he also hoped that she was having sweet dreams about him. Just as he was drifting in his trance about her.

As the endless night wore on Ethan's elation turned to irritation. This was not what he'd signed up for. Lying awake thinking about a woman? *No deal!*

He couldn't afford to have that kind of preoccupation in his life. None of his plans included a woman.

Sure, he could enjoy the company of the exotic and enticing females that his travels put him in contact with. That was a game he could play indefinitely. He wanted something from them that they'd readily give in exchange for a taste of his affluence and the limelight. Then they would want more and he would move on. He knew the routine well.

For all his aunt's prodding, Ethan hadn't ever truly acknowledged the possibility of really devoting himself to someone and building an inner circle with them. A private life together. Not after what he'd seen of the world. Not after his mother.

Blasted Holly! She'd exploded into his life and detonated every stronghold he held.

Worse still, to all intents and purposes he had reached the point of no return with her. He'd already introduced her to Aunt Louise. The gala was in three days. It would be a huge setback to back out now.

There was no choice but to see this through. However, once his aunt had stepped down and was securely ensconced in the warm Barbados sand, Ethan might have to cut the Holly engagement short. He couldn't take much more of this.

Uncle Mel had taught him that admitting and analyzing his mistakes was the crucial first step toward moving forward. Ethan had made a grave error in misjudging his own ability to keep this a purely business transaction.

Or perhaps it was just Holly. He'd chosen the wrong person for the job.

Holly was testimony that his aunt and uncle might be right—that an authentic love might be out there in the world for him. A love that was worth bowing to and sacrificing for. That defined his future and ordered everything else to work around it.

Which was not at all where Ethan was headed.

Argh! The road not taken… If only he had stuck to his original plan to hire an actress. She'd have been a consummate professional who knew exactly how to separate reality from performance. Her expertise would have shown him the way.

Just for torture, he flicked on a lamp and snatched his tablet from the coffee table. He clicked onto the website of the talent agency where he had located his original choice. The—unfortunately for him—pregnant Penelope Perkins. The website featured headshot photos of the talent they represented. Tap on the photo and a short bio appeared.

Ethan leaned back on the couch and studied Sienna Freeman. A willowy redhead with a daisy in her hair. An inquiring click told him that she had performed at regional theatres throughout the country, portraying the ingénue in famous American musicals. She looked as if she could have easily been groomed to play the fiancée in Ethan's little domestic drama. A sweet-faced young woman.

Trouble was, she wasn't Holly.

Gabrielle Rivera was a temptress with dark hair and crimson lips. A substantial list of her appearances in television comedies and commercials proved she was capable of working in a wide range of situations. Gabrielle would probably handle herself beautifully at important occasions. A fine choice.

Her fatal flaw? She wasn't Holly.

Glamazon Zara Reed was picture-perfect for a socialite wife. With her blond tresses swept into an up-do, Zara looked born to hang on a wealthy man's arm. Add in her master's degree in psychology and small roles in quirky films, and you had one convincing package. A jaw-dropper.

But—poor Zara. She simply wasn't Holly.

Enough! Ethan put the tablet down, turned off the light and attempted his now customary bent position on the sofa. Every molecule in his body screamed Holly's name.

He tossed until dawn, exhausted and annoyed.

Ethan came into the kitchen after he'd showered. Holly was picking at the apple crisp from the baking dish they had managed to stick in the refrigerator last night after Aunt Louise and Fernando had left.

Before they'd gone out looking at buildings. And at each other.

He joined her in scavenging through the mess of the kitchen for breakfast. "Is there coffee?"

She nodded. Once again, the cramped space was making her uneasy. Holly winced at every accidental slide against Ethan's starched white shirt or suit pants as she prepared two cups of java.

There had been quite enough touching him last night. She needed a break.

With him carrying the coffee, she followed him to the table with the apple crisp. She licked bits off her fingers as she folded herself into a chair.

"We could use forks," he suggested, "like evolved humans."

"Sorry if I'm not civilized enough for you."

"I did not say that."

He imitated her by gnawing his own fingerful of the leftover desert. Trying to make her laugh. Unsuccessfully.

Not that he didn't look cute doing it.

"I think it's obvious," she sneered.

Truth was, she was more than a little ticked off at what had happened last night at the Empire State Building. Even though she had asked for it. But how *dare* he kiss her like that if it didn't mean anything to him? That went way beyond the call of duty in this assignment she'd consented to.

Of course she'd had her part in it. She certainly hadn't pushed him away. The opposite, in fact. His kisses had fed a vital nutrient into her body that she had been starved of for so long she hadn't even known she was ravenous for it.

Nonetheless, she was still furious at him for stoking that hunger.

"What I think is obvious…" he paused for a sip of coffee "…is that you are angry at me and I do not know why."

"Welcome to marriage."

"No surprise I have steered clear of it."

She undid and redid her ponytail, buying a moment to regroup. Deciding to be honest.

"We went too far last night."

"I agree completely," he replied quickly.

"You do?"

His kisses hadn't offered any apology. They had been the kisses of a man entitled to his desires, who confidently took them with no cause for second guesses.

"Clearly we need to define the parameters of our physical contact," he stated, as if he was discussing an architectural floor plan. "It is important that we keep any sentiment out of the framework."

Was he admitting that he had felt as much as she had in that transcendental swirl of urgent kisses and intimate embraces? Or was he scolding her for crossing boundaries?

"It's my fault," she said, strategizing. "I asked you for some practice kissing because I don't want us to appear awkward in front of other people."

He took a minute to measure her words, carefully contemplating them before he responded.

"We simply got carried away," he concluded. "We will not do it again."

Inexplicably, her heart crashed to the floor. Which made no sense—because not passionately kissing Ethan Benton again was exactly what *did* need to happen.

"Right…" she granted. Yet sadness ricocheted between her ears.

As a diffuser, she munched on another chunk of the apple dessert.

Clearly no longer interested in the leftovers, Ethan reached for his phone. He ignored her to swipe, read and type.

She looked at her painting of him on the wall. She had never painted Ricky, nor the other couple of men she had dated. None of them had gotten under her skin like Ethan had. Filling her not only with the inclination but with the outright necessity to bring her brush to his likeness.

Ethan was like the multi-faceted diamond she wore on her finger. Every way she turned she saw something new. Something more. Something unexpected. Something unfathomable. She could paint him a hundred times and still not be done.

Eventually he glanced up and observed her, as if maybe he had forgotten she was in the room.

"So. Shall we establish some ground rules?"

"O-okay," she stumbled, unsure where he was going with this.

"I believe we *will* need to kiss on occasion. We will certainly want a convincing display of affection at the shareholders' gala, when our engagement is announced."

Holly braced herself, suddenly unsure if she was really going to be able to go through with this charade. She felt ill-suited to the task. It was too much.

"I think it will be beneficial for us to define what type of kissing is necessary," he continued.

"Absolutely," she bluffed, shifting in her seat.

"For example, I see no need for our tongues to touch, as they did last night."

Well, that was for sure. Her head and heart couldn't afford any more kisses like last night's. The kind that made a girl forget that she was only an employee of the most compelling and sexy man she had ever met. A man who had made it clear that he had hired her to help him protect his aunt, the only woman he'd ever love.

A fact she'd be wise to keep in the forefront of her mind. Which his kisses completely clouded.

"Got it—no tongues." She nodded once and reached her hand across the table to shake his in a gentlemen's agreement.

Ethan's mouth hooked up as he shook her hand. He was amused by her gesture of sportsmanship.

Except he didn't let go of her hand after the shake. In fact he fought to keep it like a possession he'd battle to the ground for. He turned it over and caressed the tops of her fingers with the pad of his thumb.

"I'd prefer it if you didn't press your body into mine." Holly yanked her hand free and continued. She sparked at the memory of last night's six feet and three inches of solid manpower searing into her.

"How far away shall I stand?" he asked, holding his thumb and forefinger apart as a measurement. "This far?"

"Further than that."

Widening the gap between his fingers, he tilted his head. “This far?”

“At least.”

“And would that be all of my body? Or just certain parts?”

Oh, Lordy, he was mocking her.

“Probably all parts.” She kept going. “Of course we should have friendly hugs, but nothing prolonged.”

“Shall I program a timer?” He smirked.

She lifted her palms in surrender. “Look, it was your idea to lay down some guidelines.”

“You are right. I did not realize how ludicrous it would sound stated aloud.” He abruptly stood and gathered his phone, tablet, keys and wallet. “For the moment we need not be concerned about our proximity to each other. My schedule today is filled with appointments.”

With that, he turned toward the front door. Holly shifted her eyes to spy him putting on his suit jacket followed by his overcoat. He picked up a roll of architectural blueprints that had been propped up beside the door, and out he went.

Holly wasn’t exactly sure why a sharp tear stung her cheek.

The left side needed more of the muddy purple she had mixed. Holly dipped thin bristles into the unusual color and applied them to her canvas. When they’d been at the art supply store Ethan had insisted on buying her a full range of brushes—a luxury she wasn’t used to. She flicked tiny lines with a brush that was ideal for the task of depicting the rain outside.

Music blared from her phone—a pop singer belting on about how it was time to move on from a man who had done her wrong.

A wild sprawl of buildings and weather… Holly couldn’t

decide whether or not she liked this painting. It didn't matter, though. The important thing was the *doing*.

Painting had always been Holly's best friend. It had kept her alive during a tumultuous childhood with an unstable mother and a man she'd called her father whom she had seen so few times she could count them on her fingers. Painting had got her through a disaster of a marriage to a selfish man-child. And then through an ugly divorce.

Painting was her escape. Her entertainment. Her coping mechanism. Her voice. Her salvation.

Early on, her brother, Vince, had found sports. And she'd discovered canvas and color. It was unimaginable where they'd be without those outlets.

In the past few years she had been fortunate enough to have been able to make some money creating artwork for paying clients. But in times of trouble she still picked up her brush purely for emotional release. For safety. For comfort.

Which was what was required now. Because she was disturbed and confused. Art gave her a little bit of a sanctuary in an unpredictable world.

So she had re-created her little studio area after packing it up for Louise and Fernando's visit last night. And she'd got back to work.

As often happened when she was painting, her problems became evident.

She had developed strong feelings for Ethan. And if that wasn't bad enough, she sensed the same might be happening for him.

How he managed to be so volatile while remaining so formal she'd never understand. He was in control of himself, yet there was a barely masked vulnerability there. Manners and restraint mixed with something brutal and pounding.

Those kisses atop the Empire State Building had come

from somewhere organic inside him. Beyond rational intent. That kind of intensity couldn't have been plotted.

In spite of that he would never care for her as anything more than an employee. Plain and simple. Even if he did, he would clamp his emotions down and lock them away as soon as he acknowledged them. He was too strong and too true ever to be swayed once he'd made a decision.

A means to an end. That was all she was to him.

And he to her.

Her phone buzzed.

"Ethan, here."

"Hi."

"I wanted to apologize for making light of your concerns about what physical interaction between us would be appropriate."

"I just don't want to mess up at the gala. I'm worried I'm going to get flustered, like I did at dinner last night. I want everything to go right for you and your plan for Aunt Louise."

"I agree that we could use more training sessions where we are surrounded by other people. I have a charity event to attend tonight. You and I will go together. As colleagues."

That was a terrific idea. She wanted to fulfill her end of the contract and make this arrangement work with Ethan. He was offering her the door into a New York that she could never open on her own. How hard could it be? He'd contracted her for a job that she was capable of doing. She just needed to keep the right mindset, purpose and goals.

An evening as colleagues. *Perfect.*

A couple of hours later the building's doorman knocked and handed Holly a delivery. She thanked him and carried the large white box to the table. Untying the gold ribbon that gave the box the appearance of a gift, she lifted the lid. A notecard was tucked on top of the gold tissue paper concealing the contents.

Tiny dress. Warm coat.
See you at the dock.
Ethan.

She unfolded the tissue to discover a black sequined party dress. It was sinfully short, with thin straps and a scooped back. Holly sucked in an audible whoosh of air. She couldn't believe that Ethan had sent her this sexy slip of a dress. Was this what his *colleagues* wore?

Tingles exploded all over her body.

For all the clothes he had already purchased for her, he must have thought none of them were just right for the charity event he was taking her to tonight.

Anticipation rocketed through her.

The warm coat—cream-colored, in a heavy wool—he had already bought her. The reference to a dock must mean they were going to be on or near a boat. The mystery of it felt hopelessly romantic, even though with Ethan she knew it wasn't. Nonetheless, she could hardly wait until nightfall.

Leonard picked her up at the scheduled time and transported her to the Battery Park dock where Ethan was waiting to open the car door. He extended his hand to help her out of the car. It was chilly, but there was no rain, and she wore her coat open over the new dress. Admittedly to show it off.

"Thank you, Leonard," Ethan called to his driver and closed the passenger door. To Holly he said, after a leisurely once-over, "I knew you would look stunning in that."

Their eyes met. She smiled. The left side of his mouth curved up.

"Shall we?" He offered his bent arm and she slipped hers through. But then he glanced down and stopped with caution. "Oh. Right." He lightly touched her engagement ring. "I generally do not bring a date to events like this.

Because our arrangement—rather, our engagement—will not be announced until the gala, would you mind terribly…?" His voice trailed out.

"No, of course not," she responded, hoping he didn't see the rush of disappointment sweep across her.

She slithered the diamond off her finger. She also hoped that, in the moonlight, he hadn't noticed that she'd been unable to remove every fleck of paint from her cuticles. She'd scrubbed her hands raw, but this was the best she could do. With any luck the stylists he'd hired to spruce her up for the gala would have some magic tricks up their sleeves.

"Shall I keep it?" he asked, and he took the ring from her and secured it in his pocket before she'd had a chance to answer. "I will introduce you as a coworker. We can have the evening to practice being comfortable with each other's company in public and nothing more."

"Exactly."

He presented his bent arm to her again. "All aboard."

As they ascended the gangway, Ethan waved politely to a few people, this way and that.

"Who was that?" Holly asked. "Where are we going?"

"Tonight is a fund-raiser for a private organization I belong to that supports maintenance of the Statue of Liberty as state funding is not sufficient. We will cruise to Liberty Island. The vantage point is spectacular. I think you will enjoy it."

The yacht set off into the New York Harbor, away from lower Manhattan. Champagne was passed on trays. Ethan and Holly mingled with a few guests onboard, sharing mainly superficial banter.

He introduced her as part of his interior design team and she shook a few hands. When they were out of anyone's earshot he instructed, "You can discuss the Chelsea Plaza project. Tell people you are currently analyzing the requirements. That you are handling the art, and much will depend on what materials the furnishings are made of."

During their next chat, around a standing cocktail table, the project came up. Holly interjected with, "We are assessing how people will move through the public spaces."

Ethan subtly nodded his approval. Holly was grateful for the positive reinforcement. She had never interacted with these mega-rich type of people before. Many of them were older than her—men in dark suits and women in their finest jewels. Wall Street leaders, heads of corporations, prominent doctors and lawyers. All of whom, apparently, with their charity dollars, were helping to keep the Statue of Liberty standing proud.

There would probably be many more people like this at the shareholders' gala on Saturday. Ethan had been smart to bring Holly here, so she could get a taste of this world she knew nothing about.

As they ferried closer to Liberty, Ethan led Holly to the yacht's railing to gain the best view.

"She is amazing."

Holly could only gawk up at the massive copper statue, famously green with its patina of age. From the spikes of Liberty's crown—which Ethan had told her represented rays of light—to the broken chain at her feet symbolizing freedom, she was a towering monument to emancipation. And her torch was a beacon of enlightenment.

Lady Liberty seemed to speak directly to Holly tonight. Holly looked into her eyes and pleaded for her wisdom and guidance.

"'Give me your tired, your poor…' Isn't that poem about this statue?" she asked Ethan.

"*The New Colossus* by Emma Lazarus."

"'Your huddled masses yearning to breathe free.'" Holly

had been suffocating in Florida. All her ghosts were there. "Maybe in New York *I* can breathe."

"What has constricted you?"

Making up for her mother's failings, with no father in the picture. Protecting her brother. Appeasing her explosive ex-husband.

"Where I come from nobody thinks big. Everyone is just trying to survive one more day."

Ethan moved a bit closer to Holly. They stood side by side while the yacht circled Liberty, allowing them to observe her from every angle.

"Fate has such irony. I know so many people who have everything," he said, "and yet it means nothing to them."

"Gratitude is its own gift."

He smiled wryly and nodded.

"As I mentioned, after Aunt Louise retires I plan to move Benton Worldwide's new construction solely into housing ventures for disadvantaged people. I like giving houses rather than just money. Because I can supply the knowledge and the labor to build them properly."

Colored lights began to flash on the deck and a band started playing in the dining room. Guests progressed to make their way inside the boat.

Ethan didn't move, and Holly stayed beside him as the boat turned and the tall buildings of Manhattan returned to their view.

"I have seen so much poverty in the world," Ethan continued musingly. "People living in shacks. In tents. In cardboard boxes. If I can help some of them have a safe and permanent home I will have accomplished something."

"You can only imagine what a house might mean to someone who doesn't have one." Holly knew about that first-hand, having moved from place to place so many times as a child.

"In any case…" Ethan shrugged "…for all my supposed

wealth and success, giving is the only thing that is truly satisfying."

Once all the other guests had filed inside, Ethan gestured for Holly to follow him in. At the dining tables they sat with some older couples who were discussing a landscaping project for the grounds around the statue.

When the band began a tamer version of a funky song that Holly loved, she stood and reached her hand down for Ethan's. "May I have this dance, sir?"

Ethan's signature smile made its slow journey from the left to the right side of his mouth. He stood and followed her onto the dance floor, where they joined some other couples.

She faced him and began to swing her hips back and forth to the music. When her hips jutted left, her head tipped right. Then she flung her head left and he hips responded to the right. Like ocean waves, her body became one undulating flow. Back and forth. Back and forth.

The dress was slinky against her skin. She loved how it swung a little with every move she made. From what she could surmise in Ethan's watchful eyes, he liked the movement of the dress, too.

At first he just rotated one shoulder forward and then the other, in a tentative sashay. But after a bit any self-consciousness dissolved and he let his body gyrate freely to the beat of the music.

He had a natural rhythm—just as Holly had known he would. It was part of that primitive side of him—the part he kept hidden away. The part she wished she could access.

Their eyes locked and their movements synchronized until they were undeniably dancing together.

There was no doubt of their attraction to each other. But they were doing a very good job of keeping the evening friendly and nothing more, just as planned.

As a matter of fact, when he had been talking on the

deck earlier, about the good feeling of giving, it had been as if Holly was an old pal he could confide in. Pals were good.

Which was why when the band switched to a slow song Holly turned to leave the dance floor. Slow dances weren't for buddies.

But a strong arm circled her waist.

"This doesn't fit in with our no touching policy this evening." Holly shook her head in resistance.

Ethan pulled her toward him and into a firm clinch. He secured her against him with a wide palm on her back.

Her breath hiccupped. Tonight was supposed to be time off from physical contact with him. After their intimacy at the Empire State Building last night had gone far outside the realm of their contract. Tonight, the last thing Holly needed was to have her face pressed against his neck, with the smell of his skin and his laundered shirt intoxicating her into a dangerous swoon.

"We may as well have a run-through, future Mrs. Benton," he murmured into her ear. "We will be expected to dance together at the gala."

He lifted one of her arms and placed her hand on his broad shoulder. He clasped her other hand in his.

"I don't know if I can do it," Holly protested.

"Surely I am not *that* irresistible."

She laughed, although that was only half funny. "What I meant was, I don't know how to partner-dance."

"Well, young lady, you are in luck. I happen to be three-time champion of the Oxford Ballroom Dance Society."

"Really?"

"No. Of course not."

He began moving and she followed in line.

"But it is not that difficult. Can you feel my thigh leading yours…?"

* * *

When they got home, before they retreated to their separate sleeping quarters, Ethan retrieved the engagement ring from his jacket pocket.

As he replaced it on her finger, he asked, "Holly, would you marry me…again?"

CHAPTER NINE

"WHO ON EARTH would notice the difference between a napkin color called Eggshell and another called Champagne?" Ethan bellowed to Holly as she made her way across the vast hotel ballroom. "And good morning."

"There's actually a big distinction." Holly jumped right in and snatched the two samples from him. She held one up in each hand to catch some of the room's light. "See—the Champagne is iridescent. The Eggshell is matte. It's a very different effect."

"Thank you for being here."

About an hour ago Ethan had called Holly and asked her to meet him here to finalize the details for tomorrow's gala. Aunt Louise was not feeling well.

"I would call in my assistant, Nathan, but I have him on a dozen other tasks right now."

Ethan's brow furrowed as he remembered yet more specifications he needed to take care of.

"What's wrong with Louise?" Holly inquired.

"She said she felt a bit weak and lightheaded."

"Will she be okay by tomorrow?"

"I hope so. She will stay upstairs today, resting in one of the suites we booked for the week. Fernando is with her. Not that *he* is of any help."

"What do you think triggered it?"

"Rainy weather is especially difficult for her. And, even though she likes to be involved in planning these galas, I think the strain is too much."

He'd feel immense relief once his aunt had retired and no longer bore the weight of continuing as CEO of their billion-dollar company. With any luck she'd be flying in from Barbados for next year's gala, with no cares other than what dress she should wear.

"I'm here to help, Ethan. What can I do?"

Holly's concern softened his tension. He gestured to the table in front of him—the only one in the bare ballroom with a tablecloth on it. Several place settings were laid out for approval, each complete with different options for china, napkins, silver and stemware. There were modern styles, and those that were more ornate. Some in classic shapes, others unusual.

"Can you make these decorative decisions? You are the artist," he said, and added with a whisper, "and the fiancée."

There was no one directly in earshot, but hotel employees bustled about doing their work. With camera phones and social media these days, Ethan wanted to be sure details of his engagement weren't released to the world any earlier than he wanted them to be.

"Oh. Good grief."

"What?"

He pointed to her hand. "The ring again. I am so sorry."

She gamely glided it off her finger, handed it to him and filled her cheeks with air to make a funny face.

"It is ludicrous. I apologize again. Now, Aunt Louise had started to select a certain color palette. She picked out this tablecloth..."

Holly lifted a corner of the linen draping the table and found an identifying label underneath. "This color is called Stone. I like its earthiness. Instead of choosing a lighter napkin, how about a darker one? Can we see samples that might be called something like Pewter or Slate?"

"Sweetheart, you can see anything you want as long as you get this taken care of."

He immediately regretted the endearment. It had fallen from his mouth spontaneously. He supposed that was what he'd need to be doing once they were announced as an engaged couple, so he might as well get used to it. Still, he wasn't in the habit of referring to women by pet names. Holly's widened eyes told him she was surprised by it as well.

Thankfully, one of the hotel's event managers was passing by. Ethan flagged down Priya to come talk to Holly. And to get him out of the moment.

As the two women conferred he stepped away to return a couple of missed phone calls. Which was a bit difficult because the napkins weren't the only things that reflected light from the ballroom's massive chandeliers.

Holly's lustrous hair, flowing freely long past her shoulders, framed her face with a glowing halo. Her sincere smile came easily during her conversation. Sidetracking him from his call to the point when he had to ask his site supervisor on the Bronx project to repeat what he had just said. Which was both embarrassing and unacceptable.

How many reminders did Ethan need that a woman had no place in his life?

She bounded over to him after her consultation with the event manager.

"I hope you don't mind, but I've had a vision. I did go with a pewter napkin. And a minimalist kind of china and flatware..." She rattled off details at a mile a minute. "With a silver napkin ring to give it a sort of elemental look. Earth and metal, kind of thing."

He mashed his lips to suppress a smile, although he was charmed at her zeal.

"And, if it's okay," she persisted, "I thought we could do a sleek centerpiece with white flowers in clear glass vases, to bring in a water element as well. I think it'll all tie together with the lighting." She pointed up to the modern chandeliers with their narrow pieces of glass. "Do you think your aunt would like that?"

"She will appreciate your creativity," he said after Holly's debriefing. "Miss Motta, it sounds like you have a knack for this sort of thing."

She shrugged. "I guess it's just a painter's eye. And at my own wed—"

Ethan's phone rang. He lifted one finger to signal to Holly to hold that thought while he took the call. "Yes, Nathan?"

Holly's cheeks turned pink. She bit her lip.

Something he wouldn't mind doing.

Sweetheart. He'd accidentally called her *sweetheart.*

"Schedule me for a late lunch with him next Tuesday at that restaurant he likes on Jane Street. Thank you." He turned his attention back to Holly, "Sorry—what were you saying?"

"Oh. Um… Just that Priya says the tech crew are here if you're ready to go to the podium."

"Come with me."

He took her hand. After taking the few stairs from the ballroom floor up to the stage, Ethan and Holly turned to face the empty event space. Tomorrow night Benton Worldwide Properties would once again fête many of their shareholders with an evening of appreciation. Close to a thousand people—some from nearby, others who had traveled far—would fill this grand room for the annual event.

Holly whistled. "What a breathtaking location for a dinner." She pointed to the large gold wall sculptures that circled the back of the room. "Those give the idea of waves in an ocean, don't they?"

Ethan surveyed the familiar surroundings. "The burgundy carpeting is new this year. It used to be a lighter color. That is about the only change I have noticed."

"You hold the dinner here every year?"

"We have been using this room for as long as I can remember. These galas are as ingrained into my family as birthdays and Christmas are to others."

This year's event wouldn't be a run-of-the-mill evening, though, when his and Holly's engagement was to be announced.

Holly gestured with her head toward the podium on the stage. "Will you be giving a speech?"

"The baton will pass to me next year," he said. Uncle Mel had always given the speech and, after he died Aunt Louise had taken over the duty. "Only a few of us know that this is the last time Aunt Louise will deliver the CEO's report."

Louise's retirement wouldn't be revealed at the gala. Ethan and his aunt had decided that the first step in her exit strategy would be to introduce his fiancée. That would cause enough pandemonium for one evening.

Shareholders could be tricky. They didn't like too many changes all at once. Benton Worldwide had already made them a lot of money by sticking to the original principles Uncle Melvin and Ethan's father had established when they'd started the company with one small apartment building in roughneck South Boston.

So only the engagement announcement would come at the gala. In a month, they'd inform the shareholders in writing that Louise Benton was retiring after a distinguished career. A month after that they'd throw a splashy retirement party.

Tomorrow night would belong to him and Holly Motta. In addition to their proclamation to the shareholders, a press release would notify the world that Ethan Benton had finally chosen a bride. Photos of them would appear in the business sections of newspapers and websites across the planet.

Ethan peered at Holly by his side on the stage. Sudden terror gripped him. What if this masquerade was too risky? This pretty young woman appeared to be genuine and of good will. But what if she wasn't? What if she was like every other woman he'd ever met? Deceptive. Manipulative. Out for herself.

He'd only met her a few days ago, for heaven's sake. It wasn't long enough to put her intentions to the test. And he still didn't know much about her other than what she'd chosen to disclose. Hopefully his head of security, Chip Foley, would get back to him soon with any information he had found. If there was something he didn't want exposed he'd need to figure out how to bury it so that the press didn't have a field-day.

Doubt coursed through him. What if Holly simply wasn't as capable a performer as he'd hired her to be? Maybe she'd crack under the spotlight and the attention. Confess that this was all a set-up, causing Benton Worldwide embarrassment and loss of credibility.

His mind whirled. What had he been thinking? In his haste to plan Aunt Louise's departure from public life before her medical condition diminished her position of respect, Ethan had made an uncharacteristically rash decision. If it was the wrong one his family would pay dearly for it for the rest of their lives.

However, there was no choice now but to take a leap of faith.

"Are you ready for this?" He took Holly's hand, as he would tomorrow. Her fingers were supple and comforting, and immediately slowed his breath.

"I may faint afterward, but I promise to put on a show," she answered amiably, lacing her fingers in his.

"Imagine every table filled with people in tuxedos and evening gowns. Staring at you."

Her shoulders lifted in a chuckle. "Gee, no pressure there!"

Her humor reassured him that she could pull this off. She wouldn't have agreed to it if she didn't know in her heart that she could handle it. And she'd done fine on the yacht last night.

Aunt Louise wanted this one thing for Ethan before she stepped away and let him officially run the company. He was determined to give it to her.

An astute woman, his aunt knew that Ethan's constant travel was to avoid settling down. He didn't have any sustained commitments outside of work. Hardly had a base other than his rarely visited corporate flat near their headquarters in Boston. He dated women—and then he didn't. He spent months alone on a boat. Socialized, then disappeared into a foreign country. He was free. There was nothing to tie him down. He could do whatever he wanted, go wherever he pleased. And he did.

His aunt believed that a fulfilled life took place on terra firma. She wanted him to find a home. A home that would shelter him from the topsy-turvy world of highs and lows, change and disappointment.

Home wasn't a place.

Home was love.

An all-encompassing love that he could count on. That could count on him. That made life worth living day after day. Year after year.

Because of Holly, Ethan had now had a glimpse into what it might be like to coexist with someone. Like he had last night on the Liberty cruise, easily sharing his thoughts and plans and hopes.

But he would stay firm in his resolve to go it alone.

And that was that.

That was his fate.

That was his destiny.

So he'd give Holly to his aunt as a retirement gift. Deliver her on a silver platter. Let the one woman who had ever been good to him hold the belief she most wanted.

But Ethan would not forget the truth.

"Mr. Benton?" A voice boomed from a dark corner of the ballroom. "We'd like to do a sound-check from the podium, if you wouldn't mind."

"Of course," Ethan said to the unseen technician.

Still clutching Holly's hand, he led her to the side of the stage before they parted. His fingers were reluctant to let go. Yet he dutifully took his place at the lectern and adjusted the microphone. Substituting for Aunt Louise, who would be introduced tomorrow to deliver her speech.

"Thank you for joining us this evening at Benton Worldwide Properties' annual shareholders' gala. We are so delighted you are here… Test, test. Test. Testing…"

Ethan dummied through as the technician made adjustments to the sound system.

"Without our shareholders we would not have experienced the global development… Hello, hello. You give us the inspiration… Thank you, thank you. Testing one, two, three."

He turned to wink at Holly. She grinned in response.

"Thank you, Mr. Benton," the technician called out. "Now we'd like to run the video, if you'd like to watch and okay?"

"Will do."

Ethan escorted Holly back down the steps to one of the tables. They took their seats as a screen was lowered from above the stage.

"Hey, do we get to sample the food?" Holly asked. "Quality control?"

"No, that is one department Fernando *is* actually handling. He was here earlier, approving everything with the chefs, before he went to attend to Aunt Louise."

"Rats!" She snapped her fingers, cute as could be.

Which made him want to kiss her.

Which was more irrational thinking he'd need to get a handle on.

Kissing was only for show, when people were watching. No more recreational kissing. The Empire State Building kissing shouldn't have happened. Where he'd thought he might have been able to keep kissing Holly until the end of the world.

His body quirked even now, remembering.

He locked his attention on the screen as the presentation began with a graphic of the company logo and some sprightly music. A slick narrator's voice explained a montage of all the Benton Worldwide projects that had been started or completed during the past year.

In another montage employees were shown holding babies, celebrating their children's college graduations, tossing a football at company picnics.

A historical section flashed older photos—one of Uncle Mel and Ethan's father, Joseph, holding shovels at a groundbreaking ceremony.

"That is my dad." Ethan pointed. His heart pinged as the image quickly gave way to the next photo. Joseph had died when he was nine. Twenty-five years ago. "I do not remember much about him anymore," he admitted.

Holly put a hand on his shoulder. He prickled, but didn't pull away despite his automatic itch to do so.

"Tell me one thing you do remember about him."

"That photo shows him in a suit. I can only think of him in a casual work shirt. Uncle Mel was the businessman. My father was always at the construction sites."

One glimpse of memory Ethan did have of his father was of when he'd come home from work at night. He'd greet Ethan and then head straight to the shower to wash off his honest day's work.

His mother was not a part of that picture. She would sequester herself in her private bedroom before Ethan came home from school, and there she'd stay throughout the evening. It had been a nanny who'd tended to Ethan in the afternoon.

Another older photo had clients at a job site, with Joseph in a hard hat on one side of them and Uncle Mel and Aunt Louise on the other side.

"Do you have any pictures that include your mother?"

"Oh, she was in that shot. We had her edited out. We cut her out of every photo."

Holly tilted her head, not understanding. "Why?"

Now he shook Holly's hand off his shoulder. He couldn't take her touch.

"Because we did not want her in any way associated with Benton Worldwide."

"But *why*?"

"My father and Uncle Mel worked hard for every dollar they made. They earned it. They deserved it. And they were loyal to the people who were loyal to them. Values my mother cared nothing for."

Ethan's blood pressure rose, notifying him to end this conversation. When Holly started to ask another question, his glare shut her down.

Another photo documented him and Aunt Louise in front of a gleaming high-rise building. "Ah, the Peachwood Center in Atlanta. One of my favorites."

The last photo had Aunt Louise surrounded by ten or so Benton executives in front of their headquarters. Even though in reality Ethan had been running the company since Aunt Louise's health had begun to fail, he still made sure that she got all the credit and glory.

"Is everything correct on the video, Mr. Benton?" the technician called from the back of the ballroom.

"Yes—thank you."

"May I trouble you for one more thing, sir? Can I get an okay for sound and lighting on the dance floor?"

Ethan stood and made his way to the polished wooden floor in the center of the ballroom. Fully surrounded by the burgundy carpet and the tables defining the perimeter, the dance floor was its own little world, and it was lit as such with a yellow tint and spotlights beaming down from the ceiling.

"Mr. Benton, we'd like to check the lighting with some movement. Would you be able to find someone to do a quick waltz around the dance floor for me?"

Naturally Ethan gestured to Holly. Stretching out his arm, he beckoned. "So, we dance again."

Holly stood and navigated between the tables in the empty ballroom to reach Ethan on the dance floor. She envisioned what he had described—how tomorrow night the room would be filled with well-dressed shareholders gaping at her. Not giving in to panic, she reminded herself that she was here to do a job. To supply what she'd offered.

A love ballad suitable for ballroom dancing began from the sound system. Ethan started to dance and Holly's body fell in line with his.

He'd taught her well last night, and although she didn't think she could pull off any fancy ballroom dance moves she didn't trip all over his feet.

The lights were so bright on the dance floor that she could hardly see out to the tables. Which didn't matter that much because she really only wanted to close her eyes and enjoy the moment. The croon of the singer… Ethan's sure steps… His rock-sturdy chest…

Dancing with him, she thought they really were a couple—an entity that was larger than the sum of two individuals.

Ah... Her head fit so well underneath his chin as they danced. Being tall, she'd always had a sense of herself as being gawky around Ricky and the other men she had dated. She loved being encompassed by Ethan's height and width. As they glided across the dance floor, she felt graceful. A fairy princess. A prom queen. The object of attention.

All things she wasn't.

How would it be tomorrow, with a roomful of guests scrutinizing her? They wouldn't think she was beautiful enough for a man like Ethan! Everyone would know that she wasn't pedigreed and educated. They'd wonder why a Benton had settled for someone as ordinary as her.

Although she would be wearing the magnificent sky-blue gown covered in crystals. That gown alone would convince leaders and kings that she was one of them. Her hair and makeup would be professionally done. The smoke and mirrors tricks would be believable.

She'd hobnobbed with the New York elite last night and no one had guessed that she was not of their social standing. They hadn't known that she'd grown up in a trailer park with an unmarried mother who'd been too drunk to get out of bed half of the time.

Of course at the gala Ethan's fiancée would be under closer examination.

She tilted her head back to study her hand on Ethan's shoulder. Just as she had last night, she actually missed wearing the gargantuan diamond ring that labeled her Ethan's intended. She thought back to the paper ring he had used to propose to her. When he had bent down on one knee with a ring made from a beer bottle label.

And then she flashed back to the shopping spree on Fifth Avenue. To the blue topaz ring she had loved. But

Ethan was right, of course. The ring he'd chosen was one befitting the future Mrs. Benton.

Leaning back further, to look up into Ethan's handsome face, she asked him, "Being in the spotlight doesn't faze you in the least?"

"I suppose I have always been visible to the shareholders. They watched me grow up."

"You came to the galas as a child?"

His muscles twitched. "When I was younger I was kept upstairs in a suite with my mother, who hated these evenings. We would come down and make an appearance."

Holly had noticed that Ethan's voice became squeezed every time his mother came up in conversation. Hints of rage had come spitting out when he'd explained how they had edited her out of all the photos in the slideshow.

"Wasn't your mother obligated to attend?" Holly persisted.

"She would call the kitchen to find out exactly what time dinner was being served. A half-hour before she would trot me down here in a tuxedo. We would do our annual mother-and-son spin around this dance floor. Then she would tug me to the exit, offering excuses that it was my bedtime or that she had a migraine."

"What about your dad?"

"He was not much the tuxedo-and-martini type, but he would soldier through alone. My mother was not gracious, like Aunt Louise. She would not mingle and exchange pleasantries with the guests. Not even to support my father. He knew that she was not an asset to the company."

"Was it awful for you, being paraded around?"

"Not really. I understood at an early age that my mother was not good for business but that I was. Whether it had been a profitable year or a struggle, seeing that there was a next generation of leadership instilled confidence in the shareholders. I have always been proud to represent our company."

"Is your mother still alive?"

"I have no idea," he bit out. "Nor do I care in the least. I have always assumed the shareholders believe that she went into seclusion and retired from public life after my father died."

With that, he tightened his hold around Holly's waist, bolted her against him and guided her with an absolute command that started at the top of his head and ended at the tip of his toes.

Holly molded herself to him and allowed his confident lead. Knowing that talk of his mother had unleashed the beast that he had now locked back into the cage inside him.

As they circled the music got louder, then softer. The low bass tones became more pronounced and then were corrected. Lights were adjusted as well, becoming hotter, then diffused and milky.

"Just one minute more, Mr. Benton!" the technician announced.

The music changed to a swinging standard.

Ethan relaxed his grip and backed Holly away to arm's distance ready for a quickstep. He twirled her once under his arm. She stumbled and they chuckled into each other's eyes.

His head tilted to the side. They leaned in toward each other's smiles. Drawn to each other.

Out of the corner of her eye Holly saw Aunt Louise's husband, Fernando, enter the ballroom and scurry toward them.

When they had come to the apartment for dinner she had noticed the way Fernando walked with small, mincing steps. She hadn't liked how he had snooped at the things on Ethan's desk and taken a fax from the machine. And she had overheard him telling Ethan that he didn't want to spend his life in Barbados when Louise retired.

But at this moment it was important for them to unify for the sake of Louise. Since the older woman wasn't well today, Ethan and Fernando had taken charge of the final details for the gala. Ethan had to be grateful for whatever help Fernando was offering. Perhaps he had a report on the status of the menu…

"I've been trying to call you!" Fernando approached and yapped at Ethan.

Ethan glanced over to one of the empty tables, where he had left his phone while he was on stage at the podium and while he and Holly had danced. "Is everything in order?" he asked.

"No, it's not. Louise has taken a bad fall. I've called the paramedics."

CHAPTER TEN

ETHAN LED THE charge out of the ballroom and toward the hotel elevators, with Fernando and Holly racing behind him to keep up. When they reached the bronze elevator bank Ethan rapped the call button incessantly until one set of doors opened. Pressing for the twenty-sixth floor as soon as he'd stepped in, he backed against the gilded and mirrored wall of the elevator car.

His neck muscles pulsed. As the elevator ascended he kept his eyes peeled on the digital read-out of the floor numbers.

One, two, seven, twelve...

"What happened?" He forced the question out of a tight throat.

"Louise had been resting on the sofa in the suite's living room," Fernando reported. "She stood up and said she was going to make a phone call. Then, as she started to walk, she tripped on the coffee table and fell face-forward."

"Why did you not help her get up from the sofa in the first place?" Ethan seethed.

"She didn't tell me she was going to stand up. She just did it. I rushed to her, but it was too late."

Ethan's jaw ground as he fought to keep himself together. This incompetent idiot should have never been allowed to care for Aunt Louise. She was going to need full-time nurses. He'd arrange that immediately.

The read-out reached twenty-three, twenty-four…

On the twenty-sixth floor, Ethan pushed through the elevator doors before they had fully opened. Holly and Fernando followed. At the room's door, he snatched the key card from Fernando's hand.

Ethan rushed into the suite. "Aunt Louise?"

Louise sat on the floor with her back against the sofa. Angry scrapes had left red stripes across her right cheek and her knees. She massaged her wrist.

"I'm all right, dear," she assured him in a fairly steady voice. "Don't embarrass me any more than I've already embarrassed myself."

"There is no reason to be embarrassed," Ethan said, trying to soothe her. These incidences must be so humiliating for her. She'd always been such an able woman.

"Falls happen," Fernando chimed in. "We've been here before, Louise. You'll be fine."

Ethan fired a piercing glower at Fernando. He didn't need to try to make light of the situation.

"Oh, goodness. Holly!" Louise spotted Holly standing back from them. She managed a dry smile. "Somehow I've become an old woman."

"Thank goodness you weren't hurt worse." Holly nodded her respect.

"At this point we do not know if or how much she is injured," Ethan snapped, angry with everyone. "She needs to be examined."

Right on cue, there was a soft knock on the door. Ethan let in the hotel manager, who confirmed that they were expecting paramedics. Two emergency medical technicians filed in.

One checked Louise's vital signs, such as her blood pressure and heart-rate. He shone a small light into her eyes. Another technician asked questions about her medical history and what had happened.

While that was going on Ethan noticed Fernando pouring himself a cocktail. Holly had noticed too.

He and Holly raised eyebrows at each other. This was hardly a time for drinks.

Ethan clenched his fists and mashed his lips tightly. He stood silently.

Fernando had accused Ethan at dinner the other night of finding himself a wife just so that Louise would retire. Fernando had said he had no intention of spending his life on boring Barbados, as he characterized it, with Louise.

So, following that logic, Fernando should be doing everything he could to try to keep Louise as healthy as possible. Yet he obviously didn't bother with trivial matters, such as protecting her from falling. And now—with paramedics in the room, no less—he clearly thought it was cocktail hour.

"There don't appear to be any broken bones," one of the technicians informed them. "But, given her overall medical condition, we're going to transport her to the hospital for a more complete evaluation."

Ethan brought a hand over his mouth, overcome with worry. This woman had shown him so much love—had gone above and beyond the call of duty for him his entire life. Maybe his caring so much for his aunt was a sign. That he was capable of loyalty. Of devotion.

He refused his inclination to look over to Holly.

The technician issued instructions into his phone.

Fernando walked over to pat Louise gently on the shoulder in between sips of his drink.

"Can we take her down in a private elevator?" Ethan asked the manager, who waited quietly beside the door. "And out through a private garage? Many of our shareholders are staying here at the hotel, and we would like to keep this matter to ourselves."

"Of course, Mr. Benton."

Fernando settled himself closer to where Ethan was standing. "Clever..." he said under his breath. "Always thinking about image. I've got a little surprise for you with regards to that."

Ethan whipped his head to look into Fernando's eyes. "What on earth are you talking about at a time like this?" he demanded.

Two more paramedics came through the door with a stretcher.

Louise protested, "Oh, please, gentlemen—a wheelchair would do."

"It's for your protection, ma'am."

"I will ride in the ambulance with Louise," Ethan declared.

"No. *I* will," Fernando countered.

"Family only, please," one of the technicians said over his shoulder as he secured Louise onto the stretcher.

"I'm her husband."

"I am coming as well," Ethan insisted.

To the outside eye they must look like an odd sort of family. Elderly Aunt Louise. Nephew Ethan, who was probably being mistaken for her son, and Holly for his wife. Then Fernando, with his tanning salon skin and overstyled hair, who looked exactly the part of a cougar's husband.

The hotel manager headed the pack as the technicians began wheeling the stretcher out of the suite. Fernando and Ethan followed closely behind.

Ethan turned his head back to Holly. "You go home to the apartment."

"I'd like to come to the hospital, too."

Irritated at even having to discuss this further, Ethan

repeated his order. "There is no need for you to be at the hospital. Go back to the apartment."

The hotel manager led them to a private elevator and swiped her access card.

Ethan dashed a text into his phone.

"I could take a taxi and meet you there," Holly pleaded. "I want to be there for you and—"

He cut her off. "I have just instructed Leonard to pick you up in front of the hotel."

This was a private matter that Holly had no place in, despite appearances. While he had certainly become accustomed to having her around, she was still only an employee, and Louise's health was a personal thing. Ethan did not want Holly to overhear any discussions with doctors, or any information regarding a prognosis for his aunt. What Holly had just witnessed in the suite was beyond what his fiancée-for-hire should be privy to.

Ethan feared that he was starting to lose his better judgment around Holly. It was becoming so easy, so natural to let her into his life. If he allowed himself to, he might long for her support at the hospital. He knew it would be hours of waiting and worrying while Aunt Louise was examined.

He had nothing to say to Fernando. Wouldn't sitting with Holly in the waiting area, sharing a paper cup full of coffee, huddled together, be a comfort?

No! Once again, he reminded himself of Holly's place in this dynamic. Despite how they might appear, to the paramedics or anyone else, Holly was not part of this family.

Not. Family.

He pointed down the hall toward the public elevator they had ridden up to the suite. "Holly, please return to ground floor and retrieve my things from the ballroom. Thank you."

Louise was wheeled into the private elevator, and everyone but Holly got in.

Just as the doors were closing Ethan saw in Holly's eyes that he'd upset her by not allowing her to come along. But this was no time to focus on her. She should know and respect that.

"I will phone you as soon as I hear anything, all right?"

He didn't wait for an answer.

So much for being part of the family.

Holly made it through the car ride home from the hotel, and it wasn't until she opened the door to the dark, empty apartment that tears spilled down her face.

Louise's condition was heartbreaking, and Holly hoped that she wasn't seriously injured after the tumble she'd taken. That she would be able to make it to the gala tomorrow night.

Ethan and Louise had such a finely tuned strategy to keep the extent of her illness hidden from the public. Holly admired their efforts. And thankfully the paramedics were only taking Louise to the hospital as a precaution.

She flipped on the lights. Slung her jacket on the coat rack. Kicked off her boots. And then she allowed in some self-pity. If she ever needed a reminder that this engagement was all a front, she had her proof. She was not, and nor would she ever be, a member of this clan.

Once they'd arrived at Louise's hotel suite Ethan had barely acknowledged her presence. Not that she would have expected him to pay lots of attention to her, but she had to admit she was surprised at how completely he had shut her out.

Holly had offered to go along to the hospital to be there for Louise *and* for Ethan—as a friend who rallied round when maybe a hand to hold would be welcome. But Ethan would have none of it, and hadn't been able to get her out of the picture swiftly enough.

Everything had moved so fast this week. How had she

got here? To feeling sorry for herself because she was left behind? How had she come to care so much for these people so quickly? She'd become so involved in Ethan's life she could hardly remember a time when she hadn't been. Had she forgotten who she was?

Holly Motta was an artist who had spent four long years married to the wrong man.

Ricky hadn't made it easy for her to leave. Even after she'd moved out of the last place they'd been living he'd shown up at her work and insisted on talking to her. Or he'd followed her car and confronted her at a supermarket or in a bank parking lot. It had got to the point that she'd had to change her phone number. Month after month he had refused to sign the legal documents divorcing them, leaving her hanging in limbo. Finally he'd given up and cut her loose.

It had taken her two years to feel truly unshackled from the demanding and possessive hold Ricky had on her. Now she was determined to move forward with her life. This prospect with Ethan had presented itself and she'd snatched it. The job, this apartment, the clothes…the promise of a glamorous escapade with an exciting man.

Nothing wrong with any of that. Life was throwing her a bone, for once. And she was taking it. Life on life's terms.

The problem was the illusion was so convincing that she was starting to buy it.

Twenty-nine years of hurt overtook her. She wasn't tough, like New York. She couldn't endure another defeat. Withstand another wound. Her heart functioned in broken pieces that were only taped together and could collapse at any minute. Maybe this masquerade was too dangerous. She didn't think she had it in her to bounce back from anguish yet again.

Restless, she went to the kitchen. Drank a full glass of water in one gulp. It had been hours since she'd eaten. A few slices of cheese and bread went down easily as she munched them standing up.

She hoped Ethan would get a bite to eat at the hospital. He'd be hungry, too. *Ugh!* She needed to stop caring about things like whether or not he had eaten. Had to break her habit of always looking after people.

She paced back to the living room. Judged the paintings she had been working on in the little studio area she had created by the window. They were a good start to the ideas she had in her head. A drawing pad perched on the easel. She mindlessly picked up a stick of charcoal and began to put it to paper.

After a few minutes she cranked up some funky music and swung her hips from left to right to the beat. A little sketching, a little boogie-woogie—that was always how she got through everything in her life.

Curved lines on the page. A man's jaw. Not square and chiseled like Ethan's. That buzz-cut hair. The thick swash of eyelashes.

A smile crossed her lips.

Small ears. The rounded shoulders. The only person she could count on. Her brother.

Yet she hadn't been honest with Vince about the events of the past few days. She had called him the first night she was here, when the mix-up with the apartment had started everything that had come since. She'd hinted that something had come her way. Vince had reminded her that it was *her* time now. That she should take hold of any prospect life threw at her.

They'd had so little in the way of support as kids. They'd always had to be each other's cheering section.

Straight up or fall down... Holly mouthed their childhood chant.

They had been texting every day, as they always did. She'd told him that New York was amazing. That it was mostly raining. But she hadn't told him about this weird arrangement she'd agreed to. Which had become a wild rollercoaster of feeling so right and then, in the next moment, feeling so wrong.

She hadn't even told Vince about meeting Ethan. And she hadn't told Ethan about her rat ex-husband, Ricky. It wasn't like her to keep secrets. But she didn't know where anything stood anymore. She didn't want to make things more complicated than they already were. Even if nothing were to work out for her here in New York, Holly needed to make sure that Ethan kept his word about helping Vince.

Her brother was a good man. She was so proud of him. Every day she hoped and prayed for a bright future for him. That separately, yet bound in spirit, they'd rise up like phoenixes from the ashes of their childhood.

She thumbed her phone.

"Holz?" Vince used his nickname for his sister.

"Vinz!" Holly sandwiched the phone between her ear and her shoulder as she finished drawing her brother's arm. Their builds were so different… It was only in the eyes of their mother where the resemblance was undeniable.

"How's New York treating you?"

"Oh… I kinda got involved in something I thought was one thing but now it seems like it's another."

As in tonight. Which had been reinforcement of the fact that Ethan would never regard her as anything more than a hired hand. That the feelings she'd started to have for him could only lead to misfortune.

"What are you talking about?"

"I don't know… I met a man."

"Well, sis, it's about time you met a man. You haven't dated anyone since you left the Rat."

"I know. But this might not be the right thing."

Somehow she couldn't bring herself to tell him that the man she was talking about was Ethan Benton. The billionaire vice president, soon to be CEO, of the company Vince worked for.

"So you'll move on to something else. We've done that enough times in our life, haven't we?"

"That we have, bro."

How often had their mother made promises? Then broken them.

"Straight up or fall down!" they recited in unison.

"Get some sleep, Holz. You sound tired."

Holly continued sketching after the call. Line after line, listening to song after song. More glasses of water downed in one go.

Finally she sprawled across the sofa and pondered the painting of Ethan on the wall. His mouth… That urgent mouth that had covered hers a few midnights ago atop the Empire State Building. He had kissed her lips. Along her throat. Behind her ear. Her eyelids.

They fluttered with the memory.

The phone woke her up.

"Hello?" Her voice was gravelly.

"Ethan, here."

"How's Louise?'

"Stable. She was not badly injured by the fall."

"Thank heavens."

Holly's eyes didn't want to open fully. The sound of his voice caressed her, but didn't erase the sting of him banning her from the hospital yesterday. Despite wishing he'd make mention of it, she knew he wouldn't.

She had to carry on forward. "What time is it?"

"Eight in the morning."

Tonight was the gala. Her end of the bargain was due.

"Are you still at the hospital?"

"No, I came back to one of the hotel suites to get some sleep. I did not want to wake you by coming in during the middle of the night."

Holly stroked the leather of the sofa where Ethan had been sleeping the past few nights. If he had come home he'd have found her conked out on it after she simply hadn't been able to stand at the easel any longer.

She'd done eight different renderings of Vince. Must have been some sort of homesickness, she mused to herself now, in the gray haze of the cloudy morning.

She stretched her neck. "What happens now?"

"Aunt Louise will be discharged in a couple of hours. Then I will send Leonard to pick you up. He will help you manage my tuxedo and your gown and whatever else you need. We can get dressed in this suite. I have ordered food. And a makeup artist and hairstylist are coming."

"Okay."

Ethan had everything so organized it made her head spin. How did he keep himself together? She needed a shower and coffee.

"Be prepared for a busy day and night," he continued. "I hope you are ready, my fiancée. Because it is showtime."

When the makeup and hair people departed the hotel suite, Holly and Ethan were finally alone for the first time all afternoon.

The last few hours had flown by. People from Benton Worldwide and from their public relations firm had come and gone from the lavish suite that had a bedroom, living room and dining table in addition to the spacious dressing area where they were now.

All of the suite's Zen-like furnishings and décor were made from precious woods and fine fabrics, while floor-to-ceiling windows provided panoramic views of the Manhattan skyline, where the gloomy and rain-drenched day had turned to dusk.

It had been a whirlwind of introductions as Ethan had presented Holly, although of course he hadn't yet revealed their engagement. Members of the shareholders' board of directors had been in to confer with Ethan. And Holly had finally met Ethan's trusted assistant, Nathan—a young man wielding four electronic devices in his two hands.

A sandwich buffet and barista bar had kept everyone fortified. Then the glam squad had arrived to give Ethan a haircut and work their magic on Holly, before filing out just now to do the same for Louise.

In the first quiet moment since she had arrived, Holly inspected herself in the mirror. She wore a white satin robe, but had already put on her jewelry and heels.

Shimmery eye makeup and soft pink lipstick gave her skin a luminous glow. The style wizards had managed to remove every speck of paint from her cuticles, so that a pearly pink manicure could complement the gown. Her hair was magically doubled in volume, thanks to the expert blow-dry she'd just received.

They had experimented with hairstyles, but gave Ethan veto power. Every time she'd asked his opinion of one of the looks they'd tried he had taken a long gander at her. He'd stopped to scratch his chin, or shot her a wink or half a smile. The way he'd studied every inch of her had been almost obscenely exciting.

And seemingly had had little to do with her hairstyle. Because each time he had decreed that he liked her hair better down.

Now she observed Ethan's reflection behind her in the mirror. He was perched on a stool in the dressing area, reading over some papers, already in tuxedo pants and dress shoes. His stiff white shirt was on, but had not yet been buttoned. She imagined her fingers tracing down the center of his bare, lean chest.

This was really happening. She was in this castle of a hotel, about to be crowned as princess and then ride off on a majestic horse with this regal prince.

Of course in real life at the end of the night they'd shake hands on a con well played. But what the heck? She might as well enjoy it.

"Louise was okay when you talked to her a little while ago?"

"Under the circumstances." Ethan didn't look up from his work.

"I have an idea for tonight that might make it easier on her," Holly said as she tightened one of her earrings in front of the mirror.

"Oh?"

"You were telling me that when it's time for her to give her CEO speech you'll escort her from the table up the stairs to the stage?"

"Yes."

"I was thinking it may be difficult for her to walk up the stairs after her fall. And it won't help to have a thousand people staring at her."

"What is the alternative?"

"I noticed that there is a side entrance to the stage from the waiters' station. While the video montage is playing, and it's dark in the ballroom, we could help Louise get away from the table and up to the stage that way. With no one watching her. Then, when she's introduced, all she has to do is come out from the side of the stage and go to the podium."

Holly followed Ethan's reflection in the mirror as he walked toward her. He came up behind her and circled his arms around her shoulders. He hugged her so authentically, so affectionately, she melted.

"Thank you for thinking of that," he said softly into her ear. "Thank you for thinking about it at all. My, my…. You have already gone far beyond what I expected of you. Please accept my gratitude."

She wanted to tell him how horribly it had hurt when

he hadn't let her go to the hospital yesterday. How much she'd wanted to be part of his family, and not just what her obligations required. How she longed to be there for him in good times and in bad.

She still had so much of her heart left to share. Nothing in her past had squelched that out of her.

But she'd never get to give that heart to him.

Even though she was now positive that he was the only man to whom she ever could.

Fearing she might cry, and tarnish her stellar makeup job, she flicked an internal switch and squirmed away from him.

"Can you help me into my gown? It weighs about ten pounds!"

Ethan went to back to the stool he had been sitting on and patted his tablet for music. A smooth male voice sang a romantic song.

Not taking his eyes off her, he drank a sip from his water bottle and then recapped it. "I would love to help you into your dress."

She raced over and punched into his tablet the upbeat music that she favored.

Ethan's grin swept across his lips.

Holly couldn't resist sashaying her hips to the rhythm as she turned and headed to the closet where her gown hung. She was sure she heard him gasp when she let her robe fall to the floor to reveal the skimpy undergarments underneath.

And so the pretend soon-to-be-married couple helped each other get dressed for the gala.

"Careful with the base of the zipper—it's delicate."

"Blast! Do this right cufflink for me. I am no good at all with my left hand."

"I hope this eye makeup doesn't look too dark in the photos."

"I do not know how women can dance in those heels. I am booking you a foot massage for tomorrow."

"Is my hair perfect?"

"Shoulders back."

"How do I look?"

"How do *I* look?"

The supposed future Mr. and Mrs. Ethan Benton exited the suite preened, perfumed and polished to perfection.

Just as they reached the entrance to the ballroom Ethan remembered he had the engagement ring in his pocket. He skimmed it onto Holly's finger.

Yet again.

They entered the gala to a cacophony of guests, cameras and lights befitting a royal wedding.

CHAPTER ELEVEN

THE BALLROOM VIBRATED with the din of a thousand people. Holly's heart thundered in her chest as Ethan maneuvered them from table to table for introductions. He charmed all the women and the men regarded him with great respect.

"Ethan, how has another year passed already?"

"Lovely to see you, Mrs. Thorpe. Good evening, Mr. Thorpe." Ethan pecked the older lady's cheek and shook the hand of her white-haired husband. "I would like to introduce you to Holly Motta."

Mrs. Thorpe's crinkly eyes lit up. "Well, now, Ethan, are we to believe that you have given up the single life at last?"

"Only because *you* are already spoken for," Ethan said, flattering her.

Holly was dumbstruck and could only squeak out, "Nice to meet you."

She felt horribly out of place. The giddy fun of getting dressed was gone now, and in this moment she felt like a young child in a Halloween princess costume. It was one thing to imagine being the fiancée of a respected and victorious billionaire. But it was another thing entirely actually to be presented as such.

"You look exquisite," Ethan whispered in her ear, as if he sensed her discomfort.

It offered no reassurance.

This wasn't going at all the way she'd thought it would. She hadn't felt this kind of pressure on the yacht the other evening, when Ethan had made small talk with casual acquaintances. The people here tonight knew him well, and she felt as if everyone—but *everyone*—was inspecting her. Panic pricked at her skin like needles, even while her brain told her she must not let Ethan down.

Taking short and fast breaths, she shook hands with a plastered-on smile.

"Henri!" Ethan clasped the shoulder of a mustached man. *"Cela fait longtemps."*

"Ça va?"

"Marie. *Magnifique, comme toujours.*" Ethan kissed the man's wife on both cheeks. "*Je vous présente* Holly Motta."

French. Naturally Ethan spoke perfect French. As men who take showers on private planes were likely to do.

As they walked away he told her, "Mr. and Mrs. Arnaud made a substantial personal donation to a low-income housing project we did outside of Paris."

"Merci!" Holly threw over her shoulder.

Ethan's eyes always took on a special shine when he mentioned those charity projects that were so important to him.

They approached a stone-faced man whose huge muscles were all but bursting out of a tuxedo that was a size too small. He stood ramrod-straight, with his arms folded across his chest. Holly saw that he wore a discreet earpiece with a barely noticeable wire.

"Holly Motta, this is Chip Foley, our head of security," Ethan introduced her.

Chip bent toward Ethan's ear. "I take it you received that fax with the information you requested, sir?"

Ethan looked confused. "No, I did not."

A Japanese couple were coming toward them.

"Ethan. *Ogenki desu ka?*"

The woman wore an elaborate kimono.

"Hai, genki desu," he answered back.

French wasn't intimidating enough. He had to speak Japanese, too.

The evening was starting off like a freezing cold shower.

Holly had imagined it was going to be easier. And more fun. What girl wouldn't want to be at the ball with the dashing prince she was madly in love with?

Madly. In. Love. With.

The four words echoed through her as if someone had yelled them into her ear. Especially the third word. Because there was no denying its truth.

She was in love with this sophisticated, handsome, brilliant man beside her.

Had it happened the very night she'd arrived in New York, when she'd opened the door to the apartment and found him reading his newspaper with that one curl of hair hanging in front of his eyes?

Had it been when he'd bought her all the painting supplies she'd been able to point to, because took her seriously as an artist in a way that no one else ever had?

Maybe it had been atop the Empire State Building, when those earth-shattering kisses had quaked through her like nothing she'd known before?

Or had it been on the yacht, under the tender shadow of the Statue of Liberty, when they'd danced together as one, late into the night?

It didn't matter.

Because she was in love with Ethan Benton.

And that was about the worst thing that had ever happened to her.

"We should make our way to the table now," Ethan said, after finishing his small talk in Japanese.

He took her hand and led them toward the head table, where Aunt Louise and Fernando were already sitting.

Awareness of his touch was a painful reminder that Holly would never have a bona fide seat at this family table. There would be no keeping the glass slippers. The Ethan Bentons of this world didn't marry the Holly Mottas. She was a commoner, hired to do a job—hardly any different from either a scullery maid or an office assistant in his corporation.

Ethan's world was a tightly coiled mechanism of wheels. She was but one small cog. Loving him was going to be *her* problem, not his.

She willed herself not to fall apart now. Overall, Ethan had been kind and generous to her. She had to hold her end up. That much she owed him. Despite the fact that she was crumbling inside.

Love was awful.

"Louise, you look wonderful tonight." Holly greeted the older woman with a kiss on the cheek.

The style magicians had worked wonders. None of the scrapes and bruises from her fall were visible. No one would guess she wore a wig that was thicker and more lustrous than her own thinning hair. Shiny baubles complemented her black gown.

Holly nodded hello to Fernando who, in return, lifted his nose and looked away.

Fernando sat on one side of Louise and Ethan the other. Holly sat next to Ethan. Rounding out their table were company VIPs whom she'd been introduced to earlier today but couldn't remember their names.

As the ballroom's lights were slightly dimmed a spotlight was aimed on Louise, and a waiter brought her a microphone. Louise stood, subtly using the table for leverage and balance. Holly saw a grimace pass quickly across her face.

"Good evening, Benton Worldwide extended family," Louise greeted the guests. "It's been another profitable and productive year for us, which you'll hear about in my report later. As you know my late husband, Melvin Benton, and his brother, Joseph Benton, began this company with the purchase of a one-bedroom apartment in South Boston. And look where we are today."

The ballroom filled with the sound of applause.

"Together we have made this happen. Melvin taught me many things. The most important of which is that money in our wallets means nothing without love in our hearts."

Louise smiled at Ethan and Holly.

"And so," she continued, "if you'll indulge an old woman before we get on to pie charts and growth projections, I'd like to share something personal with you."

A hush swept the room.

"Many of you have watched my nephew Ethan grow up over the decades. I hope you share in my pride at the man he's become. He's a leader who drives himself hard, a savvy negotiator who insists on fairness, and a shrewd businessman with a philanthropic spirit."

The guests applauded again.

Ethan bowed his head, clearly embarrassed by the accolades. Holly touched his arm. He turned his head slightly toward her.

"Yet there's been one thing missing. It has always been my greatest wish for Ethan that he would find a partner to share his life with. To rejoice with in triumph and to weep with in sorrow. To have a home. To have children. To know a love like Mel and I had. And it's with great joy tonight that I announce that Ethan has found that soul mate. And, although it's asking a lot of her to meet her extended family of one thousand all in one evening, I'd like to introduce you to Ethan's fiancée: Miss Holly Motta."

Ethan and Holly looked at each other, both knowing this was their moment. They rose from their chairs in unison and turned to face the crowd. Holly's chest crackled at the irony of the moment.

Applause and good wishes flooded the room.

"Bravo!"

"Bravo!"

"It's about time!"

"Holly!"

"Ethan!"

They smiled and waved on cue—as if they were a royal couple on a palace balcony. Guests began tapping their knives against their water glasses in a signal for a couple to kiss.

Without hesitation, Ethan leaned in to Holly's lips. Thankfully not with a passionate kiss that would have thrown her off balance. But it wasn't a quick peck either. Perhaps he was incapable of a kiss that didn't stir her up inside.

She felt herself blushing. When she giggled a little the guests cheered.

As planned, the chandeliers were dimmed further and the dance floor became bathed in a golden light. Ethan took Holly's hand and brought her to the center of the dance floor, this time as two thousand eyes fixed on them.

The love song from their practice session boomed out of the sound system.

Holly lifted one hand to Ethan's shoulder. One of his fastened around her waist. Their other hands met palm to palm.

They floated across the dance floor, bodies locked, legs in sync. The moment was so perfect Holly wanted to cry.

It was a moment she would never forget. Yet, in time she must learn to forget, if she was ever to love someone who could return her love.

With the gleam of lights beaming down on the dance floor and the rest of the ballroom darker, it was hard to see. Yet Holly's eyes landed on the table where they had been seated. Ethan turned her as they danced, but she kept craning her neck to focus on a strange sight.

Louise was chatting with a couple who had come over to the table. Meanwhile Fernando finished his drink and stood up. He reached into his tuxedo jacket's pocket and pulled out two pieces of paper. He placed one on the chair where Holly was sitting and the other on Ethan's seat. Then he smirked with a satisfied nod.

Holly was so spectacularly beautiful Ethan couldn't help glancing down at her as they danced. She was really just as fetching—if not more so—casual and barefoot in a tee shirt and jeans, having breakfast at the apartment. But tonight… The dance floor lights cast an incandescent glow on her face. The baby pink of her lipstick emphasized the sensual plumpness of her mouth.

It made him want to brand her with kiss after kiss, until he had to hold her up to keep her from falling to the ground. His body reacted—in fact overreacted—to the intimate feel of her breasts, belly and hips pressed to him as he held her close.

Every now and then the sobering fact that Holly wasn't really his fiancée would flit across his mind. There wasn't ever going to be the wedding, home and children that Aunt Louise had spoken of during her toast. He batted away the reality of those thoughts every time they came near. If only for tonight, he actually did want to believe the masquerade was real.

He could risk that much.

Yet a voice in his gut pleaded with him to stop. Told him that he knew better. That his mission had been to guard and defend. That dangerous fantasies would confuse his intentions and lead to irrevocably bad decisions.

Opposing forces argued within him. So his rational

mind welcomed the distraction when he followed Holly's eyes to the table where they'd been sitting. He watched with curiosity as Fernando placed a piece of paper on his and Holly's chairs.

As soon as the dance was over Ethan nodded politely at the applauding guests to the left and to the right. When the next song began he gestured for others to join in the dancing. Couples stood and approached. Once the rhythm was underway, and the dance floor was well populated, he gestured to Holly to return to their table.

Ethan slipped the piece of paper on his chair into his jacket pocket and sat down, trying not to draw any attention to the action. When everyone was occupied with their first-course salads and dinner conversation, he'd discreetly look at it.

Holly held her piece of paper in her lap. She looked downward to read it.

Her face changed instantly. The rosy blush of her cheeks turned ashen white. The blue in her eyes darkened to a flat gray. She blinked back tears.

Trancelike, she slowly stood.

Her murmur was barely audible, and directed to no one in particular. "Excuse me…"

Fortunately, with the dance floor in full swing and one of the video presentations playing on several screens throughout the room, Holly's exit from the table didn't appear too dramatic.

Ethan watched her cross the ballroom as if she was headed to the ladies' lounge.

Instead she opened a sliver of one of the French doors that led to the ballroom's terrace. She slipped through and closed it behind her.

At the table, Ethan caught Fernando's eye. He grinned at Ethan like a Cheshire cat. Ethan's blood began to boil.

But he kept his cool as he rose. He moved slowly toward the terrace. And slid out through the same door Holly had.

The frigid and windy evening slapped across his face and straight under the fabric of his tuxedo. Holly stood across the large plaza of the terrace with her back to him. He figured she must be chilled to the bone.

What was it that had upset her so much that she'd had to leave the ballroom and retreat to this empty space that was not in use during the winter months?

With dread in his heart, Ethan pulled the paper from his pocket.

His temples pulsated louder with each word he read.

Fax to Ethan Benton from Chip Foley, Head of Security, Benton Worldwide Properties.

Regarding Holly Motta.

Per your request, I have gathered the following intelligence.

Holly Motta, age twenty-nine, last known residence Fort Pierce, Florida.

Internet and social media presence significant only as it relates to her occupation as an artist.

No criminal record.

Sometimes known as Holly Dowd.

Married until two years ago to a Ricky Dowd, age twenty-eight, also of Fort Pierce.

Married and divorced.

"Holly!" he spat.

Her shoulders arched at the sound of his voice.

She spun around and they marched toward each other. Meeting in the middle of the grand stone terrace.

"You had me *investigated*?" she accused, rather than questioned.

"You were *married*?" he fired back.

"Without telling me?"

"Without telling me?"

"That must simply be business as usual for you, Mr. Benton. Background checks on the hired help and all that."

"As a matter of fact, it is. My family has spent two generations building our empire. We had better damn well protect it with every tool we have."

"You might have let me know."

The hammering at Ethan's temples threatened to crack open his skull as he read the fax aloud.

"'Ricky Dowd, also known as Rick Dowd and Riff Dowd, indicted for armed robbery at age nineteen. Served twenty-two months in prison, released early due to penitentiary overcrowding. Indicted six months ago, again for armed robbery. Currently serving a sentence at Hansen Correctional Facility in central Florida.'"

Ethan broke away from the page to glare at Holly.

"Twice indicted for armed robbery?"

He felt heat rise through his body in a fury that, for once, he might not be able to contain.

Holly's face was lifeless. Her eyes downcast. She didn't even seem to be breathing.

Finally she muttered softly, "I didn't know Ricky was in prison again."

"But you knew who you married." Ethan's jaw locked.

"The first robbery was before we were married. This new incident happened after our divorce. I haven't seen or talked to him in two years."

"Yet you married a convicted criminal? And deliberately withheld that from me? How will that look to my shareholders? Do you not understand the importance of an impeccable reputation?"

Ethan was approaching cruelty. Rubbing salt into her wounds. But he couldn't stop himself.

Women were never who they seemed! Once again a female had betrayed him. Had not been honest. The same as every other woman he had known. The same as his mother.

This was exactly what he'd been warning himself of, despite his growing attachment to Holly. Why would she turn out to be any different from the others? How dense was he still not to have learned his lesson?

They'd spent so much time together this week. Yet all along she'd withheld the information that not only had she been married, but to someone convicted of serious crimes. She obviously didn't understand how, if that information was to be revealed publicly, it would become an integral part of people's perception of her. Of them.

What else was she hiding? Omission was its own form of lying. And he'd always known that if this engagement façade was to work, they'd have to be straightforward with each other. He'd told her about his future plans for Benton Worldwide. She knew about his aunt's health problems. He'd even let her witness Louise being wheeled out on a stretcher by the paramedics. Without measuring the risks of his actions, he had, in fact, trusted Holly.

Trust. Every year, at every shareholders' gala at this hotel, Ethan got a reminder that *trust* was a dirty word. One that he should never factor into an equation. After all, a boy whose father had just died should have been able to trust that his mother had his best interests at heart.

To read this background information about Holly, to confirm that he didn't know her at all, was an unbearable confusion. Just like the one he'd suffered as a boy, never really knowing his mother, or what could make a woman betray her only child.

A familiar fist pummeled his gut more viciously than ever. He wanted to scream. For the nine-year-old boy who'd lost both his parents within a few months of each other. One in a horrifying car accident.

To complicate matters even more, he was also seething

with jealousy that Holly had given her hand in marriage to another man. *Any* other man! Irrationally, he wanted her only for himself.

Ethan clenched his teeth and read on while Holly clutched her own copy of the fax.

Brother Vincent Motta, age twenty-six.

Well-regarded employee at Benton Miami office.

Mother Sally Motta, age forty-eight.

Dozens of jobs, ranging from waitress to telemarketer to factory employee. No position held longer than six months. Never married. Motta appears to be maiden name.

Father of Holly Motta—unknown.

Father of Vincent Motta—unknown.

Unknown whether Holly and Vincent have the same father.

It was hard to say whose story was sadder—his or Holly's.

Her lower lip trembled uncontrollably until a sob erupted from her throat. "So now you know everything, Mr. Benton!" she cried. "Do you want to share my humiliating past with everyone in the ballroom?"

As tears rolled down her face she shivered in the cold and used both hands to rub at her bare arms.

"I do not know *what* I want to do!" Ethan shouted—uncharacteristically.

He yanked off his tuxedo jacket and wrapped it around her shoulders. "If you had given me all this information at the outset I could have discussed it with my team."

"Discussed it with your team?" She pulled the jacket closer around her. "What would you have done? Created a new identity for me? Erased the past? You masters of the world think of everything, don't you?"

"That is exactly what we have been doing, is it not? We have dressed you up and presented you as a suitable bride for me. Which is what we agreed upon in the beginning."

"Yes. Playing dress-up. Pretending someone like me could be *suitable* for someone like you. My mistake, Ethan. I thought we had become more than our contract. I thought we had..." She eyed the ground again. "I thought we had become friends."

He blamed himself for this predicament. It had been insanity to hire someone he'd only just met for this charade. In fact the whole ruse had been preposterous. Paying someone to pose as his fiancée in order to get Aunt Louise to retire. His heart had been in the right place, but he'd had a temporary lapse in judgment.

In fact he'd been deceitful to Aunt Louise. The one and only woman in his life who had always been truthful with him. Although he knew that no matter how big a mess he'd made of everything his aunt would still love him. That he could depend on.

For one of the only times in his life Ethan didn't know what to do. Didn't know how to reckon with all the events of the past few days. Just as he didn't know where to put the decades of shame that had mixed with the years of phenomenal successes.

And he surely didn't know how to make sense of his feelings for Holly. For once he was out of his league.

After a stare-down with her that had them both turning blue with cold, logic set in.

He wondered aloud, "How did Fernando get this fax from Chip Foley?"

Holly explained how she had seen Fernando take a fax from the machine when they'd had him and Louise over for dinner. Because Fernando used the apartment during his trips to New York, she hadn't thought it unusual that he'd receive a fax there.

"That weasel…" Ethan scowled with disgust.

All along Fernando had been conjuring up ways to ruin Ethan's engagement because he didn't want to move to Barbados with Aunt Louise. He no doubt planned to use Holly's history as a way to prove her an unbefitting bride.

"I will deal with him later. We will sort *all* this out later. For now, we will go back inside and finish the evening as planned."

"Okay," Holly whispered, but it wasn't convincing. She looked utterly shell-shocked with his jacket grasped tightly around her. The rims of her eyes were red and her makeup had smeared.

"I will slip back into the ballroom. You will go up to the suite and pull yourself together. I will meet you back at the table."

"Yes," she consented.

Ethan only hoped she'd be able to get through the rest of the night.

Once inside, Holly handed him his jacket and ducked toward the exit. Ethan soon got roped into a conversation with a Swedish architect. He returned to the table just as the wait staff cleared the salad plates. His and Holly's were untouched.

Ethan made small talk with his tablemates as the main course was served. Over and over again the information in the fax repeated itself in his brain. And he kept glancing in the direction Holly should be returning from. It seemed to be taking her an inordinate amount of time.

Guests were enjoying their surf-and-turf entrées of lobster and filet mignon. A pleasant buzz filled the ballroom.

Still no Holly.

Maybe she'd fallen and hurt herself.

Maybe she'd been taken ill.

Maybe she'd been so upset by the fax that she was crying her eyes out.

Ethan had to go find her. But just as he was about to get up the president of the board of shareholders, Denny Wheton, stood from his seat at the next table. A spotlight landed on him. A waiter gave him a microphone.

"Ladies and gentlemen…" Denny began.

Ethan scanned the whole ballroom for Holly, his insides filling with fear that Denny was going to make a toast to them.

"On behalf of the shareholders' board," Denny continued, confirming Ethan's worry, "I want to express our delight at the news of Ethan's engagement. As Louise said earlier, we've watched Ethan become the driving force of Benton Worldwide. His father and uncle would be proud. As to his bride…we haven't had a chance to get to know her yet, but we're sure Ethan has chosen her with the same diligence and discernment he puts into all his endeavors. To Holly and Ethan! Congratulations!"

Guests at the other tables lifted their glasses.

"Congratulations!"

Voices came from every corner of the room.

Ethan froze as a second spotlight beamed onto him. Hadn't Denny stopped to notice that Holly was not in her seat? He'd probably had too much to drink.

"Holly?" Denny called into his microphone.

The congratulations ceased. The room became silent.

"Holly?"

A microphone was handed to Ethan.

Who had to think fast.

"Thank you for your good wishes," Ethan stated robotically.

He'd kill himself if something bad had happened to her.

"I apologize that Holly is not present for this toast. She is feeling a bit under the weather."

"Under the weather?" Denny boomed into his microphone. "*Under the weather?* Will Benton Worldwide be introducing the next generation's CEO nine months from now?"

The ballroom exploded with applause and cheers.

CHAPTER TWELVE

HOLLY HAD NEVER been so relieved to be home in her entire life. She toed the apartment door closed and leaned back against it. With a deep sigh she dropped the couple of bags she had retrieved from the hotel suite before catching a taxi.

She closed her eyes for a few breaths, hoping to shut out all that had happened.

When she opened them again everything was still the same.

Only she had made matters worse by running away from Ethan and the gala.

En route to the bedroom, she heard her crystal gown swish audibly in the quiet of the apartment. A sound that hadn't been heard under all the activity at the gala. The sky-high heels were killing her, so they were quickly nudged off.

It was a struggle to reach the zipper of her dress. Much nicer earlier tonight, when Ethan had zipped her in. Eventually she was carefully able to wriggle out of the dress. Her impulse was to leave it pooled on the floor, but the adult in her at least managed to put it on the bed.

This gown wasn't her life.

Her jeans and tee shirt were familiar friends.

This wasn't her home.

It was time to go.

Time to cut her losses.

Holly had too much experience with that. Her marriage. Her mother. False hopes and grand promises that hadn't panned out. This was simply another.

With her tail between her legs, it was time to take two steps backward and keep striving for that next step ahead.

Sure, memories of New York would sting. Memories of Ethan would slice deeper than any wounds she'd ever endured before. But she was no stranger to pain.

Besides, she was supposed to be working on herself. Not getting mixed up in someone else's priorities. Not falling in love. This was the wrong road. Time to change direction.

Packing her clothes took less time than she'd thought it would. It was still the middle of the night. With plans to leave in the morning, she paced the apartment.

In the living room, the paper ring Ethan had made from his beer bottle label still sat on the coffee table. The one he'd used to propose to her with. When he had asked her to embark on a business venture that was *not* to become a matter of the heart. For the moment she still wore the enormous diamond that had been on and off her finger all week.

Holly rolled the ring round and round on her finger. She thought about the symbolism of rings—how the circle could never be broken. It had no beginning and it had no end. Continuous. Lasting. Eternal.

Undying love was *not* her and Ethan's story.

Their tale was of two people who had crossed paths in a New York City apartment. Now they both needed to continue on their separate journeys. Ethan built skyscrapers, but was determined not to build love. Holly had a past she could never escape.

His investigation into her hadn't even uncovered all her dirty laundry. He hadn't found out that she wasn't sure if the man who'd shown up every few years while she was growing up was really her father. Despite her mother's insistence that he was.

Wayne had been nice enough to her and Vince when he'd pass through town. He'd take them to get some cheap clothes that he'd pay for with a short fold of twenty-dollar bills he'd pull from his front pants pocket. Then they'd be shuffled off to a neighbor's house so that he could spend time alone with their mother.

Neither Holly nor Vince looked like him. But nor did they look like each other. It wasn't something they talked about much. They couldn't be any closer than they already were. What difference did it make? They could have DNA testing, but it wouldn't matter.

So she had never known whether she and her brother were half or full siblings. Or who their father—or fathers—were. They shared the same eyes as their mother. That was all Holly could be sure of.

Sally's blue eyes had been cloudy and bloodshot the last time Holly had seen her, five years ago.

Vince! Sorrow rained down on her. Her actions—lashing out at Ethan about the investigation and then abruptly leaving the gala without a word to him or to Louise—would cast an unprofessional shadow on Vince.

Her knees buckled and she sank down to the edge of a chair, vowing never to forgive herself if she had ruined her brother's chances at the promotion he'd worked so hard for.

Head in hands, she began to cry for all she and Vince had lacked when they were children. Not just material things, but adults to provide the care that every child needed. As much as they had looked out for each other, they'd always have holes in their hearts.

She wept for this week—for this failed chance to catapult her career to a potential high. For this lost opportunity to turn her goals into reality.

And she sobbed because she'd unexpectedly found a love in Ethan truer than any she could have imagined.

A love that the crux of her knew she would never have again. But she wasn't able to claim it.

Numbly, she picked up her phone. "Vinz…?"

"What's wrong?"

Only her brother would know after one syllable that she was shattered.

With the back of her hand she wiped the tears from her face. "I guess New York is not how I thought it would be."

"You wouldn't be the first person to say that."

"The thing is, I sort of think I've let you down."

Holly stopped herself there. She didn't have to explain everything right now. Maybe Ethan wouldn't hold all this against Vince. At this point she didn't have any control over the situation. All she had was regrets.

"Why would you have let me down? Because you took a shot and it didn't pan out? At least you did it."

"I'm just licking my wounds. I want to come home."

Where was home? She'd given up her dingy apartment in Fort Pierce to pin everything on her future. Neither she nor Vince had any current information on their mother's whereabouts.

"Fly here to Miami. My garage is yours to paint in. And my sofa bed has your name on it. I'll pick you up at the airport."

After the call, Holly took inventory of the mini art studio she'd set up by the window. Methodically she cleaned brushes. Tucked sketches into portfolios. She organized neatly, remembering the open tube of paint that had started this magical ride in New York. Cobalt Two Eleven all over her face.

Her gaze darted to the blue-painted sketch of Ethan on the wall. She was so proud of that piece—felt that she had caught his spirit in each line. Power and gravity and sensuality, with demons fighting behind his eyes.

As a matter of fact she would take the painting with her. It would either be a testament to the legacy Ethan would hold in her heart forever. Or it would be a torment that would haunt her for the rest of her days. Either way, it was hers and she wanted it.

With a small knife she found in the kitchen she carefully removed the staples attaching the canvas to its frame. She'd roll up the painting and buy a tube to transport it in before she left town.

There was nothing more to do.

She wasn't interested in sleeping. Didn't want to give up even one last minute of this magical city and its hex that made people believe dreams could come true. These moments were all she had, and she'd treasure them for a lifetime.

She stared out the window. A million stories were unfolding in the city. Hers would end here.

Inching off the diamond engagement ring, she placed it next to the paper ring on the coffee table. Beside each other they were as odd a couple as she and Ethan.

As usual, not knowing what else to do with her feelings, Holly said goodbye to her fancy manicure and reached for her charcoals.

Ethan closed the door on the hotel room where he'd managed a few hours of tortured sleep in a chair. He walked down the hall to Aunt Louise's suite. Still in his tuxedo pants, although his tie was off and the first two buttons of his shirt were undone, he scratched his beard stubble. He'd been unable to face a shower just yet, and had promised his aunt they'd reconvene their discussion during breakfast.

"Come in, Ethan," Louise called out as soon as she heard the keycard click to unlock the door.

"I have not had coffee!" Ethan managed a trace of a smile for his beloved aunt.

"I'll pour you a cup." Louise wore a dressing gown and slippers. She sat at the dining table in her luxury suite, heavy drapes open to the city.

Ethan took the seat across from her.

"Does anything look different to you in the light of morning?" She tipped her eyebrow to him in a familiar way.

When he was a teenager, living with her and Uncle Mel, if he'd been grappling with a dilemma or regretting a bad choice, Aunt Louise would always tell him to sleep on it and see if a new day brought any fresh insight.

The insistence in her arched brow today told him that she had decided what realization he should have come to. His intuition told him what her conclusion was. He peered into his coffee cup to try to shut the thought down.

Something like a tribal drum pounded inside him, urging him to lift his eyes and embrace the truth.

"Where is Fernando?" Ethan tried to change the subject—at least for a moment.

But on and on the internal drum sounded.

"Gone. Good riddance," Louise clipped. "Before dawn this morning I called Bob Parcell to draw up a nondisclosure agreement."

Ethan snorted. "Lawyers work around the clock."

"Ours do. I signed a generous check, contingent on the fact that Fernando never speaks a word about our family, our company or anything to do with us. If he does, our people will make sure the rest of his life is spent behind bars."

"Well done."

Louise took a sip of her coffee, then smacked the cup loudly back onto the saucer. "And *that*, my dear nephew, is the end of my foray into having a younger companion."

After Holly had disappeared last night he and Louise

had held their heads high until the last guest had left the gala. Then they'd sat up together until the wee hours. He'd confessed about the engagement ploy and his motivation behind it. Begged for her forgiveness. Told her about the fax and Fernando's part in it.

Now Ethan lifted his aunt's hand and gently kissed the back of it. "I am so sorry you fell prey to him"

"Don't you think I knew what he was doing?" she retorted. "His trips down here to New York while I stayed in Boston. The restaurant bills that were surely more expensive than dinner for one. Charges to women's clothing shops although I never received any gifts. Fernando was clearly taking advantage of me from the beginning."

"You never told me."

"The vanity of a rich old woman… Perhaps I thought I could simply buy myself something to replace the emptiness left by your Uncle Mel's death. But even with all the money in the world you can't purchase or declare love. You can't arrange it. It's love that rearranges *you*."

Ethan knew what she was telling him. The drum beat louder in his ears. Yet he couldn't. Mustn't. Wouldn't.

"I know that you're torn inside…" Louise continued.

For all her health problems, when Louise Benton was clearheaded she was a shrewd and intelligent woman.

"It's what I feared for you. That after so much loss you wouldn't be able to love. When your mother went—"

"You were the only mother I ever had," Ethan interrupted, taking her hand again. "Everything I have achieved is because of you."

Louise's eyes welled. "I must have done something right. You're a rare man to go through all this trouble to get me to retire. When I said I wanted you to be married and settled before you took over, I never imagined you'd concoct such an elaborate scheme just because I've been too hardheaded to see that my time has come. And I had no idea I'd raised such a skilled imposter!"

She snickered, forcing a crack through Ethan's tight lips.

"We Bentons do what we have to, do we not?" he joked in a hushed voice.

"My guess is that your playacting became real and you've fallen in love with Holly. Am I right, Ethan?"

He wanted to cover his ears, like a young child who didn't want to hear what was being said. *Love* her? Those drumbeats inside him sped up like a jungle warrior charging toward his most threatening battle.

Yes, he loved Holly. He loved her completely—like nothing he'd ever loved before. He wanted to give her everything she'd never had. Wanted to have children with her. Wanted to spend every minute of his life with her. Wanted to hold her forever as both his wife and his best friend.

That invisible opponent marched toward him and pushed him back behind the battle lines.

He lashed out without thinking. "Holly deceived me about her past. She lied to me. Look at what she came from."

"Oh, hogwash!" Louise dismissed. "How about what *you* came from? What *I* came from? Your father and Uncle Mel were brought up on the tough streets of South Boston without a dime or a university degree between them. I was a poor Southie girl whose father skinned fish for a living. It's not shame about Holly's past that you're concerned with. The time has come for you to let go of shame about your own."

Of course he wore shame—like a suit of armor. Who wouldn't be ashamed that his own mother didn't want him?

He studied his aunt's face. Hard-earned wrinkles told the story of a life embraced. Could he let go of his pain and open up to the fullness the world had to offer?

Could he gamble again on trust?

Gamble on Holly?

On himself?

In an instant he knew that if he didn't now, he never would.

He sprang to his feet. Leaned down to Louise and kissed both her cheeks. Moved to the office desk in the well-appointed suite. Wrote a quick note and then sent it through the fax machine.

"Wish me luck," he said as he flew out the door, too impatient to wait for a response.

In his hotel room, he shaved and showered. Called Leonard to bring the car around. He placed a second call to George Alvarez, manager of the Miami office.

"What are your thoughts about the site supervisor position?" Ethan asked him.

Liz Washington, the previous supervisor, had transferred to the Houston office.

"I've had a young guy apprenticing with Liz for a couple of years now. Done a terrific job," George pitched. "He's ready for the step up. Name of Vince Motta."

"Yes, Vince Motta," Ethan approved with relief.

He valued George, and wouldn't want to go against his expertise. But he knew that if he was able to help Vince it would mean a lot to Holly. That was the kind of sister she was. The kind of woman she was.

The kind of woman he was going to make his.

He raced down the hotel corridor to the elevators, and then out through the front entrance of the hotel. Because once Ethan Benton had made up his mind about something, it couldn't happen fast enough.

"To the apartment," he instructed Leonard as he got into the car.

After Holly had vanished from the gala last night Ethan had checked the hotel suites. She had been nowhere to be found. Even though there had been no answer on her cell phone, or at the apartment, that was where he figured she'd gone. A midnight phone call to the building's doorman had confirmed that Holly had indeed arrived by taxi.

Yes, he had called the doorman to investigate her whereabouts! How could she blame him for an action like that? He oversaw a corporation with thousands of employees all over the world. He couldn't possibly command that without being on top of all available knowledge. Information was power. Artistic Holly Motta might not understand that, but he relied on it. She'd have to get used to the way he thought.

Just as he'd have to get used to her freewheeling ways. How she slammed doors closed with one foot. Ordered pizza with everything but the kitchen sink on it. Said whatever came into her mind. Needed to devote hours of scrubbing to getting her hands clean of paint. Ethan thought he wouldn't mind spending a lifetime looking at and holding those graceful fingers that brought art and beauty into the world. Seeing the ring on her finger that proclaimed her lo—

"Leonard! I need to make a stop first. Take me to Fifth and Fifty-Seventh."

Holly winced when she heard the key in the door. If only she'd stuck to her original plan and left at the crack of dawn after her sleepless night. She'd known that Ethan would make his way back here to the apartment. It would have been easier to slink away than to say goodbye in person. What was it that had kept her from going?

Her heart dropped in freefall to the floor as he strode through the door. She wanted to run to him. To put her arms around him. To kiss him until all the problems of the world faded away and there was just the two of them.

"Why did you leave last night?"

His eyes looked weary. His cheeks were flushed.

That one perfect curl of hair that always fell forward on his forehead was dotted with snowflakes. So was his coat.

Holly shifted her gaze out the window to see that it had started to snow. The whole week she'd been in New York it had rained and been cold and dreary. But it hadn't snowed.

She'd fantasized about walking the city streets during a snowfall. Seeing the soft powder billowing down as she crossed busy intersections and marveled at architectural landmarks that stood proudly dusted with white.

Instead she'd be returning to the sunny Florida winter. Snow—*ha!* That was what fantasy was. By definition not real.

"Answer my question," he insisted.

Holly's voice came out hoarse. "I'm truly embarrassed by my behavior. I know it was completely unprofessional."

She cut her eyes toward the floor.

"Look at me. How about the fact that I was worried about you?"

"What do *you* care? Let's be honest."

He stepped in and took her chin in his hand, lifting her face to meet his. "Certainly you leaving the gala without a word was not good business…" he began.

"I'm so sorry."

"But this is not business anymore, and if you want to be honest you know that."

"Know what?"

He moved his hand to caress her cheek tenderly, sending warmth across her skin.

"I love you, Holly. I *love* you. And I suspect you love me, too."

Tears pooled somewhere far behind her eyes. She fought them before saying what she needed to. "Now that you know the truth about me from your investigation, you've found out that I'm not who you want. I'm not a match for you. I'm damaged goods."

"You think you are the only one?"

"What do you mean?"

He let the hand that was touching her face fall to his side. His mouth set in a straight line.

"After my father died..." he started, but then let the words dangle in the air for a minute.

Holly anxiously awaited what he was so hesitant to say.

"Within a few months of my father dying, my mother—who was not much of a mother to begin with—met a man. And together they came up with an idea."

Bare pain burned in Ethan's eyes. Holly knew he was going to tell her something he had to dig out from the rock bottom of his core, where he kept it submerged.

"My mother told Uncle Mel and Aunt Louise that she and this man were going to take me away. That they would never see or hear from me again unless..."

He swallowed hard, his breath rasping and broken.

He regained his voice, "Unless *they* wanted to keep me instead. Which she would allow them to do in exchange for five hundred thousand dollars. In cash. She specified cash."

Agony poured from every cell in Holly's body. Grief for the little boy Ethan. And for herself. For her brother, Vince. For all the children unlucky enough to be born to parents who didn't give them the devotion they deserved.

"So, you see, my mother sold me to my aunt and uncle. I believe that means that you are not the only package of damaged goods around here."

The spoken words swirled around the room.

Again Holly wanted to hug the man she loved.

And again she didn't.

It was time for her to go.

He thought he loved her. He'd fallen for the drama they were starring in.

She'd have to have the cooler head. If she let him believe he loved her, one day he'd wake up and realize that he didn't want something this raw. That instead he could stuff his hurt right back down and act in a different play, with another kind of woman. With someone who'd never have to know about the betrayed and discarded child. About the gashes that still bled, the sores that would never heal. In his next pantomime he could be with a woman who knew only the functional and successful adult he'd managed to become.

She averted her eyes to the diamond ring on the table. To the beer wrapper ring beside it. She bent down for them and handed both to Ethan.

"I am glad you've returned these rings," he said. "They do not belong on your finger."

His words confirmed what she already knew. That it was time to leave.

He reached in his pocket and pulled out a small turquoise box. Holly's breath quickened.

He knelt down on one knee and held it out to her in the palm of his hand.

"Because an ordinary diamond ring does not fit the uniqueness of you. Like this, you are one of a kind."

He opened the box. Inside was the blue topaz ring she had admired from the private gemstone collection they'd seen that day they had gone shopping.

Uncontainable tears rolled down Holly's cheeks.

"I love you, Holly. I have loved you since you bounced through the door with that ridiculous blue paint on your face. I have never met anyone like you. Pretending to be engaged to you has shown me something I never thought I could see."

"What?" Holly asked, her spirits soaring.

"That our pain does not have to define us. That a past and a future can coexist. That there is beauty to be had every day. I want to share those miracles with you. To walk through life together. Please. *Please.* Will you marry me? This time the ring will never leave your finger."

She had to take the chance if he was willing to. To trust their authentic selves—scars and all. Together.

"I will." She nodded as he fitted the ring onto her finger.

Ethan stood. Holly reached her arms up around his neck and drew him into a kiss that couldn't wait a second longer.

Many minutes later he whispered, "Did you check the fax machine?"

"No." She'd heard the sounds and beeps of the machine before he arrived, but she hadn't looked to see what had come. She'd had quite enough of faxes already.

"Go," he prodded.

The piece of paper contained a two-word question.

Will you?

Had she read it earlier, she'd have known he was coming to propose.

She flirted with her fiancé. "Will I…?"

The smile kicked at the corner of his mouth. "Will you teach me how to draw?"

"It's a deal." Her grin joined his.

They pressed their lips to each other's in an ironclad merger, valid for eternity.

* * * * *

UNVEILING THE BRIDESMAID

JESSICA GILMORE

For Kristy, roommate, cocktail enabler
and partner in crime extraordinaire.

Here's to many more RWA conferences—
and another evening in the rum bar some day. xxx

CHAPTER ONE

BEEP, BEEP, *BEEEEEP.*

Hope McKenzie muttered and rolled over, reaching out blindly to mute her alarm, her hand scrabbling to find the 'off' button, the 'pause' button, the *'Please make it stop right now'* button. Only… Hang on a second… She didn't *have* an alarm clock here in New York; she used her phone on the rare occasions when the sun, traffic and humidity didn't wake her first. So what was that noise? And why wouldn't it *stop*?

Beeeeeep.

Whatever it was, it was getting more and more insistent, and louder by the second. Hope pushed herself up, every drowsy limb fighting back as she swung her legs over the metal frame of the narrow daybed and staggered to her feet, glancing at the watch on her wrist. Five-thirty a.m. She blinked, the small room swimming into dim focus, still grey with predawn stillness, the gloom broken only by the glow of the street light, a full floor below her sole window.

Beeeeeep.

It wasn't a fire alarm or a smoke alarm. There were no footsteps pounding down the stairs of the apartment building, no sirens screeching outside, just the high insistent beep coming from the small round table in the window bay. No, coming from her still-open laptop on the small round table in the window bay.

'What the…?' Hope stumbled the few short steps to the table and turned the laptop around to face her. The screen blared into life, bright colour dazzling her still-half-closed eyes, letters jumbling together as she blinked again, rubbing her eyes with one sleepy hand until the words swam into focus.

Faith calling. Accept?

Faith? At this time? Was she in trouble? Hurt? Wait, where was she? Had she left Europe yet? Maybe she'd been framed for drug smuggling? Maybe she had been robbed and lost all her money? Why had Hope left her to travel alone? Why had she swanned off to New York for six months while her baby sister was out there by herself alone and vulnerable? With a trembling hand Hope pressed the enter key to accept the call, pushing her hair out of her eyes, scanning the screen anxiously and pulling up the low neckline of the old, once-white vest top she slept in.

'Faith?' Hope took a deep breath, relief replacing the blind panic of the last few seconds as her sister's tanned, happy face filled the screen. 'Is everything okay?'

'Everything is fab! Oh, did I wake you? Hang on, did I get the time wrong? I thought it would be evening in New York.'

'No, it's morning, we're behind not ahead. But don't worry about that,' she added as her sister's face fell. 'It's lovely to hear from you, to *see* you. Where are you?' Still in Europe somewhere, she thought, doing a quick date calculation. Despite Faith's promises to call and write often, contact with her little sister had been limited since Faith had boarded the Eurostar, just over three months ago, to start her grand tour. She was spending the summer Interrailing around Europe before flying to Australia to begin the global part of her adventures but, unlike her big sister, Faith preferred to go with the flow rather than follow a meticulously thought-out plan. Which meant she could be anywhere.

Hope grinned at her sister, the early hour forgotten. It was okay that Faith had been a little quiet; she was busy exploring and having fun. The last thing she wanted to do was call her fusspot of a big sister who would only nag her about budgets and eating well.

'I'm in Prague.' Faith pulled back from the screen a little to show the room—and view—behind her. She was in some kind of loft, sitting in front of French windows, which led out to a stone balcony. Hope could just make out what must be dazzling views of the river and castle behind. Wow, youth hostels were a lot fancier than she had imagined.

'I thought you arrived in Prague six weeks ago?' Faith hadn't intended spending more than a few days in any one place and Hope was pretty sure her sister had texted her from Prague at the beginning of July.

'I did. I never left. Oh, Hope, it's like a fairy tale here. You would love it.'

'I'm sure I would.' Not that she had been to Prague—or to Paris or to Barcelona or Copenhagen or Rome or any of the other European cities so tantalisingly in reach of London. Their parents had been fans of the great British seaside holiday, rain and all—and since their deaths there had been little money for any kind of holiday. 'But why did you stay in Prague? I thought you wanted to see everything, go everywhere!'

'I did but...well...oh, Hope. I met someone. Someone wonderful and...' Hope peered at the computer screen. Was Faith blushing? Her sister's eyes were soft and her skin glowing in a way that owed nothing to the laptop's HD screen. 'I want you to be happy for me, okay? Because I am. Blissfully. Hope, I'm getting married!'

'Married?' She couldn't be hearing correctly. Her little sister was only nineteen. She hadn't been to university yet, hadn't finished travelling. Heck, she'd barely *started* travelling! More to the point Faith still couldn't handle her own bills, change a fuse or cook anything more complicated than pasta and pesto—and she burnt that two times out of three. How could such a child be getting married? She could only think of one question. 'Who to?'

Her sister didn't answer, turning her head as Hope heard a door bang off-screen. 'Hunter! I got the times wrong. It's still early morning in New York.'

'I know it is, honey. It's not even dawn yet. Did you wake your sister?'

'Oh, she doesn't mind. Come and say hi to her. Hope, this is Hunter, my fiancé.' The pride in Faith's voice, the sweetness in her eyes as she raised them to the tall figure who came to stand next to her, made Hope's throat swell. Her sister had been deprived of a real family at such a young age. No wonder she wanted to strike out and find one of her own. Hope had done her best but she was all too aware what a poor substitute she had been, younger than Faith was now when she took over the reins. Maybe this boy could offer the stability and opportunities she had tried so hard to provide.

And if he couldn't she would be there, making sure he stepped up. She forced a smile, hoping her fierce thoughts weren't showing on her face. 'Hi, Hunter.'

'Hi, it's great to meet you at last. I've heard so much about you.' She summed him up quickly. American. Blond, blue-eyed, clean-cut with an engaging smile. Young. Not quite as young as Faith but barely into his twenties.

'So, how did you two meet?' Hope forced back the words she wanted to say. *Married? You barely know each other! You're just children!* She had promised herself nine years ago she would do whatever it took to make sure Faith was happy—and she had never seen her sister look happier.

'Hunter's an artist.' Pride laced every one of Faith's words. 'He was doing portraits on the Charles Bridge and when I walked past he offered to draw me for free.'

'You had the most beautiful face I'd ever seen,' Hunter said. 'How could I charge you when all I wanted to do was look at you?'

'So I insisted on buying him a drink as a thank you and that was that.' Faith's dark eyes were dreamy, a soft smile playing on her lips. 'Within an hour I knew. We've been inseparable ever since.'

A street artist. Hope's heart sank. However talented he was, that didn't sound too promising as far as setting up a home was concerned and Faith had no career or any idea what she wanted to do after this year was up. She forced another smile. 'How romantic. I can't wait to see the portrait—and meet Hunter in person rather than through a screen.'

'You will! In just over two weeks. That's when we're getting married! In New York and…' Faith adopted a pleading expression Hope knew only too well. 'I was really hoping you'd take care of some of the details for me.'

Hope froze. She knew what 'taking care of some of the details' meant in Faith speak. It meant do everything. And usually she did, happily. Only this was her first time away from her responsibilities in nine years. It was meant to be Hope Getting A Life Time.

Admittedly she hadn't actually got very far yet. Oh, she'd rushed out her first week here in New York and splashed out on a new wardrobe full of bright and striking clothes, had her hair cut and styled. But she couldn't rid herself of feeling like the same old boring Hope. Still, there were three months of her job swap left. She still had every opportunity to do something new and exciting. She just needed to get started.

'Details?' she said cautiously.

'Hunter and I want a small, intimate wedding in New York—just close family and a few friends. His mother will host a big reception party a couple of days later and Hunter says she'll go all out so I think the wedding day should be very simple. Just the ceremony, dinner and maybe some entertainment? You can handle that, can't you? I won't be there until a couple of days before the wedding. Hunter hasn't finished his course and I don't want to leave him alone. Besides, you are so good at organising you'll do a much better job than I ever could. You make everything special.'

Hope's heart softened at the last sentence; she'd

worked so hard to give Faith a perfect childhood. 'Faith, honey, I'm more than happy to help but why so very soon? Why not have it later on and plan it yourself? Travel first, like you arranged.' *Give yourself more time to get to know each other*, she added silently.

'Because we love each other and want to be together as soon as possible. I'm still going travelling—only with Hunter on our honeymoon. Australia and Bali and New Zealand and Thailand. It's going to be the longest and most romantic honeymoon ever. Thank you, Hope, I knew I could rely on you. I'm going to send you some ideas, okay? My measurements for dresses, flowers, colours, you know the kind of thing. But you know my taste. I know whatever you pick will be perfect.'

'Great. That will be really good.' Hope tried to keep her voice enthusiastic but inside she was panicking. How on earth could she work the twelve-hour days her whole office took for granted and plan a wedding in just two weeks? 'Thing is I do have to work, you know, sweetie. My time is limited and I still don't know New York all that well. Are you sure I'm the best person for the job?' She knew the route between her apartment and the office. She knew a nice walk around Central Park. She knew her favourite bookstore and where to buy the perfect coffee. She wasn't sure any of that would be much use in this situation.

Faith didn't seem to notice any of her sister's subtext, ploughing on in breathless excitement. 'There's no budget, Hope, whatever you think is most suitable. Don't worry how much it costs.'

Hope swallowed. 'No budget?' Although she and Faith had never been poor exactly, money had been tight for years. Her parents had been reasonably well insured and the mortgage on their Victorian terrace in north London had been paid off after they died, but after that tax had swallowed up most of their inheritance. She had had to raise Faith on her wages—and at eighteen with little work experience those wages had been pretty meagre. 'Faith, I know that you have your nest egg from Mum and Dad but I don't think it'll stretch to an extravagant wedding.' Was Faith expecting Hope to contribute? She would love to buy her sister her wedding dress, but the words 'no budget' sent chills down her spine.

'Oh, Faith doesn't need to touch her money—I'm taking care of everything,' Hunter said, reappearing behind Faith. 'I've arranged for a credit card to be sent to you.' Hope's eyes flew open at this casual sentence. 'For expenses and deposits and things. Anything you need.'

'For anything I need?' Hope repeated unable to take the words in. 'But…'

'Only the best,' Hunter continued as if she hadn't spoken. 'Anyone gives you any trouble just mention my name—or my mother's, Misty Carlyle. They should fall into line pretty quickly.'

'Mention your name. Okay.' She seemed incapable of doing anything other than parroting his words but the whole situation had just jumped from bizarre to surreal. How did a street artist in Prague have the power to send credit cards for a budget-free wedding shopping spree across the ocean without batting an eyelid? Just who was Faith marrying? A Kennedy?

'Actually, the best person to speak to will be my stepbrother Gael. Gael O'Connor. He only lives a few blocks away from you and he knows everyone. Here,

I'll email you the address and his number and let him know to expect you.' He beamed as if it was all sorted. For Faith and him it was, she supposed. They could carry on being in love in their gorgeous attic room staring out at the medieval castle while Hope battled New York humidity to organise them the perfect wedding.

Well, she would, with the help of Hunter's unexpected largesse. She would make it perfect for her sister if it killed her. Only she wasn't going to do it alone. She was all for equality and there was nothing to say wedding planning had to be the sole preserve of the bride's family after all. As soon as it was a respectable hour she would visit Mr Gael O'Connor and enlist his help. Or press-gang him. She really didn't mind which it was, as long as Faith ended up with the wedding of her dreams.

Gael O'Connor glanced at his watch and tried not to sigh. Sighing hadn't helped last time he checked, nor had pacing, nor had swearing. But when you hired a professional you expected professional behaviour. Not tardiness. Not an entire twenty minutes' worth of tardiness.

He swivelled round to stare out of the floor-to-ceiling windows that lined one whole side of his studio. Usually looking out over Manhattan soothed him or inspired him, whatever he needed. Reminded him that he had earned this view, this space. Reminded him that he mattered. But today all it told him was that he was taking a huge gamble with his career and his reputation.

Twenty-five minutes late. He had to keep busy, not waste another second. Turning, he assessed once again the way the summer morning light fell on the red velvet chaise longue so carefully positioned in the middle of the room, the only piece of furniture in the large studio. His bed and clothes were up on the mezzanine, the kitchen and bathroom were tucked away behind a discreet door at the end of the apartment. He liked to keep this main space clutter-free. He needed to be able to concentrate.

Only right now there was nothing to concentrate on except the seconds ticking away.

Gael resumed pacing. Five minutes, he would give her five more minutes and if she hadn't arrived by then he would make sure she never worked in this city again. Hang on. Was that the buzzer? It had never been more welcome. He crossed the room swiftly. 'Yes?'

'There's a young lady to see you, sir. Name of…'

'Send her up.' At last. Gael walked back over to the windows and breathed in the view: the skyscrapers dominating the iconic skyline, the new, glittering towers shooting up around him as New York indulged in a frenzied orgy of building, the reassuring permanence of the old, traditional Upper East Side blocks maintaining their dignified stance on the other side of his tree-lined street. He shifted from foot to foot. He needed to use this restless energy while it coursed through him—not waste it in frustration.

The creak of the elevator alerted him to his visitor's imminent arrival. No lobby, not when you had the penthouse; the elevator opened right into the studio.

And he did have the penthouse. Not as a gift, not as a family heirloom but because he had worked for it and bought it. Not one of his friends would ever understand the freedom that gave him.

The doors opened with an audible swish and heels

tapped tentatively onto the wooden floor. 'Er…hello?' English. He hadn't expected that. Not that he cared what she sounded like; he wasn't interested in having a conversation with her.

'You're late.' Gael didn't bother turning round. Usually he made time to greet the women, put them at their ease before they got started but he was too impatient for the niceties today. 'There's a robe on the chaise. You can change in the bathroom.'

'Excuse me?'

'The bathroom.' He nodded to the end of the room. 'There's a hanger for your clothes. Go and strip. You can keep the robe on until I've positioned you properly if you prefer.' Some did, others were quite happy to wander nude from the bathroom across the floor to the chaise. He didn't mind either way.

'My clothes? You want me to take them off?'

'Well, yes. That's why you're here, isn't it?'

He moved around to face her at the exact same moment she let out a scandalised-sounding, 'No! Of course not. Why would you think that?'

Who on earth was this? Dark-haired, dark-eyed, petite with a look of outraged horror. She was pretty enough, beautiful even—if you liked the 'big dark eyes in a pale face' look. But he was expecting an Amazonian redhead with a knowing smile and whatever and whoever this girl was she certainly wasn't that.

'Because I was expecting someone who was supposed to be doing exactly that,' Gael said drily. 'But you are not what I ordered. Too short for a start, although you do have an interesting mouth.'

'Ordered?' Her cheeks reddened as the outrage visibly ratcheted up several notches. 'I'm sorry that I'm not your takeout from Call Girls Are Us but I think you should check before you start asking complete strangers to strip.'

'I'm not the one who has gatecrashed their way past the doorman. Who are you? Did Sonia send you?'

'Sonia? I don't know any Sonia. There's clearly been some kind of mix-up. You *are* Gael O'Connor, aren't you?' She sounded doubtful, taking a cautious step back as if he might pounce any second.

He ignored her question. 'If you don't know Sonia then why are you here?'

She took a deep breath. 'My sister is getting married and…'

'Great. Congratulations. Look, I don't do weddings. I don't care how much you offer. Now, I'm more than a little busy so if you'll excuse me I have to make a call. I'm sure you can find your own way out. You seemed to have no trouble finding your way in.'

The dark-haired woman stared at him, incredulity all over her face as he pulled his phone out of his pocket. Ignoring his unwanted visitor, Gael scrolled through what felt like an endless stream of emails, notifications and alerts. His mouth compressed. Nothing from the agency. With a huff of impatience he found their name and pressed call. They had better have a good explanation. The phone rang once, twice—he tapped his foot with impatient rhythm—three times before a voice sang out, 'Unique Models, how may I help?'

'Gael O'Connor here. It's now…' He glanced up at the digital clock on the otherwise stark grey walls. 'It's nine a.m. and the model I booked for eight-thirty has yet to show up.'

'Gael, lovely to speak to you. I am so sorry, I meant to call you before but I literally haven't had time. It's been crazy, you wouldn't believe.'

'Try me.'

'Sonia was booked yesterday for a huge ad campaign—only it was a last-minute replacement so she had to literally pack and fly. I saw her onto the plane myself last night. International perfume ad, what an opportunity. Especially for a model who is…' the booker's voice lowered conspiratorially '…outsize. So we are going to have to reschedule your booking I am so sorry. Or could I send someone else? We have some lovely redheads if that's what you require or was it the curvier figure you were looking for?'

With some difficulty Gael managed not to swear. Send someone else? An image of the missing Sonia flashed through his mind: the knowing expression in her green catlike eyes, the perfect amount of confident come-hitherness he needed for the centrepiece of his first solo exhibition. 'No. I can't simply replace her, nor can I rebook. I've put the time aside right now.'

After all, the exhibition *was* in just five weeks.

'Sonia will be back in just a couple of days. All I can do is apologise for the delay but…'

It would help, he thought bitterly, if the booker sounded even remotely sorry. She would be—he would never use a Unique model again. He hung up on her bored pretence for an apology. Once Sonia was back she would be of no use to him. Unlike his photographs Gael didn't want the subjects of his paintings to be known faces. Their anonymity was part of the point. He spent too much time documenting the bright and the beautiful. For this he wanted real and unknown.

His hand curled into a fist as he faced the bitter facts. He still had to paint the most important piece for his very first exhibition and he had no model lined up. He mentally ran through his contacts but no one obvious came to mind. Most of the models he knew were angular, perfect for photography, utterly useless for this.

Damn.

'Mr O'Connor.'

Palming his phone, Gael directed a frustrated glance over at his unwanted intruder. 'I thought you'd left,' he said curtly. She was standing stiffly by the elevator, leaning towards it as if she longed to flee—although nobody was stopping her, quite the contrary. Gael allowed his gaze to travel down her, assessing her suitability. Before he had only looked at what she lacked compared to the model he was expecting to see; she was much shorter, slight without the dramatic curves, ice to Sonia's fire. She wore her bright clothing like a costume, her dark hair waving neatly around her shoulders like a cloak. Her eyes were huge and dark but the wariness in them seemed engrained.

She took another step back. 'Do you mind?'

'It is my studio…' he drawled. That was better; indignation brought some more colour into her cheeks, red into her lips.

'I am not some painting that you can just look at in that way. As if…as if…' She faltered.

But he knew exactly what she had been going to say and finished off her sentence. 'As if you were naked.'

He had lit the fuse and she didn't disappoint; her eyes filled with fire, her cheeks now dusky pink. She would make a very different centrepiece from the one he had envisioned but he could work with those eyes, with that innocent sensuality, with the curve of her full mouth.

He nodded at her. 'Come over here. I want to show you something.'

Gael didn't wait to see if she would follow; he knew that she would. He strode to the end of the studio and turned over the four unframed canvases leaning against the brick wall. There would be twenty pictures in total. Ten had been framed and were stored at the gallery, another five were with the framers. These four, the most recent, were waiting their turn.

He heard a sharp intake of breath from close behind him. He took a step back to stand beside her and looked at the paintings, trying to look at them with fresh eyes, to see what she saw even though he knew each and every brush stroke intimately.

'Why are all the women lying in the same position?'

Gael glanced over at the red chaise standing alone in the middle of the studio, knowing her eyes had followed his, that she too could see each of the women lying supine, their hair pulled back, clad only in jewellery, their faces challenging, confident, aware and revelling in their own sensual power.

'Do you know *Olympia*?'

Her forehead creased. 'Home of the Greek gods?'

'No, it's a painting by Manet.'

She shook her head. 'I don't think so.'

'It was reviled at the time. The model posed naked, in the same position as each of these,' he waved a hand at his canvases, at the acres of flesh: pink, cream, coffee, ebony. 'What shocked nineteenth-century France wasn't her nudity, it was her sexuality. She wasn't some kind of goddess, she was portraying a prostitute. Nudes at that time were soft, allegorical, not real sensual beings. *Olympia* changed all that. I have one more painting to produce before my exhibition begins in just over a month.' His mouth twisted at the thought. 'But as you must have heard my model has gone AWOL and I can't afford to lose any more time. I want you to pose for me. Will you?'

Her eyes were huge, luminous with surprise and, he noticed uncomfortably, a lurking fear. 'Me? You want *me* to pose? For you? On that couch? Without my clothes? Absolutely not!'

CHAPTER TWO

HE WANTED HER to *what*? Hope stepped back and then again, eyeing Gael O'Connor nervously. But he lost interest the second she uttered her emphatic refusal, turning away from her with no attempt to persuade her. Hope could see her very presence fading from his mind as he began to scroll through his phone again, muttering names speculatively as he did so.

Maybe she should just go, try and arrange this wedding by herself. She looked around, eyes narrowing as she took on the vast if largely empty room, the huge windows, the high ceiling, the view... This much space, on the Upper East Side? Hope did some rapid calculations and came up with seven figures. At the very least. Her own studio would fit comfortably in one corner of the room and the occupant probably wouldn't even notice she was there. Hunter had said that his stepbrother could get her into all the right places and this address, this room, Gael's utter certainty that he commanded the world indicated that her brother-in-law-to-be hadn't been lying.

Hope cleared her throat but her voice still squeaked with nerves. 'Hi, I think we got off on the wrong foot. I'm Hope McKenzie and I'm here because your brother—stepbrother—is engaged to my sister.'

He didn't look up from his phone. 'Which one?'

'Which what?'

'Stepbrother. I have…' he paused, the blue eyes screwed up in thought '…five. Although two of those are technically half-brothers, I suppose, and too young to be engaged anyway.'

'Hunter. Hunter Carlyle. He met my sister, Faith, in Prague and…'

'Hunter isn't my stepbrother. He *was*,' Gael clarified. 'But his mother divorced my father a decade ago, which makes him nothing at all to me.'

'But he said…'

'He would, he clings to the idea of family. He's like his mother that way. It's almost sweet.'

Hope took a deep breath, feeling like Alice wrestling with Wonderland logic. 'As I said, he's engaged to my sister and I was wondering…'

'I wouldn't worry. I know he's young. How old is your sister?'

Was she ever going to say what she had come here to say? It had been a long time since she had felt so wrong-footed at every turn—although being asked to strip by a strange man at nine a.m. would wrong-foot anyone. 'Nineteen, but…'

He nodded. 'Starter marriages rarely last. There will be a prenup, of course, but don't worry, the Carlyles are very generous to their exes. Just ask my dad.' Bitterness ran through his voice like a swirl of the darkest chocolate.

'Starter marriages?' This was getting worse. Was

she going to be able to formulate a whole sentence any time soon?

He raised an eyebrow. 'That's why you're here, isn't it? To ask me to stop the wedding? I wouldn't worry. Hunter's a good kid and, like I said, the prenups are generous. Your sister will come out of this a wealthy woman.'

Hope's lips compressed. 'My sister is marrying Hunter because she loves him.' She pushed the part of her brain whispering that Faith had only known Hunter for six weeks ruthlessly aside. 'And I am sure he loves her.' Based on a two-minute conversation through a computer screen but she wasn't going to give Gael O'Connor the satisfaction of seeing her voice any doubts. 'They want to get married, here in New York, two weeks on Thursday and they asked me to organise the wedding.'

Gael's mouth pursed into a soundless whistle. 'I wonder what Misty will say to that. She prides herself on her hostessing skills.'

'I believe she is holding a party on Long Island shortly after. A small and intimate wedding, that's what Faith's asked for and that's what I am going to give her. But it's going to be the best small and intimate wedding any bride ever had. Hunter thought you would be able to help me but it's very clear that you are far too busy to get involved in anything as trivial as a starter marriage. I won't bother you any more. Good day.'

Head up, shoulders straight and she was going to walk right out of here. So she might not have Gael O'Connor's connections; she had a good head on her shoulders and determination. That should do it.

'Hope, wait.' There was a teasing note in his voice

that sent warning shivers through her. Hope was pretty sure that whatever he wanted she wasn't going to like it.

'Pose for me and I'll help you give your sister the perfect wedding. I can, you know,' he added as she gaped at him. 'My little black book…' he held up his phone '…is filled with everyone and anyone you need from designers to restaurateurs. You do this and your sister will have the wedding of her dreams. And that's a promise.' His gaze swept over her assessingly, that same lazy exploration that made her feel stripped to the skin. She shivered, her heart thumping madly as each nerve responded to his insolence.

Mad, bad, definitely dangerous to know. She was horribly out of her depth. 'I…look, this isn't something you can just throw at someone. It's a big deal.'

A small smile curved his mouth. It didn't reach his eyes; she had a sense it seldom did. 'Hope, life modelling is a perfectly respectable thing to do. Men and women of all ages and body shapes do it day in, day out.'

She cast a quick glance at the canvases still facing out, at the exposed flesh and the satisfied, confident gazes. 'But these aren't men and women of all ages and shapes,' she pointed out. 'They are all women and they are all beautiful, all sexy.'

'That's because of the theme of the show. If Olympia had been a middle-aged man then we wouldn't be having this conversation. It'll be quite intensive. I'll need a week or so of your time, first a few sketches and then the actual painting. The first session is the most important—I need to know that you're comfortable with the pose, with the jewellery you choose and its symbolism. The tricky bit is finding the right mood.

The other models have spent some time thinking about their past, about their sexuality and what it means to them; the original Olympia saw sex as business and that comes across in her portrait. She is in control of her body, what it offers.'

Which meant, she supposed, that he thought she could portray sexuality. Awareness quivered through her at the idea. Awareness of his height, of the lines of his mouth, the steeliness in his eyes. It was an attractive combination, the dark hair, such a dark chocolate it was almost black, and warm olive skin with the blue-grey eyes.

Eyes fastened solely on her. Hope swallowed. It had been a long time since anyone had intimated that they found her sexy. Attractive, useful, nice. But not sexy. It was a seductive idea. Hope stared at the red couch and tried to imagine it: her hair piled up, pulling at the nape of her neck, the coolness of a pendant heavy on her naked breast, the way the rubbed velvet would feel against the tender skin on her thighs and buttocks, against her back.

How it would feel to have that steely gaze directed intently on her, to have him focus on every hair, every dimple, every curve—Hope sucked in her stomach almost without realising it—every scar.

Hope's cheeks flamed. How could she even be having this conversation? She didn't wear a bikini, for goodness' sake, let alone nothing at all. If she could shower in her clothes she would. As for tapping into her sexuality...she swallowed painfully. How could you tap into something that didn't actually exist? Even if she had the time and the inclination to lie there exposed she didn't have the tools.

'You're talking to the wrong woman.' Her voice was cold and clipped, her arms crossed as if she could shield herself from his speculative sight. 'Even if I wanted to model for you—which I don't—I don't have the time. I have a job to do, a job which takes up twelve hours of every day and often my weekend as well. I have no idea how I am going to sort out a wedding in less than three weeks and still keep Brenda Masterson happy but, well, that's my problem. I will manage somehow. I don't need or want your help. Goodbye, Mr O'Connor. As you don't consider Hunter to be part of your family I doubt we'll meet again.'

Hope swivelled and turned, heading for the door, glad of the heels, glad of the well-cut, summery clothes and the extra confidence they gave her. She was new Hope now, new Hope in New York City. She had time to invest in her career, a little money to invest in herself and the way she looked. Any day now she would try her hand at salsa or Zumba or running, join a book club and go to interesting lectures. So she had missed out on being a young adult? It wasn't too late to become the person she once dreamed of being.

But first she would organise her sister's wedding. And not by taking off her clothes and posing for some artist no matter how much she liked the way his eyes dwelled on her. Eyes she could feel follow her as she crossed the room, and pushed the button to summon the lift. Eyes that seemed to strip her bare and see straight through the thin veneer of confidence she had plastered on.

If he did paint her she knew it wouldn't just be her body that would be bared for the world to see. It would be her soul as well. And that was a risk she would never be able to take.

'Did you say you work for Brenda Masterson?'

She paused. One minute he was dismissing her, the next making her an outrageous proposal—and now small talk? She turned and glared at him, hoping he took her impatient message on board. 'Yes, I work at DL Media. I'm in New York on a job swap as Brenda's assistant.' Brenda's very late assistant. She was probably focussing that famously icy glare right at Hope's vacant desk right this moment.

Gael kept her gaze as he pressed his phone to his ear, a mocking smile playing on his well-cut lips. 'Brenda? Is that you?'

What? He knew Brenda? He had said he knew everybody but she didn't think he meant her boss.

'Hi. It's Gael. Yes, I'm good, how about you? I've been having a think about that retrospective. Uh-huh. It's a good offer you made me but there's some work I need to do first, going through the old blogs, through the old photos.' He paused as Brenda spoke at some length, her words indiscernible to Hope.

She shifted from foot to foot, wishing she had worn less strappy heels in this heat—and that she had catlike hearing. This job was her chance to be noticed, to stop being Kit Buchanan's loyal and mousy assistant and to be someone with prospects and a real career—if Gael O'Connor messed this up for her she would knock him out with one of his own paintings…

'As it happens,' Gael continued smoothly, 'I have your assistant here. Yes, very cute. Love the accent.' He winked at Hope and she clenched her jaw. 'It would be great if you could spare her for a couple of weeks to help me with the archiving and labelling, maybe start to put together some copy. Yeah. Absolutely. You're a doll, Brenda. Thanks.'

A what? Hope was pretty sure nobody had ever called Brenda Masterson a doll before and lived through the experience. Gael clicked his phone off and smiled over at Hope. 'Good news. You're mine for the next couple of weeks.'

She *what*? In his dreams. And she was going to tell him so just as soon as she had the perfect withering put-down—and when she had answered the call vibrating insistently through her phone. Hope pulled the phone out of her pocket and the words hovering on her lips dried up when she saw Brenda's name flashing on the screen. She didn't need to take a course in fortune telling to predict what this call would be about. With a withering look in Gael's direction, which promised that this conversation was totally not over, Hope answered the call, tension twisting in her stomach.

'Brenda, hi. Sorry, I'm on my way in.' Damn, why had she apologised? She hadn't realised just how much she said 'sorry' or 'excuse me' until she moved to New York where no one else seemed to spend their time apologising for occupying space or wanting to get by or just existing. Every time she said sorry to Brenda she felt her stock fall a little further.

'Absolutely not. Stay right where you are. I didn't realise you knew Gael O'Connor.' Was that admiration in Brenda's voice? Great, three months into her time here and she had finally made her boss sit up and take notice—not through her hard work, initiative or talent but because of some guy she'd only met this morning.

'My sister is engaged to his stepbrother. Ex-stepbrother.'

She couldn't have this conversation in front of him, not as he leaned against the wall, arms folded and an annoying *Gotcha* smirk on his admittedly handsome face. Hope walked past him, heading for the door she'd seen at the other end of the apartment. It might lead to his red room of pain or whatever but she'd take the risk. Actually it led to a rather nice kitchen—an oddity in a city where nobody seemed to have space to cook. It was a little overdone on the stainless-steel front for Hope's tastes and ranked highly on the 'terrifying appliances I don't know how to use and can't even guess what they're for' scale but it was still rather impressive. And very clean. Maybe having a kitchen was a status thing, the using of it optional.

She shut the door firmly behind her. 'I don't know Gael O'Connor exactly. I only met him today to discuss wedding plans.'

'You've obviously impressed him. Let's keep it that way. I'm seconding you to work with him over the next two weeks. I want regular updates and I want him kept sweet. If you can do that then I can promise that all the right people will know how helpful you've been, Hope. It wouldn't surprise me if you got your pick of roles at the end of this secondment here or back in London. After all, as you've probably heard by now, Kit Buchanan's resigned from the London office inconveniently taking my assistant with him. Maybe we could arrange for you to stay here, if you wanted to, that is...'

Hope's breath caught in her throat. *Keep him sweet?* Did Brenda know just what he wanted her to do? Was she suggesting that nude modelling was part of her job description? Because Hope was pretty sure she'd missed that clause unless it fell somewhere under 'any other business.'

But Brenda had also tapped into a worry that Hope had been trying very hard not to think about. Her role in London had been working as a PA for the undoubtedly brilliant if often frustrating Kit Buchanan. Yet in less than three months he had fallen in love with Madison Carter, her job-swap partner and owner of the tiny if convenient Upper East Side studio Hope was currently living in. And that had changed everything. She hadn't expected to feel so *lost* when she'd heard the news, almost grief stricken. It wasn't that she was jealous exactly. She wasn't in love with Kit. She didn't really have a crush on him either, although he had a nice Scottish accent, was handsome in an 'absent-minded professor' kind of way and, crucially, was the only single man under thirty she spent any time with. But Kit's resignation meant that in three months she would be returning to a new manager—and possibly a different, less fulfilling role.

It was a long time since Hope had dreamed of archaeology; she'd pushed those dreams and any thought of university aside after her parents died, starting instead as an office junior at a firm of solicitors close to her Stoke Newington home. But when she had moved to DL Media three years ago Kit had been quick to see potential in his PA and ensured there had been a certain amount of editorial training and events work in her duties. There was no guarantee a new manager would feel the same way. But if Brenda was impressed with her then who knew what opportunities would open up? Hope took a deep breath and tried to clear her head.

'Why does Gael need an assistant from DL Media?' *And why me?* she silently added.

'Because Gael O'Connor is planning a retrospective of his photographs and the blog that catapulted him into the public eye and I want to make sure that he chooses DL Media as his partner when he does so. I've been courting him and his agent for nearly a year and got nowhere. They say that his archive is incredible, that he could bring down careers, end marriages with his photos,' Brenda's voice was full of longing. 'I can smell the sales now. This could be huge, Hope, and you could be part of it straight from the start. I want you to get me those photos and the anecdotes that accompany them. Help him sort out his archive and make sure that at the end he is so impressed he signs on the dotted line of the very generous contract we offered him. Take as long as you need, do whatever you have to do but get that signature for me. You have an in. He asked for you, your sister is marrying someone he's close to. Anyone would kill for that kind of connection. Exploit it. If you do then I guarantee you a nice promotion and a secure future here at DL Media…'

Hope didn't need to ask what would happen if she failed—or if she refused. Back to England in ignominy and coffee-making, minute-taking and contract-typing-up for the rest of her days. If she was lucky. But if she agreed then she was not only getting a huge boost up the career ladder but she would also be away from the office, out from under Brenda's eye and could grab the time to sort out Faith's wedding. Damn Gael O'Connor, he had her exactly where he wanted her.

'Okay,' she said, injecting as much confidence into

her voice as she could manage. 'I'll do it. You don't have to worry, Brenda. I won't let you down.'

Gael couldn't hear Hope's conversation with her boss but he didn't need to. Hope was as good as his. He'd met Brenda Masterson several times and he knew her type; her eyes were fixed firmly on the prize and she wasn't going to let anything or anyone get in her way.

The kitchen door opened and Hope stalked through, her colour high but her eyes bright with determination. 'I suppose you think you are very clever,' she said. 'Of course some might call it blackmail…'

'Call what blackmail? Your boss wants my archive and I need help organising it. Seems like a fair trade to me.' But Gael couldn't stop the smile playing around his lips. 'You should thank me. I'm much less of a clock watcher than Brenda. You might even get some wedding organising done while you're here. In fact you can have today to get started. Consider it my wedding gift to the happy couple.'

'Is there even an archive or is this just some kind of ruse to keep me here?'

Gael stilled. He was so used to people knowing who he was, what he was, that the scorn in her all too candid eyes took him back. Back to the days before *Expose*. The days when he was nothing. 'I see. You think this is a ploy to get you to pose? Get real, princess. I may have asked you to sit for me but I don't beg and I certainly don't coerce. Every one of those women over there…' He nodded over at the canvases. 'They came to me freely.'

Her forehead creased. 'So why did you ask Brenda if I could work for you?'

'Because I was planning on saying yes to Brenda's offer anyway and this saves me the hassle of finding an assistant. Because I won't mind how you organise your time as long as the archiving work gets done so this way you can pop out to look at venues or cakes or whatever else you need to do. Not to force you into anything. Nobody is keeping you here against your will, Rapunzel, there's no escape ladder needed. You can leave at any time.'

Hope looked over at the chaise, a frown still creasing her forehead. 'I'm sorry, I just thought…you said you wouldn't help me with the wedding and then this all happened so fast.'

'I'm *not* helping you. I'm giving you time but that's all you'll get out of me. I have a model to find and paint, an exhibition to put on and an archive to explain to you and oversee. The wedding's your problem, not mine. Unless you change your mind about the picture, in which case I'll keep my end of the bargain and help you but, like I said, your decision. It's not part of your duties here. I have no interest in a reluctant subject.'

She took a visible deep breath, her eyes clouded, her forehead still wrinkled with thought. She was close to a decision but whether that decision was changing her mind and posing or walking out and telling him to go to hell he had no idea.

It was intriguing, this unpredictability.

'If I said yes…' She stopped, her eyes wary again.

He should be feeling triumphant. He almost had her, he could tell. But Hope McKenzie wasn't like his usual subjects. They were all eager for him to tell their stories with his paintbrush—she was all secrets and disguises. 'Before we go any further, I need you to know exactly what you're getting into.'

'I lie there and you paint me. Right?' The words were belligerent but her eyes dark with fear.

'It's not easy being a life model. It's a skill. You have to keep the same pose for hours. No complaining about being cold, or achy or hungry.'

'Okay.'

'I asked each model to wear some jewellery that meant something to them. Something very personal.' He pointed over at one canvas. 'That girl there, Anna? She's wearing pins in her hair she wore on her wedding day. This lady, Ameena, she's wearing gold necklaces and bangles gifted to her by her parents when she emigrated to the US.'

'And they have to be naked. I mean, I would have to be. Totally. I couldn't, instead of jewellery have a scarf or something. It's just…'

'Sorry.' And he was. It wasn't easy for even the most seasoned model to lie there so exposed to him and even though his other models had been enthusiastic about the project they had still found posing difficult, embarrassment covered in a multitude of ways, by jokes, by attempted seduction, by detachment.

'That's okay.'

It didn't seem okay; her hands were twisting together in an attempt to hide a slight shake.

'The last thing is probably the most important. If you model then I need you to think about sex. What it means to you, good and bad. I need you to think about that the whole time I paint you. I know that's an odd request but it's the theme of the paintings and it needs to show in your eyes, on your face. If it helps I can play any music you want, audiobooks, relaxation tapes—whatever makes you comfortable.'

It was odd, he'd had this conversation many times before and he had never felt so like some kind of libertine before. Every other model had known exactly why she was there, had volunteered for this. It was business, not personal.

But this time it felt horribly personal and he had no idea why.

'Think about sex?'

'Is that a problem?'

'It might be.' Her colour was even higher, rivalling the red of the chaise. 'You see, I haven't actually… I don't… I'm not…what I'm trying to say is…' she swallowed '… I'm a virgin. So I don't think I can lie there and think about something I know nothing about. Do you?'

CHAPTER THREE

'THANK YOU. NO, I see. Yes. Absolutely. Thank you.' Hope clicked her phone off and resisted the urge to throw it off the fire escape and let it smash into smithereens. Another hotel she could cross off her 'possibles' list. Three hours of calling and emailing and she still hadn't made one appointment.

She scanned the list she'd made the second she'd arrived home. It had all seemed so simple then.

1. Find a dress
2. Sort out flowers
3. Ceremony—where????
4. Read through Brenda's six zillion emails
5. Try and show Gael O'Connor that you're competent and professional and not a complete basket case...

Hope resisted the urge to bang her head on the wrought-iron railing she was propped up against. She might have managed to steal one day of wedding planning from Gael O'Connor's manipulative hands but where had it got her? Every venue she had phoned had either laughed at her incredulously or sounded vaguely scandalised. 'A wedding? In two weeks? Ma'am, this isn't Vegas. I suggest you try City Hall.' And as for a dress…you would think she had asked them to spin straw into gold, not supply one white dress, US size four.

And yes, she could try City Hall. And she could pop into any one of a dozen shops and pull a dress off the racks and it would do. And she could book a table in a five-star restaurant and the food would be great. But it wouldn't be special. It wouldn't show Faith just how much Hope loved her. It wouldn't make up for the fact that Faith would have no proud father walking her down the aisle, no mother in a preposterous hat wiping away tears and beaming proudly. Faith deserved the best and Hope had vowed nine years ago that she would have it. This wedding wasn't going to beat her, no, not if it killed her. Her baby sister would have the finest and most romantic whirlwind wedding New York had ever seen. She just needed to work out how and where.

Hope took a sip of coffee and stared at her laptop, balancing precariously on her open window ledge, hoping it would give her some much-needed inspiration. Maybe if she had spent a little more time actually in the city itself and less time either in the office or here, sunning herself on the fire escape outside her apartment window, she might actually have some unique and doable ideas. Okay. She was in the greatest city in the world, how could her mind be so blank? 'New York,' she muttered. 'New York.'

A ping from her laptop broke her half-hearted reverie and Hope looked across at it, sighing when she saw yet another email from Brenda flashing on her screen. What was going on? She had never seen her famously ice-cool boss this het up over anyone. Hunter had said that Gael knew everybody and what was it Brenda had whispered? He had the power to finish careers and destroy marriages? Remembering the mocking smile and the coldness in the blue-grey eyes, Hope didn't doubt it.

Setting her coffee cup to one side, she scrambled onto her knees and pulled up her internet browser. 'Who exactly are you, Gael O'Connor?' With a guilty look around, as if the starling on the rail above could see her snooping, Hope pressed Enter and waited. She wasn't sure what to expect but it wasn't the lines and lines of links that immediately filled her screen. Headlines, photos, articles—and a comprehensive Wikipedia entry.

Gael O'Connor. Photographer. Blogger. Society darling. It looked as if he didn't just *know* the New York scene—he dictated it, moving through it, camera at the ready, creating instant stars.

Nowhere would say no to him. Nowhere would tell him that two weeks was impossible. No one would suggest that Gael O'Connor tried City Hall…

Damn.

Her choice was stark. Either she compromised on the wedding or she agreed to Gael's demands and posed for him. If he still wanted her, that was, after her moment of hysterical oversharing. Hope groaned, slumping back again against the sun-hot railing. It was going to be bad enough facing him the next day in a working capacity, how on earth could she bring up the whole naked posing thing? Maybe she should run away instead. Somewhere no one would ever find her—she'd bet Alaska was nice and anonymous and a nice bracing contrast to this never-ending humidity.

At that moment her phone rang. She didn't recognise the number and answered it cautiously. After this morning's 'blurting out secret personal information to a stranger' debacle she'd probably tell the telemarketer about the time she wet herself in playgroup or when she shoplifted a chocolate bar when she was five—and how her mother made her take it back with a note of apology. 'Hope speaking.'

'How's the wedding planning coming along?' A gravelly voice, like the darkest chocolate mixed with espresso.

Hope glared at her laptop. How had Gael known she was thinking of contacting him? Maybe he had sold his soul to the devil and just thinking about him summoned him? 'Great!' Just a little lie.

'That's good. I was worried that two weeks' notice might be too tight for any of the really good venues.'

'How sweet of you to worry but actually I have it all under control.' Another little lie. Any moment her nose was going to start growing.

'Excellent. So you'll be here nice and early tomorrow to start work?'

'I can't wait.' Yes, she'd better hope that long noses were going to be fashionable this year because the way she was going hers was going to be longer than her outstretched arm.

'All you need is your laptop and a lot of patience. I do hope you like cataloguing.'

'I love it. I'd hate to get in your way though, while you're painting. I could work from the office or from mine if that's more convenient.' *Please let it be more convenient.*

'There's nothing to get in the way of. I haven't found

a model yet.' The mockery slipped from Gael's voice, his frustration clear.

'Oh.'

It was a sign. A big neon sign. He still needed a model and she, like it or not, needed his help. Hope took a deep breath. 'Look, Gael. I hate to deprive you of the joy of wedding planning and it looks like we're going to be spending some time together anyway so...' It was even harder to say the words than she'd anticipated.

'So?'

He knew, she could tell, but was no doubt taking some unholy satisfaction from making her spell it out.

'So I can pose. For your picture. If you still want me after, well, if you still want me...' She wasn't going to own up to her virgin status again. She still couldn't believe she had mentioned it at all, said it out loud. To a complete stranger. A state of affairs she had barely acknowledged over the last few years, pushing the thought away as soon as it occurred. Her own secret shame. Hope McKenzie, old before her time, withered, sexless.

'An intriguing offer.'

She tried not to grind her teeth. 'Not really,' she said as breezily as she could. 'I didn't exactly give you an answer, if you remember.' No, she had backed away, muttered something about needing to get things sorted, said, 'Thank you for the offer to take today to start planning and see you tomorrow, thank you very much...' and scarpered as fast as her feet could carry her, out of the studio and back to the safety of her own apartment.

'I thought your mad dash out of the studio was answer enough. Why the sudden change of heart?'

Hope never admitted to needing anyone; she didn't intend to start now. 'You need someone to start straight away and spend the next two weeks at your beck and call. Well, whether I like it or not I am already at your beck and call. It makes sense.'

'How very giving of you. So you're offering because it's convenient?'

Her fingers curled into a fist. *He'd asked her*—why on earth was she the one working to convince him? 'And although I am more than capable of sorting this wedding alone it would be foolish of me not to use all the resources available. I barely know the city but you live here, your input could save me a lot of wasted effort—and this is the only way you'll help. I'm big enough to admit that if I want Faith to have the best wedding possible then I need to involve you.'

'Another altruistic motive.' Hope's cheeks heated at the sardonic note in Gael's voice. 'And very laudable but you've seen the other portraits. Sacrificial victim isn't the look I'm going for. It's not enough for you to agree to pose. I need you to want it. Tell me, Hope. Do you want it?' His voice had lowered to a decadent pitch, intimately dark. Hope swallowed.

Did she want to pose for him? Lie on that chaise, his eyes on every exposed inch of skin?

Hope stared out through the black iron railings. She knew the view by heart. The buildings opposite, the tops of the trees. This was where she hung out with a coffee and a book or her laptop, too scared to venture out of the comfort zone she'd carved for herself. She didn't mean to speak but somehow the words came spilling out. Another sad confession. ‘I meant to shake things up when I moved here. New York was my chance to reinvent myself. I started, I bought new clothes and chopped off some of my hair and thought that would be enough. But I’m still the same. I don’t know how to talk to people any more, not when it doesn’t involve work or superficial stuff. I don’t…’ She hesitated. ‘I don’t know how to make friends, how to have fun. Maybe this will help me loosen up. It’ll be a talking point if nothing else.’

‘You want me to help you loosen up?’ Her pulse quickened at the velvet in his voice.

‘Yes. No! Not you exactly. What I mean is that I need to try something different, to be different. Posing for you will be new, unexpected.’

‘Okay. Let’s try this.’

She hadn’t known how tightly she was wound waiting for his answer, how the world had fallen away until it was just the two of them, sharing an intimate space even though they were half a mile apart, until he agreed.

‘Great.’ She inhaled a shaky breath. ‘So what now? Do you want me to come over and…?’ Her voice trailed off. How was she going to do it if she couldn’t even say it?

The laughter in his voice confirmed he was probably thinking the same thing. ‘Not today. I think we need to warm up a little first. You, Hope McKenzie, have just admitted you need me to help you discover new things.’

That wasn’t what she had said. Was it? Certainly not in the way she thought he was implying. ‘And you think you can do that for me, do you?’

'Maybe.'

She didn't have to see him to know that he was smiling. Anger rose, sharp, hot and a welcome antidote to the sudden intimacy—but she wasn't entirely sure if she was more angry with Gael for his presumption or herself for laying herself open like that. 'How very altruistic of you, and what's in it for you? A better painting or the virtuous glow of helping poor, virginal Hope McKenzie? Sprinkle a little of your privileged, glamorous Upper East Side fairy dust on me and watch me transform? Well, Professor Higgins, this little flower girl doesn't need your patronage, thank you very much.'

'Are you sure about that?' Before she could respond Gael continued smoothly. 'In that case why don't we get started on planning this whirlwind wedding? Any venues you want to see?'

Hope glared at the laptop as if it were to blame for her lack of possibilities. There was no way she wanted to admit she didn't have one idea as yet. 'Yes. Meet me…meet me on top of the Empire State Building in an hour and a half.' Did they do weddings? It almost didn't matter. It was iconic and it was a start.

'On top of the Empire State Building? How romantic. What a shame it isn't Valentine's Day. Am I Cary Grant or Tom Hanks in this scenario?'

'Neither, you're not the hero. You're the wisecracking friend who ends up handcuffed to a stripper on the stag night.'

'I must have missed that scene. Oh, well, there are worse things to be handcuffed to.' And he hung up leaving Hope with a disturbing image involving Gael O'Connor, handcuffs and the red chaise longue. What was more disturbing was the swirl of excitement in her stomach at the very thought…

It was predictably busy at the top of the Empire State Building, the sun and the wind combining to make the walkway uncomfortable in the early afternoon heat, but none of the tourists seemed to be complaining, too busy taking selfies and pointing out landmarks to notice the conditions.

And they would all be tourists. No self-respecting New Yorker would be up here at this time, during the height of the sightseeing buzz. In fact Gael couldn't remember the last time he had set foot up here. It had probably been for a photo shoot—that was why he visited most tourist locations.

Which was a shame because, even hardened local that he was, he had to admit the view was pretty spectacular, the blue of the ocean merging with the blue of the sky and the city rising from the ocean's depths like some mythological Atlantis.

Gael walked around three sides of the viewing platform before he spotted Hope, bright in the same red dress she'd been wearing earlier. She was standing half turned away from him, leaning on the railing staring out over the city, the dark strands of her hair whipping in the wind. It was odd, he'd only met her this morning but her image was indelibly printed on him—probably because most women didn't gatecrash his studio, demand he help them with a wedding and then blurt out their sexual history—or lack of—before nine a.m.

A smile tugged at his lips. He hadn't seen that one coming and at this stage in the game he could have sworn he'd seen it all. Dammit, he had to admit he was intrigued. How old was Hope? He looked at her assessingly. Somewhere in her mid to late twenties, he'd guess. Which meant she had to be either holding out for true love or had a considerable amount of baggage and neither of those things appealed to him. Not that he was interested in Hope in that way. He just needed a model.

She shifted and her full profile came into view. Nice straight nose and a really good mouth—full bottom lip and a lovely shape to the top one. Almost biteable. Almost… 'So, is this it? The perfect spot?'

She jumped as he joined her at the barrier, her cheeks flushing as she threw a stilted smile his way. 'I don't know. It looks a bit busy for a wedding.'

'Which is a good thing because it turns out you can only get married up here on Valentine's Day and only then if you win a competition. I checked…' he added as she raised an enquiring eyebrow. 'They could marry elsewhere and then come up here for photos but to be honest with you Hunter isn't that keen on heights.'

'He isn't?'

'Turns green on the Brooklyn Bridge,' Gael confirmed.

'Why didn't you tell me any of this before I arranged to meet you here?' She turned and glared, hands on her slim hips in what was clearly meant to be an admonishing way. She looked more like a cute pixie.

'And ruin your Deborah Kerr moment? Or are you Meg Ryan? Isn't it every girl's dream to arrange a meeting on the top of the Empire State Building?'

'I already told you, your role is the wisecracking best friend, not the hero.'

'What about your role, Hope? Who are you?' No

woman he knew was content to play the supporting role in their own lives.

'Me? I'm the wedding planner.' She stared out over Manhattan, her face softening. 'Isn't it breathtaking? I can't believe I haven't been up here yet.'

'Seriously? I thought this was the first destination on every tourist's wish list.'

'I'm not exactly a tourist. I live here. Well, for three more months I do. I mean to do the tourist trail at some point but I haven't had a chance yet.' Her voice was wistful.

Not the heroine of her own story, neither a tourist nor a native. If he didn't have a pose in mind he'd paint Hope as something insubstantial, some kind of wandering spirit. 'Why are you here, Hope?'

She turned, blinking in surprise. 'To meet you and make a start on the wedding, why?'

'No, why are you in New York at all? Here you are in the greatest city on earth but you're barely living in it, not experiencing it.'

''I'm planning to.' But her words lacked any real commitment and she looked away. 'But I want a real career, to make something of my life that's about me. All this…' She waved her hand over Manhattan. 'This can wait. It will still be here in ten years' time. I'm here because for the first time in nine years I don't have to worry about anyone but myself. I can put my career and my choices first.'

'Is that what this is? Putting yourself first? Because from where I'm standing you've agreed to all kinds of things you don't want to do for other people. For Brenda, your sister…'

'Brenda's my boss, of course I'm going to do what

she asks me to do. As for Faith, it's complicated. Our parents died when I was eighteen and Faith was only ten. I've raised her. I can't turn my back on her now, not when she needs me, wants me. Besides, she's marrying Hunter in two weeks. She won't be my responsibility any more. This is the last thing I can do for her and I want it to be perfect.' Her mouth wobbled and she swallowed. 'It will be perfect.'

She'd raised her sister? That explained a lot. 'Of course it will. I've agreed to help. Besides, as soon as you mention the Carlyle name any door in the city you want opening will swing open.'

'There's no budget for the wedding at all. Hunter's sending a card. But seriously, what does that even mean? Everyone has some kind of budget.'

Gael couldn't help his grin. It was so long since he'd spoken to someone who didn't live in the rarefied Upper East Side bubble. 'No, not the Carlyles. You've heard people say money's no object?' She nodded, dark eyes fixed on him. 'The Carlyles take that to a whole new level. I have no idea how rich they are but filthy doesn't even begin to cover it.'

'Wow.' She looked slightly stunned. 'And I was worrying that Faith was marrying a street artist with no prospects. I think I was worrying about all the wrong things. I don't think Faith and I are going to fit in with people like that. We're very ordinary.' She hesitated and then turned to him, laying her hand on his forearm. 'Will she be okay? They won't look down on her, will they?'

He might be standing on a platform hundreds of feet up in the air but the air had suddenly got very close. All Gael could feel was that area of skin where Hope's hand lay, all he could smell was the citrus notes of her perfume. He tried to drag his concentration back to the conversation. 'Misty doesn't think like that. She's the least snobby person I've ever met and, believe me, living where I live and doing what I do I have met a *lot* of snobs.' A thought struck him. 'She'll be delighted I'm helping with the wedding. In her head Hunter and I will always be brothers even though he was an annoying three-year-old brat when I moved into their house and we've never hung out in the same circles.' Truth was Hunter had always idolised him. He'd even decided to follow in his footsteps and study art rather than the business degree Misty Carlyle had picked out for her only son.

'She sounds nice, Misty. If she was such a good stepmother then maybe she'll be good for Faith.' Hope's mouth trembled into a poor attempt at a smile. 'Poor Faith has only had me for so long, she deserves a real mother.'

Gael suspected that Misty would be delighted to have a young and pliable daughter-in-law. She still introduced herself as *his* mother even though she'd divorced his dad ten years ago. Still, that was more than his own mother did. 'She is nice,' he conceded. 'By far the best of my parents.'

Hope blinked. 'How many do you have?'

'Are we counting discarded steps? Misty is my father's second ex-wife. My mother was his first. His current wife is number four. We all try and forget about number three.'

Her eyes widened. 'That's a lot of wives.'

'Misty's just divorced husband number five and my mother is on her third marriage.' He shrugged. 'No one in my family takes the whole "as long as you both shall live" part very seriously.'

'My parents met at university, married as soon as they graduated and that was that. I used to think they were really boring. Old before their time, you know? Now I envy them that. That certainty.'

'Oh, my parents are certain every time. I'm not sure if it's more endearing or infuriating, that eternal optimism. They were dancers, Broadway chorus dancers, when they met.'

'No way.'

'Oh, yes,' he said wryly. 'It was very *Forty-Second Street*. Right up to the minute my twenty-year-old dad knocked up my nineteen-year-old mom and carried her back to Long Harbor to the family bar.' His poor young mother, a streetwise Hispanic girl with stars in her eyes, wasn't content with a life serving drinks to the moneyed masses who flocked to the Long Island resort in the summer. 'I don't remember much about that time, but I do remember a lot of yelling. She's Cuban and my dad's Irish so when they fought crockery flew. Literally. Just before my fifth birthday she packed her bags and walked out. Never came back.'

He hadn't realised that he was clenching his fist until Hope's hand covered his, a warm unwanted comfort. He'd shed the last tear he would ever shed on his mother's behalf on his fifth birthday when she'd failed to turn up to her own son's birthday party. 'I'm so sorry. Do you see her now?'

'Occasionally, if I'm near Vegas. She has a dance troupe there, she's doing well but the last thing she needs is a six-foot, twenty-nine-year-old son reminding her that she's nearer fifty than thirty.'

'So you were raised by your dad?'

'And my grandparents, aunts, uncles—anyone else who wanted to tame the wild O'Connor boy. Not that there was much time to run wild, not with a family business like the Harbor Bar—there's always a surface to clean, a table to clear, an errand to run if you're stupid enough to get caught. And Dad wasn't brokenhearted for long. It seemed like there was a whole line of women just dying to become my stepmom. But they all were swept away when Misty decided she was interested. She was fifteen years older than my dad and it was like she was from a different planet. So calm, so together. So one minute I'm that poor motherless O'Connor boy living on top of a bar with a huge extended family, the next I'm rattling around a huge mansion with a monthly allowance bigger than my dad's old salary. It was insane.'

'It sounds like a fairy tale. Like *Cinderella* or something.'

'Fairy tales are strictly a girl thing. It's okay for Cinderella to marry the prince, not so okay for an Irish bartender to marry his way into the upper echelons of society. The more polite people called him a toy boy, but they all wore identical sneers—like they knew exactly what Misty saw in him and didn't think it should be allowed in public. And as for me? Breeding counts, money counts and I had neither. When Dad became Misty Carlyle's third ex-husband then I should have returned to the gutter where I came from.'

By unspoken accord they moved away from the railing and began to walk back to the elevator lobby. 'What happened?

'Misty. She insisted on paying for college, persuaded my dad to let me spend my holidays with her, Christmas skiing, spring break in New York, the summers in Europe. Of course everyone at school knew I was there on charity—not even her stepson any more.' It was hard looking back remembering just how alone he had been, how isolated. They hadn't bullied him; he was too strong for that—and no one wanted to incur Misty's wrath. They had just ignored him. Shown him he was nothing. Until he'd started *Expose* and made them need him.

'That must have been tough.' Her dark eyes were limpid with a sympathy he hadn't asked for and certainly didn't want.

'Expensive education, great allowance and a suite of rooms in one of the oldest and grandest houses in the Hamptons? Yeah, I suffered.' But Gael didn't know if his words fooled Hope. He certainly never managed to fool himself. He greeted the elevator with relief. 'Come on, I'll buy you a coffee and fill you in on everything you need to know about life with the Carlyles. I'll warn you, you may need to take notes. There's a lot to learn.' For Gael as well as Hope. He wasn't entirely sure why he'd decided to go all *This is Your Life* with her but one thing he did know. He wouldn't let his guard down again.

CHAPTER FOUR

'IT'S ALL SET UP and ready to go. Where do you want me to start?' Hope was perched on one achingly trendy and even more achingly uncomfortable high stool, her laptop set up on the kitchen counter, her bright yellow skirt and dotted cream blouse feeling incongruously feminine and delicate set against the stainless steel and matt black cupboards and worktops.

To one side was Gael's own laptop and several backup drives plus a whole box of printed photos, most of which had names and dates pencilled on the back. Hope had spent the morning looking through the box and scanning through a couple of the hard drives before setting up the spreadsheets and database she was planning to use.

Gael strolled into the kitchen carrying yet another box, which he set next to the first. Great. Even more photos. 'I think you are best off starting with the old blog posts. They're all archived and filed.' He pushed one of the hard drives towards her and Hope plugged it into the side of her laptop.

'Okay. So what do you want? Names obviously so we can cross reference them, dates—what else?'

'Any references made to the subjects in *Expose.*

Once we've finished with that we'll move on to the photos I either didn't use or were taken after the blog closed down. We'll only need names and dates unless they were used professionally in which case the magazine will need referencing as well. Most are saved with all the relevant information but any that aren't put aside into a separate folder and I'll go through them with you at the end of each day.'

She was scribbling fast, taking notes. 'Got it. I don't think it'll take too long. You've kept good notes and everything seems to be labelled…' She hesitated and he looked at her. Really looked at her for the first time since they had left the Empire State Building yesterday afternoon. Oh, she'd spent time with him. Had coffee, learned some tips on handling her new in-laws-to-be, drawn up a list of possible venues for her sister's wedding, but he had retreated behind a shield of courtesy and efficiency. She barely knew him and yet that sudden withdrawal left her feeling lonelier than she had for a long time.

'Everything okay?'

'Yes, it's just… Obviously I know that you're a photographer.'

'Were,' he corrected her. 'Hence the retrospective. I'm a struggling unknown artist now.'

Hope looked around at the kitchen full of gleaming appliances, each worth the same amount as a small car, and repressed a smile. There were few signs of struggling in the studio. '*Were* a photographer. And you do—did—a lot of society shoots and fashion magazines and stuff…'

'And?'

'Where does the blog fit in? If I'm going to catalogue properly I need to know what I'm dealing with.' Somehow Brenda had failed to make this clear in any one of her excitable emails, most of which just reminded Hope how important this assignment was.

Gael leaned on the counter close beside her. He was casually clad in dark blue jeans and a loose, short-sleeved linen shirt. Hope could see every sharply defined muscle in his arms, every dark hair on the olive skin. '*Expose* was a blog I set up when I was at prep school. My plan, not surprisingly given the name, was to expose people. The people I went to school with to be more precise. I took photos chronicling the misadventure of New York's gilded youth. It just skated the legal side of libellous.' His mouth curved into a provocative smile. 'After all, there was no proof that the senator's son was *going* to snort that line, that couple on the table weren't necessarily going to have sex, but it was implied.' The smile widened. 'Implied because generally it was true.'

Hope thought back to the hundreds of black and white photos she had already seen today, stored on hard drives, in the box, some framed and hung on Gael's studio walls, the attractive, entitled faces staring out without a fear in the world. What must it be like to have that sort of confidence ingrained in you? 'And they let you just take photos, even when they were misbehaving?' She cursed her choice of word. Misbehaving! She was living her own stereotype. She'd get out a parasol next and poke Gael with it, saying, 'Fie! Fie!' like some twenty-first-century Charlotte Bartlett.

He laughed, a short bitter sound. 'They didn't even notice. I was invisible at school, which was handy because nobody suspected it was me. They simply didn't see me.' How was that possible? Surely at sixteen or seventeen he would still have been tall, still imposing, still filling all the space with his sheer presence? 'By the time I was outed as the photographer the blog had become mythic—as had its subjects. To be posted, or even better named and the subject of a post? Guaranteed social success. The papers and gossip magazines began to take an interest in the Upper East Side youth not seen for decades—and it was thanks to me. Instead of being the social pariah I expected to be I found myself the official chronicler of the wannabe young and the damned. That was the end of *Expose*, of course. It limped on through my first years at college but it lost its way when people started *trying* to be in it. I became a society photographer instead as you said, portraits, fashion, big events; lucrative, soulless.'

'But why? Why set it up in the first place? Why run the risk of being caught?' She could understand taking photographs as a way of expressing his loneliness—after all, she had been known to pen the odd angsty poem in her teens. But that was a private thing—thank goodness. She shivered at the very thought of anybody actually *reading* them.

Gael straightened, grey-blue eyes fixed on Hope as if he saw every secret thought and desire. No wonder he'd been so successful if his camera's eye was as shrewd as his own piercing gaze. She swallowed, staring defiantly back as if she were the one painting him, taking him in. But she already knew as much as she was comfortable with. She knew that his hair was cut short but there were hints of a wild, untamed curl, that his eyes were an unexpected grey-blue in the dark, sharply defined face. She knew that he could look at a girl as if he could see inside her. She didn't want to know any more.

'Because I could. Like I say, I was invisible. The people at the schools I went to cared about nothing except your name, your contacts and your trust fund. I had none of the above, ergo I was nothing.' His mouth twisted. 'The arrogance of youth. I wanted to bring them down, show the world how shallow and pathetic the New York aristocracy were. It backfired horribly. The world saw and the world loved them even more. Only now I was part of it for better or for worse. Still am, I suppose. Still, at least it should guarantee interest in the show. Let's just hope the paintings are as successful as the photographs were.'

'But why change? You're obviously really successful at what you do.'

'Fame and fortune have their perks,' he admitted. 'The studio, the invitations, the parties, the money...' the women. He didn't need to say it; the words hung in the humid New York summer air, shimmering in the heat haze. She'd seen the photos: pictures by him, pictures of him—with heiresses, actresses, It Girls and models.

Hope didn't even try to suppress her smirk. 'It must have been very difficult for you.'

'I'm not saying my lifestyle doesn't have its benefits. But it wasn't the way I thought I'd live, the way I wanted to earn a living. *Expose* was just a silly blog, that was all. I thought anyone who saw it would be horrified by the excess, by the sheer waste, but I was wrong.' He shrugged. 'My plan was always art school and then to paint. Somehow I was sidetracked.'

'So this is you getting back on track?'

'Hence the retrospective. Goodbye to that side of my life neatly summed up in an A4 hardback with witty captions. Right, lunch was a little on the meagre side so I'm going to go out and get ice cream. What do you want?'

'Oh.' She looked up, unexpectedly flustered. 'I don't mind.'

He shot her an incredulous look. 'Of course you mind. What if I bought you caramel swirl but really you wanted lemon sorbet? The two are completely different.'

'We usually have cookie dough at home. It's Faith's favourite.' Hope's mind was completely blank. How could she not know which flavour she preferred?

'Great, when I buy Faith an ice cream I'll know what to get. What about you?'

'No, seriously. Whatever you're having. It's fine.' She didn't want this attention, this insistence on a decision, stupid as she knew that made her look. Truth was she had spent so long putting Faith's needs, wants and likes before her own it was a slow and not always comfortable process trying to figure out where her sister ended and she began. 'Thank you.'

Gael didn't answer her smile with one of his own; instead he gave her a hard, assessing look, which seemed to strip her bare, and then turned and left leaving Hope feeling as if she'd failed some kind of test she hadn't even known she was meant to study for.

'Any more? I don't think you tried the double chocolate peanut and popcorn.'

Hope pushed the spoon away and moaned. 'No more, in fact I don't think I can ever eat ice cream again.' She stared at the open tubs, some much less full than others. 'And even after eating all this I don't know which my favourite flavour is.'

'Mint choc,' Gael said. 'That one has nearly gone. Impressive ice-cream-eating skills, Miss McKenzie.'

'If I ever need a reference I'll call you.' She paused and watched Gael as he placed the lids back onto the cartons and stacked them deftly before carrying them to the industrial-sized freezer. She hadn't known what to say, what to think when he'd returned to the studio carrying not one or two but ten different flavours of ice cream.

'You wouldn't pick,' he'd said in explanation as he'd lined the pots up in front of her. A bubble of happiness lodged in her chest. Nobody had ever done anything so thoughtful for her. Maybe she could do this. Work with this man, pose with him, because there were moments when she crossed from wariness to liking.

After all it would be rude not to like someone who bought you several gallons of Italian ice cream.

The pictures on the computer screen blurred in front of her eyes. 'I feel sleepy I ate so much.'

'Then it's a good thing you're about to get some fresh air. There's no time to slack, not with your schedule.'

'Fresh air?'

'Central Park. I spoke to a couple of contacts yesterday and they might just be able to accommodate your sister.'

Central Park! Of course. One of the few iconic New York landmarks she had actually visited and spent time in. Hope obediently slid off her stool, pressing one hand to her full stomach as she did so. She couldn't remember the last time she'd indulged so much. The last time she'd felt free to indulge, not set a good example or worry about what people thought.

Central Park was barely a ten-minute stroll from Gael's studio. Hope had spent several hours wandering around the vast city park but it felt very different walking there with Gael. He clearly knew it intimately, taking her straight to a couple of locations that had availability on Thursday in two weeks' time.

'What do you think?' he asked as they reached the lake. 'Romantic enough or did you prefer the Conservatory Garden?'

'The garden is lovely,' she agreed. 'It's a shame the floral arch is already booked. I think Faith would love it. But with such short notice she'll just have to be grateful we found her anywhere at all.'

'Why on earth is it such short notice? Is it a religious thing? Is that why your sister wants to marry Hunter on six weeks' acquaintance? Why you are still a virgin? You're waiting for marriage? For true love?' She could hear the mockery inherent in the last phrase.

The small bubble of happiness she'd carried since the moment she'd seen the bags heaped with ice cream burst with a short, sharp prick. He thought she was odd, a funny curiosity. 'I don't see that it is any of your business.'

'Hope, tomorrow, or the day after or the day after that, the moment I think you are ready, that you can handle it, you are going to pose for me for a painting which is supposed to symbolise sex. If this is going to work I need to understand why you have made the choices you have. I'm not going to judge you—your body, your decisions. But I need to understand.'

Hope stopped and stared out over the lake, watching a couple in a boat kissing unabashedly, as if they wanted to consume each other. Her stomach tightened. 'Honestly? Is it that unbelievable that a twenty-seven-year-old woman hasn't had sex yet? Does there have to be some big reason?'

'In this day and age, looking like you do? You have to admit it's unusual.' Happiness shivered through her at his casual words. *Looking like you do.* It was hard sometimes to remember a time when she had felt like someone desirable, bursting with promise and confidence, confident in her teeny shorts and tight tops as only an eighteen-year-old girl could be.

'It's no big mystery. It's not like I have been saving myself for my knight in shining armour.' She didn't believe in him for one thing. 'It just happened.' Hope turned away from the lake, dragging her eyes away from the oblivious, still-snogging couple with difficulty. For the first time in a really long time she allowed herself to wish it were her. Oblivious to everything but the sun on her back, the gentle splash of the water, his smell, his taste, the feel of his back under her hands. She had no idea who 'he' was but she ached for him nonetheless.

'I told you I raised Faith after our parents died. My aunt offered to help. She had a couple of kids Faith's age and would have been happy to have had her. But I wanted her to grow up where I grew up, in the family house, stay at her school with her friends.' She twisted her hands together. It all sounded so reasonable when she said it but there had been nothing reasonable about her decision at the time. Just high emotion, bitter grief and desperate guilt.

'So you put everything on hold?' He sounded disbelieving and she couldn't blame him; it sounded crazy said so bluntly. But she had had no real choice—not that she wanted to tell him that. To let him know she was responsible for it all. She had to take care of Faith—if it wasn't for Hope she would have had her family intact.

She swallowed, the old and familiar guilt bitter on her tongue. 'I didn't mind. But it meant my life was so different from my friends' new worlds—they were worrying about boyfriends and exams and going out and I was worrying about paying bills and childcare. It was no wonder we drifted apart. My boyfriend went to university just a few weeks after the funeral and I knew it would be best to end it then, that I wouldn't be able to put anyone else first for a long time.' It had seemed like the logical thing to do but she had hoped that he would fight for her, just a little.

But he had disappeared off without a word. He was getting married in just a few short weeks, his life moving on seamlessly from grungy teen to pretentious student to a man with responsibilities, just the way it was supposed to. Just as hers was supposed to have done.

Gael was like a dog with a bone. 'Let me get this straight: you didn't date at all? Since you were eighteen you have been single?'

How could she explain it? It all sounded so drab and dreary—and in many ways it had been. Those first few years when she earned so little, the long nights in alone while Faith slept, studying for her Open University degree, the ever-widening chasm between herself and her school friends until the day she realised she had no one to confide in. Too young for the mums at the school gates and the other secretaries at her law firm, too old at heart and shackled by responsibilities for the few girls around her age she managed to meet.

And then there was the rest: the lack of money or time to take care of herself and the slow dawning realisation she had lost any sense of style or joy in clothes and hair. It was hard when she had no budget to indulge herself and little time or talent to make the most of what she could afford. But there had been other things that compensated—watching Faith star in her school play, taking her ice skating at Somerset House, organising sleepovers and pamper evenings and home-made pizza parties for her sister and her friends and seeing her sister shine with happiness. Surely that was worth any sacrifice?

'No, I dated. A little. But I didn't like to stay out late, even when Faith was older and no one could stay over, it didn't seem right. And so the few relationships I had never really went anywhere. It's really no big deal.'

'Okay,' but she could hear the scepticism. Hope didn't blame him. How could she fool him when she had forgotten how to fool herself? 'Come on.'

Gael took her arm and turned her down a path on their left, his walk determined and his eyes gleaming with a devilish glint she instinctively both distrusted and yearned for. 'Where are we going?'

He stopped in front of a red and yellow brick hexagon and grinned at her. 'When's the last time you rode on a carousel, Hope?'

Was he mad? He *must* be mad. Hope stared over at the huge carousel. It was like a step back in time, wooden horses, their mouths fixed open, heads always thrown up in ecstasy, their painted manes blowing in a non-existent breeze as the circular structure turned to the sound of a stately polka. 'I don't know when I last rode on one,' she said and that was true. She couldn't pinpoint the date but she knew it was before Faith was born. Before she had elected to opt out of family life. She vividly remembered standing by the side of a carousel in the park as her parents took her laughing baby sister on one. She had refused to accompany them, had said it was too babyish. Instead she had stood by the side feeling left out and unloved, hating them for respecting her word and not forcing her to ride.

'You'll always be able to answer that question from now on. The eighteenth of August, you can say confidently. In New York, around...' He squinted at his wrist. 'Around two-forty in the afternoon.'

'No, I can say the eighteenth of August is the day some crazy person tried to persuade me to go on one and I walked away.' She swivelled, ready to turn away, only to be arrested by a hand closing gently around her wrist. She glared at Gael scornfully. 'What, you're going to force me to go on?'

'No, of course not.' He sounded bemused and who could blame him? She was acting crazy. But she could still see them, the two forty-somethings cradling their precious toddler tight while their oldest child stood forgotten by the exit.

Only she hadn't been forgotten. They had waved every time they passed by, every time. No matter that she hadn't waved back once. Hope swallowed, the lump in her throat as painful as it was sudden. Why hadn't she waved?

Gael leaned in close, his fingers still loose around her wrist. His breath was faint on her neck but she could sense every nerve where it touched her, each one shocking her into awareness. 'Doesn't it look like fun?'

Maybe, maybe not. 'I'll look ridiculous.'

'Will you? Do they? Look at them, Hope.'

Hope raised her eyes, her skin still tingling from his nearness, a traitorous urge to lean back into him gripping her. *Stop it*, she scolded herself. *You've known him for what? Two days? And he's already persuaded you to pose nude, holds your career in his rather nicely shaped hands and is trying to make a fool of you. There's no need to help him by swooning into him.*

But now he was so close she could smell him, a slight scent of linseed and citrus, not unpleasant but unusual. It was the same scent she had picked up in his studio. A working scent. He might be immaculately dressed in light grey trousers and a white linen shirt but the scent told her that this was a man who used his hands, a physical being. The knowledge shivered through her, heating as it travelled through her veins.

'Hope?'

'Yes, I'm looking at them.' She wasn't lying, she was managing somehow to push all thoughts about Gael O'Connor's hands out of her mind and focus on the carousel, on the people riding it. Families, of course. The old pain pierced her heart at the sight; time never seemed to dull it, to ease it.

But it wasn't just families riding; there were groups of older children, laughing hysterically, a couple of teens revelling in the irony of their childish behaviour. Couples, including a white-haired man, stately on his golden steed, smiling at the silver-haired woman next to him. 'No,' she admitted. 'They don't look ridiculous. They look like they are having fun.'

'Well, then,' and before she could formulate any further response or process what was happening she was at the entrance of the building and Gael was handing over money in crisp dollar bills.

'Go on, pick one,' he urged and she complied, choosing a magnificent-looking bay with a black mane and a delicate high step. Gael swung himself onto the white horse next to hers while Hope self-consciously pulled her skirt down and held on to the pole tightly. He looked so at ease, as if he came here and did this every day, one hand carelessly looped round the pole, the other holding a small camera he had dug out of his jeans pocket.

'Smile!'

'What are you doing?'

He raised an eyebrow. 'Practising my trade. Watch out, it's about to go. Hold on tight!'

The organ music swelled around them as the carousel began to rotate and the horses moved, slowly at first, before picking up speed until it was whirling around and around. At first Hope clung on tightly, afraid she might fall as the world spun giddily past, but once she settled into the rhythm she relaxed her grip. Gael was right, it was fun. More than that, it was exhilarating, the breeze a welcome change on the hot, sticky day. Above the organ music she could hear laughter, children, adults and teens, all forgetting their cares for one brief whirl out of time. She risked a glance at Gael. He was leaning back, nonchalant and relaxed, like a cowboy in total control of his body; his balance, his hand was steady as he focussed the camera and snapped again and again, watching the world through a lens.

And then all too soon it was slowing, the walls

slowly coming back into focus, the horse no longer galloping but walking staidly along as the music died down. She looked over at Gael and smiled shakily, unable to find the words to thank him. For a moment then she had been free. No one's sister, no one's PA, no expectations. Free.

'Another go?'

'No, thank you, one was enough. But it *was* fun. You were right.'

'Remember that over the next two weeks and we'll be fine.' Gael dismounted in one graceful leap, holding a hand out so that Hope could try and slide down without her skirt riding up too far. 'Come on, let's have a drink at the Tavern on the Green and you can decide if you like it enough to shortlist it for the wedding drinks.'

'Good idea.' Damn, why hadn't she thought of that? Celebrating her sister's wedding in such an iconic venue would certainly be memorable.

Hope stopped, suddenly shy, trying to find the right words to frame the question that had been dogging her thoughts since their conversation at the lake. 'Gael, when will I be ready? To be painted?'

It wasn't that she felt ready; she wasn't sure she ever would be. But knowing that at some point it would happen, at some point she would have to keep her word, made it almost possible for her to relax.

Gael didn't answer for a moment, just stared at her with that intense, soul-stripping look that left her feeling as if she had nowhere left to hide.

'When you start living,' he said and turned and walked away. Hope stood still, gaping at him.

'I am ready,' she wanted to yell. Or, 'Then you'll be waiting a long time.' Because the truth was she was scared. Scared of what would happen, scared of who she was, scared of what might be unleashed if she ever dared to let go.

CHAPTER FIVE

HOPE STOOD IN her walk-in wardrobe and stared at the rack of carefully ironed clothes, fighting back almost overwhelming panic. Panic and, she had to admit, a tinge of anticipation. Every day for the last nine years had followed its own dreary predictable pattern and even here, in the vibrant Upper East Side, she had managed to re-establish a set routine before she'd worked out the best place to buy milk.

But not today. She had no idea what Gael had in store for her. He'd told her to be ready at ten a.m. and that he would call for her. Nothing else.

He'd mentioned risks. Allowing herself to live. Unlocking herself. Hope swallowed. She liked the sound of that, she really did. She just wasn't sure whether it was possible, that if she stripped away the layers of self-sufficiency and efficiency and busyness there would be very much left.

'Okay,' she said aloud, the words steadying her. 'What's the worst that could happen?'

Oh. She shouldn't have even thought that because now, now she had opened up the floodgates, it turned out she could think of *lots* of worst things. Maybe he was going to suggest skydiving or bungee jumping off the Brooklyn Bridge—illegal but even Hope had heard the rumours and she bet Gael O'Connor didn't give two figs for legality anyway. Or climbing up some skyscraper—or walking a tightrope between them. She inhaled shakily. No, she was pretty sure she could strike the last one off her list.

Or maybe when he said he wanted her to loosen up he was talking about her V card. He might be a member of one of those exclusive clubs where expensive call girls and even more expensive cigars and whisky were shared by men in ten-thousand-dollar suits. Possibly. She'd seen a TV show once where the detective went undercover in exactly that kind of club right here in New York City…

Or maybe he would want her to explore her own sexuality in a burlesque class or pole dancing or actually perform in some kind of club or…or no. Ten minutes would be nine minutes and fifty nine seconds longer than she needed to convince any stage manager that she most definitely didn't have what it took. After all, how many four-year-olds were asked to leave baby ballet?

'Stop thinking.' Hope grabbed a pair of high-waisted orange shorts and a cream *broderie-anglaise* blouse and marched out of the wardrobe, throwing them onto the daybed, which doubled as a sofa and place to sleep. Living in a studio so compact it practically redefined the word had meant she needed to find new levels of neatness and organisation or resign herself to living surrounded by everything she had brought with her in disordered chaos. And that, obviously, would be intolerable.

Dressed, her hair brushed and tied back into a high ponytail, and her feet encased in a comfortable pair of cream and tan summer loafers, she should, she reflected, have felt better. That was what her new, eye-wateringly expensive wardrobe was supposed to do. Make her feel ready for anything. Make her feel like someone. Instead she felt all too often like a little girl playing dress up in the bold colours, designs and cuts. Maybe she should get changed…

Right on cue, as if Gael knew the exact moment she was feeling the most insecure, the buzzer went. No doorman here, no lift or fancy hallway. Just a buzzer and several flights of stairs.

Not that the four flights of stairs seemed to faze him. He was annoyingly cool when she opened the door, his breathing regular, not a damp patch to be seen on the grey short-sleeved shirt he'd teamed with a pair of well-cut black jeans. His clothes gave no clue to the day's activities although she could probably rule out the gentleman's club. Her eyes met his and, as she took in the lurking laughter, all the calm, welcoming words she had prepared and practised fell away.

'Do you want to get going?'

He took a step forward until he was standing just inside her threshold. 'Are you in a hurry? It's usually considered polite to invite a guest in. Or is there something you don't want me to see?'

As if. Her life was an open book. A very dull book, which had been left to gather dust on the library shelf, a little like her. 'Not at all. I just thought you might want to get started. Ah, come in. Although you are. In.'

How had he done that? Eased himself in through the door and past her so smoothly she had barely noticed. She should add magician to his list of talents.

Come on, Hope, get some control. 'Tea?' When in doubt revert to a good national stereotype.

'Iced?'

'No, the normal kind. I have Earl Grey, normal, Darjeeling and peppermint.'

His mouth quirked. 'Seriously?'

'Er...yes. I found this little shop which sells imported British goods and I stocked up...' *Stop talking right now, Hope.* But her mouth didn't get the message. 'Tea and pickle, sandwich pickle, not gherkins. And real chocolate, no offence. There's many things the US does better, like coffee and cheesecake, but I would give my firstborn for a really mature cheddar cheese and pickle sandwich followed by a proper chocolate bar.'

Just in case he had any doubt she was socially awkward she was spelling it out for him loud and clear. She hadn't always been this way; if only she could turn the clocks back nine years—although if it was a choice between getting her confidence back or her parents there was no contest. She'd happily be awkward for ever.

Mercifully Gael didn't pursue the conversation. He stood in the middle of the room, dominating all the space in the tiny studio. 'Nice address.'

'Location is everything. Apparently it makes up for the lack of actual space—at least that's what Maddison says. It's her apartment,' she explained as his eyebrows shot up in query. 'We swapped homes when we swapped jobs.' Not that Maddison was currently occupying either Hope's home or her job; instead she was cosied up in the home of Hope's old boss, Kit Buchanan, planning a future together. Hope had worked with Kit for three years and he had never stepped even a centimetre over the professional line but barely a couple of months with Maddison and he had given up his job and was planning a whole new life with the American. Hope couldn't help wondering how the job swap had turned Maddison's life so radically upside down while hers was left untouched.

And look at Faith. Less than three months into her travels and she was engaged to the heir to a multimillion-dollar fortune, which was an awful lot more than most people managed on a gap year. What had Hope done in the city that never slept? Tried a few new bagel flavours and experimented with her coffee order. Hold the front page.

Maybe today wasn't going to be so horrendous after all. Whatever Gael had planned at least it would be *new.* Maybe this was all for the best—what was the point in bemoaning the dullness of her life if she didn't grasp this chance to shake things up a little?

Gael strolled over to the window in just four long strides. 'I like it. Nice light.' The apartment didn't compare with his, of course, but thanks to the gorgeous bay window the light did flood in, bathing the white room with an amber glow. The window opened far enough for Hope to climb out onto the fire escape so she could perch on the iron staircase, cup of tea in one hand, book in the other, soaking up the sunshine.

'It does for me. I don't need much space.' Which was a good thing. A tiny table and solitary chair sat in the bay of the window, the daybed occupied the one spare wall lying opposite the beautiful and incongruously large fireplace. The kitchen area—two cupboards and a two-ring stove—took up the corner by the apartment door and a second door to its right led into the walk-in closet equipped with rails and drawers, which opened directly into the diminutive but surprisingly well appointed bathroom. Two people in the studio would be cosy, three a crowd, but this was the first time Hope had shared the space with anyone else. Unless she counted the Skype conversations with her sister.

Loneliness slammed into her, almost knocking the breath out of her.

Gael's mouth quirked into a knowing smile. 'I'm sure you don't. More used to accommodating others than demanding space, aren't you?'

'There's nothing wrong with being able to live simply. What do I need? For today? A coat? Different shoes?' She wasn't going to ask what they were doing, show any curiosity, but she wasn't above digging for a clue.

Gael turned and looked her over slowly and deliberately. It was an objective look, similar to the way he'd looked at her when he asked to paint her, as if she were an object, not a living, breathing person and certainly not as if she was a woman or in any way desirable. And yet her nerves smouldered under his gaze as if the long-buried embers remembered what it felt like to blaze free.

'You'll do as you are.' That was a fat lot of help.

'Great.' Hope grabbed her bag. 'Lead on, then. The sooner we get this over with, the sooner I can get on with some wedding planning for Faith. Don't think I'm here for any other reason.'

But even as she said the words Hope knew she wasn't being entirely honest, not with him, not with herself. She could tell herself as much as she liked that she was only spending time with Gael for her sister, for her job. But the truth was she needed a way out of the rigid constraints and fears she had built around her. And whatever happened over the next two weeks or so Hope knew that she would be changed in some way. And that had to be a good thing, didn't it? Because this life swap had shown her that it wasn't her old job, or raising Faith or living in her childhood house that had imprisoned her. It was Hope herself. Which meant there was no handsome prince or fairy godmother waiting in the wings to transform her life, to transform her.

This was her chance and she was going to grab it.

'So, where exactly are we going? Do we need to get a cab?' Hope was trying to sound nonchalant but Gael could tell that she was eaten up with curiosity. What had she been imagining? Probably the worst—after all, hadn't he told her that he wanted her to take some risks? To start living? She'd probably put those remarks together with the paintings and come up with some seduction scenario straight out of a nineteen-seventies porn movie.

But it wasn't her body he needed to start exploring, no, not even in those shorts, which hugged her compact body perfectly, lengthening her legs and rounding nicely over what was a very nice bottom. He had never deflowered a virgin, not even in his school days, and had no intention of starting now. Inexperience physically meant inexperience emotionally and Gael had no intention of dealing with crushes or infatuation or anything else equally messy. No matter how enticing the package.

Hang on—when had Hope gone from convenient minion and model to enticing? He'd been so busy with the exhibition he'd been living like a monk for the last few months—which was more than a little ironic, considering how much naked female flesh had been on display in his studio. It wasn't *her* per se. No, Hope was just the first woman he had spent any time with in a social capacity in a while. Obviously boundaries would blur a little.

Not that this was really social. Sort out the wedding, crack open that shell she'd erected around herself and she'd be ready for him to paint. That was why he was here, why he'd spent yesterday afternoon wandering around Central Park encouraging her to forget her dignity and enjoy the carousel ride. At the end of the day it was all business.

And he refused to dwell on just how enjoyable the business had ended up being… 'No cab needed. It's just a few blocks.'

'Okay.'

She still sounded apprehensive and Gael's conscience gave him a small but definite nudge. His skill, talent aside, had always been to put people at their ease, so much so that they almost forgot he was there. That was how he managed to take so many fly-on-the-wall photos; no paparazzi tricks for him. No, just the ability to blend in, to become part of the furniture. But something about Hope McKenzie had him rubbed up all the wrong way; he liked seeing her bristle a little too much, couldn't resist winding her up. But a brittle, wary subject wasn't going to give him the kind of picture he needed. It was time to turn up the charm. 'We're going to the Metropolitan Museum of Art. I want you to look at an original Manet and some portraits to get an idea of what I want from you—and then we can look at the roof terrace. It's beautiful up there and you might want to consider it for the reception. They don't usually hire it out but I might be able to pull some strings.'

'That sounds great.'

Gael repressed a grin as Hope exhaled a very audible sigh of relief. 'What, did you think I was going to send you on some kind of Seduction 101 course? Starting with the dance of the seven veils and ending up in some discreet bordello?'

'Of course not,' but the colour in her cheeks belied her words. Interesting, her imagination had definitely been at play. Had he figured in it at all? The seducer, the cad, the lover? The architect, leading her through her seductive education? Gael tore his mind back to the matter at hand, refusing to allow it to dwell on the interesting scenes so effortlessly conjured up.

He stopped as Hope halted at a snack stand to pick up a bottle of water and an apple. She turned, the apple in one hand, like Eve tempting him to fall. 'Would you like anything?'

'No, thanks.' He'd forgotten that girls, that women, did that. Bought their own water, a normal bottle of water from a normal silver metal snack stand just outside Central Park. The women he dated demanded fancy delis and even fancier water imported from remote places with prices to match.

And they never paid their way. Hope hadn't even sent him a hopeful sideways look; instead she'd offered to treat him. To water and a piece of fruit, but still. It was a novel experience—and not a displeasing one.

'So.' She had sunk her teeth into the apple, juice on her lips. He tried not to stare, not to be too fascinated by the glistening sweetness, but his eyes were drawn back to the tempting plumpness. The serpent knew what it was doing when it selected an apple; Adam had never stood a chance. 'Do we have to go into special rooms to look at the paintings or are they respectable nudes?'

'It's all perfectly respectable,' he promised as they turned the corner and walked towards the steps leading up to the arched entrances of the museum. As usual the steps were crowded: groups of girls gossiping while sipping from huge coffee cups, lone people scrolling through phones, sketching or reading battered paperbacks, couples entwined and picnicking families. The usual sense of coming home washed over him. The museum had been a sanctuary when he had lived in Misty's town house, the place he had come to on exeats from school. The only place where he had felt that he knew who he was. Where his anonymity wasn't a curse but a blessing as he moved through the galleries, just another tourist.

Hope tossed her apple core into a trash can and wiped her hands on a tissue before lobbing that in after her apple. 'I pass this every day on my way to work,' she said as they began to climb the stairs. 'I always meant to come in.'

'What stopped you? It's open late and at weekends.'

Hope shrugged. 'I don't know, the usual, I suppose.'

'Which is?'

'That because I haven't before I don't know how to. And before you say anything, yes, I know it's stupid. But even though we lived in London my parents weren't really museum people or theatre people—they were far more likely to take us for a walk. They liked nothing better than driving out to a hill somewhere so we could walk up it and eat sandwiches in the drizzle. It was always drizzling!'

'My parents didn't take me to museums either—Misty's interest only runs to showing off her philanthropy and my dad only stepped foot inside when it was the annual ball and only then under duress. I think that's why I loved it so much; it's somewhere I discovered for myself. What did you do as a teenager?'

'Hung out with friends, the usual.' But her voice was constrained and she had turned a little away from him, a clear sign she didn't want to talk about it.

They reached the doors and entered the magnificent Great Hall with its huge ceilings and sweeping arches. Gael palmed his pass, steering Hope past the queues waiting patiently to check their bags in and pay for admittance until he reached the membership desk.

The neatly dressed woman behind the desk smiled, barely looking at his pass. 'Good morning, Mr O'Connor. Is this young lady your guest?'

'Good morning, Jenny. How's the degree going? Yes, Hope's with me.'

'First-name terms with the staff?' Hope murmured as he led her down the corridor, expertly winding his way around tour groups and puzzled clumps of map-wielding visitors.

'I may come here fairly regularly.' Plus he was a patron—and Misty sat on the prestigious Board of Trustees but Hope didn't need to know that. He didn't want to dazzle her with his connections; he'd learned long ago that women impressed with those were only after one thing—influence. He'd vowed long ago never to be used again. He might be enjoying Hope's company but, just like every other woman, she was with him because of what he could do for her. It was a lesson he was unlikely to forget.

Hope sank onto the couch with a grateful cry. 'I wore my most comfortable shoes and *still* my feet ache. We must have walked miles and miles and miles without ever going outside. And my eyes ache just as much as my feet.'

Gael suppressed a smile. 'It's not easy compressing two thousand plus years of art history into a four-hour tour.'

'Five hours and only a twenty-minute coffee stop,' Hope said bitterly. 'I almost fainted away right in front of the Renoir—or was it Degas?'

'Better get it right or you'll fail the written test later. I've ordered a cheese plate, water and a glass of wine. Do you think that will fortify you?'

'Only if I don't have to move again. Ever.'

'Not for the next half hour,' Gael promised. 'But then we have a private tour of the roof garden and the Terrace Room. Your sister can't get married here but she can certainly have the reception. Do you know how many you're organising it for yet?'

Hope rubbed her temples. 'Not exactly but because Misty is planning such a lavish party and a blessing two days later the wedding day itself is to be kept small and intimate. Last email she said that she would like to keep it down to me, you, Hunter's mother of course. His father—will that be awkward in such a small group?'

'I don't think so. Misty and he still move in all the same circles. I told you yesterday, she specialises in civilised divorces.'

'Then a couple of the groom's friends and apparently they are paying for two of Faith's school friends and our aunt and her family to fly over. So that will be...' she totted up the amount on her fingers '...fifteen.'

'Hmm, we might rattle around a bit in the Terrace Room. Let's have a look and see what you think.'

'Faith emailed yesterday to say she would definitely like to have two dresses, which is great because finding just one isn't proving to be at all awkward. Something subtle for the wedding because it's so small, but I think she wants to go all out for the party, especially as they will be repeating their vows.' Hope bit her lip. 'It's such a responsibility. The couple of places I spoke to yesterday seemed to imply that it was easier to learn to do heart surgery in a fortnight than it is to buy and fit a wedding dress. And it's not just the dress. There's a veil, tiara, jewellery. Underwear. And she wants me to sort out bridesmaids' dresses for just me for the ceremony but for both friends and our cousin for the party as well.'

Gael got that Hope felt responsible for her sister, that she had raised her. But this amount of stress all for someone else? He couldn't imagine a single member of his family—including all the exes and steps—putting themselves out for someone else. He had them all on the list for his exhibition's opening-night party and knew Misty would be there if she possibly could. His father if there was nothing better to do. But his mother? She hadn't made his graduation from school or college, he doubted she'd make the effort for a mere party. Funny how, much as he told himself he didn't care, her casual desertion still stung after all these years—only he was so used to it that it was more of a pinprick than anything really wounding.

He didn't know if it was better or worse that she adored his two half-brothers so much, every occasional email a glowing testimonial to their unique specialness. No, he might still have two living, breathing parents but Faith was luckier than he was. What would it be like to have someone like Hope on your side? Someone you could count on? 'You could say no. Ask her to come and organise it herself.'

But she was already shaking her head. 'No. I promised her that I would take care of everything. If things were different she'd have a mother to help her. Well, she doesn't, she only has me. I won't let her down.' There was a telltale glimmer in her eyes and her words caught as she spoke. She looked away, swallowing convulsively as the waitress brought their food and drink over.

Gael sat back, smiling his thanks as the waitress placed their drinks and the cheese platter onto the table. Hope swallowed again and he gave her a moment to compose herself, glad that it was so quiet in the members' only lounge he had brought her to. 'What about you, Hope? Who takes care of you?'

She stared at him, her eyes wide in her pale face. 'I take care of me. I always have.'

'And you're doing just fine, is that what you're saying? You don't know how to step out of your limited comfort zone. You pour all your energy into work and looking after your sister and you're lonely. But you don't need anyone. Sure. You keep telling yourself that.'

What was he saying? He was all about the self-sufficiency himself. But it was different for him. He was toughened whereas Hope was like a toasted marshmallow—a superficial hardened edge hiding an utter mess on the inside. He'd only known her for less than three days but he'd diagnosed that within the first day. And it was a shame. She was a trier…that was evident. She cared, maybe a little too much. A girl like that should have someone to look out for her.

'Thanks for the diagnosis, Doc.' Hope picked up her wine glass and held it up to him in a toast. 'I'll make sure I come to you every time I need relationship advice. Especially as I spent a lot of time yesterday looking through photos at your place and do you know what I didn't see? I didn't see a single photo of you having fun. Oh, yes…' as he tried to interrupt. 'There are pictures of you posing next to women. Sometimes you have your arm around their waist. But you never look like you're enjoying yourself, you never look relaxed. You're as alone as I am—more so. I have Faith. Hunter said you were his brother but you were very quick to deny any relationship with him at all.'

Touché. Gael clinked her glass with his own. 'But I prefer to be by myself. It's my choice. Is it yours, or are you just too afraid to let anyone in? Either way, here's to Hunter and Faith, getting their wedding and this painting out of the way and returning to our solitary lives. Cheers.'

CHAPTER SIX

WHAT WAS IT about Gael O'Connor that made her bristle like an outraged cat? Hope usually hid her feelings so well sometimes it seemed, even to her, that she didn't have any. Slights, slurs and digs passed her by. It didn't rankle when the girls at work went out without her, when they chatted about nights out in front of her as if she weren't even there. She barely noticed when photos of school reunions she hadn't been invited to showed up on her social-media pages or when wedding photos were circulated and she wasn't amongst the guests. Hope had chosen to remove herself from the human race, had chosen to devote herself and her life to Faith; she wasn't going to complain now her job was almost done.

Why would she when she had raised a happy, confident, bright girl who had her whole future before her? She could never fully make things up to her little sister but she had done as much as was humanly possible—and if she had sacrificed her own life for that, well, that felt like a fair trade. She was at peace with her decision.

At peace until Gael opened his mouth, that was. As soon as that mocking note hit his voice her hackles rose and she responded every single time. Was it because he didn't care for the official 'Hope is wonderful to give everything up for Faith' line, instead making her sound like a pathetic martyr living life vicariously instead of in reality? She didn't need it pointed out. She knew she wasn't wonderful or selfless but she didn't feel like a martyr. Usually.

Still, she couldn't complain too much when in one afternoon he had managed to sort out the wedding venues and in such smooth style. It helped that they were looking at a Thursday afternoon wedding and not the weekend but Gael had known all the right people to talk to, to ensure the tight timescales weren't a problem. After consulting with the blissful and all too absent couple they had decided to hold the ceremony in Central Park itself, at a beautiful little leafy spot by the lake, followed by cocktails at the Tavern on the Green. The Met's Roof Garden closed to the public at four-thirty p.m. and wasn't usually available for private hire, but Gael had managed to sweet talk the event coordinator into letting them in after hours for drinks and dinner. So all Hope needed to do was organise afternoon entertainment, evening entertainment, flowers and clothes. She still had just over ten days. Easy.

Now all she wanted to do was fling herself onto the surprisingly comfortable daybed and sleep for at least twelve hours. Her feet still throbbed from the whistle-stop tour through the history of art and her head was even worse. But sleep was a long, long way away. Instead she had less than an hour to shower and get ready. 'I'll pick you up at eight,' Gael had said brusquely as they'd finalised the details with first the event organiser at the Met and then with the Central Park authorities. 'It might be worth eating first.'

Okay. This wasn't a date. Obviously. It was part work, part family business but still. Hope would bet her half of her overpriced London home that not one of the beauties she had seen hanging off Gael's arm in photos had ever taken less than three hours to get ready—and he would have always bought them dinner.

She crammed the rest of her Pop-Tart into her mouth and grabbed a banana reasoning that the addition of fruit turned her snack into a balanced meal.

Thirty minutes later she was showered with freshly washed and dried hair and dressed in one of her new dresses. She hadn't dared wear it before, much as she liked the delicate coffee-coloured silk edged with black lace; it was just so short, almost more of a tunic than a dress… She fingered a pair of thick black tights; surely they would make the dress more respectable? But it was still so hot and humid and her own legs were the brownest they had ever been thanks to weekends spent reading on her fire escape. Hope stared down at what seemed like endless naked flesh before cramming her feet into a pair of black and cream sandals she'd bought on sale but not yet worn because she wasn't entirely sure she could walk in them.

Hope steeled herself to look in the mirror. It was like looking at a stranger: a girl with huge eyes, emphasised with liquid liner and mascara, hair swept back into a low, messy bun, tendrils hanging around her face. This girl looked as if she belonged on the Upper East Side; she looked ready for anything. This girl was an imposter but maybe, just maybe, she could exist for a night or two.

The sound of the buzzer brought her back to the room, to the evening ahead, and Hope blinked a couple of times, getting her bearings back, returning to reality. Rather than buzz Gael up she grabbed her bag and slowly, teetering slightly as she adjusted to the height of the shoes, made her way out of the studio and down the stairs into the evening heat.

Gael took one look at her feet and hailed a cab, much to Hope's relief. She breathed a deep sigh of satisfaction as she sank into the back seat and swapped the evening humidity for the bliss of air conditioning. She had spent twenty-seven years in London considering air conditioning a seldom-needed luxury—less than a day in the New York summer and she'd changed her tune for ever.

She didn't recognise the address Gael gave the cab driver and so sat back, none the wiser about her destination, watching the streets of Manhattan slide slowly past. They were heading west and down, towards the busy tourist hotspots of Times Square and Broadway. She lived barely half an hour's walk from the lively theatre district and yet had only visited once, quickly defeated by the crowds and the heat. Hope stared out of the cab window at the crowded streets thronged with an eclectic mix of tourists, locals and hustlers—the busiest district of New York City by far.

The cab made its slow progression along Fifty-First Street until just after the road intersected with Broadway and then pulled up outside a small, dingy-looking theatre. Hope hadn't been entirely sure what to expect but it wasn't this down-at-heel-looking place. She pulled the dress down as she got out of the cab, wishing she had worn the black tights, feeling both overexposed and overdressed. Gael took her arm. 'This way.' They were the first words he had said to her all evening.

He ushered her through the wooden swing door into the lobby. It was a study in faded glory: old wooden panelling ornately carved and in need of a good dust, the red carpet faded and threadbare in places. It was the last place she had expected Gael to bring her. He was smart in a pale grey suit, his hair sleeked down, as incongruous a contrast to the tatty surroundings as she was. He handed two tickets to a woman dressed like a nineteen-forties usherette and then led Hope down the corridor into the theatre.

It was like stepping into another world. The huge chandeliers hanging from the high ceiling gave out a warm, dim glow, bathing the gold-leafed auditorium in flattering lowlights. The seats had been removed from the stalls and instead it was set up cabaret style with round tables for two, four or six taking up the floor space instead. Many tables were full already, their laughing, chattering occupants wearing anything from jeans to cocktail dresses.

The stage was set up with a microphone and a comfortable-looking leather chair. Nothing else. Steps led up from the floor to the stage.

Gael led her to a small table with just two chairs near the front, pulling a chair out for her with exaggerated courtesy. 'Two glasses of Pinot Noir, please,' he said to the hovering waitress, who was also dressed in nineteen-forties garb. Hope opened her mouth to change the order, she preferred white wine to red, especially on a hot night like this, but she closed it again as the waitress walked away, not caring enough to call the woman back.

'What is this?' she asked as she took her seat. 'Are you thinking this will be suitable entertainment for after the wedding meal?'

'What? Oh, no. We're looking into that later. Right now, this is all about you.' The wolfish look in his eyes did nothing to reassure her and she took the glass the waitress handed her with a mechanical smile. This wasn't some kind of comedy improvisation place, was it? Oh, no, what if it was audience participation? She would rather dance in public than try and tell jokes. And she'd probably prefer to strip naked rather than dance. Maybe that was the point.

Just as she tried to formulate her next question the lights dimmed and one lone spotlight lit up the chair and the microphone. The buzz of conversation quietened as, with an audible scrape and squeak, all chairs turned to face the stage. It remained empty for what was probably less than a minute but felt longer as the anticipation built, the air thick with it. Hope clasped her glass, her stomach knotted. She doubted she was here to see an avant-garde staging of Shakespeare or some minimalist musical.

Finally, a low drum roll reverberated throughout the room, the low rumble thrumming in her chest as if it were part of her heartbeat, and a woman stepped out onto the stage. She was tall, strikingly dressed in a floor-length black dress, a top hat incongruously perched on her head.

'Good evening, ladies and gentlemen, I am delighted to welcome you to the Hall of Truth tonight. As you know the entertainment is you and the stage is yours. This is where you are able to free yourselves of an unwanted burden. You are welcome to share anything—a secret, something humorous, a sad tale, a confession, a rant, a declaration, anything you like. Here are the rules: what's said in the Hall of Truth stays in the Hall of Truth unless it's illegal—there's no confessor's bond here, people.' A nervous laugh at this as people turned in their seats as if searching out any potential villain.

The blonde Master of Ceremonies smiled as the laugh faded away. 'No slander, no judgement and—most importantly—no lies. And no singing or dancing. There are no directors here searching out their next star! Oh, and please switch your cell phones off. Anyone caught recording or videoing will be prosecuted and, besides, it's bad manners. Okay. As is customary on these occasions I'll start. Anyone who would like to contribute please let a waitress know and you'll be added to tonight's set list.' She took in a deep breath, her rich tones captivating the audience. 'Tonight I am going to share with you the story of my daughter's hamster and my parents' dog and I must warn you that I can't guarantee that no animals were harmed during the making of this tale.'

'You've brought me to a place that tells pet snuff tales? Shame on you,' Hope whispered and a gleam of amusement flickered on Gael's face.

'Compared to some of the stories I've heard here this is practically fluffy and warm.'

'I bet that's what the dog said.' But Hope's mind was whirling. He'd come here before? More than once. Did he sit here and listen, just as he'd sat to the side and taken photos when he was younger? Or did he join in? What did he have to confess? She couldn't imagine him telling a funny story.

'Have you done this?' she whispered as the first audience participant stumbled up onto the stage, pale and visibly nervous as he launched into a tale of wreaking revenge at a school reunion on the bullies who had made his school life a misery. Gael leaned in, his mouth so close to her ear she could feel the warmth of his breath on her bare shoulder. Hope shivered.

'I can't tell you that, I'm afraid. You heard her. What's said in the Hall of Truth stays in the Hall of Truth.' He leaned back and the spot on her shoulder tingled, heat spreading down to the pit of her stomach. Hope drew in a shuddering breath, glancing sideways at Gael. He was concentrating on the stage, his eyes shuttered. Why did he come here to hear strangers speak? And more importantly why had he brought her?

Hope wouldn't have thought it possible that so many people would be prepared to stand up and bare their souls to a room of strangers but, as the first hour ticked by, there was no shortage of willing volunteers. There was a pattern, she noticed. Most ascended the steps nervously, even the ones with confident grins showed telltale signs, the way they tugged at their hands or pulled at their hem. But they all, even the woman who confessed to crashing her husband's car and blaming it on their teenage son, bribing him to take the fall, descended the steps with an air of a weight having been removed from their shoulders, a burden lessened. It was an appealing thought.

The red wine was heavier than she cared for and yet the first glass was finished before she noticed and replaced with a second, which also disappeared all too easily. Gael motioned the waitress over to get their glasses topped up again and a wild idea seized Hope. Maybe she too could lessen some of her burdens. True, she didn't deserve to. But she'd been carrying the guilt around for nine long, long years. Would it hurt to share it? To let this crowd of strangers be her judge and jury.

Her breath caught in her throat, the very thought of speaking the words she'd buried for so long out loud almost choking her. But as the man on stage finished relating a very funny tale of neighbourhood rivalry taken to extremes her mind was made up and when the waitress came over in response to Gael's gesture Hope handed her the slip, slumping back in her chair as the waitress nodded.

What have I done? Her chest was tighter than ever, nausea swirling in her stomach as her throat swelled—her whole body conspiring to make sure she didn't say anything. She glanced at Gael and saw his eyes were fixed on her. Was that approval she saw in their blue-grey depths? He'd brought her here for this, she realised. Wanted her to expose herself emotionally before she did so physically. He was probably right—posing would be a doddle after this.

If she went through with it.

She barely took in the next speaker, her hands clammy and her breath shallow. She swigged the wine as carelessly as if it had been water, needing Dutch courage in the absence of actual courage. She didn't have to do this; she could get up and walk away. She *should* get up and walk away. What was stopping her? After all, her sister's wedding was almost sorted—and if this was the price she had to pay for her career then maybe she needed to reassess her options.

True, Gael wasn't making her do this. Just as he wasn't making her pose for him and yet somehow she was agreeing to do both. He was her puppet master and she was allowing him to pull her strings.

Her head was buzzing, the noise nearly drowning out every other sound and she barely heard her name called. Just her first name, anonymity guaranteed. *She didn't have to do this*...and yet she was stumbling to her feet and heading towards the steps and somehow walking up them, even in the heels from hell, and heading towards the microphone. She grasped it as if it were the only thing keeping her anchored and took in a deep breath.

The spotlight bathed her in warmth and a golden light and had the added bonus of slightly dazzling her so that she couldn't make out any faces on the floor below, just an indistinguishable dark grey mass. If she closed her ears to the coughing, throat clearing, shuffling and odd whispers she might be alone.

'Hi. I'm Hope.' She took a swig of the water someone had thrust in her hand as she had stepped onto the stage, glad of the lubrication on her dry throat. 'I just want to start by saying that I don't usually wear heels this high so if I stagger or fall it's not because I'm drunk but because I have a really bad sense of balance.' Actually after three glasses of Pinot Noir following a dinner comprising of two Pop-Tarts and a banana she *was* a little buzzed but, confessional or not, she didn't see the need to share *that* with the crowd.

Hope took another long slow breath and surveyed the grey mass of people. It was now or never. 'My parents loved to tell me that they named me Hope because I *gave* them hope. They planned a big family, only things didn't work out that way until, after four years of disappointment and several miscarriages, I was born.

They thought that I was a sign, that I was the beginning of a long line of babies. But I wasn't.' She squeezed her eyes shut for a long moment, remembering the desperation and overwhelming need in their voices when they recounted the story of her name to her.

'My childhood was great in many ways. I was loved, we had a nice house in a nice area of London but I knew, I always knew I wasn't enough. They needed more than me. More children. And so my earliest memories are of my mother crying as she lost another baby. Of tests and hospital appointments and another baby lost. I hated it. I wanted them to stop. No more tears, no more hospitals, no brothers or sisters. Just the three of us but happier. But when I was eight they finally gave me the sister I didn't want. They called her Faith…' was that her voice breaking? '…because they'd always had faith that she would be born. And although they still didn't have the long line of children they had dreamed of, now Faith was here they could stop trying. She was enough. She completed them in a way I hadn't been able to.'

The room was absolutely still. It was like speaking out into a large void. 'Looking back, I know it wasn't that simple. They didn't love her more than they loved me. But back then all I knew was that she wasn't told to run along because Mummy was sad or sick or in hospital, her childhood wasn't spent tiptoeing around grief. She had everything and I… I hated her for it. So I pulled away. Emotionally and physically, spending as much time at friends' houses as I could. I pushed my parents away again and again when all I really wanted was for them to tell me I mattered—but they had no idea how to deal with me and the longer they gave me space, the angrier I got and the wider the chasm became. Once I hit my mid-teens it was almost irreparable.

'I wasn't a very good teen. I drank and stayed out late. I wore clothes I knew they'd hate and got piercings they disapproved of. Hung out with people they thought trouble and went to places they forbade me to go. But I wasn't a fool, I knew my best shot at independence was a good education and I worked hard, my sights set on university in Scotland, a day's travel away. And still they said nothing, even when I left prospectuses for Aberdeen lying around. I thought they didn't care.' She took another sip of water, her throat raw with suppressed tears.

'The summer before I was due to go away they booked a weekend away for my mother's fiftieth birthday and asked me to look after Faith. You have no idea how much I whinged, finally extorting a huge fee for babysitting my own sister. I was supposed to have her from the Friday till the Monday morning but on the Sunday I called them and told them they had to come home because I had plans.'

This was the hard bit. True, she had never told anyone what a brat she'd been, how miserable she'd made her family—and herself—but that was small stuff. This, now, was her crime. Her eternal shame. 'I'd been seeing someone, a boy from school, and his parents had made last-minute plans to spend the Sunday night away. I thought I might be in love with him and I didn't want to go to university a virgin, and this seemed like the perfect opportunity to finally sleep together—in his house, in a bed with total privacy.

'I called my parents and told them they needed to

finish their weekend early. That I would be leaving the house at four and if they weren't back then Faith would be on her own. It was their choice, I told them, they were responsible for her, not me. And I put the phone down knowing that I had won. I had. Right that moment they were packing their things, their weekend ruined by their own daughter.' She swallowed, remembering the exact way she had felt at that moment. 'I knew even then that I was being unfair, I didn't feel victory or anticipation, just bitterness. At myself for being such a selfish idiot—and at them for allowing me to be. I hadn't left them much time to get home so I think they were distracted, hurrying. They weren't speeding and my dad was a really good driver. But somehow he didn't react in time to the truck that pulled out right in front of him. It was instant, the police said. They probably didn't feel a thing. Probably.'

Utter silence.

'I didn't lose my virginity that night but I did become a grown-up. I had deprived my sister of her parents and so I took on that role. I gave up my dreams of university, gave up any thought of carving out my own life and dedicated myself to raising my sister.' Hope couldn't stop the proud smile curving her lips. 'I think I've done okay. I spoiled her a little but she's a lovely, warm-hearted, sweet girl. And she loves me. But I've never told her what I did. And I don't know if I ever will. Thank you for listening.'

He only had himself to blame. He'd wanted to know what she was hiding, had wanted her to open up and now she had.

He should be pleased, Hope had shed a layer of armour, allowed her vulnerability to peek through just as he had planned. It would make her picture all the rawer. So why did he feel manipulative? Voyeuristic in a way he hadn't felt even as a teen taking secret photos to expose his classmates?

Because now he knew it all. He knew why she was still a virgin, why she would put her whole life on hold to plan her sister's wedding, why she put herself last, didn't allow herself the luxury of living. And Gael didn't know whether he wanted to hug her and make it better—or pull her to him and kiss her until all she could do was feel.

The way she looked on that stage was terrifying enough: endless legs, huge eyes, provocative mouth. But the worst part was it wasn't the way she looked that had him all churned up inside. It was what she said. Who she was. He had never met anyone like her before.

For the first time in a long time he wasn't sure he was in control—and hadn't he sworn that he'd never hand over control to a woman, to another human being ever again? Because in the end they always, always let you down.

Hope slid into the seat next to him, shaking slightly as the adrenaline faded away. He remembered the feeling well, the relief, the euphoria, the fear. 'Can we go?' she asked.

'Sure. Let me just pay.'

'Great, I'll wait for you in the lobby.' And just like that she was gone, walking tall and proud even in the heels she could barely balance in. His chest clenched painfully. He'd never met anyone like her before. Brave and determined and doing her best to cover up how lost she actually was. He'd spent so long with society queens obsessed with image, with money, with power that he had forgotten that there were women out there who played by a whole different set of rules.

It didn't take long for him to settle up and join her. Hope was standing absolutely still, lost in a world of her own, her dark eyes fixed on something he couldn't see. Guilt twinged his conscience. 'That was a brave thing you did in there.'

'Was it?' She looked at him pensively. 'I don't know. Letting go would be brave. Telling a room full of strangers? I don't know if that's enough.'

'Who else could you tell?'

'Sometimes I wonder if I should let Faith know the truth. If she should know just what kind of person I really am, not worthy of her love and respect.'

'Punish yourself more, you mean? What would that accomplish? Look at me, Hope.' He took her chin gently in one hand, forcing it up so her eyes met his gaze. They were so sad, filled with a grief and regret he couldn't imagine and all he wanted was to wipe the sadness out of them. 'What matters is what you have done in the last nine years and that makes you more than worthy of her love and respect. Don't make her feel that she wasn't a responsibility you accepted joyfully but a burden that you took on through guilt. Think that she's the reason you've spent the last nine years locked away from any kind of normal life. Honesty isn't always the best policy, Hope.'

'You think I should keep lying?'

'Do you love her?'

'Of course I do!'

'Would you sacrifice everything for her?'

'Yes!'

'Then that's your truth. How you got to this point is just history. Goddammit, Hope, the girl lost one set of parents. Don't threaten the bond she has with you as well.' He knew all too well what it felt like to have that bond tossed aside as if it—and he—had meant nothing. 'Come on, I'll take you home.'

But she didn't move. 'I thought we were going out afterwards. You said you knew the perfect place we could go to after the wedding dinner and we should try it out tonight.'

'Haven't you had enough excitement for one night?' He knew he had. He wanted to get back to his studio and draw until all these inconvenient feelings disappeared. This sense of responsibility, of kinship. This stirring of attraction he was trying his damnedest to ignore. So her legs went on for ever, so a man could get lost in her eyes, so he never quite knew what she would say or do next, one minute opinionated and bossy and the next strikingly vulnerable. So he wanted to make everything that had ever gone wrong in her life better. None of this meant anything. Once he'd painted her all these unwanted thoughts and feeling and desires would disappear, poured into the painting where they belonged.

Irritation flashed in her eyes. 'Don't tell me what I have or haven't had, Gael O'Connor. You may have orchestrated tonight but I've been looking after myself for a long, long time. You promised me that I would loosen up and have some fun—well, right now I'm more tense that I think I've ever been so what I need is for you to keep your word and for you to show me a good time.'

Her words were belligerent but the look in her eyes was anything but. She wanted to forget; he understood that all too well. He weighed up the consequences. He should put her in a cab and go somewhere where he could drink until every word she had said on stage was no longer seared into his brain. But common sense seemed less than desirable, everything seemed less than desirable while she stood there in a dress that barely skimmed her thighs, need radiating from her like a beacon. He swore under his breath. He was a fool—but at least he was aware of it. 'Come on, then, what are you waiting for?'

CHAPTER SEVEN

IT WAS A short walk to their destination but, after a swift assessing look at her feet, Gael flagged down a cab, tipping the driver well in advance to make up for the swift journey. It took less than five minutes before the car pulled up and Hope blinked as she took in their surroundings, unable to keep the surprise off her face as she looked around at the massive hotel they'd been dropped off by. As she turned she could see the bright lights of Times Square flashing brashly just a few metres away. 'Every time you take me somewhere you surprise me,' she said. 'Art museums, funny little theatres and now a hotel?'

'We're not going into the hotel proper,' he assured her and steered her past the darkened windows of the hotel to the bar tucked into the ground floor. 'Just into here.'

'Okay,' but she wasn't convinced as he opened the anonymous-looking door and stood aside to allow her to precede him inside. 'It's just this is a hotel bar and it's not really the kind of thing I think Faith is wanting…' She stopped as abruptly as if her volume had been turned down, her mouth still open as she slowly turned and surveyed the room. It was perfect.

Wood panelled and lit with discreet low lights, the piano bar evoked a long-gone era. Hope half expected to see sharp-suited men propping up the bar, their fedoras pulled low and ravishing molls, all red lipsticks and bobs, on their arms.

The long wooden bar took up most of the back wall, a dazzling array of drinks displayed on the beautifully carved shelves behind. A line of red-leather-topped stools invited weary drinkers to sit down and unload their cares into the ever open ears of the expert bartenders. Gael nodded towards a table, discreetly situated in the corner. 'Cocktail?'

Hope weighed up the consequences. A cocktail on top of all that wine? But the five minutes she had spent on stage had sobered her up more effectively than an ice-cold shower and she needed something to alleviate the buzz in her veins. 'Yes. Please. I don't mind what. I know, I'll try one of the house specialities.'

She took a seat, watching Gael as he ordered their drinks. He fitted in here, sleek and handsome with an edge that was undeniably attractive, probably because it was unknown, slightly dangerous. She looked away quickly, hoping he hadn't caught her staring, as he joined her. 'This place is awesome. It's like the New York I hoped to find but haven't yet, if that makes sense.'

'It's exactly like a film set,' he agreed. 'Piano and all. They'll have a jazz band playing on the night of your sister's wedding...'

'So we can come here after the dinner? Oh, Gael, thank you. What a brilliant idea. Faith is going to be so happy. The only thing is it's not that big and there will be fifteen of us. Can we reserve a table?'

He nodded. 'They don't usually but I should be able to…'

'Pull a few strings? I've noticed that. Hunter was right. You know everyone.'

'That's why he sent you to me.'

'Yes. I could never have done this on my own, thank you.'

'I'm not helping you out of the goodness of my heart,' he reminded her.

'Oh, I know, I owe you a debt.' She did but she couldn't begrudge him that, not now. Hope had seen a lot of weddings recently, mostly vicariously through photos shared on social media, far too cut off from her old social group to merit an invitation. They all varied in location, in expense, but the trend seemed to be for huge, extravagant, glitzy events. This small but very sweet wedding she and Gael were putting together in record time made the rest seem tawdry and cheap. It was, she realised with a jolt, the kind of wedding she would want for herself.

The realisation slammed into her and she gripped the table. Would she ever have the opportunity to do this for herself? She wasn't sure she'd know how to date any more, let alone fall in love—and suddenly it was dawning on her just how much she wanted to. Spending the last three days with another human being, a very male human being, had been eye opening. She wasn't entirely sure she always liked Gael; she certainly wasn't comfortable around him. But he challenged her, pushed her, helped her. Attracted her.

Yes. Attracted. Was that so wrong? She was twenty-seven, single, presumably with working parts. Attraction was normal. Only she was a beginner and she was pretty sure he was at super-advanced level. Far too much to handle for her first real crush in a decade. She should start slow. With a man who wore tweed and liked fossils.

Thank goodness, here was her cocktail and it was time to stop thinking. With relief Hope took an incautious sip, eyes watering as the alcohol hit her throat. 'Strong,' she gasped.

'They're not known for their half measures. How are you?'

'Choking on neat gin?'

He raised an eyebrow and she sighed. 'I feel like I've been for a ten-kilometre run or something. It's exhausting baring your soul to complete strangers.'

'I know.'

It was obvious that he did. Either the alcohol or the knowledge he truly had seen everything she was emboldened her to push deeper. 'What did you say? When you went up? You did go up, didn't you? That's how you know it's what I needed.' It had been, she realised. She'd needed to drain some of the poison from her soul.

Gael didn't answer at first, fingering the rim of his glass as he stared into the distance. Hope watched his capable-looking fingers as they caressed the glass in sure strokes and something sweet and dark clenched low inside her.

'I first went there because I was looking for inspiration. My photos felt stale, uninspired. I had just been asked to shoot a series for *Fabled* about the next generation of Upper East Side, all unimaginatively dressed up as Gatsby and co. There they were, ten years younger than my friends and just as entitled, just as arrogant, nothing had changed. I came to the Truth night looking for hope. I didn't expect to be getting up on stage and bearing my soul.' His mouth twisted. 'It could have been professional suicide. I know it's supposed to be confidential but if a journalist had heard me confess how much I hated my work they could have destroyed me.'

'Is that what you said?'

'It's not what I meant to say but near the end it hit me. I was miserable. I needed to change, get back to what I'd originally planned to do—paint.'

'So what did you say?'

'I don't know why but I wanted to tell them about the first time I went to Paris, about the effect the whole city had on me. I'd spent days in the Louvre and so when I went to the Musée d'Orsay I was a little punch-drunk.'

'I can relate to that after this afternoon.'

He grinned. 'Not so punch-drunk that I mixed up Renoir and Degas.' Hope pulled a face at him, absurdly pleased when he laughed. 'Then I saw her, Olympia. I don't know why she struck me the way she did. It wasn't that I found the painting particularly sexy or shocking or anything. But her honesty hit me. I didn't know that relationships could be that honest.'

Hope set her drink down and stared. 'But isn't she a courtesan?'

He nodded. 'And she's upfront about it. There's no coyness, no pretence. "Here I am," she says. "Take me or leave me but if you take there's a price." Everyone knows where they stand, no hard feelings.'

Hope tried to put his words into a context she understood. 'But a relationship, a real one, a lasting one, that's based on honesty, surely.'

'Is that what you believe?'

Was it? She was doubting herself now. 'It's what I'd like to believe.' That much she knew.

'Exactly! You've been sold the fairy tale and you want to believe it's true, but you and me, we live in the real world, we know how rare true honesty is.'

'Hey, don't drag me into your cynical gang of two! What happened to make you so anti love?'

He smiled at that, slow and serious and dangerously sweet. 'Oh, I believe in love. First love, love at first sight, passion, need. I just don't believe in happy-ever-after. Or that love has anything to do with marriage. The marriages I see are based on something entirely different.'

'What's that?'

'Power. Either one person holds all the power and the other is happy to concede it—that's how the whole trophy-wife—or husband, in my father's case, it can be equal opportunity—business works. One half pays, the other obeys. Once they stop being obedient, or they live past their shelf life, then they get replaced.'

'In your crazy world of wife bonuses and prenups maybe, not in the real world.'

'In every world. It may not be as obvious or understood but it's there.'

'But if that was the case then all marriages would fail eventually,' she objected. 'And they don't. Some, sure. But not all.'

Gael shrugged. 'Some people are happy with the imbalance. Or they have equal power and can balance each other out, but that's rare. Now my dad, he keeps marrying women with money. In the beginning they like that he's younger, they think he's handsome, it gives him status—he holds the power. But once they are used to his looks and the lust dies down and they realise their friends aren't so much jealous as amused by their marriage then the power shifts. That's where he is right now. Again.'

'Does he love them? The women he marries?'

'He loves the lifestyle. He loves that they don't demand anything from him. My mom, she held the power because he was absolutely besotted. He tried everything to make her happy. That's her trick. Only in her case she always stays on top. She leaves them when a better deal comes along. Although she's been with Tony for ten years and they have two kids so who knows? Maybe this one she'll stick out.'

'Not all marriages are like that. Your parents were so young when they married.'

'Like Hunter and Faith?'

'Yes.' She wanted to say things would be different for them but how could she when they were still such strangers? But her sister's marriage was hers, to succeed and fail as it would. Hope would help where she could but in this her sister, for the first time in her life, was on her own. 'But they are hardly typical either. Look, you have spent your whole life watching these absurdly rich, absurdly spoilt people play at marriage, play at love, grabbing what they want and walking away the second it gets tough. The real world isn't like that. My parents survived seven miscarriages—seven—IVF. Me,' she finished sadly. She was all too aware just what a strain her behaviour had been on her parents. She would give anything to go back and do it all over again. Yes to Saturday night pizza and films, yes to Sunday walks in the country, yes to that damn carousel ride.

She tried again. 'Look, I might have little real-time experience of love or relationships. I've obviously never been married. But I know something about living up to expectations. If you go around believing everyone is looking to shaft everyone else then that's what you'll find. I don't believe that. I won't.'

His eyes narrowed. 'Look at that, Hope McKenzie all fired up. I like it.'

And she was. She was on fire, living, completely in the moment for the first time in nine years. Her chains loosened, her self-hatred relieved. 'In that case,' she said slowly, scarcely believing the words coming out of her mouth, 'I believe we have a painting to start working on.'

Time stilled as Gael studied her, his eyes still narrowed to intense slits, his focus purely on her. Hope made every muscle still, made herself meet that challenging stare as coolly as she could. If they didn't start this now she wasn't sure she'd ever have the guts to go through with it. But right here, right now, she was ready.

He pushed his stool back and stood up in one graceful, almost predatory movement. 'Yes, it's time,' he said and a shiver ran through her at his words. 'Let's get this painting started.'

The scene was set. He'd planned it all out the day he met her and it was the work of seconds to pull the chaise round to exactly the right angle and to set up the spotlights he used for his photographs to simulate the sun. 'Here,' he said, throwing a clean robe over to her. 'Go and get changed. Can you screw your hair up into a high knot?'

Hope nodded. She had barely said a word since they had left the bar, since her unexpected challenge. But she'd lost that wide-eyed wariness that had both attracted and repelled him. Tonight she was filled with some other emotion, an anticipation that pulled him in. She was ready, ripe for the unveiling.

Gael swallowed. She wasn't the only one full of anticipation. His hands weren't quite steady as he threw a white sheet over the chaise, adding a huge pillow and a rumpled flowery shawl. The other models had brought in their own jewellery, pillows, throws to lie on, things that had significance to them, but he was painting Hope in almost identical colours and attitude to the original. The virgin posing as the courtesan.

'Wait, take this as well.' He handed her a bag.

Hope took it, opening it and peering at its contents. A thick gold bracelet, a pair of pearl earrings and a black ribbon to tie around her neck. Mule slippers. An orchid for her hair. 'Okay. What about make-up?'

'You don't need any. You have perfect skin.'

A blush crept up her cheeks at his words and she threw him a quick smile before heading off to the small bathroom he had directed her to just three days ago. Was that all it was? He'd lost count but what he did know was that it felt like weeks, months since he had met her and he didn't want to analyse why that might be.

It didn't take him too long to set up his tools: paints, palette, brushes, linseed oil, rags. They evoked a fire deep inside that his camera and lenses never could; the messy, unpredictable elements appealed even as he tried to impose order on his emotions. Gael ran a hand through his hair as he took stock one last time. The setting was perfect, all he needed was his model.

'Hi.' She appeared at the door as if summoned by his thoughts, the white robe clasped tightly around her waist, the mule slippers on her feet. She'd fastened her hair up as directed, the orchid set above one ear, the vibrant pink contrasting with the paleness of her face. Two pearls dangled from her lobes.

'Hi.'

'So where do you want me?' She grimaced. 'Stupid question.'

She walked over to the chaise, slow, small steps, obviously steeling herself as she neared the middle of the room. She halted as she reached the chaise and looked at him enquiringly. 'Do I just…?'

Gael nodded. 'You can drop your robe behind the chaise or hand it to me, whichever.'

'I don't expect it makes much difference. I'm going to end up the same way whichever I do.' But she didn't loosen the robe although her hands were knotted around the tie.

'I could put on some music? If that helps?'

'I don't think so, thank you. Not tonight anyway. Do you need silence while you work or could we talk?'

'I don't mind either way unless I'm focussing on your face. Your mouth will want to stay in one position then but that won't be for a few days.' He usually left conversation up to the models. Some liked to chat away, almost as if they were in a therapy session, others preferred silence, lost in a world of their own. Gael didn't care as long as he got the pose and expression he needed.

Hope walked around the chaise and stared down at the sheet, the pillow, the rumpled shawl. 'Looks comfy.'

'Okay, you've seen the painting. You're propped up on the pillow, your head slightly raised and looking directly at me. One leg casually over the other with the slipper half on, half off—but I can adjust that for you. The arm nearest me bent and relaxed, the other resting on your thigh.' Although she would be fully nude the pose preserved a little bit of modesty, a nod to the Renaissance nudes that had inspired the original pose.

'Got it.' With a visible—and audible—intake of breath Hope untied the robe and slipped it off, handing it to him as she did so. Gael turned away to place it on the floor behind him, deliberately not looking as she lay on the chaise and positioned herself. He had done this exact thing nineteen times before and not once had he had this dizzy sensation, as if the world were falling apart and rearranging itself right here in front of him. Not once had he been both so eager and so reticent to turn around and examine his model.

It's just another model, another painting. But he knew this girl, knew her secrets and her hopes. Had coaxed them out of her so that he could capture her in oils and hang her up, exposed, for all the world to see. Only right now he didn't want the world to see, he wanted to keep this unveiling for himself, her secrets to himself. It was his turn to take a deep breath, to push the troubling, unwelcome thoughts out of his mind and turn, the most professional expression he could muster on his face.

She was magnificent. Almost perfect, as pale as the original except for her legs, tanned to a warm golden brown. Petite and curvy with surprising large breasts proudly jutting out and the sexy curve of her small belly. Every woman Gael had dated boasted prominent ribs and a concave stomach; they looked fantastic in the skimpy designer clothes they favoured but felt insubstantial, as if the real joys in life eluded them. Not surprising when they considered dressing on a salad a treat and cheese the invention of the devil.

She was almost perfect, in a way he hadn't even considered, conditioned as he was by the gym-going gazelles he had been surrounded by for the last fifteen years. Her only flaw was the silver scars crisscrossing the very top of her thighs. There were more lines than he could count, covering the whole thigh from the side round to the fleshy inner thigh. They stopped just where a pair of shorts would end. Where the dress she was wearing tonight had ended, hidden from the world.

She stiffened as his gaze lingered there and when he looked back into her eyes all he could see was shame mingled with hurt pride and something that might be a plea for understanding. 'It hurt when my parents died. It hurt giving up my dreams. It hurt how much I blamed myself. Sometimes it hurt so much I couldn't stand it.'

'You don't have to explain anything to me.' He picked up the yellow ochre and squeezed an amount onto his palette before adding in some cadmium red light, the titanium white close at hand ready to lighten the blend to the exact shade of Hope's upper half.

'Every time I swore it was the last but then the pressure would get too much and the only thing that let it out was blood. For that second, when the blade sliced, I had peace. But then the blood would start to well up and I would feel sick again, hated myself, knew I was so weak. Faith used to ask why I wore old-fashioned swimsuits, you know, with skirts and I pretended it was because I liked the vintage look. In reality I couldn't bear for anyone to see my thighs.' She stopped. 'They will though, won't they? They'll see them on this.'

'I can't exclude them. It would be like editing you. Not quite real.'

'I knew that's what you'd say.'

'When did you stop?'

'When I'd accepted the situation. When it became my reality and not this horrible nightmare with no escape. When I put my old self and my old dreams away and devoted myself to Faith. Then I could cope.'

'Or you exchanged one mechanism for another? How long have you been locked in that box, Hope? How long have you suppressed who you are, what you want, what you need?' His voice had deepened and he wasn't even pretending to mix colours any more, the palette lying in his lap, the brush held casually in his hand as his eyes bore into hers.

'I don't any more. I'm at peace with who I've become.' *Liar*, a little voice inside her whispered.

'That teen rebel who kept a clear head on her shoulders while she did just what she wanted? The girl who had her future planned out down to where she wanted to study and when she was going to sleep with her boyfriend. The girl with dreams which took her away from the family home, away from London. Has she really gone?' His words sent an ache reverberating through her for the lost dreams and hopes she barely even acknowledged any more.

'I am away from London.'

'Still anchored to your family home. To your sister. Still doing the sensible thing.'

'This isn't that sensible,' she whispered.

His eyes pinned her to the pillow; she couldn't have moved if she'd wanted to. 'No.'

Hope had a sense she was playing with fire and yet she couldn't, wouldn't retreat. 'I'm bored of being sensible. So very, very bored.'

'Your hand,' he said hoarsely. 'I just need to position it.'

Hope's mouth was so dry she couldn't speak, couldn't do more than nod in agreement as Gael put the palette down and walked towards her. He had changed into old, battered, paint-splattered jeans and a white, equally disreputable shirt, buttons undone at the neck. She could see the movement of his muscles, a smattering of hair at the vee of the low neck and something primal clenched low down inside her.

She had never been so aware of her own body before, not as a teenager, her mouth glued to her boyfriend's as she fended off his hands, not as she'd stood in the bathroom, razor blade in hand. Every nerve was pulsing, jumping to the increasingly rapid beat of her heart. She could sense Gael over the ever shortening distance, sense him physically as if she were connected to him on some astral plane.

'This hand.' His voice was now so hoarse it was almost a rasp. 'I need it here.'

The second he touched her she gasped, unable to bear the pressure building up so slowly inside her any longer. His fingers on hers, the coolness against the heat of her skin, the sight of those deep olive tones on her own pale hand, the gentle strength inherent in his touch as he moved her. It was as if she had been craving his touch without even knowing it and that one movement opened up a deep hunger inside her.

But she had no doubt, no hesitation. She might be inexperienced but she instinctively knew what to do. She half closed her eyes, watching him through her lashes. 'Here?' She slid her hand a little way along her thigh and, with feminine satisfaction, watched him swallow. 'Or here?' She slid it slightly further so the tips of her fingers met his and, almost of their own volition, caressed the roughened tips.

'Hope…' She didn't know if he was uttering a warning, an entreaty or both but she was past caring. The last few days this man had laid her bare, exposed her deepest secrets and made her confront them. She was tired of confronting, tired of hiding, she just wanted to feel something good—and if her nerves were tingling like this from the mere touch of hand on hand then she had the suspicion this could get really good really soon.

'I think here, don't you?' Her fingers travelled up his hand to explore the delicate skin at his wrist. Gael closed his eyes and Hope thrilled at the knowledge that one simple touch could have such a potent effect, only to draw in a breath of her own as he captured her hand in his, his thumb sliding down to return the favour. One digit, one tiny area of skin but her whole body was lit up like Piccadilly Circus and she knew she couldn't, wouldn't walk away.

She should feel shame or embarrassment lying here wearing nothing but a flower in her hair, a ribbon round her neck while he was still dressed but she didn't feel either of those things. She felt powerful as she tugged at his hand, powerful as in answer to her command he sat at the side of the chaise, powerful as she raised her hand to his face and allowed herself the luxury of learning the sharp cheekbones, the dimple by the side of his mouth, the exquisitely cut lips.

'Hope,' he said again, capturing her hand once again, this time holding it still while he looked deep into her eyes. She saw concern and chafed at it. She saw need and fire and thrilled to it. 'This isn't right. It's been an emotional evening. I can't take advantage of you…'

'Right now I feel like I'm taking advantage of you.'

A primal fire flashed in his eyes and her whole body liquefied as his mouth pulled into a wolfish grin. 'You believe that if you want, sweetheart.'

'Would you be pulling back if I was any other woman?'

'I wouldn't be here if you were any other woman.' The admission was low, as if it had been dragged from him.

Oh.

'That's not what I meant and you know it. If I wasn't a virgin, if you knew I'd been swinging from the chandeliers with a whole regiment of lovers, then would you be pulling away?'

'No,' he admitted. 'But you are and the first time, Hope, it should be special. With someone you love. I don't do love, I don't do long term and I don't want to hurt you. You deserve better.'

'How very teen drama of you. I'm twenty-seven, Gael. I don't know how to flirt or date or *be* in that way. The way things are going I'll be a thirty-eight-year-old virgin and you holding my hand will be the single most erotic thing that's ever happened to me and it would be most unfair of you to condemn me to that. I'm not holding out for a knight on a white charger, you know that. If things were different I'd have lost it to Tom Featherstone nine years ago, in his parents' bed with a White Musk candle to create the mood and James Blunt on the speakers telling me how beautiful I was. I liked Tom. I liked him a lot. I wanted to sleep with him, but I didn't love him and I promise not to fall in love with you. I know you think you're good but you can't be *that* good.'

His mouth curved into a reluctant smile. 'That sounds like fighting talk.'

'It was supposed to be seductive talk.'

The virgin seducing the playboy. It was completely the wrong way round but it turned out that this playboy had scruples. Hope respected them, she just wanted him to get over them already and respect *her* choice.

Gael studied her for a second longer and Hope stared back more brazenly than she ever had, allowing all her need and want and desire to spill out until, with a smothered groan, he leant in, arms either side of her head, his face close to her, mouth within kissing distance, almost.

Hope moistened her lips.

'Let's get this straight,' he said. 'If there's going to be any seducing tonight then I'll be the one who's doing it.'

Her body liquefied again, every bone melting so she felt as if she could simply slide off the chaise to lie in a puddle on the floor—and he wasn't even touching her.

Only then he was, one hand tilting her chin up before he claimed her mouth with his and the last coherent thought Hope knew was that when it came to seduction Gael was right: he was definitely the one in control.

CHAPTER EIGHT

IT WAS ALMOST like a relationship. Almost. The doorman let her straight up without even buzzing first, she had a bag with hot bagels and two coffees in one hand and a Bloomingdale's bag in the other, her toothbrush and a change of underwear in the handbag slung over her shoulder, just in case.

But it wasn't a relationship. When the lift doors opened and she walked into the studio Gael looked up and smiled—which was an improvement on his old non-greeting—but he made no move to come over and kiss her. They didn't kiss, or hold hands, or feed each other titbits or cuddle. They had sex. Every night for the last week and a couple of times in the day as well—after all, she was spending most of the day naked—but they weren't affectionate.

It was as if life was in two halves: the normal half filled with wedding planning, painting, archive sorting and anything else that needed doing—and the secret half. The half when Gael's eyes darkened to a steely blue and just the look in them made her stomach swirl and her pulse speed up. And the two halves were totally disconnected.

That very first night, afterwards, he had asked if

she was okay. Probably still worried that she was going to transfer twenty-seven years of singledom into one giant, all-encompassing *'thank you for the first orgasm I didn't sort out on my own'*, wholly inappropriate crush. Obviously all the serotonin and oxytocin had been a little overwhelming; she'd wanted to be completely absorbed in and by and round him while her heartbeat returned to its normal pace and her breathing slowed. Hope completely understood, for the first time, how knee-weakening, chest-tightening, dry-mouthed lust could be mistaken for love.

But she'd spent the last nine years ignoring her wants and wasn't going to let a little bit of—okay, a lot of—sex change the carefully ingrained habits. A wide-eyed, 'So that's what all the fuss is about,' followed by, 'I can't believe it's taken me so long,' wrapped up with a 'thank you' was all that she allowed before wrapping the handy robe around herself and disappearing into the bathroom.

And so she'd reassured him—and herself—that she was more than okay, that she understood exactly what this was. Temporary, fun, no strings, no expectations. Hope guessed that this was what was meant by friends with benefits. Not that they were exactly friends either. Soon to be kind of in-laws with benefits?

Gael threw a pointed look at the industrial clock on the wall. 'Got lost? I thought you were heading back to yours for a change of clothes. Last time I looked your apartment was a ten-minute walk from here.'

Hope felt a slight twinge of guilt. She *was* supposed to be cataloguing again this morning. 'I know I took longer than expected, but I did bring coffee and bagels because, honestly, it is far quicker to go and buy coffee than it is to work that fiendish machine of yours.'

'Coffee from Bloomingdale's?' He nodded at the huge bag in her hand.

'Well, no. I just popped in while I was passing…'

'Passing? Your apartment is straight north from here. How were you passing Third Avenue?'

'Okay, I took a little detour. I know we have an appointment at the bridal shop this afternoon…yes. *We*,' she added firmly as he pulled an all too expressive face. 'I am not going on my own. But Faith needs two gowns and it's stressful enough getting one made up on time, so as the New York dress can be a lot less formal I thought I'd look elsewhere. Besides, I haven't really had a chance to flex the credit card Hunter gave me yet. Shopping with an unlimited budget is a lot more fun than bargain hunting, let me tell you. This might not be an actual wedding dress but it cost more than most entire weddings. I seriously thought they'd added an extra digit by mistake.'

She placed the bag carefully on the floor and opened it. 'What do you think? It was the last in her size so I bought it straight away but now I'm worrying I didn't look at enough options.' She pulled out a delicate cream dress with a lace overlay on the short bodice and cap sleeves, the silk almost sheer around the high waist before cascading into a long pleated skirt. 'I wanted something floaty and unstructured which will be comfortable to wear. After all, she's moving around a lot on the wedding day—Central Park, then to the boat for the afternoon cruise.'

Hope had been unsure what to do with the fifteen guests in the four hours between the cocktails at the

Tavern on the Green and dinner at the Roof Garden. They were such an odd selection of people from Hunter's multimillionaire socialite mother to her aunt and uncle who lived in a small village in Dorset and hated big cities. Luckily inspiration had led her to a small business that chartered boats out and she had booked an old-fashioned sailboat for the afternoon to take the guests on a cruise around Manhattan. It would probably be a little unsophisticated for Misty, who actually owned her own yacht, but Faith and her UK guests would love it.

'Then she's at the Met and finally the piano bar. It's a busy day and she wants white for the party and blessing so I wanted to make sure there was a contrast. It's such a beautiful shimmery cream as well. I got a gorgeous cashmere wrap in a soft gold and both flat shoes and heels so she can swap. What do you think?'

Gael didn't just nod and say, 'Very nice, dear,' as her father used to do. She guessed that was the advantage of wedding planning with an artist and former society photographer. Instead he took the hanger from her and hung the dress from a hook on the wall, standing back, brow creased in concentration.

'Gold accessories?'

Hope felt a little as if she were taking a test. 'Soft gold, not metallic. Because of the thread in the lace.'

'So Hunter and I will need ties in that colour. His dad too probably.'

Hope stared at him, horrified. Suits? She hadn't even thought about suits. Dear God, she wasn't expected to sort the rings out as well, was she?

To her relief Gael carried on. 'My tailor has already started on the suits for the party. A light grey with white linen shirts. You can work with that? We'll order the ties once you have chosen the bridesmaids' dresses. I think we'll want a darker, almost charcoal suit for the wedding, to go with the soft gold accents in the cream of the dress. And a lightweight fabric.' He pulled his phone out and started tapping. How could it be that simple?

Easy, she reminded herself, he had connections. Besides, dress number one had been pretty easy for her thanks to the limitless budget. She'd met up with a personal shopper and this dress was the second she'd seen. She'd fallen for it instantly—more importantly she knew Faith would love it.

Gael looked up from his phone. 'What about you? Have you sorted a dress out yet?'

'No, not yet but I still have a few days. Besides, I don't have a limitless budget so an hour with a personal shopper isn't going to cut it for me. I thought I'd head downtown tomorrow and see what I can find in a soft gold. It's Faith's day anyway so as long as I complement her in the photos it's all good.'

'Hope, just use Hunter's card. He'll be expecting you to use it.' He threw her a shrewd glance. 'But sure, hide away in the background as usual.'

'I'm not! It's her wedding. Some sister I would be if I tried to overshadow her.' Besides, that huge canvas right there? She was in the foreground there. Enough in the foreground to last her a lifetime. 'I'll find something, I promise. Besides, Hunter wants me to put the bridesmaids' dresses for the party on the limitless card so this afternoon I'll spend big. You won't recognise me, my dress will be so attention seeking.'

'I'd know you anywhere,' he said softly and her heart trembled. *No*, she scolded herself. *No reading meanings into words. No thinking this is more than it is. You escaped awkward if sweet fumblings with Tom Featherstone for toe-curling, out-of-body-type sex. How many people go straight to advanced levels, huh? It's just your emotions are still stuck on beginner level. Give them a chance to catch up.*

Besides. She wasn't that stupid. She trusted Gael with her body but there was no way she would trust him with her heart. She was pretty sure he couldn't handle his own, let alone somebody else's. No, she would enjoy this for what it was and when it was over take the confidence and belief she was gaining day by day and go out and make herself a happy life. One day she might even feel that she deserved to.

'We're due at the shop in four hours. Do you need me to pose?' Airily said but each time she still needed to take a deep breath before she let the robe slip. Habits of a lifetime were hard to escape and after years of keeping in the background being under such intense scrutiny was hard. More than hard.

'No, there's not really enough time. I'm doing some work on the background so I don't need you. Why don't you get on with the archive?'

And there she was. Relegated from lover to muse to wedding planner to assistant in four easy steps. *Know your place*, she told herself sternly as Gael snagged the brown bag to take out his coffee—black, two shots—and bagel—pumpkin seed with cream cheese and smoked salmon. Both a stern contrast to her own more adventurous orders but she was a tourist, it was her duty to experiment. She grabbed her own food and headed off into the kitchen where her workstation was set up. She enjoyed the work but this time away from the office was making her face some uncomfortable truths. She'd hoped this job swap, working with Brenda, would give her the time she needed to work on her career—but instead it was becoming increasingly clear that although she was good at office work and ran events smoothly and meticulously she was bored. In fact she had been bored for a long time if she was honest with herself—something was missing and she couldn't put her finger on exactly what that was.

Hope had fallen into a rhythm over the last week. Gael kept good records and she was beginning to recognise many of the faces so she barely had to put any aside for future clarification. She had already worked her way through his junior year at school and made a good start on senior. The photos were all taken anonymously up to this point but there was a step change the second he was outed: less candid, more posed, less scandalous.

And more of Gael himself. Set-up group shots, time delays. He didn't look at ease, didn't pose, a faraway look on his face as if he was dreaming of being safely back behind the camera.

It wasn't just Gael who made more of an appearance. Time after time the camera lingered lovingly on a willowy blonde girl. She had possibly the most photogenic face Hope had ever seen, the sharp angles and exaggerated features made for the lens. It wasn't just the camera who loved her, judging by the close-ups. The photographer had too.

Hope checked the face against the records she was building up. The girl had been in the junior year pictures as well, only in the background, watching the main players as yearningly as the camera. At some point, like Gael, she had come out of the shadows to shine on centre stage. Tamara Larson.

With half an eye on Gael through the open door, Hope brought up her internet browser and typed in the name. In less than a second it presented her with thousands of possibilities. She pressed randomly on one link. She almost knew what she'd see before the picture loaded: Gael looking down at Tamara, almost unrecognisable. It wasn't just that he was more than a decade younger, slim to the point of skinny, still wearing the gangliness of a very young man. It was the softness in his face, the light in his eyes, the warmth in his smile that made him so alien. Hope had never seen him look that way, not even in their most intimate, unguarded moments.

'I believe in love,' he had said. The proof was right here. He had loved. Adored.

Hope's breath caught in her throat and her fingers curled into fists. It wasn't that she was *jealous*—well, she conceded, maybe just a teensy weensy bit in a totally irrational way but no, in the main it wasn't jealousy consuming her, it was curiosity. Something had happened to wipe that softness out so complexly replacing it with cynicism. What was it?

She clicked back and scrolled onwards until a headline caught her eye. '*Expose* photographer and muse to wed' it screamed in bold type over a picture of a beaming Tamara Larson showing a gigantic—and tacky, Hope sniffed—ring, Gael standing proudly behind her, his hands possessively on her shoulders.

Engaged! He must have still been a baby, younger even than Hunter.

What had happened? There was definitely no socialite living here in the loft. Of course Gael had no obligation to tell her if he was divorced, none at all.

Hurt flickered inside her. Small but scalding. He knew everything about her from the scars on her thighs to the scars on her heart and yet he had shared nothing that wasn't already public knowledge. No, this definitely wasn't anything like a relationship. For him she was a convenience; a convenient model, a convenient assistant, a convenient lover.

Which was *absolutely* no problem. She just needed to remember, remember exactly what this was—and exactly what it wasn't.

'Researching?' How had she not heard him come into the kitchen? Hope jumped guiltily. 'How very keen.'

'I didn't know you were engaged.' There was no point in prevaricating; she'd been caught red-handed.

His mouth twisted. 'Briefly. It was a long time ago.'

'What happened?' She saw the shutters come down and pressed on. 'You're going to have to tell me at some point. She's going to feature heavily in the retrospective; half your pictures from that time are of her.'

'Tale as old as time: boy meets girl, girl sees opportunity, boy falls for girl, it ends tragically. The end.' The mocking tone was back but this time it was entirely self-directed. That was worse in some ways than when he employed it against her.

She tried for a smile, wanting to lighten the suddenly sombre mood. 'Fairy tales have darkened since my day.'

'Oh, this is no fairy tale. It's an old-fashioned morality tale of lust, hubris and greed.' He hooked a stool out and sat down opposite her, leaning on the steel countertop, eyes burning with sardonic amusement. 'They rarely have a happy ending.'

Hope was right. He couldn't have a retrospective and not include his own secrets and shame. What would be the point in that? Besides, Tamara was no secret. Their relationship was well documented as the long list of web links on the laptop attested.

Gael spun the laptop round and stared at the photo. All he felt, all he wanted to feel was pity for the poor fool. Standing there looking as if he had won life's lottery, as if the right honeyed words from the right girl were all he needed to count in this world. 'It's really no big deal. It wouldn't be worth a footnote in the retrospective if I hadn't been stupid enough to think I was old enough to get married.'

'But you did get engaged?'

'Does it count as an engagement if the blushing bride-to-be had no intention of going through with the wedding?' He didn't wait for an answer. 'It's not that exciting, Hope. No big romance. Tamara was in the year behind me at school. She was…' he paused, searching for the right word '…she was ambitious. She felt that she belonged at the very top of the social strata; she was beautiful, smart, athletic, rich—but our school was full of beautiful and smart rich girls and somehow she couldn't even get into the inner circle, let alone rule it. She was left out on the fringes.'

'Like you.'

Like him but so much more ambitious. 'Like me. But I knew my place and had no desire to move upwards. I think she knew who I was before I was outed. Sometimes I think she was the one who outed me, because a couple of months before it happened, a few months into my senior year, she started to make a very subtle and clever play for me. Of course I, sap that I was, had no idea. I thought it was the other way round and couldn't believe that this gorgeous girl would ever consider a commoner like me. But the more I noticed her—and she made sure I did—the more I photographed her, the more she made it into *Expose* and the more she featured on the blog the higher her status grew.'

'She might not have planned it. You make her sound like Machiavelli.'

Proof Hope didn't belong on the Upper East Side; the boys and girls he'd gone to school with had studied Machiavelli at preschool. 'Oh, she planned it. She played me like a pro—like father, like son. Suckers for a poor little rich girl every time. No one can make you feel as special as a society goddess, like Aphrodite seducing a mere mortal. We started dating spring break that year and right through my first year at college. I asked her to marry me when she graduated from high school. Can you even imagine?' He couldn't. He couldn't begin to imagine that kind of wild-eyed optimism any more. You'd think his own parents would have taught him just how foolish marrying the first person you fell for was. Turned out it was a lesson he needed to learn for himself.

'She said yes?'

He nodded. 'Oh, she wasn't finished with me yet, and such a youthful engagement ensured she was in the headlines, just where she wanted to be. She dropped out of college to play at being a fashion intern, did some modelling and dumped me for the heir to a hotel empire. I don't think she has any regrets. Her penthouse apartment, properties in Aspen, Bermuda, Paris and the Hamptons more than make up for any lingering feelings she may have had.' He ran into Tamara every now and then. She usually tried to give him some kind of limpid look, an attempt at a connection. He always ignored her.

'You were much better off finding out what she was like before you got married.'

'That's what Misty said. She sent me to Paris for my sophomore year as a consolation prize and that's when I really fell in love.'

'With Olympia?'

He smiled then. 'Olympia and all her sisters.'

'You're lucky.'

'Lucky? Interesting interpretation of the word. Foolish, I would have said.'

'Not for Tamara, for Misty. To have someone who cares. Okay, you lost out a little in the parent lottery. They were too young, too self-absorbed to know how to raise you.'

'Were?' Neither of them had ever grown up, at least where he was concerned.

'But it sounds to me like Misty has always been there for you. Not everyone has that.'

Interesting interpretation. But there was a kernel of truth there that niggled at him uncomfortably. He'd never asked why Misty had kept him after she divorced his father; he'd been more focussed on the fact both biological parents had walked away rather than appreciating the non-biological one who'd stayed. But she *had* kept him. Supported him, still expected him to come and stay every Christmas, Thanksgiving, every summer. She'd have bought him the studio, made him an allowance if he weren't so damned independent. Her words.

He'd always thought that somehow he was fundamentally flawed, unlovable; that was why his parents didn't stay, why Tamara could discard him without a qualm. That was why he only dated women with short-term agendas that matched his, never allowed himself to open up. But maybe he wasn't the one who was flawed after all.

Because it wasn't just Misty who believed in him. He might have bribed Hope into posing, manipulated her into helping him, but she'd responded with an openness that floored him. The painting was almost taking on a life of its own, rawer and more honest than he had thought possible. And then there was the sex…

He'd be lying if he said that was unexpected. There had been a spark between them from the first moment and although he'd been reluctant to take her virginity in the end he'd been powerless when confronted by the desire in her eyes. She was a grown woman and she had made it clear she knew exactly what she was doing.

What was unexpected was how calmly she accepted the situation. No expectations for anything beyond his limited offer. He should be relieved. He wasn't sure what it meant that he wasn't. He was very sure that he didn't want to know.

CHAPTER NINE

LUCKY. SEVERAL HOURS later Hope's words were still reverberating around Gael's head. He'd been called lucky before—when his father married Misty and he stopped being one of 'us', a local, and became one of 'them', the privileged summer visitors. Lucky when he started seeing Tamara, lucky as his career progressed. It had been said with envy, with laughter, with amusement but never before with that heart-deep wistfulness.

He'd never been able to think about that time with anything but regret and humiliation. Tamara's manipulation had been the final confirmation of everything he had suspected since the day his mother had walked out, her next lover already lined up. His subsequent relationships hadn't done much to change his mind, a series of models, socialites and actresses whose beautiful eyes were all solely focussed on what he, his camera and his influence could do for them. The only thing in their favour was that they knew the score, were only interested in the superficial and the temporary and made no demands on his heart or future.

Of course he had never dated outside that narrow world. Never searched for or wanted anything more meaningful. Why would he when so many easy opportunities presented themselves with such monotonous regularity?

Until Hope. She broke the mould, that was for sure. The first woman he had met who seemed to want nothing for herself—he didn't know whether he admired her or wanted to shake her and shout at her to be more selfish, dammit. To *live.* It would be so easy to take advantage of her, to hurt her. Every day he told himself that they should end their affair. And yet here they still were.

Maybe he wasn't the one with the power here after all; in his own way he was as bad as she was, living safely, ensuring his emotions were never stirred, that he remained safe.

Gael scowled, pushing the unwanted thought out of his mind. He *was* challenging himself, opening himself up to potential ridicule with his change of direction. In a few weeks his paintings would be exhibited at one of the most influential galleries in town, exposing his heart and soul in a way that his photos never had. Besides, look at him now. Wedding planning, ordering suits, playing happy families so that his pain of a little brother could have the perfect wedding.

Little brother? He was usually so quick to disassociate himself from any close relationship with Hunter by a judicious 'ex' and 'step'. Just as he always added the 'half' qualifier onto his mother's two children.

Gael shifted, uncomfortable on the overstuffed velvet seat. A few phone calls had led Hope and he here to the exclusive bridal salon popularised on the TV show *Upper East Side Bride.* Women from all over the States—and further afield—travelled here, prepared to pay exorbitant prices for their one-of-a-kind designs, hoping for a sprinkle of rarefied fairy dust to cast a sparkle over their big day.

'I have your sister's measurements and her choices from our available stock,' the terrifyingly elegant saleswoman had said, eyeing Hope as if she were a prize heifer. 'You're a couple of inches too short and a little larger around the bust but I think it's best if you try on the dresses I have selected. That way you'll know how they feel, how your sister will feel when she puts it on.'

Hope had gaped at her, looking even more terrified than when Gael had first asked her to model. 'Me?' she had spluttered but had been whisked away before she could formulate a complete sentence. That had been half an hour ago and Gael had been left in splendid isolation with nothing to occupy him except several copies of *Bridal World* and a glass of sparkling water.

Tamara had never tried on a wedding dress. They hadn't even discussed the guest list. In fact, looking back, she'd shown no interest in anything but the ring—the largest he could ill afford and one she hadn't offered to return.

'Don't laugh.' Hope's fierce whisper brought him back to the here and now. Finally. He'd begun to wonder if this was some form of purgatory where he would be left to ponder every wrong move he had ever made.

Hope teetered into the large room, swaying as if it was hard to get her balance. The private showroom was brightly lit by several sparkling chandeliers and a whole host of high and low lights, each reflecting off the gold gilt and mirrors in a headache-inducing, dazzling display. The walls were mirrored floor to ceiling so he couldn't escape his scowling reflection whichever way he turned. The whole room was decorated in soft golds and ivory from the carpet to the gilt edging on every piece of furniture. A low podium stood before him, awaiting its bride.

Or in this case a bridesmaid masquerading as the bride. A pink-faced, swaying bridesmaid.

'Because Faith's two inches taller they've made me wear five-inch heels,' she complained as she gingerly stepped onto the podium. 'I'm a size bigger as well but they have these clever expanding things so hopefully we'll get an idea but bear in mind that Faith won't spill out the way I am.'

Of course he was going to stare at her cleavage the second she said that—he was only flesh and blood after all—and she was looking rather magnificent if not very bridal, creamy flesh rising above the low neckline of the gown.

The huge, ornate, sparkling gown. It looked more like a little girl's idea of a wedding gown than something a grown woman would wear.

But what did he know? Gael understood colour, he understood texture, he understood structure. Thanks to the work he had done for many fashion magazines he knew if an outfit worked or not. But in this world he was helpless. The second they'd sat down he'd been ambushed with a dizzying array of words: lace, silk, organza, sweetheart necklines, trails, mermaids—mermaids? Really? People got married in the sea?—ball gowns, A-line, princess, crystals. This was beyond anything he knew or understood or wanted to understand, more akin to some fantasy French court of opulent exaggeration than the real world. Marriage as an elaborate white masquerade.

'Say something!'

Hope looked most unbridal, hands on hips and a scowl on her face as she glared at him.

'It's…' It wasn't often that Gael was at a loss for words but he instinctively knew that he had to tread very carefully here. His actual opinion didn't matter; he had to gauge exactly what his response should be. What if this was Faith's dream dress—or, worse, Hope's? He swallowed. Surely not Hope's. Her body language was more like a child forced into her best dress for church than that of a woman in the perfect dress, shoulders slumped and a definite pout on her face.

Gael blinked, trying to focus on the dress rather than the wearer, taking in every detail. There were just so *many* details. A neckline he privately considered more bordello than bridal? Check. Enough crystals to gladden the heart of a rhinestone cowgirl? Check. Flounces? Oh, yes. A definite check. Tiers upon tiers of them spilling out from her knees. It seemed an odd place for flounces to spill from but what did Gael know?

'It doesn't look that comfortable.' That was an under-exaggeration if ever he'd made one; skintight from the strapless and low bust, it clung unforgivingly all the way down her torso until it reached her knees, where it flowed out like a tulle waterfall. If Gael had to design a torture garment it would probably resemble this.

'It's not comfortable.' She was almost growling. 'Worse, I look hideous.'

'You could never look hideous.' But she didn't look like Hope, all trussed up, tucked in and glittering.

Hope pulled a face. 'Now you start complimenting me? Don't worry, Gael, I don't need your flattery.'

Was that what she thought? 'I don't do flattery. But

if you want honesty then I have to say that dress doesn't suit you. But you're not looking for you and I don't know your sister at all.'

She studied herself in the mirror. 'She did short-list it but I don't think she'd like it. I can't imagine her picking it in a million years but who knows? Even the sanest of women, women who think a clean jumper constitutes dressing up, get carried away when it comes to wedding dresses. This was designed for a reason. Someone somewhere must think it's worth more than a car. But no, I don't think Faith would. Still, it's not up to us. Take a photo and email it to her.'

The next dress was no better unless Faith dreamed of dressing up as Cinderella on steroids. The bead-encrusted heart-shaped bodice wasn't too bad by itself—if copious amounts of crystals were your thing—but it was entirely dwarfed by the massive skirt, which exploded out from Hope's waist like a massive marshmallow. A massive marshmallow covered in glitter. Gael didn't even have to speak a word—the expression on his face must have said it all because Hope took one look at his open mouth and raised eyebrows and retreated, muttering words he was pretty sure no nicely brought-up Cinderella should know.

He very much approved of dress number three. Very much so, not that it was at all suitable unless Faith was planning a private party for two. Cream silk slithered provocatively over Hope's curves, flattering, revealing, promising. Oh, yes. He approved. So much so he wanted to tear it right off her, which probably wasn't the response a bride was looking for. Regretfully he shook his head. 'Buy it anyway, I'll paint you in it...' he murmured and watched her eyes heat up at the promise in his voice as she backed out of the room.

'I like this but I think it's too simple. She's already wearing one flowy dress, I think she wants something a bit more showy for the party.'

Gael looked up, not sure his eyes could take much more tulle or dazzle, only to blink as Hope shyly stepped onto the podium. 'I like that,' he said—or at least he tried to say. His voice seemed to have dried up along with his throat.

He coughed, taking a sip of water as he tried to regather himself. Brought to his knees—metaphorically anyway—by a wedding dress? Get a grip. Although Hope did look seriously…well, not hot. That wasn't the right word, although she was. Nor sexy nor any of the other adjectives he usually applied to women. She looked ethereally beautiful, regal. She looked just like a bride should look from the stars in her dark eyes to the blush on her cheek.

Looked just like a bride should? Where had that thought come from? He'd attended a lot of weddings, many of them his parents', but right up to this moment Gael was pretty sure he'd never had any opinion on how a woman looked on her wedding day. It was this waiting room, infecting him with its gaudiness, its dazzle, its femininity.

But Hope did look gorgeous. The dress was deceptively simple with wide lace shoulder straps, which showed provocative hints of her creamy shoulders, and a lace bodice, which cupped her breasts demurely. The sweetheart neckline was neither too low nor too high and the skirt fell from the high waist in graceful folds of silk. She was the very model of propriety until she turned and he saw how low the back of the dress swooped, almost to her waist, her back almost fully exposed except for a band of the same lace following the lines of her back.

'I've seen statues of Greek goddesses who look like you in that dress.'

'I look okay, then?' But she knew she did. Look at the soft smile curving her mouth, the way she glowed. Not only did she look incredible, she obviously felt it too.

'Is this the one, then?' An unexpected pang hit him as he asked the question. Not at the thought of the day's purgatory finally ending, but because Hope should buy that dress for herself, not for someone else. It was hers. It couldn't be more hers if it had been designed and made for her. But here she was, ready to give up the perfect dress to her sister, just as she had given up everything for Faith every day for the whole of her adult life.

'I don't know.' Hope was obviously torn. 'I really, really love it. It's utterly perfect. But is it right? She asked for a showstopper for the party and this is too simple, I think. Take a photo and send it but I'm not sure she'll pick it.'

Gael disagreed. His show had been well and truly stopped the second Hope appeared in the dress. 'Whatever that dress is it isn't simple.'

'It *is* the most gorgeous dress I have ever seen. I can't imagine finding anything more beautiful. But I'm not sure it's what Faith has in mind.'

'There is a whole salon of showstopping dresses you haven't tried on yet,' Gael said, heroically reconciling himself to another several hours of dazzling white confections. 'Let's fulfil the brief and get your sister what she wants. But, Hope, you look absolutely spectacular in that dress. You should know that.'

She looked at him, surprise clear on her face. Surprise and a simple pleasure, a joy in the compliment. 'Thank you. I feel it, for once in my life I really do.'

Gael stood back and surveyed the painting before looking over at Hope, lying on the chaise in exactly the same position she had assumed every day for the last eleven days. She had complained that she was so acclimatised to it she was sleeping in the same position now. 'I think we're done.'

'Really done? Finished and done? Can I see?' Gael hadn't allowed her to take as much as a peep at her portrait yet and he knew she was desperate to take a look. 'I need to, to make sure you haven't switched to a Picasso theme and turned me blue and into cubes. Actually, that might be easier to look at. I vote Picasso.'

'No to the blue cubes, possibly to taking a look and no, not finished, but I don't need you for the second pass, that's refinement and detail. I have photos and sketches to help me for that. But I am absolutely finished for now. I'm going to let it dry for a few days and then work on it some more.'

Hope was manoeuvring herself off the couch, as always reaching straight for the white robe, visibly relaxing as she tied it around herself. 'It's good timing. Faith gets here in what, three hours? We've got a fitting almost straight away. Tomorrow I am going to walk her through the whole wedding day and then we have afternoon tea with Misty. I hope Faith's happy with the decisions we made. Not that she has much choice at this late hour.'

'If she isn't then just point out that rather than frolic in Prague she could have sorted it all out herself.'

Hope ignored him. 'Wednesday is the hen do all day—that's a spa day, afternoon tea, Broadway show followed by dinner and cocktails and then Thursday is the actual wedding. Friday we recover while the happy couple love it up in the Waldorf Astoria and then it's the blessing and party on Saturday. So it's a good thing you don't need me. I don't have any time to pose this week. I've just about finished the archiving as well. Brenda has a designer and a copywriter ready to start working with you the second that contract is signed.'

Which meant they were done. He didn't need her to cross-reference any more photos or pose and the wedding was planned. So where did that leave them? Funny how they had been heading to this point for nearly two weeks and yet now they were here he felt totally unprepared.

Because he *was* unprepared. The wedding was the end date; they both knew it. He'd finish his paintings and prepare for his show, she'd go back to DL Media and complete her time here in New York before heading back to London. Yet he felt as if something wasn't finished. As if *they* weren't finished.

Gael swallowed. It had been a long time since he'd cared whether a relationship was over or not. And this wasn't even a relationship, was it?

It wasn't meant to be... His chest tightened. Of course, it most definitely wasn't. He didn't do relationships, remember? Because that way he didn't get hurt. Nobody got hurt. And he'd told her that right from the start.

So why was he feeling suddenly bereft?

Hope kicked off the mule, stretching out her leg. 'Thank goodness that's over with. Do you know how uncomfortable it is holding your leg in that one position for hours at a time? So, may I see?' Hope nodded at the easel and gave Gael her most appealing smile. 'I know nothing about art anyway, so you know my opinion isn't worth anything.'

He narrowed his eyes. 'Why do you do that?'

'Do what?'

'Put yourself down. Your opinion is worth a lot more than most of those so-called critics who will make or break me in three weeks' time. Because it's genuine. Because somewhere hidden deep inside you have heart and passion and life if you'd just let yourself see that. But you never will, will you? Far easier to wallow and self-deprecate and hide than put yourself out there, risk falling or heartbreak again.'

He wanted to recall the words as soon as he'd said them as she physically recoiled, staring at him, her face stricken. 'I put myself out there. Good God, in this last two weeks all I've done is try new things.'

He could apologise. He *should* apologise but he kept going, dimly aware he wasn't so much angry with Hope as he was with himself. Angry because at some point he'd broken his own rules and started caring—and he hadn't even noticed. Angry because yet another person was about to walk away out of his life and not look back—and he had no idea how to stop her. 'You've let me lead you into new things. You followed. That's not quite the same thing.'

She straightened, her colour high and her eyes bright with anger. She looked magnificent. 'Oh, excuse me for not walking in here and stripping off and begging you to paint me. Of course, where I come from that behaviour can get a girl arrested but why should that have stopped me?'

'You never tell me that no, you don't want steak you want Thai, you never say no, I don't want red wine I'd like white even though I *know* you prefer white. You don't tell me what ice cream you prefer so I end up buying out the whole store. You don't tell me when your legs have cramps and the pose hurts. You don't tell your sister that organising a wedding in two weeks is impossible.'

'Because those things don't matter to me. I wanted to help Faith. I genuinely don't care what wine I drink. Why are you saying this?'

Gael stood back from the easel, his eyes fixed on her, expression inscrutable. 'Tell me this, Hope. Tell me what you want to happen next. Tell me what we do tomorrow when you no longer have to come here. What we say to your sister, to Hunter. Tell me how it ends.'

Tell me how it ends. There was no point telling him anything because no matter what he said there was no real choice. It would end. Today, Sunday, when she went back to the UK—only the date was in doubt.

She had to focus on that because if she thought about everything else he had said she would collapse. Was that how he saw her? She always thought of herself as so strong, as doing what was needed no matter what the personal cost. But Gael didn't see a strong woman. He saw a coward.

I know you prefer white.

She did. Why hadn't she said so? Because she was so used to putting other people's needs, their feelings first at some point it had become second nature. Well, no more.

'It has ended. It ended when you put that paintbrush down. We no longer have anything to offer each other.'

'So that's what you want,' he said softly.

Yes! No! All she knew was that it wasn't a choice because if he could make her feel like this, this lost, this hurt, this needy, after less than two weeks then she had to walk away with her heart and pride intact. Or at least her pride because it felt as if something in her heart were cracking open right now. It shouldn't be possible. She knew who he was and what he was and she had kept her guard up the whole time and yet, without even trying, he had slipped through her shields.

Without even trying. How pathetic was she? He didn't need to do anything and she had just fallen in front of him, like her aunt's dog, begging for scraps. The only consolation was that he would never know.

'You knew I preferred white and bought red anyway?'

The look he shot her was such a complicated mixture of affection, humour and contempt she couldn't even begin to unravel it. 'All you had to do was say.'

Affecting a bravado she didn't feel, she walked forward until she was standing next to him then turned and looked at the painting.

It was at once so familiar and yet so foreign. The pose, the setting so similar to the painting she had now seen so many copies of she could probably reproduce it blindfolded—but this was magnified. No dog, no servant, no backdrop, the attention all zoomed in on Hope. Her eyes travelled along her torso, from the so casually positioned slipper along her legs. She winced as she took in the scars, each one traced in silvery detail, an all too public unveiling.

The actual nudity wasn't as bad as she'd feared, not compared to the scars. She was curvier, paler, sexier than she had expected; she looked like a woman, not like the girl she felt inside. Her breasts full and round, even the slight roundness of her stomach suggested a sensual ease.

But her face… Hope swallowed. 'Do I really look that sad?'

Unlike Olympia she wasn't staring out at the viewer with poise and confidence. She wasn't in control of her sensuality. She looked wary, frightened, lost. She looked deeply sad.

Gael was watching her. 'Most of the time, yes. I paint what I see, Hope. I tried to find something else, thought if you confronted some of your sadness I could reach a new emotion but that's all there was.'

All there was. She wasn't just a coward, she was a miserable one.

'Between the scars and my emotions you have exposed everything, haven't you?' Hope whispered.

'I didn't expose anything, Hope, it was all right there.'

But it wasn't, it hadn't been, she'd hidden it all under efficiency, under plans, under busyness, until even she had no idea how she felt any more. It had taken his eye to see it and strip her bare until she couldn't hide any more. 'I hope you're satisfied, Gael. I hope this painting brings you fame and fortune. I hope it's worth it. But at the end of the day that's all you'll have. You tell me I'm a coward? I'm not the one recreating pictures of an idealised woman. I'm not the one cold-shouldering the family who love him, who care for him, who have done nothing but support him even when they no longer had any legal link. I'm too afraid to go for what I want? I'm not the only one. You'd rather photograph life, paint life than live it.'

Hope would have given anything to make a dramatic exit but unless she wanted to walk through the grand marble foyer, past Gael's doorman and out into the streets in a white robe that was never going to happen. She changed as quickly as she could, gathering all her belongings and stuffing them into a bag. It didn't take long. She'd practically lived here for the past eleven days, heading back to her own tiny apartment every couple of days to get a change of clothes, but she had left no residue of herself. Her bag didn't even look full and it was as if she had never stepped foot inside—apart from the painting, that was.

She walked back through the vast studio. At what point had the picture-covered brick walls, the cavernous empty space, the mezzanine bedroom begun to feel like home? Hope took one last look around; nothing would induce her to return.

Gael certainly wasn't going to make the effort. He was leaning by the window, a beer in one hand, looking out at the skyline. He barely turned as she walked by.

'I guess I'll see you at the wedding,' Hope said finally, glad that her voice didn't wobble despite the treacherous tears threatening to break through the wall she was erecting brick by painful brick.

'I guess.'

She pressed the lift button, praying it wouldn't take too long. 'Bye, then.'

He looked up then. 'Hope?'

Her namesake flared up then, bright and foolish. 'Yes?'

'You deserve more. You should go and find it. Believe it.'

She nodded slowly as the flare died down as if it had never been, leaving only a bitter taste of ashes in her mouth. 'You're right, Gael. I do deserve better. See you around.'

CHAPTER TEN

'DO I LOOK OKAY?'

Gael turned to see Hunter pull at his tie, trying to fix it so it was perfectly aligned, pulling at the knot with nervous fingers until it tightened into a small, crumpled heap. Otherwise he looked like a young man on the cusp of a life-changing moment, shoulders broad in the perfectly cut suit, eyes bright and excited and a new maturity in his boyish face.

'Here,' Gael said gruffly, trying to hide the pride in his voice. 'Let me.'

He had taught Hunter how to tie a tie in the first place, how to ride a bike, how to swim. He'd bought him his first beer and listened through his first infatuations. And now his little brother was moving on without him, going forward, past Gael into a whole new life. 'There you go.' He stood back and surveyed him. 'I don't know what Faith sees in you but you'll do.'

Hunter still looked pale but he managed a smile. 'She's wonderful, isn't she? I don't know what I did to deserve her. I'm the luckiest man alive.'

He really believed it too; there was sincerity in every syllable. All credit to Misty for bringing up such a decent young man. Gael had known plenty of men with lesser looks, lesser pedigrees and lesser fortunes who prowled the earth believing themselves young gods. Hunter genuinely didn't believe his face, name or income made him any better than anyone else—it just made him work harder to prove he deserved his privilege. Gael had only met Faith once briefly, two days ago after her afternoon with her new mother-in-law, but had quickly decided that either she was the world's best actress or as genuinely besotted by Hunter as he was with her.

He had hoped to see Hope, to try and make some kind of amends so that the next few days wouldn't be too awkward, but Hope hadn't been with her sister. He hadn't seen her since she'd walked away without a backwards glance. Not since he'd allowed her to. It was better for them to be apart; they both knew it. So why that bitter twist of disappointment when Faith had announced that her sister had gone shopping—and why this even more twisty and unwelcome anticipation as he savoured the knowledge that in just an hour's time she would be by his side?

They were both adults. They had spent two enjoyable weeks together. She had inspired him to create one of the best paintings he had ever done, even if it wasn't exactly what he'd set out to paint; he was thinking of calling it Atlas—because she looked as if she were carrying all the cares in the world on her slim shoulders. They could meet to celebrate this wedding as friends, surely? But when he thought of her in that wedding dress, glowing, when he thought of her lying on the chaise, posed and perfect, when he thought of her in his bed, then 'as friends' seemed a cold and meagre ambition.

But what was the alternative? Ask her out properly? They had said everything that needed to be said; he knew her more intimately than some men knew their wives of fifty years. How could he go from that to the kind of dating he did? The kind of dating he was capable of? Premieres, dinners in places to be seen, superficial and short-lived. He couldn't but he knew no other way.

He didn't *want* to know any other way. Because his way couldn't go wrong. It ended without tears, without acrimony, without devastation. It was safe. There was nothing safe about Hope and the way he was with her—harsh, unyielding, pushy. He wanted too much from her and she let him demand it. But, oh, how he liked it when he surprised her; her face when he had laid out all the different tubs of ice cream. Like a small child set loose in a toy store. She almost made him believe he could be the kind of man who lived a different way. Almost.

He pushed the thought away. Today wasn't about him and, despite his attempts to deny kinship, he was proud that Hunter had asked him to stand by his side. 'You ready?'

Hunter nodded. 'I was ready the first day,' he said simply. 'I saw her walking towards me and I just knew.'

Gael's mind instantly flashed back to the moment he had first seen Hope. What had he known? Surprise that she wasn't the woman he was expecting, yes. Annoyance at the delay in his plans? Absolutely. Recognition? He would like to deny it but something had made him keep her there, manipulate the situation so she stayed with him. He didn't want to dwell too much on what his reasons might have been. He attempted humour instead. 'Knew she was hot?'

'Knew she was the one for me. I was prepared to learn Czech or German or French, whatever I had to do to talk to the girl with eyes like stars—you can imagine my relief when I discovered she was English! Not that it would have made any difference whatever nationality she was. We would have found a way to communicate.'

'Hunter, you've known her what, two months? And it's not like your mom has had the best track record with the whole happy-ever-after thing. Are you sure you're not rushing into things?'

'Man, I am totally rushing into marrying Faith. Full pelt. I just know that she's the one for me and I'm the one for her and I can't wait to get started on our adventures together. As for Mom? She'd be the first to say she never listened to her heart. She didn't trust it not to lead her astray so she married strategically, for fun, for friendship—and then ended up divorced anyway.'

When had Hunter got so wise? Gael straightened his own tie, unable to look the younger man in the eye. 'I don't know what a good marriage is. What makes a relationship worth fighting for.' The confession felt wrought out of him and he turned slightly so that Hunter wouldn't be able to see his expression.

'I think it's when you trust someone completely and their happiness means more to you than your own—and when you know that they feel exactly the same way. You balance each other out, make the other person safe.'

Balance. What had he said to Hope? That marriage was about power? Hunter was saying the same thing only he saw it as a positive thing. That allowing someone else the power just made you stronger. Gael was almost light-headed as he tried to work it out. But looking at Hunter, so happy and so *confident*, he couldn't help but wonder if he possessed a knowledge Gael just couldn't—or wouldn't—understand.

He didn't have much time to dwell on his stepbrother's words as the next hour was a flurry of activity, first meeting up with Hunter's father and the two friends the groom had invited to this small, intimate celebration, and then they had to make their way to Central Park and the little lakeside glade where Hunter and Faith would be making their vows. Hunter didn't seem at all nervous, laughing and joking with his friends and patiently listening to all his father's last-minute advice—and who knew? Maybe Hunter's father did know what he was talking about because not only had he stayed good friends with Misty but he had clocked up fifteen years with his current wife, a record amongst all the parental figures in Hunter's and Gael's lives.

In no time at all they were at the lake, which had been made ready according to Hope's detailed instructions; a few chairs had been arranged in a semicircle either side of the little rustic shelter under which Hunter and Faith would make their vows. White flowers were entwined in the shelter and yellow and white rose petals were scattered on the floor. All against Central Park's stringent regulations but the Carlyle name had persuaded the officials that an exception could be made.

Gael looked up at the cloudless sky and smiled; somehow Hope had even persuaded the weather to comply and the rain and wind which sometimes heralded the beginning of September had stayed away. Hunter's father and friends took their places while Gael stood beside his brother at the entrance to the pavilion, making polite conversation with the official who was conducting the short service. But what he said he hardly knew. In just a few minutes he would see her—and the spell her absence had cast would be broken. She'd walked away before he had decided it was time. That was all this sense something was amiss was. Nothing more.

He turned as he heard feminine voices, his heart giving a sudden lurch, but it wasn't Hope, merely a group of hot-looking women dressed in bright, formal clothes, fanning themselves and giggling as they took their seats. They were accompanied by one harried-looking elderly gentleman who breathed a sigh of relief as he took in the other men. Hope's uncle must have felt fairly overwhelmed by all the womenfolk he had spent the last three days escorting around the city.

He took a brief headcount as Misty wafted in, looking as elegant and cool as ever. The five men in Hunter's party, Misty, the bride's uncle and aunt and four young women who must be her two cousins and two friends. They were all here except for the bride herself—and her bridesmaid. He took a deep breath and steeled himself. It had been a brief fling, that was all. He bumped into old flames all the time and didn't usually turn a hair. There should be nothing different this time.

Shouldn't be and yet there was.

And then the string quartet, placed just out of sight around the curve in the path, struck up and the small congregation rose to their feet and turned as one. Every mouth smiled, every eye widened, many dampening as Faith floated towards them in the ethereal designer dress Hope had chosen for her beloved sister. Her hair was twisted into loose knots with curls falling onto her shoulders, she carried a small posy of yellow and white roses and her eyes were fixed adoringly on her groom. But Gael barely took any of it in, all his attention on the shorter woman by her side. Faith had asked her sister, the person who had raised her, to walk her down the aisle both today and for the blessing in two days' time.

Gael was the only person there who knew how much this gesture cost Hope. How touched she was but also how full of grief that their father wasn't there to do it—and that she would be symbolically relinquishing the last of her immediate family to someone else. That the moment she stepped back she truly would be alone.

His chest swelled with empathic grief because although her full mouth was curved in a proud smile and her carriage straight her eyes were full of tears and the hand holding a matching posy was shaking slightly.

Hope's hair was also tied up in a loose knot with a cream ribbon looped around, contrasting with the darkness of the silky tresses. She wore a knee-length twenties-style dress in a slightly darker shade than her sister's soft golden cream; she was utterly beautiful, utterly desirable. Damn. That wasn't the reaction he had been hoping for at all.

Hope looked up as if she could feel the weight of his gaze. Her lips quivered before her eyelashes fell again. *Look at me*, Gael urged her silently. *Let me work out what's happening here.* But his silent plea fell flat and although she smiled around at the gathered audience she didn't look at him directly again, not once.

* * *

The day was at once eternal and yet it passed in a flash. One moment Hope was kissing her sister's cheek, knowing that this was the last time she would be her next of kin, her first confidante, her rock, the next she was listening as Hunter promised to take care of Faith for ever.

She believed him. They were absurdly young but there was a determination and clearness amidst the starry-eyed infatuation that made her think that maybe they had a shot at making it work. Faith had grown up so much it was impossible to take in that the sisters had only been apart for three and a half months.

They moved seamlessly from ceremony to drinks, from drinks to the boat, which dreamily sailed around Manhattan in a gentle ripple of sparkling waters and blue skies before the cars took them to the now shut Met for a VIP tour followed by dinner. Now, at the end of the day, they were back at the speakeasy, reserved exclusively for the wedding party until midnight; there had been a last-minute panic when Hope realised that Faith's age meant she would be unable to enter the premises if it was open to the public. The bar didn't usually do private parties but a quiet word from Gael had ensured their cooperation; she wouldn't have been able to organise half of the day without him. He knew exactly who to speak to, how to get the kind of favours Hope McKenzie from Stoke Newington wouldn't have had a cat in hell's chance of landing. She should say thank you.

She should say *something.* They had been in the same small group of people for ten hours and somehow avoided exchanging even one word. She should tell him that he was wrong about her, that when it mattered she would always stand up for herself; she should tell him that, uncomfortable as his painting made her, she still recognised what a privilege it was to be immortalised that way. She should thank him for all his help with the wedding. She should tell him that two weeks with him had changed her life.

But she didn't know where to begin. She was just so aware of him. They could blindfold her and she would still reach unerringly for him. She knew how he tasted, she knew how his skin felt against hers. She knew what it felt like to have every iota of his concentration focussed on her. How did people do it? Carry this intimate knowledge of another human being around with them? She hadn't expected this bond, not without love.

Because of course she didn't love him. That would be foolish and Hope McKenzie didn't do foolishness. She wasn't like her sister; she couldn't just entrust her heart and happiness to somebody else. Especially somebody who didn't want either and wouldn't know what to do with them even if he did.

The sound of a spoon tapping on a glass recalled her thoughts to the here and now and, as the room hushed, she looked up to see Faith balancing precariously on a chair, her cheeks flushed.

'Attention,' her sister called as the group clapped and whistled. 'Bride speaking.'

Hope slid her glance over to Gael and, as she met his eyes, quickly looked away, her chest constricting with the burden of just that brief contact.

'I know we're doing speeches on Saturday,' Faith said when she had managed to quieten the room. 'So you'll be glad to hear this isn't a speech. Not a long one anyway. I just wanted to say thank you to my big sister.'

Hope started as everyone turned their attention from Faith to her. She shifted awkwardly from foot to foot, cursing her sister as she met the many smiles with a forced one of her own. Faith knew how much she hated attention.

'There are so many thank-yous I owe her that I could keep you here all night and not finish. Most of you know that Hope raised me after our parents died. You might not know that she gave up her place at university to do it, that she planned to study archaeology and travel the world, instead she became a PA and worried about bills and balanced meals and cooking cakes for the PTA bake sale. She refused to touch the money our parents left us, raising me on her salary—and I never did without. It was only recently that I realised that while *I* didn't go without, Hope often did. But she never made me feel like a burden. She always made me feel loved and secure and like I could be or do anything.' Faith's voice broke as she finished that sentence and Hope felt an answering lump in her own throat, a telltale heat burning in her eyes.

She heard a gulp of a sob from her aunt and a murmur from Misty but her eyes were fixed on her sister. The two of them against the world one last time.

'She gave me this amazing day, the best wedding day a girl could have asked for, with only two weeks' notice. She has always, always put me first. Now it's time she put herself first and I am so happy that she's decided to quit her job and go travelling.'

'What?' Hope wasn't sure if anyone else heard Gael's muffled exclamation as the room erupted into applause. 'I know she can afford to do it by herself but, Hope, I hope you will accept this from Hunter and me.' Faith held out an envelope. 'It's a round-the-world ticket and an account with a concierge who will organise all the visas and accommodation you need. It doesn't even begin to pay you back for all you've done and all you are but I just want you to know how much I love you—and when Hunter and I start a family I just hope I can be half the mother you were to me.' Faith was clambering off the chair as she spoke and the next minute the two girls were in each other's arms, tears mingling as they held each other as if they would never let each other go. Only Hope knew as she kissed her sister's hair that this was them letting go, this was where they truly moved on.

'Thank you,' she said as she reluctantly and finally moved back. 'You absolutely didn't have to…'

'I wanted to. So did Hunter. It gives you three months to explore the US and South America before taking you to Australia, then New Zealand and from there to Japan and across Asia. You choose when and where—as long as you turn up in Sydney in three months' time because that's when we'll be there and I hope you'll join us for that leg.'

'You can count on it.' She knew this was the right thing for her to do, to start living some of the dreams she'd relinquished all those years ago. The world might seem larger, scarier—lonelier—than it had back then, but she was a big girl now. She'd cope. But as she glanced over at Gael's profile a sense of something missing, something precious and lost shivered through her. She couldn't leave without making sure things were mended between them. It wouldn't be the same, not after the things they had said, but she wasn't sure she would have had the courage to move on without him. He should know that. Because she knew he was broken too.

CHAPTER ELEVEN

IT WAS NEARLY MIDNIGHT. A car was waiting outside to whisk Hunter and Faith back to the Waldorf Astoria where they had a luxury suite booked for two nights. Hope would see Faith in less than forty-eight hours at the blessing and party in Long Island but as she hugged her new brother-in-law and kissed her sister goodbye it was as if she was saying goodbye to a whole portion of her life.

The bride and groom departed in a flurry of kisses and congratulations and the party began to disperse as the bar staff efficiently began to set the room back up ready to reopen to the public. Hope's aunt and uncle were taking their daughters and Faith's friends back to the apartment Hope had booked for them, a day of non-wedding-related sightseeing waiting for them the next day. Hope had excused herself from joining them with the excuse that she still had some arrangements to finish for the Saturday—but in reality all she wanted to do was lie in her apartment and work out the rest of her life. She fingered the envelope her sister had given her. She had a year's hiatus at least.

'Congratulations on the travel plans. It seems a little sudden though.' She shivered as Gael came up beside her, not touching and yet so close she could feel every line of his body as if they were joined by an invisible thread. Her body ached for him; she wanted to step back and lean into him and let him absorb her. Typical, first time she tried for a light-hearted fling and she was having to go full cold turkey, knowing one touch would drag her back in.

Okay, deep breath and light chit-chat. She could do this. 'Sudden or really overdue. I was always going to go travelling after university. I had my route planned out. Lots and lots of ruins. Machu Picchu, the Bandelier national monument, Angkor Wat…' Her voice trailed off as she imagined setting foot in the ancient places she had dreamed about studying.

'What about Brenda, the job you wanted so much?'

'I phoned her yesterday and handed in my notice. I know it seems that I'm just jumping into it but I'm not. It turns out there's plenty of time to think at a spa day. I lay there on a massage table covered in God knows what, baking like a Christmas turkey, and your words echoed round and round.'

He caught her wrist and pulled her round to face him. The nerves in her wrist jumped to attention, shooting excited signals up her arm.

'I was out of line.'

'You were right,' she said flatly. 'I let life happen to me—I only did the job swap because Kit told me to apply. If he hadn't I would still be in Stoke Newington, missing Faith, wearing baggy tunics with my hair four inches too long because regular haircuts feel like an extravagance, getting the same bus to work, eating the same sandwich on the same bench every lunchtime and not even allowing myself to dream of anything better. Thinking I didn't deserve anything better.'

They moved aside with a muttered apology as a waiter pulled another table into place and a waitress pulled chairs across the floor, their legs screeching as they dragged on the wood. Gael winced. 'Let's get out of here. We're going the same way, at least let's share a cab.'

A cab pulled up almost the second they hit the pavement and Gael opened the door. 'Will you come back to mine?' he asked as she climbed in. 'I have a bottle of white in the fridge. I would really like to clear the air before the party. We're almost related now, after all.'

He'd bought a bottle of white wine. It was too little too late but it was something. 'Okay.' They did need to clear the air. The last thing she wanted was for Faith to know that they had been involved; it was all too messy.

They didn't speak again until they reached his studio. It was only three days since she had last walked through the lobby, greeted the night porter and taken the exclusive lift that led up to Gael's penthouse studio but she felt as if she had been away for months, suddenly unsure of her place in this world.

'Wine?' Gael asked as they stepped into the studio and Hope nodded. He'd bought it for her after all, a peace offering, it would be rude to say no.

She kicked off the pretty, vintage-style Mary Jane shoes, uttering a sigh of relief as her feet were freed from the straps and three-inch heels. She looked around, unsure where to sit. The chaise held too many memories, there was no way she was heading up the winding staircase to the small mezzanine, which contained a bed and very little else—and there was no other furniture in the place. Hope placed her shoes on the floor and followed Gael through to the kitchen instead, perching herself on one of the high stools as he poured wine from a bottle with an obscure—and expensive-looking—label.

'To new adventures,' she said, taking the glass he slid over to her and raising it in a toast. 'My travels, your exhibition.'

'When are you off? A month's time?'

Hope took a sip of the wine. Oh, yes. Definitely expensive. You wouldn't get a bottle of this in a price promotion in her local corner shop. 'No. Next week.'

'Next week?' He set his glass down with an audible clink. 'Didn't you have to work out your notice?'

'No, thanks to you signing the contract I was so far in Brenda's good books that she's offered me a year's sabbatical. I don't know if I'll take it. Who knows what I'll want to do or where I'll want to be in a year's time but there is a job with DL Media if I need it, which is reassuring.' She grimaced. 'It's not easy being spontaneous all at once. Baby steps.'

'But next week! Don't you have to plan and pack and sort out an itinerary?'

Hope pulled the envelope Faith had given her out of her bag. 'No, thanks to Faith. These people will sort it all out. I tell them where I want to go and they make sure I do. They're already looking at converting my work visa here to a tourist one and sorting out everything I need for South America. I'll spend a couple of days shipping some things home and sorting out what I need and then I'll be ready to go. It's working out really well actually. Maddison is coming to New York to clear the rest of her things out of the studio. If I leave she can cancel her rent. I don't think she's planning on coming back to the city.'

It would be interesting to meet her life-swap partner, the woman who captured Kit Buchanan's heart. Funny how a six-month change of locations could alter things irrevocably. Maddison was engaged, moving countries, her whole world changing. Hope might be more alone than ever but at least she was no longer staying still.

'You have it all organised, as always.' There was a bleak tone in Gael's voice she didn't recognise but when she glanced at him his expression was bland.

'The plane ticket is first class as well. I can't believe they did this.'

'I can. Your sister loves you, Hope.'

'For the first time in nine years I feel unburdened. Free. I'll always miss my parents and I'll always regret the person I was but I'm ready to forgive myself.' She forced herself to hold his steady, steely gaze. 'Thanks to you, Gael. I'll always be grateful.'

'You won't be here for the opening night of the exhibition.'

'No.' She blinked, surprised at the sudden change of subject. 'I'm not sure I could have faced it anyway. People looking at me and then at the painting. It'd be a little like the nightmare when I'm walking down the street naked. Only it would be real.'

'That's a shame. I wanted you there.' He paused while Hope gaped at him, floored by the unexpected words. He wanted her at his big night? As a model—or to support him? 'Look. I wanted to let you know that I've decided not to show it, your painting.'

Time seemed to stand still, the blood rushing to her

ears as she tried to take in his words. 'But, you need it. The centrepiece. It's less than three weeks away.'

'I have nineteen pictures I am proud of. Nobody else knows I planned a larger twentieth. I'm not sure that I'll ever paint a better picture than the one I did of you but I don't need to show it. I'd rather not, knowing it makes you so uncomfortable.'

He was willing not to show the picture? After everything he had done to persuade her to pose? Even though he thought it was the best he had done? Hope had no idea how to respond, what to say. This graciousness and understanding was more than she had ever expected from anyone. She slid off the stool and walked to the door, pausing for a second as she took in the easel with the large canvas balanced perfectly on it dominating the empty space and then, with a fortifying breath, she went over to take a second look.

It wasn't such a shock this time. Her skin was as white, her body as nude, she still wished she'd done daily sit-ups so that her stomach was concave rather than curved but, she conceded, her breasts looked rather nice. Biting her lip until she tasted blood, Hope forced herself to step in and examine her scars, remembering the pain and the secrecy and the self-hatred that went into every one of the silvery lines.

She pulled her gaze away from her torso and looked into her own eyes. Sad, wary, lonely. That was who she was; there was no getting away from it, no hiding. She shouldn't blame Gael for painting what he saw. She could only blame herself. Well, no more.

'Show it,' she said. 'I want you to. It's real. Maybe one day you can paint me again and I'll be a different person, a happier one.'

'You can count on it.' He was leaning against the door, watching her, hunger in his eyes. She recognised the hunger because she felt it too. Had felt it all day, this yearning to touch him, for him to touch her. For the world to fall away, to know nothing but him and the way he could make her feel; sexy, adored, powerful. Wanted.

She was leaving in less than a week. What harm could it do, one last time?

'On Saturday we're the best man and the bridesmaid once more. We have busy, sensible roles to play.'

The hunger in his eyes didn't lessen; if anything it intensified. 'I know.'

'Sunday I'm helping Faith get ready to go off on her travels and then I need to spend a couple of days preparing for mine.'

Gael pushed away from the door frame and stalked a couple of steps closer. 'Hope, what are you saying?'

Deep breath. She could do this. 'I'm saying that this is the last time we can be ourselves, Hope and Gael. Painter and model. Carousel riders. Storytellers.' She moistened her lips nervously. 'Lovers.'

'Last time?'

She nodded.

He smiled then, the wolfish smile that sent jolts of heat into every atom in her body, the smile that made her toes curl, her knees tremble and her whole body become one yearning mass. 'Then we better make the most of it, hadn't we?'

The morning sun streamed in through the huge windows, bathing the bed in a warm, rosy glow. Gael had barely slept and now he rolled over to watch Hope slumber, the dawn light tinging her skin a light pink, picking out auburn lights in her dark hair.

He felt complete, that all was right in his world. Probably, he decided sleepily, because Hope and he had tidied up their brief relationship, ending it in a mutually agreeable and agreed manner. No more messy arguments or avoiding each other, no more hurt emotions or dramas. Instead a civilised discussion and one last night together before they went their separate ways. Neat, tidy and emotionless. Just how he liked it.

It was a shame she wouldn't be there for the opening night though; he would have liked to have seen her reaction when all the pictures were displayed together for the first time with her at the very heart of the show.

He trailed his finger over her shoulder, enjoying the silky feeling of her skin. She was right. Tomorrow they had their roles to play and those roles didn't involve making out on the dance floor. Probably for the best that they had agreed last night was to be the final time.

But right now, in dawn's early light, was in between times, neither last night nor today. They were out of time, which meant there were no rules if they didn't want there to be. And that meant he could press his lips here, and here, and here…

'Mmm…' Hope rolled over, smiling the sleepy yet sated smile he had come to know and enjoy. 'What time is it?'

'Early, very early, so there's no need to think about getting up yet,' he assured her, dropping a brief kiss onto her full mouth, shifting so his weight was over her. 'Can you think of any way to spend the time as we're awake?'

Her eyes, languorous and sleepy, twinkled up at

him, full of suggestion, but she put her hands onto his chest and firmly, if gently, pushed him off. 'Plenty, but none suitable for people who are just friends.'

'Ah.' That wasn't disappointment stabbing through his chest. He could walk away at any time, after all. 'We've reached the cut-off point, then.'

'I think it might be wise.' She sat up, the sheet modestly wound around her. The message was clear—*I'm no longer yours to look at or touch or kiss.* 'Besides, I could do with an early start. Your stepmother—ex-stepmother—has asked me to go to Long Harbor this evening and stay so that I'm there for the morning when the caterers and everyone arrives. I know this party is all her work but I think she'd appreciate some backup. You'll be with us Saturday before three p.m., won't you? That's when my family arrives, with the blessing ceremony due to start at four.'

They were back in wedding-planning mode, it seemed. Gael slumped back onto the pillows, curiously deflated. 'I'll be there.'

'Great. I'll see you then.' Hope slid off the bed, still wrapped in a sheet, and headed towards the stairs. She turned, curiously dignified despite her mussed-up hair, her bare feet, the sheet held up modestly, just her shoulders peeking out above its white folds. 'Thank you, Gael. For waking me up, for challenging me, for making me challenge myself. I'm not saying I'm exactly relaxed about giving up my job—even with a sabbatical as a safety net—and if I think too hard about travelling by myself I get palpitations here.' She pressed her hand to her stomach. 'But I know it's all really positive—and I don't think I would have got here on my own. So thank you.'

'You'd have got there,' he said softly. 'You just needed a push, that was all. You were ready to fly.' He wanted to say more but what could he say? He didn't have the words, didn't have the feelings—didn't allow himself to have the feelings—so he just lay there as she turned with one last smile and watched her walk down the stairs. And five minutes later, when he heard the elevator ping and knew that this time she really had walked out of his studio for the last time, he still hadn't moved. All he knew was that the complete feeling seemed to have disappeared, leaving him hollow.

Hollow, empty and with the sense that he might have just made the biggest mistake of his entire life.

Five hours later the feelings had intensified. Nothing pulled him out of his stupor, not working on the painting—that just made the feelings worse—not going over his speech for the next day, not proofing the catalogue for his show. The only thing that helped was keeping busy—but he couldn't keep his mind on anything. Finally, exasperated with the situation, with himself, Gael flung himself out of the apartment, deciding if he couldn't work off this strange mood he would have to run it off instead. He stuck his headphones on, selected the loudest, most guitar-filled music he could find and set off with no route in mind.

Almost inevitably his run took him through Central Park, past the carousel and down towards the lake. Every step, every thud of his heart, every beat an insistent reminder that last time he was here, the time before that and the time before that he wasn't alone.

Funny, he had never minded being alone before. Preferred it. Today was the first day for a long time that he felt incomplete.

It didn't help that everywhere he looked the park was full of couples; holding hands, kissing, really kissing in a way that was pretty inappropriate in public, jogging, sunbathing—was that a proposal? Judging by the squeal and the cheering it was. Were there no other single people in the whole of Central Park? With a grunt of annoyance Gael took a path out of the park, preferring to pound the pavements than be a bystander to someone else's love affair.

He. Preferred. Being. Alone. He repeated the words over and over as his feet took him away from the park and into the residential streets of the Upper East Side. The midday sun was burning down and the humidity levels high but he welcomed the discomfort. If you were okay on your own then no one could ever hurt you. If he hadn't loved his mother so much then her absence wouldn't have poisoned every day of his childhood. If he hadn't relied on his father so much then it wouldn't have been such a body blow when his father left him behind with Misty. If he hadn't fallen so hard for Tamara then her betrayal wouldn't have been so soul-guttingly humiliating.

You could only rely on yourself. He knew that all too well.

And yet he couldn't shake Hope's words. *You're lucky to have Misty, to have someone who cares.* Hunter had wanted—no, needed—him by his side yesterday. Misty hadn't just paid his school and college fees, she had given him a home, shielded him from his father's impulsive and destructive post-divorce lifestyle. In those tricky few days after his authorship of *Expose* became public knowledge she had stood by him. She insisted he came to her every Thanksgiving and Christmas even now.

Hope had seen that when he couldn't—or wouldn't. But then she knew all about being a mother figure, didn't she?

And now it was her time to shine. He wished he could see her as she finally visited the places she had always wanted to visit, could capture the look on her face as she finally reached Machu Picchu, in photographs, in pencil sketches, in oils. He could draw her for ever and never run out of things to say about the line of her mouth, the curve of her ear, that delicious hollow in her throat.

His steps slowed as he gulped for air, his discomfort nothing to do with the heat or his punishing pace. Somehow, when he hadn't even noticed it, Hope McKenzie had slid under his guard and he could walk away—leave her to walk away—and it would make no difference. She'd still be there. He'd still be alone but the difference would be now he'd feel it. He'd not just be alone—he'd be lonely.

He bent over, trying to get his breath back and reorder his thoughts, and as he straightened he saw a familiar sign, the shop they had visited so recently, the shop where Faith's wedding dress still hung, the last alterations completed, ready to be steamed and conveyed to Long Island in the morning. The shop where Hope had tried on a dress that, for one moment, had made him wish that he were a different man, that they had a different future. A dress that belonged to her.

Was this a sign or just a coincidence? It almost didn't matter. What mattered was what he chose to do next.

CHAPTER TWELVE

'YOU LOOK BEAUTIFUL.'

Hope smoothed down her dress and smiled at Gael, her heart giving a little twist as she did so. By tacit consent they had kept their distance from each other all day except when posing for photographs, but now the evening had drawn in and the event moved from celebration to party the rules they had set themselves didn't seem quite so rigid. They were aiming for friends, after all.

'It's all the dress. Lucky I had some expert help choosing it.' All the bridesmaids wore the same design, a halter-necked knee-length dress with a silk corsage at the neck, but while the other four bridesmaids' dresses were all a deep rose pink Hope, as maid of honour, wore a cream and pink flowered silk. 'If your show is a flop you could always turn your hand to wedding styling. You have quite the knack.'

'All I did was nod in the right places. I think you knew exactly what you were looking for.'

'Maybe. So that was a good speech you did back then.' She'd heard lots of people talking about it—and him. It was hard to keep a bland smile on her face when she kept overhearing beautiful, gazelle-like girls in dresses that cost more than her entire wardrobe discussing just how sexy they thought he was and speculating whether his net worth was high enough for a permanent relationship or whether he was just fling material.

They weren't lying about how sexy Gael looked today. Some men looked stilted or stuffy in a suit; Gael wore his with a casual elegance and a nonchalance that made a girl sit up and take notice. Even this girl. Especially this girl.

His tie was the same dark pink as the flowers on her dress. They looked as if they belonged together.

Funny how deceiving looks could be.

'Thank you. Hunter deserved something heartfelt and not too cruel. He's a good kid. Although now he's a married man I suppose I shouldn't call him a kid.'

'I suppose not.' Hope looked over at the dance floor where her sister swayed in her new husband's arms, the two of them oblivious to the two hundred or so guests Misty had invited. It was a beautiful party. Lanterns and fairy lights were entwined in the trees all around and in the several marquees that circled the dance floor, one acting as a bar, one a food tent, one a seating area and one a family-friendly place with games and a cinema screen for the younger guests.

The swing band that had accompanied the meal had been replaced by a jazz band crooning out soulful ballads as the evening fell. A sought-after wedding singer was due to come onto the purpose-built stage at nine to get the dancing really started and then a celebrated DJ would entertain the crowd into the early hours. The blessing had been beautifully staged and even though

Hope had seen her sister make similar vows just two days before she had still needed to borrow a hanky from her aunt when she welled up for the second time.

'Would you like to dance?'

The question took her by surprise. 'I don't know if that's wise. Maybe later when the music is less…'

'Less what?'

'Less sway-like. I hear the wedding singer does an excellent Beyoncé. I'll dance with you to that.'

'It's a deal.'

So they had made small talk and it wasn't too hard, made civilised plans for later. No one looking over at them would think that they were anything but the best man and the maid of honour relaxing after a long day of duties. Good job on both sides. It was probably time to drift away to opposite sides of the dance floor so Hope could resume sneaking peeks at him while pretending even to herself, especially to herself, that she wasn't.

The night after the wedding had been her gift to herself. A chance to be bold and brave. A way of ensuring that something sweet and special didn't turn sour, that her memories of Gael and her time with him were something to savour. A time for her to take control and show them both just what she could do, who she could be. And then she had walked away with her head held high. Chosen when, chosen how.

So why did her victory feel so hollow? She had a sinking feeling it was because things weren't finished between them, much as she tried to fool herself that they were. There had been a tenderness that night she hadn't felt before. A closeness that she wasn't sure she believed was real and not just a figment of her overheated imagination. Truth was, Gael knew her better than anyone else in the entire world. How did she walk away from that?

But she didn't know what the alternative was or if she was brave enough to explore it. Hope turned away from the dance floor. Ahead of her, through the small scrub-like trees, was a private path that led directly to the beach. She'd been meaning to take a look at the ocean but hadn't had a chance to. 'I'm going to take a walk,' she said, kicking her shoes off, taking a couple of steps away. She didn't know if it was devilry or the moonlight that made her swivel back around and aim a smile in Gael's direction. 'Coming?'

He didn't answer but his movement was full of intent and she didn't demur as he took her hand, leading her through the trees with sure steps. The path through the trees was lit with tiny storm lanterns swaying in the slight breeze like an enchanted way.

All Hope knew was the salt on her lips, the sea breeze gentling ruffling her elaborately styled hair, the coolness of the sand between her toes and the firmness of Gael's grip. 'What was it like living here?'

He didn't answer until they cleared the trees and reached the top of the dunes. The beach spread out before them, dim in the pearl glow of the moon, behind them Hope could hear music and laughter, ahead the swish of the waves rippling onto shore.

'I didn't feel like I belonged,' he said finally. 'I was a scrubby kid who biked around Long Harbor getting into trouble, the kind of kid begging for a chance to go out on a boat, trying to find ways of earning a few dollars through running errands. Home was chaotic, living with my grandparents, I always fell asleep listening to the music in the bar downstairs. And then I came here. A driver to take me where I needed to go, money, more than I could spend, a boat that belonged to the family I could take out whenever I wanted complete with a crew. And when I fell asleep at night it was to total silence. I had a room, a study and a bath all to myself.'

'How did it feel?'

'Like I didn't know who I was.' His hand strengthened in hers. 'I still don't. Except…'

She wasn't sure she dared ask but did anyway. 'Except what?'

'These last couple of weeks I've had an inkling of who I could be, the kind of man I'd like to be.'

'Me too. Not the man part but the seeing a new way. It's not easy though, is it?'

Letting go of his hand, Hope sank down into the soft sand, not worrying about stains on her dress or if anyone was looking for her or if there were things she should be doing. All those things were undoubtedly true but she didn't have to take ownership of them. Gael folded himself down beside her with that innate grace she admired so much and Hope leaned into him, enjoying his solid strength, the scent of him. The illusion that he was hers.

'You've made a good start though. Travelling, carefree, no plans.'

'Hmm. On the surface maybe,' she conceded. 'I want to go, don't get me wrong, but there's still the little voice in my head telling me I don't deserve it. And another little voice shrieking at me to plan it all down to the final detail, account for every second because if it's planned it can't go wrong.'

'Sounds like it's getting crowded in your head.'

'Just a little. Planning makes me feel safe so trying to learn to be more spur of the moment is, well, it's a challenge. My real worry is…' She hesitated.

'Go on.'

'Being lonely,' she admitted. 'Even lonelier than I have been because I have always had Faith and a job, a routine. I'm not good at talking to people, Gael. I suck at making friends. A whole year of just me for company looms ahead and it terrifies me.'

'Oh, I don't know. It sounds pretty good to me.'

Surprise hit her *oomph* in the chest. In her heart. Not just the words but the way he said them. Low, serious and full of an emotion she couldn't identify. Her pulse began to hammer, the blood rushing in her ears, drowning out the sound of the sea. She'd always wanted to matter to someone, be worthy of someone, but at some point in the last two weeks her goalposts had shifted.

She wanted to matter to Gael.

Proud, cynical Gael. A man who gave no quarter and expected none. A man who knew what he wanted and pushed for it. A man who had made her confront all her secrets and sins and forgive herself.

A man who made her feel safe. Worth something.

'You could travel,' she said, looking down at her feet, at the way her toes squished into the sand. 'Do the whole Gauguin thing.'

'Been reading up on your history of art?'

'I remember some things from my whistle-stop tour.'

'I could. I could travel, stay here, move to Paris or

Florence or Tahiti. I'm not sure it would make much difference though. I'd still be hiding.'

'What from?'

'Myself. From emotion. From living. Do you know why that painting of you is the best thing I have ever done?'

She still couldn't look at him, shaking her head instead.

'Because I felt something when I painted it. Felt something for you. Complicated, messy, unwanted human emotions. Lust, of course. Exasperation because I could see you hiding all that you are, all that you could be. Frustration that you didn't see it. Annoyance because you kept pushing me, asking awkward questions and puncturing the bubble I had built around myself.'

Exasperation, annoyance. Frustration. At least she had made him feel something.

'And I liked you. A lot. I didn't want to. The last thing I needed was a dark-eyed nymph with a wary expression and a to-do list turning my carefully ordered world upside down.'

'Is that what I did?' She raised her head and looked directly at him, floored by the unexpected tenderness in his smile.

'I think you know you did. I have something to show you. Will you come?'

She nodded mutely.

Gael pulled Hope to her feet and led her back along the path to the house, skirting the party and the merrymaking guests, neither of them ready or able to make small talk with Hunter's Uncle Maurice or Misty's drunken college room-mate. He took a circuitous route round the Italian garden and in through a side door that only he and Hunter had ever used as it led straight into a boot room perfect for dropping sandy surfboards and towels and swim trunks with a shower room leading right off it. It was empty today, no towels folded on the shelves, no boards hanging on the wall, no crabbing nets leaning in the corner. For the first time Gael felt a shiver of fond nostalgia for those carefree, summer days. He might not have ever admitted it but this huge nineteen-twenties mansion had at some point become his home—just as its mercurial, warm-hearted, extravagant owner had become his mother.

The boot room led into a back hallway, which ran behind the reception and living areas, avoiding the famous two-storey main hallway with its sweeping, curved staircase and ornate plasterwork. Instead Gael led the way up a narrow back stairway, once used solely by the army of servants who had waited on Misty's great-grandparents, the original owners of the mansion.

'I feel like I'm a teenager again, sneaking girls up to my room through the back stairs.'

'Was there a lot of that?'

'No, sadly not. I was too grand for the girls I grew up with and not grand enough for the girls Misty introduced me to. Besides, there wouldn't have been any sneaking. Misty would have offered us wine and condoms and sent us on our way. She was embarrassingly open-minded. Nothing more guaranteed to make a teen boy teetotal and celibate—even if he wasn't a social pariah!'

'I bet there were hundreds of girls just waiting for

you to look in their direction,' Hope said. 'I would have been.'

'Maybe,' he conceded. He had been so filled with his own angst he would never have noticed.

A discreet door led onto the main landing. Closed again, it blended into the wooden panelling. The house was riddled with hidden doors and passageways and he knew every single one of them.

'Don't think I'm not appreciating this behind-the-scenes tour of one of Long Island's finest houses but where are we going?'

'Here,' Gael said and, opening the door to his own suite of rooms, ushered her inside.

It hadn't changed much since he first took possession of the rooms as a boy. A sitting area complete with couch, a TV and a desk for studying. The computer console was long gone and the posters of bikini-clad girls replaced with paintings he admired by local artists, but the window seats still overlooked the beach and the Victorian desk was still piled with his paints and sketchbooks. A door by the window led into his bedroom.

'These are yours?'

'Misty apologised when she assigned them to me, said she hoped I wouldn't be too cramped but she thought I'd prefer not to be stuck out in one of the wings.'

Hope wandered into his bedroom, her eyes widening as she took in the king-size bed, the low couch by the window, and she opened the door to his bathroom complete with walk-in shower and a claw-foot bathtub. 'You poor thing, it must have been such a chore making do with just the two huge rooms and a bathroom fit for an emperor.'

'I managed somehow.'

Now she was here, now the moment was here, unexpected nerves twisted his stomach. What if he had got her, got them, got the situation wrong? For a moment he envied Hunter his certainty. He'd known, he'd said, the second he'd seen Faith. They had been together for just two months and there they were downstairs, husband and wife.

He'd known Hope for less than three weeks but he couldn't imagine knowing anyone any better after three years.

He looked over at her as she stared out of the window at the moon illuminating the sea. Her hair was still twisted up, held with a rose-pink ribbon, the dress exposing the fine lines of her neck and the fragile bones in her shoulders. Desire rippled through him, desire mixed with a protectiveness he had never experienced before, an overwhelming need to protect her from life's arrows. She'd already been pierced too many times. 'I got you something.'

She turned, a shy smile lighting up her face. 'You didn't have to.'

'I know. It's not a parting gift. It's an *I hope you come back* gift.'

Her mouth trembled. 'Really?'

Words failed him then, the speech he'd prepared during the sleepless night. Words telling her he wanted her to go, to experience, to live. But at the end of it all he hoped she'd choose to come back. To him. 'It's in the closet.'

With a puzzled frown wrinkling her forehead, Hope

opened the door to his walk-in closet. It was practically empty, the few essentials he kept here folded up and put away on shelves at the back. There was only one item hanging up.

Hope stood stock-still, one hand flying to cover her mouth. 'My dress.'

'I didn't think anyone else should have it.' It was hers. They had both known it the second she had put it on. Every line, every delicate twist of lace, every fold of silk belonged to her.

'But…it's a wedding dress.'

'I don't want to confine you, Hope. I don't want you to go away tied down. I want you to live and laugh and if you love then that's the way it's supposed to be.' He swallowed as he said the words, alternate words trembling on his tongue. *Stay with me.* 'This dress is a talisman, a pledge. That if you choose to come back to me then I'll be here. And if you don't, well. It's yours anyway. If you want it.'

Did she understand? Did she know what it meant that he had asked her to come back to him? He had never asked anyone before. Never exposed himself. Taken each desertion on the chin and then wrapped another layer of protectiveness around himself.

Hope couldn't take her eyes off the dress, perfect as it hung in the closet, every fold exactly where it should be. It did belong to her, he was right. Nothing had ever felt so right—nothing but being in Gael's arms. And he had bought it for her.

The dress had been exorbitant but she knew it wasn't the dollar price that made it special, utterly unique. It was the gesture behind the gift. It was opening himself up to rejection. It was allowing her the power to reject him. That was his real gift. He was giving her power. He trusted her with his heart just as she had trusted him with her body and soul.

'Come with me,' she said. 'Travelling. You can paint anywhere, can't you? Come with me.'

'But it's your big adventure.'

'And I want to share it with you.' That was what had been holding her back. Her dream travels seemed ash grey when she contemplated doing it alone. She wanted to share each discovery, each experience with Gael. She wanted him to tease her, to push her, to make her feel, to stretch herself. 'I have done since I booked it. I knew I should be excited but instead every time I thought about getting on that plane, flying away from you, I felt sick with dread.'

'You really want me along?'

'Always.' She put her hand on his shoulder and instantly knew she was home, that no matter where she was in the world if he was there she would be settled. 'When Faith told me she was marrying someone she barely knew I thought she was crazy. Well, people will tell me I'm crazy, that two weeks is nothing at all, but I have lived a lifetime in the last fortnight. A lifetime with you. It wasn't always easy or comfortable but for the first time in a long time I was alive. You brought me to life. I didn't think that I knew what love was, that I was capable of it, that I deserved it, but you have made me change my mind. I love you, Gael. I love you and I want to spend the rest of my life having adventures with you.'

His eyes had darkened to a midnight blue as he pulled her in close, caressing her with light scorching kisses along her brow, her cheeks, her mouth. Hope pressed herself as close as she could, her hands holding on tightly as if she would never, ever let go. And she wouldn't; this man was hers. She knew it with every fibre of her being and her body thrilled with ownership. He was hers and she was his.

'I love you,' he said, the words catching in his throat. 'I didn't want to, I fought against it but I think I loved you from the first moment you unleashed your outrage on me.'

'I'd barely said hello and you asked me to strip,' she protested. 'Gael, will you come with me? I don't want to be away from you, from us, but I don't want to walk away from a chance to do something new again. If I don't travel now I never will.'

'On one condition.' He smiled into her eyes. 'Monday you put on that dress and we go to City Hall and get married. I'll need to be in New York in three weeks for the exhibition launch party but otherwise I'm yours for the next year. For the rest of my life. What do you say?'

'I say you'd better ask me properly.'

She was only teasing but Gael stepped back, dropping to one knee, like a picture from a fairy tale. Hope's heart stuttered with longing and love as he took her hand in his. 'You'd better say yes now I'm down here.'

'Ask the question and then I'll be able to answer.'

'Hope McKenzie. Would you do me the honour—the very great honour of being my wife?'

She didn't answer straight away, taking a moment to take in the devilish glint in his eye mingling with the love and tenderness radiating from him. Hope dropped down to kneel in front of him, taking his face in her hands as she did so. 'Yes. Yes, I will. Always.' And as she leant in to kiss him she knew that her adventures were only just beginning and that she would never be lonely again, not while she had Gael by her side.

* * * * *

HER MAN IN MANHATTAN

TRISH WYLIE

CHAPTER ONE

TYLER wasn't the only guy watching her. It was just a shame he didn't want to be there and resented the living hell out of the fact he didn't have a choice.

If things had been different he could enjoy the view.

Pinpricks of sparkling light swirled over the dance floor as she sashayed sideways and made a sexy rotation of her hips. She had a body made for sin: tall, slender, with full breasts and flawless, sun-kissed skin. Raising bared arms above her head lifted the hem of her silver minidress, exposing several more inches of delectably long legs encased in white platform-heeled knee-high boots. Add the sleek bob of a snowy wig, which covered her trademark hair, to darkly made-up eyes and ruby-red lips and she would make a fortune dancing on a dais.

When she bent her knees and shimmied downwards—rising with an effortlessly fluid curve of her spine—he didn't have difficulty picturing her with a spotlight following her every move. Judging by the fun she'd had fending off potential dance partners she would probably get a kick out of it. But despite her obvious comfort in the centre of so much male attention she stood out of the writhing mass of humanity too much for his liking. She was lucky no one had recognized her and if there was one thing Tyler knew, it was luck had a tendency to run out.

Even for the Irish.

Without warning her gaze collided into his with a pinpoint accuracy, which made it feel as if she'd known he was there all along. The impact created a sudden flare of heat in his body, like a spark igniting a fuse. Refusing to accept it was anything but the natural biological reaction of red-blooded male to hot female, he held his ground and waited to see what she would do next.

Rolling her shoulders and hips, she ran the tip of her tongue over glossy lips and smiled a slow, sensual smile. The silent come-on might have summoned him to the dance floor if he'd ever danced a day in his life. But even if he had he wasn't the kind of guy who came running when a woman crooked an invisible finger. If she wanted to come talk to him she could slide on over. A corner of his mouth lifted.

He was willing to bet she'd be pleased as punch when she found out who she'd been flirting with.

When something was yelled in her ear by her friend she laughed and turned away. A moment later she flashed another smile over her shoulder and swayed, drawing his gaze to the curve of her rear.

Tyler dragged his gaze away. It didn't take a genius to work out she was going to be trouble. He'd known *that* before he laid eyes on her.

Lifting the beer bottle in his hand, he took a long pull and frowned at the label in disgust as he swallowed. Light anything had never been his style; when associated with the word beer it was just all kinds of wrong.

As he experienced a visceral demand from his body to watch her again he forced his gaze elsewhere. Even if he was officially on the clock he wasn't paid to watch her every move. He had to focus on his surroundings; survey the room for potential threats and monitor the crowd. Being attracted to her was a problem he didn't need, especially when it felt as if they'd been tumbling down on him like boulders after a landslide of late.

He missed the days when he had more control over his life. How had it got so screwed up?

When it came to why he was standing there the path was easy to track. A guy had a friendly word of warning for one low life too many and suddenly the brass were tossing around phrases like 'desk duty' and 'temporary leave of absence.' Granted, the fact he was unrepentant probably had something to do with it, but what he still didn't get was why his punishment involved babysitting.

Despite his ability to provide what she was looking for, he had better things to do with his time than spend it reining in an entitled rich kid in search of a few thrills to liven up her—

A familiar face caught his gaze as the music changed to a faster beat and raised an enthusiastic cheer from the crowd. Immediately on alert, Tyler swiftly scanned the rest of the room, targeting two more likely subjects before he hit another face he recognized.

He had to get her out of there.

Setting the bottle down on the nearest table, he looked at the dance floor and frowned when he discovered she wasn't there. Gripping the brass railing in front of him, he played a short game of Where's Waldo? before locating her on her way to the bar with her friend. After checking the nearest exit point, he headed straight for her.

He was two steps away when the music stopped and voices yelled out, *'NYPD. Everyone stay where you are!'*

With her focus on what was happening on the other side of the room, she jumped in surprise as he grabbed her hand. Her eyes widened when she looked up at him. 'What—?'

'This way.'

She tugged against his hold as he dragged her towards the exit. 'Let me go!'

'You want to get arrested?'

'No, but—'

'Then follow my lead.'

Hauling open the door, he stepped them into a dimly lit hallway and looked from side to side. A lightning-fast inventory revealed restrooms, a payphone, steps to what Tyler assumed was a basement on their left and enough banging from the right to indicate they were about to have company. The basement was the most viable option if it had a loading bay that opened onto the sidewalk, but before he could check he heard a crash. Out of time and in need of a distraction, he backed her into the wall and smashed his lips against hers.

Big mistake.

The fuse she'd lit from the dance floor set off the equivalent of an explosive charge. Plumes of fire engulfed him, incinerating rational thought as the invitation of her parted lips was met with the instinctual thrust of his tongue. Need pulsed through his body as an appreciative moan vibrated in her throat. His hand gripped her hip and slid lower. In response she lifted her leg off the ground and hooked it around the back of his knee, allowing him to cradle a silky thigh and lift it higher.

It didn't matter if they were seconds away from being discovered in a highly compromised position. If anything it immediately turned his thoughts to the position his body desperately wanted to be in—his imagination adding fuel to the fire with the suggestion her underwear was as sexy as her dress. Or, better still, non-existent.

'You seeing this?' a voice asked.

'Hey! Break it up over there,' another voice demanded.

Wrenching his mouth free, Tyler hauled in much needed air before squinting at the beams of light aimed their way. Allowing the leg he was holding to lower to the floor he took a step forwards to block her body with his.

'Stay right where you are, buddy,' the first voice said in warning.

Recognizing who it was, Tyler raised his arms at his sides, palms forwards, and waited for the penny to drop with the heavily armed cop. Since silently willing the younger man not to do anything stupid was pointless when saying the words out loud had never had any effect, he added an almost imperceptible shake of his head. When the torch nodded a little he assumed the point had been made and lowered his arms. But when it moved in an attempt to see who was behind him Tyler frowned. 'Problem, Officer?'

'You know there's a raid going on next door?'

'Can't say I'd noticed...'

'We can guess why.' The cop cleared his throat before asking, 'Do we need to search you two for narcotics?'

Funny guy. 'What we're high on doesn't have anything to do with drugs.' Tyler smirked.

A fine-boned hand snaked around his arm and flattened on his chest. 'Can we get arrested for not being able to keep our hands off each other?' the woman behind him asked in a passable, not to mention sultry Southern accent.

Tyler made a note of the fact it obviously wasn't the first time she'd acted her way out of a tricky situation. 'If we can I'm willing to do the time.' He glanced over his shoulder. 'How about you?'

'Are there co-ed jails in the state of New York?' She chuckled throatily, the sound strumming across the taut strings of his libido. 'Just think how much fun we could have sharing a room.'

When she gently caught his ear lobe between her teeth and touched it with the wet tip of her tongue, he felt the impact of the contact all the way to his toes.

'Getting a room *somewhere* sounds like a plan to me,' the officer in front of them said before he lowered his torch. 'Get outta here before I change my mind.'

Grasping hold of the hand on his chest, Tyler headed down the hall and through the busted door. As they entered an alley bathed in flashing red and blue lights one of the cops by a line of vehicles lowered his hand from the radio on his shoulder and waved them through. If he'd been her, he would have had questions about the ease of their escape, but apparently she was too busy jogging on her platform heels to keep up with his determined stride to ask.

'My friend—'

'Unless she's carrying drugs she'll be fine.'

When she tripped he simply tugged on her hand and kept walking, the anger he felt directed as much at himself as her. He could still taste her on his lips: a combination of strawberries, spice and liberation. He couldn't remember a time he'd wanted a woman so badly he would have risked everything for a brief moment of mutual release. What he *could* remember were the days when his timing—not to mention his judgment—had been better.

'Where are we going?' she asked a little breathlessly as they rounded a corner onto a wide street where they stood a better chance of finding a cab.

If she'd been any other woman who reacted the way she had when he kissed her, they'd be headed straight for his place. But he couldn't use her to make him feel good for a few hours even if he made certain she felt the same way. Until he completed his assignment, went back to where he was supposed to be and handed out some justice, he didn't have the right to live his life as if nothing had happened.

To focus his mind he summoned the memory of another woman's face and the words he'd said to her. *'I won't let anything happen to you,'* he'd lied. *'You can trust me.'*

'I'm not taking you anywhere.' When he spotted a flash of yellow he raised an arm in the air to flag down the cab. 'He is.' Digging in his pocket for a handful of bills as the vehicle drew to a halt beside the kerb, he handed them through the window to the driver. 'That should cover it.'

He held open the rear door and waited for her to get inside, his gaze lowered to watch long legs fold gracefully into place before he looked into the shadows of her eyes.

'I don't get a name?' she asked.

'You already have one.'

Her mouth curved into a smile. 'I meant *your* name.'

Tyler shook his head at the liquid cadence of her voice. Next she'd be asking for a phone number and when she could see him again. It was all just one big game to her. He could have been anyone—drug dealer, kidnapper, serial killer—she had no idea how dark the world could be.

But he did.

'You're welcome.' He closed the door and turned away without mentioning she'd be seeing him again real soon.

Why ruin the surprise?

Since it was the last one she'd have in a while, he hoped she'd enjoyed her little adventure. Come Monday she would be playing by *his* rules.

Cross him and he'd make her sorry they ever met.

CHAPTER TWO

AFTER checking that Crystal made it out of the nightclub okay and apologizing profusely for abandoning her, Miranda spent the rest of the weekend fantasizing about her rescuer.

She'd felt his gaze on her before she saw him, which was rare for someone who had spent most of her life being watched. Understandably curious she'd sought him out, her breath catching when she laid eyes on him.

He was the most compelling man she'd ever seen.

From what she could tell he was handsome in a rough-edged kind of way, but that wasn't what made him exciting. What *did* was that even while standing tall and straight he gave the impression of a predator crouched to spring on its prey. Brazenly answering his interest in her with a smile of encouragement had felt like playing with fire, the associated rush of adrenaline addictive.

And when it came to that kiss, *oh, my...*

Smoothing her palms over her elegantly tailored linen dress, she followed the curve from breast to waist to hip. She closed her eyes and allowed herself to imagine the hands touching her body were larger and more masculine; a deep voice was rumbling in her ear, describing everything he was going to do to her in explicit detail.

A sigh of regret left her lips.

If they hadn't been interrupted…

None of her small acts of rebellion had ever given her the same rush she got when she thought about doing more than kissing him. But how would she find him again in a city the size of New York when she didn't know his name?

A familiar three-tapped knock on her bedroom door snapped her out of her reverie.

'Come in,' she called as she stepped over to sit on the stool in front of her dressing table.

'Good morning, Miranda.'

'Good morning, Grace,' she answered cheerfully when her father's personal assistant appeared. 'Isn't it a beautiful morning? The park looks lovely from the windows. I don't suppose there's enough of a gap in my schedule today to allow for a leisurely stroll?'

'No.' Grace's reflection smiled apologetically. 'But at least you'll be outside for a while.'

'Well, that's something.'

While Miranda attached small pearl-drop earrings to her lobes, the ever efficient fifty-something who had been in her life for so long she'd become a kind of maiden aunt opened her file and got down to business.

'You have a nine a.m. appointment for a dress fitting with Ms Wang. At ten you're due at a community project in the Bronx with time for a meet-and-greet before morning coffee. At eleven-thirty—'

'Do you think the world would come to an end if we took a day off?' Miranda mused as she added a flawless string of pearls to her neck and fluffed her hair into place. 'We could pack a picnic, grab a handful of gossip magazines and spend the morning people watching…'

When she nodded enthusiastically in the mirror Grace closed her file. 'Before or after you go through the Help Wanted ads with me?'

'One little day,' Miranda cajoled with a pout and a flutter of long lashes.

'Your father would like to see you before you leave.'

'Ten bucks says it's a reminder to kiss babies.'

'I don't think they're eligible to vote.'

'No. But with any luck they'll have fathers there for me to

flirt with or mothers for me to charm with talk of how much I want kids of my own one day.' Pushing to her feet, she lifted her bag and shoes and linked their arms at the elbows as they crossed the room.

It was the kind of simple human contact she didn't stop to think about with Grace. She'd heard somewhere people needed eighteen inches of personal space but for most of Miranda's life the distance had been greater. Hence a small part of why the memory of full bodily contact with a virile male was so hard to shake, most likely.

Not that there weren't other reasons.

'It's remiss of me not to have produced a suitable grandchild by now,' she continued in the same bright tone. 'Chubby toddlers are always a hit with the electorate.'

'If you start planning ahead you could schedule it for the whispered campaign for Governor.'

'Always best to keep something in reserve.' Miranda nodded in agreement. She smiled as they stepped into the hall. 'Good morning, Roger. Is that a new tie?'

'Wife bought it for my birthday,' her father's press secretary replied with an answering smile.

'She has excellent taste.'

'Speaking of spouses, finding a husband before you have that chubby toddler might be a good idea,' Grace whispered conspiratorially.

Miranda leaned closer to whisper back, 'I've heard you don't have to have one to get the other.'

'You do when your father's the mayor.'

Another face in the hallway earned another smile. 'Good morning, Lou. How was the Little League game?'

'Two strikes and a home run,' her father's head of security replied with the swing of an invisible bat.

'Tell Tommy I said *"yay,"*' she replied with a ladylike punch to the air.

'Shoes,' Grace reminded her outside the door to her father's study.

'What would I do without you?'

'Run barefoot and be late for appointments.'

'Now doesn't that sound like fun?' She handed over her bag for safekeeping, slipped on her heels and took a step back to turn a circle. 'Am I ready for inspection?'

'You'll do.'

After a light knock on the door, she waited for the cursory 'come' and turned the handle.

'Ah, here she is,' her father said from behind his mahogany desk as she crossed the room. 'Miranda, this is Detective Brannigan. He'll be overseeing your security during the remainder of the campaign.'

Though unaware there were any changes planned, she kept a smile in place as she waited for the man to stand up and turn around. Her first impression was of his size; he was six feet two, possibly three, his build more running back than linebacker. Many people would have been surprised by that—when they thought bodyguard they pictured brute force—but while physical strength and fitness were both important the members of her family's protective details came in many shapes and sizes. Keen observation skills and an ability to think on their feet were of equal importance.

Any following thought on the subject disappeared in a flash and was instantly replaced by shock when she looked into cobalt-blue eyes. It took every ounce of her social skills to prevent the drop of her jaw.

'Miss Kravitz,' he said in a low rumbling baritone as her hand was engulfed in a firm handshake.

It wasn't what she'd fantasized he would say if they met again but the sound of his voice was enough to remind her of every imagined word. She peeled her tongue off the roof of her mouth as heat suffused her palm and rushed up her arm. Had he known who she was when he came to her rescue? Had he been watching her because he was on duty? How long had he been following her?

As she remembered to reclaim her hand and lowered it to her side—his touch still tingling on her skin—her gaze shifted to her father. There was no way to determine how much trouble she was in while he was wearing his elected official expression but if he was upset about something it was a new tactic. Usually the punishment for her supposed misdemeanors involved a lecture on responsibility—the kind she liked to think she'd endured stoically over the years.

'He'll report to Lou the same way Ron did,' he said. 'They've selected a new detail for you.'

All of her guys had been replaced—since when and, more to the point, *why?*

'Detective Brannigan suggested a shake-up,' he added so she knew who to blame.

While he turned his attention to some of the papers on his desk she looked at the man beside her to see if the reality lived up to her fantasy. Strong masculine features—short, dark blond hair, thick lashes framing his intense eyes. He was every bit as compelling as she remembered. Seeing him again reawakened the potent sensual awareness in her body. It transported her back in time to when he'd kissed her into a boneless puddle of lust and walked away.

Now she thought about it Miranda wasn't certain she'd forgiven him for that. Particularly when it was more than obvious he still had the upper hand. She'd wondered how he managed to get them past a cordon of New York's finest with such ease. In her furtive imagination he'd been everything from a mafia don with cops on his payroll to a combination of secretive billionaire by day and caped crusader by night. That he was *with* the NYPD made more sense but why hadn't he said so? Why the charade? Why kiss her instead of flashing a badge?

He blinked lazily hooded eyes. 'I believe you have a nine a.m. appointment.'

Miranda ignored him and rounded the desk to place a kiss on her father's cheek. 'Bye, Daddy.'

'Bye sweetheart. Have a good day.'

'You, too,' she replied before lifting her chin as she walked back across the room. '*Now* we can leave.'

In a few long strides he'd overtaken her and held open the

door but she didn't thank him for the courtesy while she was piqued by his duplicity.

'New bodyguard?' Grace whispered as she handed over her bag and a copy of the day's itinerary.

Miranda crinkled her nose in mock delight. *'Lucky me.'*

She led the way down the second-floor landing, past a rare five-seat settee that had been discovered in the basement of City Hall. Despite living in the mansion for the two terms her father had been mayor she never took her surroundings for granted. If anything the combination of rare paintings and antiques interspersed with modern furniture reminded her of what a privilege it was to live in one of the few surviving eighteenth-century mansions in the city. It was something she could appreciate more approaching twenty-five than she had at seventeen. But unlike most mornings she didn't take the time to greet any of her favorite pieces with a smile or to mull over her continuing need to escape such a beautifully gilded cage.

She was too distracted by the man walking behind her, her body highly tuned to his presence.

They were halfway down the carpeted stairs before she lowered her voice to ask, 'Did you know who I was?'

'Yes.'

'Did my father order you to follow me?'

'No.'

She smiled at the woman making her way upstairs. 'Good morning, Dorothy. Is it as beautiful outside as it looks through the window?'

'It is,' the maid replied with an answering smile.

The tension became heavier with each muted downward step while Miranda tried to pretend she couldn't feel an intense gaze following her every move. There was no way she could spend every day in the company of a man she'd pictured naked…and sweaty…and as aroused as he'd left her after one little kiss. She had a reputation for being cool, calm and poised in public. She wasn't about to exchange it for hot, bothered and sexually frustrated. It wasn't as if the discovery he was—*technically speaking*—a 'good guy' had done anything to dilute her fantasy, either. Even while wearing a dark suit, white shirt and patriotically striped tie he oozed the danger she'd craved since her late teens.

Skydiving, bungee jumping, swimming with sharks—they were all on an ever-growing wish list of forbidden pursuits she'd added to over the years.

Making wild, crazy whoopee with one of her bodyguards had never crossed her mind, *until now.*

Her heels clicked on the exquisitely refurbished faux marble patterning of the wooden floor in the foyer. In a matter of seconds they would be in the vestibule, away from the constantly moving crowd that never quite managed to make her feel less alone. They could take advantage of the moment and pick up where they'd left off. He would grab her hand and swing her around, press her against the wall with his muscled body, crush her lips beneath his and…

Miranda gave herself a mental smack upside the head. She needed to focus. The brief alone time they had between inner and outer doors should be used to reclaim some of the control over her life she couldn't afford to relinquish. She hadn't been fighting for her freedom so someone new could stride in and clip her wings before she had a chance to stretch them. With that in mind, the second the first door closed behind them she turned to face him.

'As it's your first day I think we should lay out some ground rules….'

'I agree.' He nodded. 'So shut up and listen.'

Miranda gaped at him in disbelief. 'You can't talk to me like that.'

'What you mean is no one else ever has, right?' He didn't wait for an answer. 'I'm willing to bet folks have been kowtowing to you since you were in diapers.' The forwards step he took seemed to suck all the air out of the vestibule. 'What you need to learn quick-smart is I don't kowtow to anyone,' he said in a low, mesmerizing rumble. 'I'm here to do a job. Make that more difficult for me than it needs to be, things will get ugly.' He jerked his brows. 'You feel me?'

Did she—? She blinked. 'I beg your pardon?'

'No begging necessary,' he replied with a small shake of his head. 'Just be a good girl and do as you're told and we'll be golden.'

'You know I can have you removed from this position?'

'Good luck with that. I've been trying to get out of it for a week.' He reached past her, held open the outer door and inclined his head. 'After you, princess.'

A dazed Miranda stepped through the door, her gaze locked on broad shoulders as he overtook her on the gravel driveway. While there was no denying part of her buzzed with the titillating after-effects of his forceful tone, another was mildly outraged. No one had ever spoken to her that way. Who did he think he was?

She narrowed her eyes. It didn't matter who he was. He was about to discover she wouldn't be easily intimidated. She was a politician's daughter. Everything she needed to know about hiding her emotions she'd learned from masters of disguising how they felt. Summoning an air of poise, she reached into her bag for a pair of oversize sunglasses and her cell phone. If he thought he was dealing with a spoilt princess she would give him exactly what he expected. Covering her eyes, she hit speed dial.

'Good morning, darling, how are you?' She purposefully spoke loud enough to be overheard. 'My day has got off to the most *dreadful* start.'

'The Queen of England called and said she wanted her accent back?' Crystal sighed dramatically. 'You're standing me up for lunch, aren't you?'

Miranda smiled smoothly. 'Absolutely not.'

It didn't matter if he was a walking sex fantasy. She planned on ditching her new bodyguard by noon.

CHAPTER THREE

'I ASSUME Detective isn't your first name.'

Tyler glanced in the rear-view mirror. She'd given him the silent treatment since they left the mayor's residence and he'd have been happy for it to stay that way. He wasn't there to make small talk. He was there to keep her safe and out of trouble; something the guys on her previous detail could have done with remembering more often.

'I'll ask Lou,' her honeyed voice said in a dismissive tone when he didn't reply. 'He's a sweetheart.'

Somehow Tyler doubted she'd think so if she knew the mayor's head of security was a big part of the reason he was there. It had been Lou Mitchell's bright idea to draft in someone who hadn't been doing the job for so long they took things for granted or was easily distracted by a pretty face. That Tyler wasn't prepared to be subtle didn't seem to be a problem, which was just as well considering where he'd been drafted *from.*

The next time he glanced in the mirror she'd placed her sunglasses on top of her head and was idly twirling a lock of hair as she read the screen of her BlackBerry. She might have been hot while wearing a disguise but without one she was a stone-cold knockout. Her skin-coloured dress left little to the imagination even with a demure neckline and its hem a respectable couple of inches above her knees. Fitted the way it was—to lovingly follow every curve of her damn-near-perfect body—it had drawn his gaze to her more often than he should have allowed.

The hair she was toying with was a particular source of

fascination: lustrous, tumbling tresses of flame blended with sunlight. He could have said his interest in it stemmed from curiosity—how had she got that much hair under a short wig?—but he'd have been lying. The truth was he didn't know why he found it so fascinating. He just did.

But the packaging didn't make up for her personality.

A few hours of watching her in action was all it took to confirm what he'd already suspected. What surprised him was how easily she fooled everyone else. When they got to the second hit of the day and she stepped into a community project for the elderly she pulled out all the stops. A flash of her hundred-watt smile, a few carefully chosen sound bites, the brush of elegant hands over selected arms and she was treated like a combination of visiting European royalty and prodigal granddaughter. By the time she left he suspected there wasn't anyone she came into contact with who didn't believe she genuinely cared what they had to say.

The folks out in Hollywood earned a gold statue for that kind of performance.

His next glance in the mirror revealed she'd shifted her attention from her hair to the pearls around her neck. The fine-boned forefinger tracing them stilled and then she blinked darkened lashes, her hazel-eyed gaze crashing into his before he returned his attention to the road.

'What was your last assignment?' she enquired after another moment of silence.

'You want a copy of my CV so you can get your friend Lou to pull my jacket?'

'Your jacket?'

'My file.' He made a turn and merged the Escalade into three lanes of busy traffic when he heard a sound. 'What are you doing?'

'It's unusually stuffy in here.'

'That's why they invented air-con.' Reaching forwards to hit the switch, he frowned when he glanced in the mirror and discovered she was leaning her face towards the open window. 'And that glass is tinted for a reason.'

'As disappointing as I'm sure it is for you,' she replied haughtily, 'I'm not high on anyone's hit list.'

'You've never read any of the letters that land at your father's office, have you?' Tyler hit another switch to slide the window shut and waited for the answer he already knew.

'We have people who do that.'

'Course you do,' he said dryly while he steered into the middle lane of traffic on Fifth Avenue.

When he drew to a smooth halt at a crossing there was a gasp from the rear seat. 'What a gorgeous dress!'

Though he'd been ready for her to try something the sound of a door being opened caught him off guard. He turned around in his seat. 'Don't get out of—'

Too late. She smiled brightly as she grabbed her bag. 'I'll meet you back here in an hour.' Next thing he knew the door slammed and she was skipping her light-footed way to the sidewalk.

Tyler's seat belt was unbuckled when the light changed, the honking of horns forcing him to ram the Escalade back into gear. With one eye on the traffic and another on where she was headed, he cut across a lane and swung around the corner. It might have taken five minutes of screeching tyres to get there but by the time she exited the rear of the store he was casually leaning against the side of the vehicle with his arms crossed.

The victorious smile on her face faded the instant she saw him. 'How did you—?'

'Clue's in the word *detective*.' He pushed upright and opened the rear door. As she reached him he swung it shut in her face. 'Which part of our talk this morning wasn't clear to you?'

She angled her chin and looked him straight in the eye. 'Which part of your job description suggested you were the boss in this relationship?'

'Who exactly is it you think I work for?'

'You're *my* bodyguard.'

'The city pays my wage.'

'Is there a bonus for being a pain in the ass?' She smiled sweetly.

'Where were you going?'

'That's none of your business.'

'Yeah, it is.' He reached into his pocket for a folded piece of paper and held it up in front of her face. "Cos if it's not on here, you don't get to go there....'

'It's a free country. I can go where I want.'

Tyler wondered how much effort it had taken not to stamp her foot. 'Let's check the schedule, shall we?'

She crossed her arms as he shrugged back the sleeve of his jacket to consult his watch. 'Eleven fifty-seven.' He glanced over the sheet of paper and shook his head. 'Nope, can't see anything on here about playing hide-and-seek. Maybe yours is different from mine.' His gaze locked with hers again. 'Since we've established other people do the reading for you, maybe I should check that one, too.'

'You carry a gun, right?' she asked with a completely dead-pan expression.

Two as it happened but she didn't need to know that. 'You gonna make me use it?'

'I was going to ask if I can borrow it.'

Drawing in a long breath, Tyler refolded the paper and put it back in his pocket. 'If I were you I wouldn't waste time thinking up ways to cut me loose. This is strike one. Three strikes and you won't get to visit a restroom alone.'

'Your last assignment was at Guantanamo, wasn't it?'

The old Tyler might have laughed at the comment. The one standing in front of her simply leaned closer and informed her, 'I'm in your life now. Get used to it.'

The flecks of gold that flared in her eyes hinted at a temper to match her hair. For a split second he wanted her to get mad enough to swing for him—to spit fire and passion and remind him of the woman he'd kissed.

As if sensing a weakness ripe for exploitation she switched tactics. The curve of her full lips became sinful, drawing his gaze to her mouth and calling him to taste her again. She slowly ran the tip of her tongue over the surface, leaving a hypnotically glossy sheen in its wake.

In an instant he remembered how she'd felt when her body was melded to his, how soft her skin had been beneath his fingertips and how badly he'd burned for her. Just as suddenly he was aware of how close they were standing. One more step and their bodies would be touching again.

It took almost as much effort not to frown at his reaction as it did to snap his gaze back up to her eyes. 'That won't work either, so you can forget it.'

'I have no idea what you mean.'

Sure she didn't. He reached for the door handle and jerked his chin. 'Back up a step.'

The order was met with a defiant lack of movement, her luminous eyes narrowed in thought. 'Is my father aware of how you got me out of the nightclub?'

Tyler's arm dropped. He'd wondered how long it would take for her to go there but if she thought she could use it against him, she was wrong. 'You want to tell him where you were?'

'He doesn't know?'

'I thought the mayor was supposed to know everything that goes on in his city.'

'You didn't answer the question.'

'Didn't I?'

The battle of wills made the air between them crackle and when her gaze briefly flickered to his mouth Tyler knew *that kiss* was as much on her mind as it had been on his. Her awareness of him was in the darkening of her eyes, in the increased rise and fall of her breasts. Any hope he'd had that what happened between them could be blamed on the heat of the moment was gone. But while he'd lost his self-control once he wasn't about to let it happen again.

'You getting in or am I putting you there?'

'You can't manhandle me like a common criminal,' she replied on a note of outrage.

'Try me.'

She glared at him as she took a step back. *'Door.'*

Tyler held it open, unable to resist an incline of his head and a sweep of his arm in invitation. 'Your Highness…'

CHAPTER FOUR

HIS attitude *sucked.*

'What is his problem?' Miranda asked as she paced her bedroom floor with her cell phone glued to her ear.

'He's rude, overbearing and obviously doesn't know his place,' Crystal replied.

'*Obviously,* but that's not what I meant. It's like I've done something to him way worse than making him open a stupid door.'

'He's *supposed* to open doors.'

'He is.' Miranda agreed. 'It's courteous.'

'It is. And how dare he speak to you that way?'

'I know, right?'

Having allowed her the customary five minutes to rant, Crystal called a halt with 'Can we stop being the mean girls from high school now?'

'Do we have to?'

'Yes,' she replied firmly. 'You were never that girl. Now take a deep breath and tell Auntie Crystal what the real problem is.'

Miranda stopped pacing and dropped heavily onto the end of her bed. 'I don't like him.'

'You liked him on Friday night,' Crystal crooned.

'That's when he wasn't a brick wall standing between me and—'

'All those nasty sex fantasies you had about him over the weekend?'

Flopping back onto the soft covers, Miranda blinked at the

ceiling and sighed heavily. 'There are at least three people I could have called who'll tell me what I want to hear right now. And yet I still called *you.* Why is that?'

'I'm your reality check,' she said in a matter-of-fact tone. 'The only reason you don't like him now is because he's switched sides. Up till this morning he was part of your dream to do what—or *who*—you want, whenever you want. Now he's part of the system keeping you in servitude.'

'I hate that,' Miranda admitted reluctantly.

'Of course you do. No one likes to have a sex fantasy ruined by reality. We all prefer to live in hope.'

'I was *really* hopeful,' Miranda said wistfully.

'And I really wanted to hear all the sordid details over lunch,' her best friend complained. 'I can't believe you let this guy outwit you.'

'I still have a few tricks up my sleeve.'

'You learnt from the best.'

'You're a bad influence.'

'I *am,*' Crystal said with pride.

'Which if you recall is part of the reason you're not my father's favourite person.'

'He's just never gonna let that reality-TV-show thing go, is he?' she said in a tone that suggested she'd rolled her eyes. 'You were on camera for like, five seconds.'

'Might have helped if I wasn't dancing on a table at the time.'

'Does he have something against people having fun?'

It was an old debate. One Miranda knew she would never win with Mayor Kravitz. As far as *hizzoner* was concerned Crystal was a publicity nightmare: rich, overindulged, and for a considerable amount of time, out of control. She might since have moved on to a lucrative career of celebrity endorsements but when her fame stemmed from notoriety…

Frankly Miranda found it a little insulting he thought she could be so easily led. If she chose to she could get into trouble all on her lonesome. She didn't need *help.* What she needed was the freedom to do what she wanted without her actions becoming fodder for the gossip hungry.

The thought added to her restlessness. She needed to get out for a while before the walls started to close in. Turning her head on the covers, she checked the alarm clock by her bed. 'I'll be at your door in a half hour.'

'Are you going to rant some more when you get here?'

'Probably,' she admitted.

'Awesome. I'll open the wine. By the time you arrive I should be two glasses more sympathetic to your plight.'

Miranda wriggled upright, tucked her phone into the back pocket of her skinny jeans with some cash and pushed her feet into a waiting pair of deck shoes. Twisting her hair into a pony-tail, she grabbed a baseball cap from one drawer and sunglasses from the collection in another. Ready for action she opened her bedroom door and checked the hall. Once she confirmed it was empty her lucky music talisman started playing in her head.

It wouldn't be the first time a combination of wits, observa-tion and an extensive study of spy movies was put to good use. As a result she knew to time her progress downstairs; to wait for the turn of the security cameras to take advantage of blind spots. She also knew the best window of opportunity for escape was at shift-change time, when the security details gathered to hand over the baton. At the foot of the stairs she stopped and held her breath, waiting for the last squeaking footsteps to disappear into the back of the house before she jogged across the foyer.

As usual the kitchen was deserted.

A bubble of exhilaration formed in her chest as she made it to the short hallway at the other side of the room. Tantalizingly close to the exit and secure in the knowledge she had an ally on the gate outside, she allowed the music in her head to become a low rhythm on the tip of her tongue. But as she reached for the handle a loud crunch made her still.

When she turned around Detective Party Pooper was leaning against the larder door with an apple in his hand.

'The *Mission Impossible* theme is appropriate,' he said with his mouth full.

Miranda gritted her teeth. 'What are you doing here?'

'Overtime,' he replied with a nonchalant shrug of broad

shoulders. 'Reckoned I'd keep an eye on things till the rest of the new detail is up to speed.'

How diligent of him.

She noted his appearance: the lack of a jacket, the loosened tie below an unbuttoned collar, the rolled up sleeves over tanned muscular forearms. When her pulse sped up she ignored it, refusing to have a physical reaction to his presence when she disliked him so much. Instead she focused on how quickly he'd settled in—standing there as if he owned the place and had been there forever.

'I'm trying to decide if this counts as another strike when you haven't left the building yet.' He nodded firmly. 'I'll get back to you on that.'

When he nudged off the wall and went into the kitchen Miranda fought the need to growl. She hadn't thrown a hissy fit since she was eight and denied a puppy, but it was tempting after a day in his company. Aiming a longing glance at the exit she sighed heavily and retraced her steps. He was standing at the island in the middle of the room when she walked in, casually flipping over the pages of a newspaper.

'No disguise,' he commented without looking at her. 'Means you were going somewhere people know you.' Another page of the newspaper flipped over. 'Narrows it down some…'

Miranda swore she would never kiss another handsome stranger. She'd learned her lesson. They could turn into frogs. Now if her fairy godmother could just drop a bolt of lightning out of the sky and incinerate him, she promised to be a very good girl for a very long time. Even if she'd already been there and felt she'd earned a break.

In the absence of magical intervention she considered the options left open to her. She'd be damned if she was retreating to her bedroom. Neither was she staying for a friendly chat over coffee the way she used to with the members of the team she'd *liked.* Giving him anything resembling an order obviously wasn't going to work and she sincerely doubted any attempt at negotiation would end in anything but a migraine.

'I was going to stretch my legs,' she said when the silence began to bother her.

He shook his head as he turned another page. 'Lying sways you closer to strike two.'

'I'm glad the trust part of this relationship is going so well.'

'Stop treating the guys in this unit like idiots and they might trust you a lot quicker.'

Miranda bristled at the accusation. 'You've been here five minutes. You don't know anything about—'

'How many of them do you reckon you got fired?'

'I…' Miranda faltered and frowned at the hesitation. She hadn't got anyone fired. If she had she would have done something to fix it. 'The bodyguards who left the mansion *chose* to leave.'

'Ever ask yourself why?'

She lifted her chin. 'Mac said he missed riding in a squad car.'

She'd liked Mac. He was a straight-up guy. Happily married with a young family, he'd done a lot of community policing when he left the academy and said he wanted to get back to it. They'd joked around about the squad car but when it came down to it he missed being in a position where he could talk to people. She understood that but was sorry to see him go. Unlike *some* people, he'd been really good about letting her make unscheduled stops for shopping or lunch when she needed to take a breather. On his last day she'd given him season tickets for the Giants because he loved football so much. She leaned back against the counter and folded her arms. Detective Smarty-pants knew squat.

'Yeah, those things are a real sweet ride compared to the low-spec models you have parked outside.' His gaze lifted. 'Don't know much about guys and cars, do you?'

'I'm reliably informed there's a little more to your job than the toys which go with it.' She nodded at the gun holstered at his lean waist beside his shield. 'It would be nice to think they don't hand those out to everyone who thinks it's cool to carry one.'

When he studied her more intently the memory of how he'd looked at her in the alley that morning entered her mind. For a second she'd thought he was going to kiss her again. A few hours in his company was all it had taken to dissolve her fantasy. At least she'd *thought* it had. But for that long stretched-out moment—as irritated as she'd been by him—she'd wanted him to kiss her.

He raised his right arm and tossed what was left of the apple through the air. As it dropped neatly into a swing-top trash can at the end of the counter he grabbed his jacket off the countertop. 'Come on, then.'

Miranda's eyes narrowed. 'Where are we going?'

'Said you wanted to go for a walk, didn't you?'

'I don't need your permission.'

'No,' he said in a low voice as he turned towards her. 'But since you don't get to go alone, either I go with you or you go back to your room—*your call.*'

'Even if it's not on the itinerary?'

'Why do you think we stick to that schedule?'

Miranda lifted her gaze to the ceiling. 'Gee, that's a tough one.' She looked into his eyes again. 'But I'm going to guess it's so I know where I'm supposed to be at certain times of the day.'

'There's another reason.'

She batted her lashes. 'So the people I'm going to see know I'll be there?'

'Try again.'

'So you know where to drive me?' She pouted.

She didn't mention it was the tip of an iceberg that could sink her if she thought about it too much. Every moment of her day was planned to the last detail: when she got up, what she ate for breakfast, the visits she made to places her parents couldn't slot into their busy days. She clawed back control where she could—getting to choose her own wardrobe had certainly been a leap in the right direction—but it wasn't enough any more.

It hadn't been for a long time.

'Every place on that list is checked by an advance.'

Oh, for goodness' sake. How long did he think she'd been doing this? 'They search every room, run any necessary background checks and organize escape routes. When they're happy they brief the security details who in turn plan the route to and from the venue.' She raised a brow. 'Are there bonus points if I can tell you everyone's call sign?'

'Don't take losing well, do you?'

'If I'm about to go for a walk in the park when I want to, how have I lost anything?'

'Guess it depends on whether or not that's where you were headed, doesn't it?' he challenged in return. 'And I didn't say anything about the park. The grounds of the mansion will do.' When she didn't reply he tossed his jacket down. 'But if you don't want to go out…'

'Fine,' she snapped as she turned on her heel and headed back towards the exit. Getting out of the house was better than nothing. 'But don't feel you need to make conversation to pass the time.'

'Just remember if you rabbit it'll be the last time we try this,' his deep voice rumbled in warning behind her.

Miranda looked over her shoulder. 'Rabbit?'

'Run,' he translated as he rolled down a sleeve.

It was as if he spoke a different language. She pushed the door open and stepped outside, the last throes of a humid summer surrendering to the first hints of autumn in the evening air. Where was he *from?*

The silent question opened the floodgate for a string of others. She wanted to know how long he'd been a cop, where he'd been before he transferred to the Municipal Security Section, what age he was, if he had a family.

As she crossed the gravel to the lawn another thought occurred to her. Since the absence of a wedding ring meant nothing she didn't even know if he was single. Asking him would be the obvious solution if he was remotely in the region of forthcoming—the fact she still didn't know his name being a prime example. If she found out he was married she would have several names for him; none of them *nice.*

Ramming the baseball cap onto her head, she frowned beneath the cover of the peak. Considering how much of her mind was occupied by thoughts of him even when he was *right there,* she didn't have a choice. She had to get to know him better.

Ordinarily it was something she enjoyed: talking to people, listening to what they had to say and getting small glimpses of lives that were so much freer than hers.

With him it felt different, more necessary to her survival, most likely because the silence was starting to turn her into a crazy person.

She just needed to figure out a way of getting him to start a conversation when she'd told him not to.

Had to pick *now* to follow an order, didn't he?

CHAPTER FIVE

AT FIRST Miranda's pace was rushed, the irritation she felt at his presence obvious, particularly when he walked beside her instead of taking up the more usual position on point or a few steps behind. When she slowed and started to take everything in Tyler studied her reaction as she breathed deep and a small smile formed on her lips.

Either she'd never walked the grounds before or she was up to something. He assumed it was the latter.

Without warning she changed direction and headed for the river, stopping to look from side to side when she got to the railing. After a couple of minutes of the same thing he inevitably asked, 'What are you looking for?'

'Mmm?' she hummed absent-mindedly.

'You're obviously looking for something.' If it was a place to jump in the river and swim to freedom she could forget it.

'Baby seals.'

'What?'

'Baby seals,' she repeated. 'Fuzzy bundles of joy that mummy and daddy seal made together as a token of their love for one another.' When she shot a sparkle-eyed glance at him from beneath the peak of her baseball cap he got the impression she thought she'd won some kind of victory. 'Didn't they teach you about reproduction in high school?'

Like most teenage boys it hadn't been the reproduction of seals he'd been interested in but Tyler didn't say so out loud. Instead he checked the grounds and the river, the water still busy with tugboats and barges. There was no immediate danger but he couldn't relax. Every muscle in his body was wound tight, ready to spring into action at a moment's notice. Without a means of release the tension grew, making him hyper-aware of the smallest details.

The name of the tugboat closest to them—the man standing on the prow of a barge—the water lapping against algae-covered rocks—the way a breeze from the river brushed a loose tendril of flame-red hair against the sensitive skin on her neck. He frowned as it swayed back and forth in a whispered touch that made his fingertips itch.

The ability to store large quantities of miscellaneous information in the back of his head until he needed to call on it was something Tyler had always taken for granted. It allowed him to focus his mind and manage the most immediate tasks. In many ways his brain acted like a computer with several open programs, a dozen others working in the background and plenty of spare memory. If that was the case she was messing with his operating system. Every time his eyes opened an image of her the screen froze.

'They're supposed to be around here somewhere,' she continued. 'There was a picture on Twitter.'

'Right,' he said dryly. He'd never been a Twitter fan but he knew she was popular there. It was the one area he hadn't been allowed to suggest changes.

From a protection standpoint he thought regularly reporting her location to all and sundry was an unnecessary risk. From the perspective of the mayor's press office her online presence was a valuable publicity tool. That they wouldn't budge on the subject still bugged him.

But not as much as all the standing around he'd been doing since he reported for duty.

'I don't think they constitute a breach in security if that's what you're worried about.' She glanced up at him again. 'Isn't it supposed to be dolphins they train to carry explosives?' When he didn't say anything, she leaned an elbow on the railing and turned toward him. 'You don't have a sense of humour, do you?'

'Would it save time if I told you I wasn't here to make friends?'

'I'm shocked,' she replied without batting an eye.

Tyler fought his nature. Normally he gave as good as he got; with a woman who looked the way she did it would probably involve a heavy dose of flirting. He could lay on the charm when he set his mind to it. But even if he hadn't been assigned to the position of babysitter his skills were a little rusty. Hadn't had much call to use them when he was buried in work was the easiest explanation. Hadn't met anyone he wanted to use them on was another.

But there was a reason for that.

When the thought conjured an image of long dark hair and soulful brown eyes it didn't improve his mood.

'That's how you got some of the others to turn a blind eye, isn't it?'

She raised an elegantly arched brow. 'What are we talking about now?'

'Your little adventures…'

'What adventures?'

Tyler cut to the chase. 'I do my homework. There isn't anything I don't know about you.'

There was a melodic burst of dismissive laughter. 'I very much doubt that.'

He summoned the necessary information without missing a beat. 'Miranda Eleanor Kravitz, twenty-four, born in Manhattan, raised in Vermont, moved back to New York prior to your father becoming mayor when you were seventeen.'

'Sixteen,' she corrected. 'Elections are in November.'

'He didn't take up office until January. Your birthday is December fourteenth. You were seventeen.' He picked up where he'd left off before she interrupted. 'You were a straight "A" student in high school, made the honour roll and in the final year took one of the leads in a stage production of *Twelfth Night.*' It was probably where she'd picked up her acting skills. 'Fluent in Spanish and French, studied English literature at NYU. By the time you left you'd danced on a table in a reality TV show and made headlines twice—once when you were caught drunk partying with the same infamous party girl who—'

'Has my bra size made it to Wikipedia yet?'

When the old Tyler made a rare appearance his gaze automatically lowered to the scooped neck of her T-shirt. 'No, but I'm willing to go out on a limb and say you're a—'

'Eyes north, Detective,' she warned in a lower voice.

Irritated he'd stepped over the line again, Tyler snapped his gaze back up. 'The investigation I did before I got here involved more than Googling your name. I talked to every bodyguard assigned to you and know exactly how you roll. There isn't an escape route I haven't plugged or a former cohort who hasn't been reassigned. The guy on the gate tonight is new, too, so you wouldn't have got far. You don't have any friends in the security team any more. What you have is people focused on doing their jobs who'll end up back in uniform if they don't.'

The gold in her eyes flared. 'What is your problem?'

'Until you accept you're not going anywhere without me or one of the other guys on your new detail, it's you.'

'You're not my keeper.'

Tyler stepped around her. 'Well, obviously they figured you needed one or I wouldn't be here.'

'Who are *"they"?*' she asked as she followed him.

'Who do you think they are?'

She muttered something incoherent below her breath but judging by her tone it wasn't a word she'd picked up from a study of English literature.

When he stopped and turned around she took a step back and frowned at the centre of his chest.

'This close to the election you're a liability,' he told her flatly. 'Three weeks back you were photographed sitting on a bar while some random guy licked salt off your neck before taking a shot of tequila.'

She lifted her chin. 'Jealous?'

'Personally I couldn't give a damn what you do.' Even if his reaction to seeing the photographs after he kissed her might have suggested otherwise. 'The only thing that concerns me is making sure it doesn't happen again. Some major favours were called in to keep those pictures out of the public eye.'

Any surprise she felt was hidden behind a mask of ice. 'It's just as well there wasn't anyone with a camera in a darkened hall on Friday night, then, isn't it?'

When she turned on her heel and headed back to the mansion Tyler let her get a few steps ahead. He needed to take a beat. Her parting shot had been bang on target but that wasn't what grated him. What did was the indifference in her voice. He wasn't the only one who got carried away in that hall. The implication he could have been just another guy lining up to lick salt off her neck bothered him a great deal more than it should.

At a very basic level he wanted to march on over there and demonstrate she was wrong. A Brannigan never backed down from a challenge. Trouble was they were also carved with deep streaks of honour and duty and while he knew how close he was to breaking one code, he had to hang on tight to the other. If he didn't there would be nothing left of the man he was before everything got so messed up.

'Go home, Detective,' she demanded when they were back in the kitchen.

'No can do,' he informed her retreating back.

When she turned he got a brief glimpse of how angry she was from the flash of fire in her eyes. Then the ice returned. 'I'll make a deal with you.'

'What kind of deal?'

'I'll give you my word I'll stay in tonight and that way you won't have to camp outside my door.' She ran an impassive gaze down the length of his body and back up. 'A good night's sleep might help with all the tension you're carrying around…'

Tyler treated her to his patented interrogation face: the one that said nothing short of a nuclear blast would change his position. 'What's the catch?'

She shook her head. 'No catch.'

'What do you get out of it?'

'Apart from a break from you?'

The thought he got to her went a long way towards evening

the playing field, but there was more to it than that. 'You want something.'

'World peace, an end to poverty, freedom and justice for all… I want a great many things, *Detective.* But for now I'll settle for your name.'

What was the big deal with his name? He ran through every possible scam she could be running and came up short. But with his Spidey-senses on alert he knew whatever she was doing was part of something bigger. That was okay, he could play the long game, and if giving her a name was what it took to give him a few hours he could put to better use than standing twiddling his thumbs or sleeping…

'Tyler.'

'Tyler,' she repeated in a lower voice as if savouring how it felt on her tongue.

Hearing her say it had a mesmerizing effect he'd never experienced before. Time stretched inexorably while she stared at him, her chin angled in contemplation. As he tried to figure out why his blood had thickened to the same consistency as magma when she hadn't done anything overtly seductive, she blinked and turned away.

'I'll see you in the morning, Tyler.'

'You leave this house, I'll know inside five seconds.'

She raised an arm and waggled her fingers in the air. 'Nighty-night.'

Tyler stood in the same spot after she left, trying to decide whether he trusted her any further than he could throw her. His word meant something—or at least it used to; he wasn't convinced hers did. Then his cell phone vibrated.

'Brannigan.'

'So what's it like with the city's version of the Secret Service?'

The sound of his partner's voice got him moving again. 'Don't ask,' he said as he left the kitchen and headed for the control room. 'Got anything new for me?'

'There weren't any DNA hits in the database.'

'It took them a month to tell us that?'

'Backed up in the lab…'

'What about the known associates we've been chasing?'

'There I might have better news.'

Tyler nodded brusquely. 'Save it for when I see you. I'll be at O'Malley's by nine.'

'If I end up divorced I'm blaming you.'

'Because all your kids look like me?'

The response made the corner of Tyler's mouth lift. It was the closest he got to a smile any more. Pretending nothing was wrong when he was around the people who knew him was wearing him down. From that point of view his day with the mayor's daughter had been a welcome respite.

He just had to get a handle on his reaction to her while he was still volatile.

There'd been a time when not getting involved had never been a problem for him the way it had for other members of his family. He'd kept his distance and remained detached, gaining a rep for being emotionally unavailable to women along the way. Once he'd made the mistake of thinking he could handle a little attachment he'd fallen flat on his face. To top it off he'd overcompensated and it had cost someone their life.

Sometimes he thought he saw her face in a crowd: dull, lifeless eyes staring at him in silent accusation. She was a ghost who followed him everywhere.

He shouldn't have left her alone.

The thought gave him a moment's pause outside the room that housed the security monitors. From inside he could hear the voices of the men whose presence meant he wasn't leaving the mayor's daughter unprotected even if there was an immediate threat.

There was no reason for him to feel torn.

A small army of people surrounded Miranda Kravitz and, though they might not have kept her out of trouble, they had plenty of practice cushioning her from the world beyond the walls of the mansion. It wasn't as if she didn't have a voice, either. Half her problem with him was he didn't let her get her own way when she was plainly accustomed to getting whatever she wanted.

Tyler stood up for the people who didn't have a voice, who didn't have the opportunities she'd been given or the ability to escape their lives when they felt like it. If she broke her word, she would pay for it. He'd see to that.

She might think he'd been tough on her the first day, but she had no idea how ruthless he could be.

CHAPTER SIX

THE small victories gained when she got him to start a conversation and give her the name she so badly wanted to know were enough to allow Miranda to cut him some slack. She wouldn't break her word. What helped him *more* was that he'd given her somewhere else to focus her ire. After a night of enforced captivity she was determined to fight for her rights.

'Good morning, Miranda.'

'Good morning, Grace.' She saw the surprise in the older woman's eyes when she appeared outside her father's office. 'Is the mayor in?'

'He's having breakfast with the chief of police.'

'Where is my mother?'

'I believe she's still in the morning room.'

When she turned on her heel Grace grabbed her file, rounded her desk and rushed down the hall after her. 'You have a nine a.m. appointment in Brooklyn at—'

'Not now, Grace.' It was rude and she was sorry for that but they both knew the morning briefing was more habit than necessity. Miranda knew where she was going days in advance—weeks for the functions that required more forwards planning. If she didn't how was she supposed to know what to wear or find time to research things she knew nothing about so she could hold a conversation?

Two sets of eyes looked across the morning room as she entered without knocking. 'Could you give us a moment, please,

Roger?' Once the door shut behind him Miranda took a deep breath. 'I won't be held prisoner in this house.'

'Sit down, darling.'

'I don't want to sit down,' she said without moving. 'What I want is to be treated like an adult.'

'Start behaving like one and you will,' her mother replied with the infinite patience that drove her daughter insane when she was upset about something. 'Now take a seat and tell me what's wrong.'

'You knew, didn't you?'

'Knew what?'

'About the changes to my security detail.'

'It's hardly the first change of personnel since we took up residence.' Her mother raised a brow. 'Don't you think you're overreacting a little?'

'When they were brought in specifically to keep me out of trouble in case I prove an embarrassment to you during the campaign?'

'Well, obviously we would prefer to avoid any negative publicity this close to—'

'I'm more than aware of the responsibilities forced on me since my teens, Mother. I don't need a reminder.'

'Yet your father and I are being given increasingly regular reports of your acts of rebellion.' She gracefully folded her hands together on her lap. 'We were elected to set an example. People expect more of this family. That's the life we live.'

'*We* weren't elected,' Miranda reminded her. '*Dad was.* I didn't choose to run for office and I wasn't elected to the position of your daughter. Doesn't the fact I've lived someone else's life for half of mine count for anything?'

'Like it or not, you're still the mayor's daughter. This is his last term in office and—'

'*If* he's elected or are we taking that for granted? Throwing pots of money at the campaign isn't an automatic guarantee of success.'

'We're a family, Miranda. We stick together through everything. Once the election is over—'

A small burst of sarcastic laughter left her lips. 'I'm supposed to do what—wait until he decides whether he wants to confirm the rumours and run for Governor? Why stop there—what about the White House?'

'That's your father's decision.'

'And how I choose to live my life is mine. If you want me to act like a grown-up you have to allow me to be one. How am I supposed to learn from my mistakes if I'm not permitted to make any?'

'Your argument might carry more weight if there was any evidence to support it,' her mother replied. 'We gave you more freedom at NYU and you repaid our trust by having your picture splashed across several tabloids.'

Miranda's frustration grew. 'I love dancing and got drunk when I turned twenty-one—how does that make me worse than any other college student in America? I could have been running around in a wet T-shirt during spring break or got arrested at student protests. I could have experimented with drugs or slept with guys who were happy to make a buck selling all the gory details to the press. I didn't but none of those things matter any more than the long hours I work. Did it occur to either one of you that turning this place into the equivalent of Alcatraz would make the need for escape more necessary? Why do you think Richie chose to attend a college on the other side of the country?'

'There's no need to raise your voice. If you would learn how to state your case calmly and sensibly the way your brother does—'

Miranda shook her head. No matter how often she tried to communicate with her mother every conversation left her feeling like a petulant teenager. The truth was her parents didn't know their son any better than their daughter. While they had disappeared off to countless business meetings, charity benefits and met with people who were keen for her father to launch his political career their daughter had become a surrogate mother.

She'd read her baby brother bedtime stories and made sure he did his homework. She'd put Band-Aids on cuts, watched cartoons when he was sick and held his hand when they'd had to face a world filled with curious eyes.

No one had done those things for her.

'I'm done,' she said flatly. 'I'll stick around for the election but once the votes are counted, I'm out. No more public appearances, no more smiling for photographers and no bodyguards following me everywhere I go. I never wanted one to begin with and I don't see why the taxpayer should suffer because my overprotective parents want to control my every move.'

It meant breaking the pact she'd made with her brother but it couldn't be helped. Not when another eight months felt like a life sentence.

There was a heavy sigh as she turned away. 'Miranda—'

'I'm going to be late for my first appointment.' When she yanked the door open and stepped into the hall her gaze lifted and crashed into cobalt-blue eyes.

Her breath caught. *Tyler.*

With her heart still beating hard as a result of a long-overdue parental confrontation she experienced the same difficulty she had the last time his name echoed in her mind. She couldn't break eye contact, was frozen in place and her brain seemed to have turned into mush.

He broke the spell with the blink of dense lashes and held out a sheet of paper. 'I told Grace I'd make sure you got this.'

'Thank you.' She took the schedule with one hand and closed the door behind her with the other.

'You ready to go?'

'I need a couple of minutes.'

He nodded. 'I'll be outside.'

Miranda turned the sheet of paper in her hands as they walked down the hall. When she stole an upward glance at his profile she saw the corner of his mouth lift.

'Bye, Grace,' his voice rumbled.

'Bye, Tyler.'

Her gaze shifted in time to catch a glimpse of what looked like a hint of warmth on the older woman's cheeks. In all the years she'd known her, she'd never seen Grace blush. Or be flustered enough to feel the need to shuffle the papers on her desk. Had he just winked at her?

The thought was surreal.

When she stole another glance as they approached the top of the stairs he caught her doing it. Adopting the same impassive expression he was wearing, she simply blinked and looked away. If there was one thing she'd learnt about him it was when he had something to say he didn't have any difficulty opening his mouth. Keeping it shut on the subject of anything he might have heard through the door would be her advice.

When he remained silent she lifted the sheet of paper and glanced over her day.

'You need any help with the big words, let me know.'

The comment made her glare at him in warning before they parted ways but as she continued down the hall to her bedroom something unexpected happened: she smiled.

Unwittingly he'd given her exactly what she needed to face the day. Combined with the knowledge that her release date was closer, it placed a spring in her step that hadn't been there before.

CHAPTER SEVEN

SOMETHING was eating at Tyler.

Usually it meant he'd missed something—a random clue or part of the puzzle that didn't quite fit. That Miranda would make another bid for freedom was a given. What he didn't get was why it suddenly felt wrong to stand in her way.

Hearing what he'd heard through the door that morning probably had something to do with it. The knowledge she hadn't wanted a bodyguard helped raise his opinion of her a notch, even if she was under the misconception she didn't need one. But then she didn't know what he knew, did she?

His gaze scanned the room, but with little cause for concern among a bunch of kids and schoolteachers it slid back to his mark. The long legs encased in sharply tailored dark grey trousers were folded elegantly to the side, one high-heeled open-toed white shoe tapping in time to the music while she smiled. Judging by the sparkle in her eyes, she would probably agree calling the recital *music* was a bit of a stretch but it didn't seem to dilute her enjoyment any.

Maybe that was what was eating him: *her mood.*

She'd been Little Miss Sunshine since she appeared outside the mansion.

When the cacophony of sound limped its way to an overly enthusiastic end she led the applause and stood up. 'Thank you, that was wonderful. The mayor would have loved this. If you keep practising and get to Radio City Music Hall I'll make sure he has front-row tickets.'

Tyler doubted there was an adult present who didn't think they would need to be practising for a very long time before that happened. Opening the door, he stepped into the empty hall, inhaling the scent he'd had so much difficulty ignoring on the trip over as she passed within inches of him. It was different from the sophisticated perfume she'd worn the day before. Since he wasn't up to date on flowers he couldn't identify what it had been but now he thought about it he reckoned it was probably something like lilies or lilac. The one she was currently wearing was sweeter, more playful and made him wonder if she matched her perfume to where she was going with as much care as her clothes.

If she did it was clever. Even if he could have done without the constant trace of strawberries in the air as a reminder of how she'd tasted on his lips.

He followed a few steps behind as the head teacher and members of the board escorted her along the hall. When his gaze lowered to the feminine sway of her hips he hid a frown of annoyance and forced it elsewhere.

'This next class is made up of children with learning difficulties,' the principal explained. 'The ratio of teacher and classroom assistant to pupil is higher.'

'What is the age range?' Miranda asked.

'Between six and eight…'

When they filed inside Tyler took up position by the door again. After a cursory inventory of his surroundings, the occupants and checking the line of sight through the windows there wasn't much else for him to do but continue watching her. He justified the action by telling himself he was searching for the clue he might have missed, examining everything from her introductory wave to how she interacted with the children as she moved from one small desk to the next. She crouched down to eye level, asked questions and listened carefully to the answers. From time to time she ruffled the odd tousled head of hair, her hundred-watt smile flashing more than once.

It wasn't dissimilar to the act she'd put on with the elderly in the Bronx the day before but Tyler couldn't shake the sensation something was different.

As the principal explained some of the ways they made it easier for the kids to stay focused somewhat ironically Miranda's attention wandered. When her gaze landed on something at his side of the room and she angled her chin with curiosity, Tyler looked to see what it was.

A little girl with blonde hair sat on padded mats on the floor a few feet away, seemingly oblivious to what was happening around her as she swapped one thick crayon for another and continued colouring a sheet of paper.

Miranda crossed the room and hunched down beside her.

'Hello.'

The girl didn't look up.

'Would you mind if I sat with you for a minute? My feet are really starting to hurt in these shoes.'

No reply.

Regardless of her expensive outfit, she sat down and tucked her legs to one side. 'That's a very pretty picture. I love the flowers. Pink is my favorite colour.'

After a moment's hesitation the girl reached for a pink crayon, her chin lifting as she held it up.

The gesture was received with an impossibly soft smile. 'Is that for me?'

There was a nod.

'Are you sure you want me to help? I can never stay between the lines when I'm supposed to.'

Tyler thought it was the most honest statement she'd made since they met. That it was said with a hint of self-recrimination was interesting. For a second he almost believed it was a glimpse of the real her.

Accepting the crayon, she brushed her hair over her shoulder and looked at the picture again. 'Which one do you want me to do?' A small finger pointed at the page. 'Okay. I'll try not to mess it up for you.'

Tyler looked at the captivated audience of adults who were watching what she was doing. He doubted any of them would forget it before they cast their vote in the election. They'd see her father's name on the voting slip and think of her. Maybe even tick the box next to his name if they'd been wavering.

He'd thought New Yorkers were savvier than that.

'You have flowers,' a small voice said.

His gaze was drawn back to Miranda as she glanced down at her blouse. 'I like the ruffles and the layers. They all feel different. Try one and see.'

A small hand reached out to one of the larger grey and white flowers pinned randomly to white linen. Catching a ruffle between a thumb and forefinger, the girl checked out how it felt. 'Soft.'

'Do you like the beads in the middle?'

'They're shiny.'

'Someone has to sew them on with a needle and thread.'

'Did you do it?'

'Nuh-uh,' Miranda sang in reply. 'Needles are pointy. It's not a good idea to play with the things that might hurt you.'

Something she could have done with remembering before she gave a stranger the come-on from a dance floor.

Tyler looked away and found a boy at a nearby desk staring at his waist with wide eyes. Lightly shrugging his shoulders, he tugged the edges of his jacket closer together to cover his sidearm and checked his watch. It was almost time to leave. Shifting his gaze to his mark, he waited for an opening to make eye contact.

'What's your name?'

'Casey.'

'I'm Miranda. Why are you sitting on your own, Casey? Don't you want to sit with your friends?'

'There are boys at my table,' she explained with the typically solid reasoning of most small girls her age.

'Some boys can be nice.'

'Some of them are mean.'

'Believe me, *I know.*' Obviously stifling amusement, Miranda shot a pointed glance his way.

Cute—with a lazy blink to indicate he'd got the message, Tyler subtly tapped his watch. *Tick-tock, princess.*

'I have to go now, Casey,' she said with a pout before turning it into a smile. 'But it was very nice to meet you. Thanks for letting me colour with you.'

'Are your feet better?'

'Much better, thank you.' She pushed upright and ran her palms over the seat of her trousers, brows lifting when the sheet of paper was held up in the air. 'I can take it home with me?'

'You can finish it at your house.'

'I will, I promise. Bye, Casey.'

'Bye, Miranda.'

She waved to the rest of the room. 'Bye, kids. Thanks for letting me come visit you today. I can't wait to tell the mayor how great you're all doing in school.'

Tyler stepped into the hall as there was a chorus of goodbyes. Lifting the mike in his closed hand, he spoke into it in a low voice.

'Rand from Brannigan, Phoenix is on the move.'

The reply sounded in his earpiece. 'Roger that—moving to primary.'

As they approached the main entrance Tyler tuned out of the conversation and went on alert. There had been a small gathering of parents outside when they arrived, but, taking into consideration how long they'd been there, the numbers might have grown. When the group in front of him stopped in the foyer he headed for the doors to check it out. What he discovered made him twice as determined to stay focused. He had to hand it to her: whatever else she might be, the woman was a crowd-puller.

When she said her goodbyes, shook hands and headed his way he stepped outside, his eyes on the crowd as he walked a few feet in front of her. What he was looking for as she approached the people yelling for attention was someone who stood out, whose actions and demeanor were different from everyone else's. While she waved and stopped to shake hands on the approach to Officer Rand at the waiting Suburban, Tyler took dozens of mental snapshots. A couple of minutes and an alarm bell went off in his head.

He went back over the last faces he'd seen while she talked to a young woman who followed her on Twitter.

At the back of the crowd there was a man who wasn't smiling or yelling. He was pale and ordinary looking, the kind of guy who normally faded into the background. Dark hair, approximately five feet eight, glasses, baseball cap with a faded lion logo—nothing unusual there. What made him stand out was how he was fixated on Miranda as if she was the only thing he could see.

Suddenly Tyler was aware of every hand reaching out for her, the weight of bodies pressed against the barricade close to where she stood and the flapping greeting banners that could obscure any of the danger behind them.

Adrenaline sped through his veins while his gaze flickered to face after face. With a sickening sense of inevitability heads moved in the crowd and he saw the one face he would never forget. Dull, lifeless eyes filled with accusation stared at him from a face streaked with blood.

It didn't matter that the man at the back of the crowd hadn't moved. He couldn't take a chance.

Stepping towards Miranda, he laid a palm on the inward curve of her spine and leaned close to her ear. 'You need to go now.'

Her body stiffened as she looked into his eyes. 'Why?'

'Just do it.' He added pressure to her spine to move her along.

To her credit she dealt with the situation a lot better than he did, smiling brightly and waving goodbye as he ushered her to safety. If he had time to stop and think about it Tyler might have realized he respected her for that. But since he was too busy getting her the hell out of there he jerked his chin at Rand, who opened the rear door and looked around.

'Problem?' he asked when Miranda was inside.

'Guy on my six at the back of the crowd.'

Rand looked over his shoulder. 'Which one?'

'Pale complexion, glasses, baseball cap.'

'Don't see him.'

Turning ninety degrees and zeroing in on the position, Tyler frowned when he discovered the man wasn't there.

'Let's go.'

'What's wrong?' Miranda asked when he opened the driver's door and got behind the wheel.

He watched Rand through the windscreen as he walked around the front of the vehicle to the jump seat. 'Nothing you need to worry about.'

'Nice try.' To his surprise her voice softened. 'I saw your face, Tyler, and—'

'We have a schedule to stick to,' he said tightly as the passenger door opened. When their gazes met in the mirror something resembling understanding passed silently between them before she glanced at Rand.

She shook her head. 'You're more obsessed with my schedule than Grace.'

It wasn't the first time she'd followed his lead. But that she hadn't pushed on the subject in front of his fellow officer made it feel as if *she* was protecting *him,* which was not a pleasant sensation for Tyler. Pulling away from the kerb, he headed them back to Manhattan and took deep, even breaths. That his heart rate still hadn't returned to normal by the time they got to the Brooklyn Bridge wasn't unusual—he'd been in plenty of situations where adrenalin continued to course through his body long after the event.

But this time felt different.

He just wasn't sure he wanted to know why.

CHAPTER EIGHT

As SOMEONE who'd been looking forwards to a little one-on-one time with her new prison warden—albeit in the form of a continuing game of one-upmanship—Miranda found the addition of a second bodyguard a tad frustrating. By midafternoon she was glad to see Lewis go, especially when she hadn't been able to get what happened off her mind. They'd barely left the civic reception at City Hall before she focused on what she could see of his reflection in the rear-view mirror and broached the subject with Tyler.

'What happened this morning?'

'I told you it was nothing to worry about.'

She scowled at his eyes when they didn't look at her. The fact he was driving through heavy traffic didn't seem to matter. 'I didn't push the subject when Lewis was here,' she reminded him. 'But I saw the look on your face and there's no way you were that spooked about nothing.'

'I wasn't *spooked*.'

'Call it what you want, I know what I saw.'

The atmosphere within the cocoon of the SUV grew darker, the lack of a response adding to her frustration. 'The whole mean, moody and mysterious thing you're working so well won't cut it with me. If you want to build a level of trust in this relationship it has to go both ways.'

'When I think you need to know something, you will.'

She tried to figure out why she'd wasted time worrying about him. Despite his denial he'd been spooked, Miranda couldn't think of a better word to describe his reaction. When she'd stolen a glance at him as he watched the crowd he was frozen in place, ramrod straight and the colour seemed to have faded beneath his tan.

Momentarily distracted by the conversation she was having with the person closest to her, she hadn't seen him move. She could still feel the pressure of his large hand on her spine, the heat of his touch branding her through the material of her blouse as an electric current zinged through her body. Adding the deep rumble of his voice so close to her ear she could almost feel his lips move left her skin feeling several sizes too small to fit over her bones. He would never know how much effort it had taken to make it look as if she hadn't been so shaken by it she wouldn't have noticed if the sky had fallen down.

As she turned her head and looked out of the side window she blamed her fantasies. The time she'd spent dreaming about having seriously hot sex with him combined with the forbidden aspect of physical contact with one of her bodyguards had left her body primed in a way it had never been for any other man.

The pang of hurt she felt was harder to justify.

When she'd looked into his eyes in the mirror, she'd thought she felt a flicker of understanding pass between them and dropped the subject until they were alone. It was the same way she'd felt in the school when she teased him about being mean and even made her wonder if giving her what she'd needed after the confrontation with her mother had been unintentional.

She wouldn't make the same mistake again.

By rejecting the olive branch she'd offered him, Detective Brannigan had sealed his fate.

Fishing in her Herrera bag for a pair of sunglasses, she hid behind them while she plotted her revenge.

CHAPTER NINE

LIKE every other guy on the planet Tyler could think of a million other things he would rather do than sit around waiting while a woman went shopping for clothes. That she felt the need to parade each outfit in front of him wasn't helping any, especially when it gave him an excuse to fill his mind with image after image of her body.

Leaning forwards on a velvet-covered chair, he rested his elbows on his knees, staring at the cream carpet while he crossed his jaw and mentally prepared for the next test of his self-control.

'This neckline might be a little too low,' her voice announced from beyond the curtain.

While he appreciated the warning he still felt the need to take a deep breath and blow it into his cheeks before exhaling. If she started modelling lingerie he would have to take a cold shower. The sound of curtain rings drawing across a rail lifted his gaze for a furtive glimpse of what was headed his way.

A *little* too low, she'd said?

The damn thing was practically at her navel.

All but painted onto her body, the black floor-length sleeveless dress plunged downwards from two thick straps on her shoulders. The globes of her spectacular breasts were barely contained, leading his gaze over the valley of her cleavage to the minuscule black band beneath and the tempting strip of skin beyond that.

She placed her hands on her hips and struck a come-and-get-me pose. 'What do you think?'

It was a bit difficult to think anything when all the blood had rushed from his brain to a point in his body that was so painfully hard he had to stifle a groan.

Silently clearing his throat, he forced a response through tight lips. 'It's nice.'

She arched a brow. *'Nice?'*

Tyler frowned as he raised his chin and looked into her eyes. 'What do you want me to say?'

'Anything other than nice, fine or not bad would make a pleasant change.' She took a deep breath that pushed her breasts forwards and loosened Tyler's grip on his sanity. Then she bent forwards, lowered her gaze and wriggled her shoulders from side to side. 'I'm a bit worried I might pop out of it.'

He sat up and ran his palms over his face. 'How much longer do we have to do this?'

Raising her hands Miranda cupped her breasts as she straightened. By the time she looked at him Tyler had his hands in his lap to hide the evidence of what she was doing to him.

'As long as it takes to get what I want…' A decadent smile formed on her lips as she dropped her hands to her sides. She shrugged. 'There's a reason this is the last appointment on the schedule today. They'll stay open late for me if I need them to. They're awfully good about that and I do love to shop.' Turning, she looked over her shoulder and asked, 'How does it look from the back?'

Like endless miles of flawlessly tanned skin he wanted to touch to discover if it was as soft as it looked. He'd start with his hands, then his mouth, would retrace the path they took with his tongue and blow gently on the wet surface to raise goosebumps while he raised her skirt and…

'I was worried about lines so I thought it was best not to wear anything underneath it.'

Tyler swore viciously inside his head. Gritting his teeth together hard enough to crack the enamel, he managed to bite, 'Where exactly are you planning on wearing that?'

'You think it's too much for something public?' She stepped over to the mirrors lining one wall so he was treated to a front and back view at the same time. 'You're probably right. Somewhere more intimate would be better. Given the right smoky atmosphere and some sultry music...' She closed her eyes and swayed her hips. 'Mmm...' Her palms followed the curve of her sides from waist to hip. Then she stilled and popped open her eyes. 'I might get this one.'

When she went back into the dressing room Tyler looked at the ceiling and silently asked what he'd done to deserve her. Didn't he have enough to deal with already? He might have miraculously managed to temporarily put his problems to the back of his mind, but it didn't mean they'd gone away. He supposed he should be thankful she hadn't made another escape attempt. But while she was making him suffer for not telling her what had happened outside the school he didn't consider it much of a silver lining.

The door to his left opened and the personal shopper who'd already rolled a rack of clothes into the changing area appeared with another one.

'How is she getting on?' she enquired with a smile as she wheeled it in.

'Slowly.'

His response earned a chuckle of laughter. 'You can't become a fashion icon in this city without putting in long hours of preparation.'

Since he didn't know anything about fashion Tyler would have to take her word for that.

'Is that Janice with the next rack?' a voice called from behind the curtain.

'Yes, I have it here,' Janice replied. 'Is it safe to come in?'

'Absolutely. If you hadn't come back I was going to have to ask Tyler to zip me up.'

While they chatted behind the curtain he pushed to his feet and began pacing the room. After the third lap—and with no new outfit to send him over the edge—he reached into his pocket for his cell phone and called his partner.

'I'm officially in hell,' he said in a low voice.

'The mayor's little girl proving too much of a handful for you?'

'She's *shopping*.'

'I feel your pain, brother.'

'Could you feel it without sounding so amused?' He walked to the other side of the room and glanced at the curtain. 'Give me some good news about the case and I won't hit you the next time I see you.'

While his partner brought him up to speed he made the mistake of turning his back to the changing room. It was only when he ended the call he realized it had gone quiet.

Immediately crossing the room, he threw caution to the wind and yanked back the curtain.

'Son-of-a—'

CHAPTER TEN

'How pissed do you think he'll be when he tracks you down?'

Miranda shrugged as they relaxed in comfortable chairs in the elegant surroundings of the iconic Waldorf Astoria. 'Don't care. He deserves it.'

She didn't mention she'd never met anyone who could irritate the life out of her one minute and make her so hot it felt as if she had a fever in the next. She'd never behaved so provocatively before, purposefully pushing the boundaries of his control to discover how much he could take. It was a perilous game—one she'd thought she had the sense not to play with a man who oozed danger the way Tyler did—but had that stopped her? *Oh, no.*

'You don't feel the least little bit guilty he might get in trouble for losing you?'

'I didn't until you mentioned it so thanks for that—I owe you one.'

Crystal lifted one of the porcelain teacups sitting on the round table between them. 'That conscience of yours has always been a problem. We still need to work on that.'

'You wouldn't have got me this far if I didn't have a natural aptitude for courting trouble.'

'I did say I saw potential in you for greatness when we met.'

'Give me a couple of months to shake off my shackles and I promise to spread my wings and soar,' Miranda vowed.

She heard the clink of the teacup touching a saucer as Crystal took a long breath. 'Nothing to tie you down…no one to get in your way…' She hummed as she exhaled. 'Put all that freedom together with the absence of a guilty conscience and I might have to abdicate my notoriety throne in favour of a worthy successor.'

Drumming her fingers on the arms of her chair, Miranda gently swayed her crossed leg while she tried to convince herself she wasn't watching the foyer for Tyler's arrival. If the stupid man could make up his mind what he wanted it would make things a lot easier.

The way he had looked at her set her body alight, her pulse hammering and her breasts aching for attention. If she had any sense she would have toned it down a little. But the more of a reaction she got from him, the hotter he made her feel, and the desire to push him to breaking point grew. She hadn't been able to stop.

She'd *wanted* him to snap.

If the first time she'd encouraged him with a smile had felt like playing with fire, using her sexuality to get to him was about to turn her into a pyromaniac.

She still didn't like him. She was still mad at him for making her feel like a fool because she'd looked for something that obviously wasn't there. But apparently the thought of angry sex with him did it for her, *big time.*

'You still confident in your fifty-dollar bet on him finding you inside a couple of hours?' Crystal asked.

'If he was as smart as he likes to think he is he would have found me already.'

'If he was as smart as you *say* he thinks he is he would have found Jimmy Hoffa by now.'

She turned her head and smiled ruefully at her best friend. 'So much for my great plan… It doesn't take away from the victory of escaping when he was so determined it wasn't possible. But slinking back to the mansion to find him waiting for me like another disgruntled parent takes the shine off it a little.'

Crystal's gaze moved. 'Well you better dig out your sunglasses because if that's who I think it is headed our way the day just got a whole lot brighter.'

Miranda's gaze immediately shifted to the foyer. The sight of him did its usual snatch and grab with her breath. When his gaze sliced through the air and slammed into hers a heady frisson of excitement travelled through her body. He wasn't just mad. He looked as if he was ready to explode.

'Wow.' Crystal sighed dreamily. 'I want to be in as much trouble as you are right now. Do you think he'll spank you? He looks like he's gonna spank you *good.*'

Her reaction to the suggestion shocked Miranda.

She really was a *very* bad girl.

Exhaling the breath she'd been holding, she smiled sweetly as he marched straight up to them. 'I don't believe you've been formally introduced. Detective Brannigan, meet Crystal—Crystal, meet Tyler.'

'Well, *hello, Tyler.* Is that a gun in your pocket or are you just pleased to meet me?'

A low burst of laughter bubbled up from Miranda's chest when he pressed his mouth into a thin line. 'He doesn't have a sense of humour but I thought it was funny.'

'Awesome,' Crystal replied.

His dark gaze remained firmly fixed on the cause of his anger. 'You're leaving now.'

'Excellent timing. I've just finished my tea. If you hadn't got here I would have had to hail another cab.' She lifted her brows. 'Did you park nearby? I can wait for you to bring the car around front.'

Rage rolled off his large body in waves. 'I'll carry you out of here if I have to.'

'How about we save that for next time?' She reached to the side for her bag and unfolded her legs.

As she got to her feet Crystal held up a set of neatly folded bills. 'The fifty dollars I owe you.'

Miranda turned towards her and flashed a grin, 'Why, *thank you.* It's been a pleasure doing business with you.'

'Any time. Don't forget about that thing at the place we talked about. It should be a blast.'

'I'll see you there.'

'No, she won't,' a deep voice said firmly.

Miranda waved a dismissive hand in his direction. 'Don't listen to him. I never do. Love you.'

'Love you, too.'

Taking the lead, she walked across the foyer with her head held high. When they got to the revolving doors she stopped and angled her chin. 'Oh, dear, this is a bit of a dilemma.' She looked up at him. 'Do you gamble on me going first or risk turning your back on me again? It must be a little like playing roulette for you.'

'Having fun?' he asked through gritted teeth as he captured her elbow in a potentially bruising grasp and bundled them both into a narrow compartment.

'I was till you got here.' But actually, while crushed so tightly against him, she still kinda was.

Wriggling experimentally, she smiled when he tensed.

'You're a piece of work.'

She tugged her elbow free when they hit the sidewalk and he'd pushed her in the right direction. 'You're just upset I slipped through your iron curtain of security. Through a velvet one, no less.'

'Did it ever occur to you if you can find a way out someone can use the same way to get to you?'

'Why would anyone want to get to me?'

'Famous brings out the crazy. I don't even care that you're famous and right this minute *I* want to kill you.'

'How did you find me?' she enquired as they walked to wherever they were going. She hoped it was far away. She was having entirely too much fun to stop now.

'Your friend Crystal needs to turn off the location option on her Facebook page. And while we're on the subject of the internet any Twittering you do about the places you're going should be done *after* you've been there.'

'They're called Tweets.'

'They're a waving flag that says "come get me, I'm over here."' As they stopped at a crossing he flicked a glare at her. 'Every whack job in the five boroughs could have been waiting for you outside that school.'

'Is that what spooked you?'

'I wasn't *spooked.*' His reaction to the word was so vicious the second time around it gave Miranda the distinct impression she'd hit a nerve. He took a long breath and frowned at how long it was taking for the light to change. 'Someone in the crowd was off.'

Miranda's eyes narrowed. 'Define *"off."*'

'Acting odd—hinky—out of place—obsessively watching your every move.' He captured her elbow again and pushed her across the street.

'You spend all day watching my every move.'

'I'm paid to do it and, believe me, it wasn't my idea.'

'Whose idea was it?' She tugged her elbow. 'You can let go of me now.'

'Not a chance.' He navigated their way through the human traffic on the sidewalk. 'Your head of security used to be my captain's partner back in the day. When he mentioned he needed an injection of new blood it was my misfortune to be volunteered as the wild card.'

Ah-h-h, so *that* was what he meant when he said he'd been trying to get out of it for a week. Considering it was the longest conversation they'd ever had, Miranda thought she should make him angry more often. 'You must have done the close-protection course.'

'Stop changing the subject.'

She sighed heavily as they rounded a corner. 'I think you're overreacting a tad to my having tea at the Waldorf, don't you? Was I dancing on a table when you got there?'

Tyler stopped so suddenly he had to yank her back into place when she got a couple of steps ahead.

'Whoopsies.' Miranda giggled when she almost tripped over, tipsy on the headiness of her success.

He let go of her elbow when she was steady on her feet. 'You don't get it, do you?'

'That this is strike two?' She rolled her eyes. 'I heard you. One more strike and—'

His body loomed over her, the tip of his nose barely an inch away from hers as his voice rumbled, 'Get in the damn car.'

Miranda hadn't even noticed it was there and, frankly, with his mouth in kissing distance, she couldn't care less. She angled her head in a move that suggested she was about to fit their lips together and lifted her chin, reducing the gap to millimetres. Then she looked deep into cobalt-blue eyes and whispered, 'Make. Me.'

The gaze glittering with promise of the danger she so desperately craved wandered lazily over her face. His warm breath mingled with hers while her heart thundered so loudly she could hear it in her ears. It didn't matter that they were standing in the middle of a street in Manhattan. It didn't matter that there were people everywhere and dozens of cars driving by and that pretty much everyone in the universe had a camera on their phone. All that mattered was how badly she wanted to be kissed.

There was nothing beyond burning need and him.

When her heavy-lidded gaze lowered to his mouth she saw a corner of it tug upwards.

'You don't want to do that,' he said in a low, husky, unbelievably sexy voice before moving his head so he could whisper in her ear. 'I'm more trouble than you can handle.'

It was as if he'd placed all of her fantasies within her grasp. Endless possibilities spun around and around in her head in ever decreasing circles with Tyler as the focal point. Miranda blinked at him while he leaned away from her and reached for the door. She turned towards the vehicle and blindly took a step forwards when a thought finally made it through her dizziness. They were just two small words but the weight of their importance felt immense.

'We'll see...'

The voice that said them wasn't hers; it was the sultry voice of the siren she'd always suspected lived somewhere deep inside but had been afraid to seek out. Now she realized the temptress had been with her each time she stepped out of the changing room, had fed on his reaction and was gaining the strength she needed to break free.

As Miranda got into the SUV and he slammed the door shut

she experienced the crippling fear that stemmed from the threat of its imminent release.

She didn't know what scared her more: having the siren's call answered by someone she would drag to disaster or having it ignored and remaining isolated and alone, endlessly calling out to someone who would sail through her life without stopping to take a second look.

CHAPTER ELEVEN

IT TOOK intense concentration for Tyler to focus through a blinding rage so he could drive them back to the mansion.

Discovering she'd slipped out through a hidden door in a mural-covered wall at the back of the changing room meant he didn't have to suffer the humiliation of knowing she'd tiptoed out behind his back. But the thought someone might have taken her made him experience his second wave of unwarranted panic in a handful of hours. The realization she'd stood *in front* of the hidden door while he checked the space both eased his mind and made him angry as hell.

The latter feeling grew when he had another moment of clarity. He'd been played since the moment they got there.

By the time he'd searched the store, tracked down Janice and interrogated her until she confessed Miranda had left in a cab there wasn't a rock in the state of New York he wouldn't have turned over to find her. The mayor's head of security would rue the day he'd given him the scope to *'do whatever he needed to do'* when he locked her in a cell and lost the key. His next move was an attempt to get the cab number off the store's security cameras. When that had failed he'd gone hunting for her partner in crime.

Throughout it all he was battling emotions he'd been unable to control since he'd let them out of the damn box. By challenging him to make a move she'd got a glimpse of him few people on the right side of the law ever saw.

That Tyler came from the dark side. He was the man who

had spent so long among the dregs of humanity no amount of scrubbing would ever make him clean. He was the lean and hungry one, the cold one, the one who would devour her until he'd taken all she had to give and left her feeling as empty as he did.

She didn't want to mess with that Tyler.

The silence coming from the back seat was a wise move. She could forget a third strike; there wasn't going to be one. What was more, it was time to play the card he'd been holding close to his chest. If she'd behaved he wouldn't have to use it. Now he didn't have a choice.

When they landed back at the mansion he followed her inside and headed straight for the control room. Yanking open one of the drawers on a filing cabinet, he searched for the file he needed and checked the contents. Then he headed for the stairs, taking them two at a time to speed up the process until he reached the hall and marched to her door.

The three sharp knocks he made on the wood were answered with an invitation to come in.

She frowned when he stepped over the threshold and closed the door behind him. 'You can't come in here.'

'You told me to come in.'

'I thought you were *Grace*.'

Holding up the file, he stepped across to the small seating area on one side of the room, pointedly ignoring the presence of her large bed. 'Little light reading for you…' Slapping it down on one of the small tables beside a deeply cushioned armchair, he folded his arms and widened his stance to claim the ground he was standing on. 'I'll wait for questions.'

'You can't *be* here,' she argued as she moved away from the windows. 'What if someone finds you?'

'So long as you don't start another fashion parade we should be fine.'

She scowled at him as she stepped over to pick up the file. 'What is this?'

While she opened the cover and bowed her head to look at the contents he studied her reaction through hooded eyes. Her gaze lifted and sought his before she sat down on the chair farthest away from him. Laying the file on her lap, she turned to the next page.

When she spoke her voice was lower and surprisingly calm. 'How many of these are there?'

'They're the ones we take a closer look at.'

'Because you consider them a potential threat?'

'It's the tone as much as the content. After they're fingerprinted and tested for DNA, a psychologist looks them over and builds a profile.' He shrugged. 'Vast majority of them are sent by fruitcakes still living in the basement of their parents' house when they're forty.'

She flicked a brief glance his way. 'Is that true or are you just saying it to make me feel better?'

'I'd be willing to bet your picture is pinned to more than one of those walls in this city.'

'Eww.' She grimaced.

He didn't mention there'd be less of them if people got to know her the way he had in the last forty-eight hours. When he questioned why he hadn't mentioned it, Tyler realized his rage had dissipated. Claiming back a little control probably had something to do with it. Added to the fact they were discussing something that felt closer to police work than babysitting, it was understandable he felt more at ease.

When he noticed the almost imperceptible tremor in her hand as she turned another page Tyler assumed she'd got to one of the more twisted letters.

'Why have I never been shown this file before?'

'They probably thought it was better you didn't know.'

'You obviously disagree.'

As her gaze flickered towards him again the hint of vulnerability he could see in her eyes made him question if he'd done the right thing. He took a short breath. 'Figured if you knew what was out there it might help you understand why things have to change around here.'

'So why not show it to me on the first day?'

Determined he could control her without it would have been

the honest answer. But since showing it to her would then be somewhat akin to admitting defeat…

'Wasn't time,' he lied.

She turned her head a little, her gaze searching the air while she gathered her thoughts. As something occurred to her there was a blink of long lashes and she looked him in the eyes again. 'You think the person you saw in the crowd this morning might have sent one of these letters?'

Tyler nodded. 'It's possible. I'll know if I see him again. I'm good with faces.'

She frowned for a moment before confessing, 'I can't believe there are people out there who would write these letters to me. Let alone *mail them.*'

'I told you, famous brings out the crazy.'

'I don't know how I'm supposed to react to this.'

'Calm is good. A lot of folks would be nailing boards over the windows and bulk buying pepper spray by now.'

The comment earned a brief if somewhat half-hearted attempt at a smile before she closed the file and stood up. One of her hands rubbed her hip while she stretched out the other. 'Can you take this with you?' She avoided his gaze. 'I don't want it in here.'

For the first time since he'd entered the room Tyler took a look at his surroundings and realized his mistake. He'd done more than introduce her to the darkness in the world beyond the walls of her cushioned existence—he'd brought some of the sickness he dealt with every day into her haven. But it didn't stop there—one mistake leading directly to another—not only shouldn't he have come to her bedroom, he shouldn't have taken a look around.

It revealed more about her than he'd wanted to know.

Large, bright flowers covered the wallpaper, crystal chandeliers and mirrored glass sparkling in the autumn sunshine pouring through the windows. The furnishings were soft and textured, reminding him what she'd said to a little girl about liking the way things felt.

The penny dropped. She was *tactile.*

It was why she touched so many arms and ruffled heads of

tousled hair. She'd demonstrated the same thing when she traced the pearls around her neck. It was part of her inherent sensuality; as witnessed when he'd watched her cup her breasts and smooth her palms over the curves of her body. With the revelation came a question: How did she deal with being surrounded by people who weren't allowed to make physical contact? The need to touch and be touched had to make her as much of a ticking time bomb as him.

It explained a lot when it came to *that kiss.*

The file nodded in front of him, her brows lifting.

Unfolding his arms, he stepped forwards and took it from her. As he walked back to the door she followed him.

'Tyler?'

He turned to look at her. 'Yeah?'

'Thank you. You're the first person who thought I could handle this and I appreciate that.'

In fairness he hadn't stopped to consider that any more than he'd thought about the repercussions of charging into her bedroom like the proverbial bull in a china shop. But the knowledge softened his stance a little. 'Does it make more sense as to why I've been so rough on you?'

The question garnered a better attempt at a smile. 'It's not just because you're mean and moody?'

'And mysterious, let's not forget that one.'

The knowing gleam in her eyes placed him about two seconds away from offering to touch and be touched, any time she felt the need. If he didn't think she would come out the other side of it a lot worse off than him, he wouldn't have any qualms about being used that way. He doubted any guy who'd watched her dance would. Though he'd never felt the urge to step on a dance floor, he knew what it meant when a woman moved the way she did.

The sexy rotation of her hips, the back-and-forth movement of her pelvis, the fluid curve of her spine, mile after mile of flawlessly tanned skin with spectacular breasts and long tresses of flame-red hair tumbling over her shoulders and down her back.

Suddenly Tyler could see such a vivid image of her naked he

could practically feel her weight on top of him as she hovered on the edge of release.

Time to go.

'I'll see you tomorrow.'

She nodded in reply.

Despite frowning on the way back to the control room he decided—as risky as it was—he would have to pay more attention. He'd missed a lot of clues that had been right in front of his face and that wasn't like him. Prejudice could cloud the evidence, he *knew that.* But now he knew he didn't have all the answers—he had to take a closer look.

If they could find a way to get along better after the tentative truce they'd struck in her bedroom, maybe things would get better and he could focus on something other than sex with a woman who was out of bounds.

Doubtful, but worth a try.

CHAPTER TWELVE

MIRANDA was determined not to let it get to her.

By thinking about the contents of the letters she was allowing whoever had written them to occupy a place inside her head. She refused to give them that but to deny she was rattled would have been pointless. In the following busy days the only time she felt secure was with Tyler around, which was a tad ironic considering the danger *he* posed.

She glanced at him as he completed a check of the room and stopped to run his gaze over the buffet table. 'I'd eat something if I were you. There's not a lot of time for snacks during the speeches stage of the campaign. I think I saw mini-doughnuts somewhere. They're a cop thing, right?'

'Not if the cop wants to stay in shape.'

'You have trouble with your weight?'

'Not everyone is blessed with my godlike physique.'

Miranda stifled a smile as she looked away. It hadn't escaped her attention he'd been working on his sense of humour lately, even if it demonstrated a distinct lack of anything missing in the ego department.

Lifting her bag from the floor beside her chair, she rooted around for the objects she'd brought with her to help pass the time. Her mother liked to sit out front in the audience and listen to the never-ending soliloquies—her daughter, not so much. Since her father was speaking to a pro-Kravitz crowd she didn't see the need to be there until they had to provide a united family front for the press.

With the sheet of paper carefully smoothed out on the table, she reached for the small box sitting beside it as Tyler pulled out a chair and joined her.

'What are you doing?'

'I promised I'd finish it.'

'She won't know if you don't.'

'That's not the point.' Miranda shrugged a shoulder as she selected a slim crayon. 'It's a karma thing.'

'Careful with those lines.'

'Studying me for a test, Detective, or is everything I say and do so memorable you can't get it out of your mind?'

'Been working long on that confidence problem?'

She lifted her chin and raised a brow. 'You're asking me that after the godlike physique comment?'

'That's just stating a fact. You can't argue them.' He selected what looked like a small samosa from the teetering pile on his plate. 'Whereas what you just did? More like wishful thinking.'

When he popped the morsel in his mouth and smirked, Miranda rolled her eyes and continued colouring.

'It's easy to be confident when everything you want gets handed to you,' he said a couple of minutes later.

'I take it we're talking about me again.' She swapped one crayon for another. 'Were you this judgmental with the last person you bodyguarded?'

'I don't think bodyguarded is a word.'

'Is now…'

When she glanced upwards he had his gaze on the open door as an announcement sounded from the auditorium and there was a wave of applause. As he lifted long arms out to his sides in a leisurely stretch the edges of his navy jacket parted, feeding her hungry gaze with the sight of a pale blue shirt stretched taut over his sculpted chest.

Godlike might have been an exaggeration but there was no arguing the man was ripped.

She wondered when he found time to work out and then pictured him hot and sweaty, pumping weights…

'This is my first gig as a bodyguard,' he confessed as he lowered his arms.

Miranda averted her gaze. 'Well, that explains a lot. What did you do before you got here?'

'Police work.'

'What do you call this?'

'Babysitting.'

'I walked right into that one, didn't I?'

'Yup.'

When she glanced upwards again and saw him press his lips together her eyes narrowed. 'Was that a smile?'

'Those little triangle things are spicy.' He tapped a closed fist against his chest. 'Probably indigestion.'

Miranda felt her mouth curve into a smile of her own.

Shifting his weight on the chair, he reached into the inside pocket of his jacket and produced a cell phone, frowning down at the screen as it flashed.

'Are you going to answer that?' she asked.

'It'll wait.'

'Player.'

He looked into her eyes. 'What makes you so sure it's a woman?'

'Isn't it?' She blinked innocently. 'For all I know it could be your wife.'

'How long you been waiting to ask that question?' When she didn't reply he rested his left elbow on the table and showed her the back of his hand. 'Do you see a ring?'

'That doesn't mean anything.'

He lowered the hand to lift something else off his plate. 'Does to me.'

Miranda liked that it did. Without saying so in as many words he'd conveyed he was the faithful type. She didn't have any proof of that without taking his word for it but she knew instinctively it was true. After all, she'd met more than her fair share of liars over the years.

People who attempted to befriend her because of what rather than who she was—who thought they could get her to speak on their behalf to her father or that dating her would deliver their five minutes of fame. She'd met them all and knew she had trust issues as a result.

She would never have the same problems with Tyler. He didn't have an agenda other than doing his job.

Knowing that should have made her feel better but, oddly enough, it didn't.

When she returned her attention to what she was doing, he took a short breath. 'Since we're playing the sharing game, how come it took you so long to have that talk with your mother?'

'Congratulations,' Miranda said dryly. 'It took you a whole four days to bring up the subject. I didn't think you'd last that long.'

'Deflection—I invented that.'

She sighed heavily. 'Mothers and daughters often have complicated relationships.'

'My sister gets on fine with our mom now she's got better about calling her.'

The comment lifted her gaze. 'You have a sister?'

'And three brothers.'

'There are three more of you out there?' The thought was a tad too much for her brain to contemplate.

A corner of his mouth lifted and for the first time—while looking directly at him as it happened—she realized the move lowered the other side. It was almost a yin and yang thing, hinting at two sides of his personality.

'There's only one of me,' he said as if denying the thought she hadn't voiced. 'The rest of them get to spend their time trying to reach the high bar I set for them.'

'You're the eldest?'

'I'm in the middle.'

'I might need you to explain to me how the high bar works if there were two born before you.'

'I raised it,' he replied without skipping a beat.

Miranda nodded. 'You tell them that, don't you?'

'Repeatedly.'

She tried to imagine what it must have been like to be part of such a large family. Apart from the freedom they had growing up, she envied the company they would have provided for one another. It made her realize how much she missed having Richie around. He'd be joining the campaign soon and they would have to find the time to talk. She just hoped he could forgive her for breaking their pact.

Pushing the thought from her mind, she jumped into the opening Tyler had given her to get to know him better. 'What do your siblings do?'

'My sister runs the legal department at her husband's company. The rest of us are cops.'

Her gaze lifted again. '*All* of your brothers are with the NYPD?'

'Third generation,' he said with an obvious note of pride. 'It's in the blood.'

'You never wanted to be anything else?'

'Nope.'

It explained where some of his confidence came from. He'd known exactly what he wanted, worked towards it and achieved his goal, whereas Miranda's confidence was born of a need to survive. It wasn't that she didn't have it *now,* but in her teens it was a different story.

'What do you want to be when you grow up?' he asked.

Ouch. But considering she probably deserved it after the way she'd been with him, Miranda let it slide. Instead she set down the crayon and pushed her chair back. 'Do you want something to wash down that mountain of food?'

'Avoidance—I invented that one, too.'

'I'm *thirsty* and a bottle of water might help with your indigestion.' She felt his gaze on her as she approached the buffet table.

'You sure you can manage to find it on your own? Don't you usually have someone to do that for you?'

'There are several things I'm perfectly capable of doing on my own.'

'You're just not given much of a chance to do them…'

'No,' she admitted before lifting a bottle of water from a bowl of ice and turning to look at him. 'You want one of these or not?'

He nodded. 'Go on.'

There was another announcement as she returned to the table, followed by loud cheering as she stopped by his chair and reached out her arm. Long, warm fingers wrapped around hers as she handed the bottle to him, providing a sharp contrast to its icily dewed surface. Miranda drew in a sharp breath in reaction to the heat travelling up her arm and tingling across her chest to her sensitive breasts. Moving downwards, it pooled low in her abdomen, creating an empty throbbing between her thighs.

When her gaze lifted the intensity in his eyes devoured her, leaving her in no doubt he knew the effect his touch had on her body. What she couldn't understand was why he hadn't done something about it. He didn't strike her as a man who would let something as trivial as boundaries stand in his way.

Part of her was disappointed, another frustrated. But he had no way of knowing she was different with him than she'd ever been with anyone else.

As far as he knew she played the tease with every guy she met, safe in the knowledge if they attempted to cross the line she could simply step behind a protective wall of security personnel and add another tick to a battle of the sexes scorecard. He didn't know how tough it was to date in high school with a bodyguard present. He couldn't imagine how long it had taken for her to lose her innocence to someone who wouldn't consider the virginity of the mayor's daughter a significant notch on their belt. He would *never* know how disappointing the experience had been or that even with determination the three other times she'd managed to find enough privacy to have sex with the same guy hadn't been a whole heap better.

In the end it had led to a bitter break-up, which left scars she covered with a veneer of self-assuredness it had taken years to perfect. Appearances could be deceptive.

A police detective should know that.

Slipping her hand free, she turned away and stepped over to her chair, curling her fingers into her palm as if she felt the need to save some of the warmth of his touch for later. While her father began his speech they both twisted the lids off their bottles and took a drink.

'You haven't answered the question,' he said.

Miranda resisted the urge to look at him. 'Because I know what you're doing. You think by sharing things about your life with me, I'll confide in you.'

'Afraid I'll sell the inside story to the press?'

'No,' she answered honestly. 'Just suspicious about your motives.'

'Cops ask questions. It's what we do,' he reasoned before adding, 'isn't sharing stuff and getting them to empathize how you usually persuade your bodyguards to cut you some slack?'

'I think we've already established I have to work harder than that with you.'

'Which is part of the attraction, isn't it?'

Miranda's gaze snapped up. They were actually going there? Before she made a fool of herself again she had to be sure. 'Attraction?'

The cobalt gaze locked to hers remained steady. 'I think you know what I'm talking about.'

'Maybe you should elaborate.'

'How explicit do you want me to be?'

Miranda ran the tip of her tongue over her lips and watched as his gaze lowered for long enough to follow the movement. 'You think I can't handle explicit?'

If he knew the number of times she'd imagined him telling her exactly what he was going to do to her…

'I think you still don't know you're swimming out of your depth.' His tone was suddenly hollow and cold.

Subliminally Miranda responded to the accompanying emptiness she thought she could see behind his eyes with the need to offer comfort and return some of the heat he'd created inside her.

She wanted to be alone with him, *really* alone. She wanted him to want the same thing; to ask questions because he wanted to get to know her better and not because he was gathering information to make his job easier.

'Miranda—five minutes.'

The sound of another voice drew her gaze to the open door. 'Thanks, Roger.'

As he disappeared she gathered her things together and placed them back in her bag without looking at Tyler. Reaching inside, she produced the prerequisite Vote Kravitz badge and pinned it to the front of her blouse. 'You want one of these? I always carry a few spares.'

'I didn't vote for him last time.'

Miranda smiled. 'You probably don't want to mention that in front of him. Unless you *want* to hear the one-on-one version of the campaign speech?'

'Any other tips you want to pass on?'

'If he says he'll take it under advisement it means he's going to ignore what you said.'

'Good to know.'

While he cleared the table and walked to the trash can beside the buffet table she checked her appearance in the mirror of a compact and fluffed her hair into place. They met at the door, Tyler waiting silently by her side as she paused to take a breath and fortify herself for the trials ahead. It was time to put on her game face but before she did she allowed him a rare glimpse of a well-kept secret.

As the chill ran down her spine instead of hiding it she shook it off with a shudder of her shoulders. Once she realized what she'd done she glanced sideways and attempted to cover up her vulnerability with a wink. *'Showtime.'*

The low huff of amusement seemed to catch him as off guard as it did her, the immediate following need to shift his gaze to the people assembled behind the stage making Miranda's chest expand with what felt a little too close to endearment. She knew he didn't smile much but suddenly she ached with the need to experience it, to see how it changed his face and hear the sound of rumbling male laughter.

'Your mother is making her way up from the audience now,' Roger's voice said, encouraging her to step forwards and focus.

When she got a brief glimpse of the packed auditorium as

her mother appeared through the curtain at the side of the stage Miranda experienced a flutter of nerves. In need of reassurance, she glanced over her shoulder at Tyler and as their gazes met she thought she could feel it again: the silent understanding she'd been wrong about before.

The nod he gave her was almost imperceptible.

I'm right here, the unexpected warmth in his eyes said. *I've got you.*

She flashed a small smile in reply and for the first time in longer than she cared to admit she didn't feel so alone. It was nice to think someone was there just for her.

Any concern she felt about the truth in the second part of his silent message she could examine later.

CHAPTER THIRTEEN

HE'D been right about one thing.

Miranda was one hell of an actress.

No one on the outside saw how much effort she put into hiding her emotions. Burying them didn't come naturally to her the way it used to for him. But when it came to the way she looked at him—as if he were some kind of tasty treat she wanted to savour—she needed to knock it off. Add their undeniable sexual chemistry to the flash of vulnerability he saw in her eyes before she faced the public and the draw he felt to her was so overpowering Tyler had to remind himself they weren't alone.

He'd have to be careful when they were. The closer she dragged him to the edge, the more likely he was to lose what was left of his footing.

The next time she glanced his way he pointed at the curtain to let her know he would be out front. She nodded in reply before arching a brow at her mother when the woman reached out to brush her hair away from the badge she'd pinned to her chest.

'Seriously?'

'I'm not permitted to make motherly gestures now?'

'Not if it takes us back to the days when you used to dress me like a Jackie Kennedy doll.'

Content she had something to distract her from any fear she felt of unseen dangers in the auditorium, Tyler moved into position. Standing where he had one-hundred-and-eighty-degrees' coverage from the front of the stage, he checked everyone else on the combined detail was where they were supposed to be before running his gaze over the crowd.

'…and with your help we can finish what we started…'

As the mayor's speech whipped the crowd into a frenzy the cheers became louder, making it difficult for Tyler to hear if anything came through in his earpiece. The ever-present tension in his body coiled tighter as he raised his hand and used his forefinger to push it tighter into place.

'We've come too far to give up now!' the mayor shouted into the microphone. 'Are you with me?'

The crowd yelled, 'Yes!'

'Are you with me?'

'Yes!'

There were too many banners and placards waving wildly in the air to allow him to check every face. It made Tyler antsy, the fingers of his gun hand flexing at his side.

'Then let's *do it!*'

'Kravitz! Kravitz! Kravitz! Kravitz!'

In the midst of the chanting there was what sounded like popping gunfire. Immediately pushing back his jacket to place a thumb on his service weapon, Tyler snapped his gaze in the direction he thought it came from. There wasn't any screaming; the crowd wasn't panicking—somewhere in his mind he knew they were both indications nothing had happened. But while his body created so much adrenaline it made his heart struggle to pump it through his veins his brain ignored the message.

In the end it took the sight of a woman scolding her son as she confiscated a bunch of balloons for him to avoid calling in the threat and drawing his weapon.

Lowering his arm, he ground his teeth together, self-recrimination searing his throat when he glanced at the stage. Miranda was standing in plain sight, smiling and waving with her parents. As her gaze sought him out the need to go to her and haul her into his arms was crippling.

He didn't want her up there. He wanted her somewhere he knew she was safe. The thing that stopped him from jumping onstage and carrying her away wasn't his job or who her father was; it was the certainty that place of safety wasn't with him.

By the time they were driving back to the mansion through a not-so-safe-after-dark neighbourhood he was strung out and close to breaking point.

'You okay?'

'Yes,' he gritted. But it was a lie. If he didn't find an outlet for some of his tension soon…

When a figure walking down the sidewalk caught his eye Tyler's brain ran through a scrolling roll of faces and hit jackpot. Checking for traffic, he turned the wheel and swung the Escalade around.

'Where are we going?' she asked.

He didn't reply as the figure turned a corner. Instead he followed it, drew to a halt and unbuckled his seat belt. 'Lock the doors and stay inside.'

'What are you—?'

'Keys are in the ignition.' He got out and slammed the door. As the man lit up by the headlights turned and looked over his shoulder he called out, 'Hey, Jimmy, remember me?'

The second he rabbited Tyler gave chase. One wrong turn later the idiot was trapped in a dead-end alley.

'Haven't you learnt you can't run from me?' He slammed him face-first into a wall before patting him down. 'Out doing a little business—what do we have here?' He took a step back and looked down at the clear plastic pouch in his hand. 'Looks like I have you on possession…'

'That's not mine. It belongs to a friend.'

'Do I look like I just got hit by the stupid stick?'

When the idiot made a predictable attempt to escape it was all the incentive Tyler needed to cut his dark side loose. Reaching for a wrist, he twisted the arm, spun him around and slammed him back into the wall. When he leaned closer his voice was purposefully menacing.

'You know what I want.'

'I heard you was off the case.'

'You heard wrong.'

'You can't rough me up. I'll file a complaint.'

'Go ahead,' Tyler told him as he twisted the arm hard enough to dislocate a shoulder and used his other hand on the guy's head to press his cheek to the wall. 'In the meantime here's what's gonna happen. You're gonna take a message to Demietrov for me. I'll keep the sentences nice and short so you can remember them. You tell him I'm coming for him. He won't know where. He won't know when. Tell him to keep looking over his shoulder.'

'You're Dirty Harry now?'

'No.' His mouth curled into a threatening smile. 'I'm his worst nightmare. You don't deliver the message I'll be yours, too. I'll spread the word you're my new best friend.' He felt his hand press harder against the man's skull and ignored the cry of pain while he fought the need to crush bone. 'No witnesses here. It'll be your word against mine and I think we both know you're the weakest link.'

'She's a witness,' Jimmy croaked.

CHAPTER FOURTEEN

MIRANDA'S breath caught when Tyler's gaze snapped towards her. Fear trickled down her spine, creating goosebumps on her skin and chilling her bones. The violent edge to the scene, the savage need for blood pervading the air—they were valid reasons to fear the man she barely recognized.

Somewhere deep in her soul she could hear a voice calling out to him, 'What are you doing? This isn't *you*.'

But how could she know that for sure?

He released his captive. *'Go.'*

As the man ran towards her Miranda took an instinctive step back. By the time she looked at Tyler again she could sense the hostility aimed at her. Tendrils of rage flowed through the air with the oppressive weight of a brewing storm. 'I told you to stay in the car with the doors locked. What part of that didn't you understand?'

'I…uh…' She cleared her throat and tried to find her voice. 'I was never that good at taking orders.'

'I suggest you start.' He stepped forwards and past her, his muscles carrying him with the same fluidity of movement she would have associated with a panther.

Her first impression of him as a predator crouched to spring on its prey had been right. She just hadn't realized how lethal he could be until she saw him in action.

She hesitated before following him, torn between the need to know what had happened and an almost childlike desire to hide. Her gaze darted to the shadows between overflowing

Dumpsters, her imagination filling them with everything from rats to Freddie Krueger.

Better the devil—even if it was plainly obvious she didn't know him that well.

'Tyler.' She had to run to catch up. 'Tyler, *wait*.'

He stopped so abruptly she almost tripped face-first into his back.

'That's the second time you've done that.' She frowned at his chest when he turned around. 'A little warning would be good.'

Chancing an upwards glance at his shadowed face she discovered he was looking at her through dark hooded eyes.

'What just happened?'

'Did you lock the Escalade?'

'Yes.'

'Where are the keys?'

She reached into the scooped neckline of her blouse to retrieve them from her bra, jangled them in front of his face and snatched them away before he lifted his arm.

Tyler waggled his fingers at her. 'Hand them over.'

'I don't think so.' She tucked them back into her bra. 'You want them you're going to have to come get them.'

'You think I won't?'

'I think I'll scream at the top of my lungs if you *try*.' As far as she was concerned he wasn't getting them back until he gave her an explanation. She folded her arms over her breasts to protect her bargaining tool. 'I'm assuming that man wasn't a friend of yours.'

'Good guess.' The corner of his mouth lifted in a move resembling a sneer. 'I haven't made many friends on the periphery of the Russian mob recently.'

Miranda's jaw dropped. 'That's a joke, right?' A small burst of nervous laughter left her lips. 'Next thing you'll be saying you like your Martinis shaken, not stirred.'

'I'm not a spy.'

'We've already established you weren't a bodyguard until recently. So what are you?'

He shook his head and turned away, glancing at her from

the corner of his eye as she unfolded her arms and fell into step beside him. 'I'm a street cop—narcotics. The bodyguard thing is a temporary gig.'

'But you're still working on a case, aren't you?'

'Stopping the flow of drugs in any city with a market for them is like trying to empty the ocean with a teaspoon. I can't afford to take time off.'

'Then why are you babysitting me?'

'I've asked that question several times.'

'But if you've never been a bodyguard?'

'I took the close protection course a few years ago,' he told her as they turned a corner. 'Back in the days when I had a career plan I was gonna spend time in every department and work my way up.'

Naturally she wanted to know what had happened to knock him off course but first things first. 'How long have you been with Narcotics?'

'Three years—transferred from Vice.'

'How long have you been a police officer?'

'Coming up on twelve years.'

She blinked in surprise. He must be older than he looked. 'What age are you?'

'Thirty-two—ask a lot of questions when you're scared, don't you?'

'I'm not scared,' she lied. 'I'm…' Her head nodded a little from side to side as she sought the right words. When none was forthcoming she opted for a smidgeon of truth. 'Okay, I was scared. I've never seen anyone… I mean, not in real life… obviously on TV and in movies but—'

'View's not so great away from the ivory tower, is it?' he said dryly. 'Down here on street level things can get dirty. I know of at least two cold-case homicides in this area in the last couple of years.'

She glared at his tense profile. 'Are you trying to scare me again?'

The question made him stop and turn towards her. 'What you just saw wasn't enough for you?'

Even in the restricted light Miranda could see his gaze burned with anger. Having faced it before—and with the recent addition of visible proof—she realized how much constraint he exercised when she pushed him. What she found more difficult to understand was how he made her feel and how swiftly it returned to the same unwavering constant over and over again.

She was drawn to him—had been from the start—and even after seeing him at his most dangerous it hadn't changed.

'That didn't look like you,' she replied.

The man she'd seen in the alley wasn't the one who had been watching over her.

'You think you know me after less than a week?' He jerked his brows. 'Is this the part where you tell me danger does it for you—that you're into bad boys and want to be taken on a wild ride?'

Yes, but there was wild and then there was suicidal.

He took an ominous step forwards. 'That's what you were looking for from that dance floor. It's why you responded the way you did when I kissed you. Do you know what happens to women who go looking for trouble? I do. But maybe what you need is a little taste of what you're getting into.'

Miranda's breath snagged in her throat as he took another step forwards, her eyes widening as she took a reciprocal step back. 'Tyler, *don't.*'

'Too late, princess.'

The man obviously had a thing with pinning people to walls because the next thing she knew Miranda had her back to one, the cold dampness of the bricks through the thin material of her blouse making her jump forwards. The move literally played her directly into his hands. Grasping her wrists, he lifted her arms above her head and pushed her back into the wall with his body.

Hard, he was hard everywhere, muscular and tight, his grip on her wrists unyielding as he trapped them in one large hand to free up the other. Miranda struggled against him, the movement merely adding to her problems when her traitorous body responded with a gush of heat to her core. He angled his head, his lips hovering above hers, tempting, teasing, the muscles in his torso so tense they rippled with each harsh breath.

'You think you can stop me now?' When he spoke his mouth whispered across hers. The hand he'd freed smoothed into the dip of her waist on the side of her body before lowering to her hip and squeezing tight enough to make her feel the imprint of each finger. Moving lower, he fisted a handful of skirt material and slowly dragged it upwards. 'Go ahead and try.'

It was pure hell not to give in to temptation and kiss him. If there was trust between them she wouldn't resist; might even have encouraged him not to stop. But no matter how desperately she clung to the belief he wouldn't hurt her, Miranda couldn't deny her desire was woven with a thread of fear. Her heart pounded painfully against her breastbone, her body shaking from the inside out. He was both stronger and bigger than her—there was no way she could fight him off. She'd never been made so aware of the weakness of her body before.

As the skirt slid higher he forced a leg between her knees and nudged them apart. 'I could take you in this position whether you want me to or not.'

She drew in a ragged breath as she stopped struggling and swore he wouldn't make her cry. 'This isn't you.'

'You don't know that,' he said harshly. 'You could have been sidling up to a monster with that little game of dress up you played. I could have brought you here because I know it's a place where people ignore screams after dark.' His voice lowered. 'I could be inside you right now—taking what I need without caring if you get any pleasure out of it. And when I'm done I could leave your broken body for someone else to find.'

'You wouldn't do that.' The crackle of emotion in her voice was impossible to disguise. Swallowing the sob she didn't want him to hear, she forced her gaze upwards to the fire escape on the wall opposite them, willing her mind to detach from her body so he couldn't touch a part of her that might never heal.

When her vision blurred she blinked rapidly but was unable to stop the tears that spilled over her lower lashes to blaze a heated trail down her cheeks.

'Isn't this what you wanted all along—you and me, together?' he asked in his coarse, cold voice. 'You've been begging for it from the start.'

'Not like this,' she choked.

Whether it was the honesty, the pain in her voice, how badly her body was shaking or that he could taste the tears trickling into her mouth, she didn't know. But suddenly his hand stilled, his fingers loosened and a deathly silence descended. It couldn't have lasted for more than a handful of seconds but felt like an eternity. Then, without warning, he released her and staggered back as if he'd been repelled by an invisible force.

When she looked at him Miranda didn't need better light to see the mixture of fury, self-loathing and guilt on his face; she could feel it swirling in a maelstrom around him. He moved sharply, pacing a restless circle while viciously spitting a litany of self-recrimination that was downright nasty. She winced as she straightened her skirt with shaking hands. The self-hatred was more than obvious and with blinding clarity she got an inkling of what he might have been doing.

It was more than a brutal warning of the consequences her actions could have with the wrong man—it was an attempt to get her to hate him as much as he hated himself.

When he stopped pacing he shook his head. 'You need a new bodyguard. I'm obviously not cut out for this.'

Gathering strength, she took a tentative step forwards and dampened her lips with the tip of her tongue. 'I don't want a new bodyguard. I want you.'

'How can you *say that* after what I just did to you?'

He snarled like a cornered animal but with new insight Miranda saw him as less of a predator and more of an angry bear with a thorn in his paw.

She took another step. 'You wouldn't have hurt me.'

'You don't *know* that!' His mouth twisted when he saw her hesitate. 'You gonna try lying to me and telling me you didn't have a moment of doubt?'

'I can't do that,' she confessed. 'But I can remember the man you were before you turned the car around.'

His chest heaved as he tried to gain control. 'What do I have to do to make you realize you'd be better keeping your distance from me?'

'I don't know. But this wasn't it.'

'I'm not like the other guys you've spent time with. There's nothing polished or refined about me.'

If he was trying to discourage her from reaching out to him, then he wasn't doing a very good job. The compulsion she'd felt to offer comfort combined with her need for physical contact, drawing her to him with a sense of what felt like inevitability. She took another step forwards and another until she was standing directly in front of him.

'Right now I need you to hold me for a minute,' she said softly. 'Do you think you can do that?'

'You should be running for the hills,' he replied in a gruffer voice. 'Not asking me to get closer.'

'I need a little shoulder action.' When she attempted a smile the fear of rejection she'd hidden since her teens made it waver. 'If you can think of anyone else I can ask for that when everyone who surrounds me isn't supposed to touch me—'

He reached out and hauled her into his arms.

Miranda gasped at the contact and let out a small sob of relief. Wrapping her arms around his lean waist, she buried her face in his chest and took several breaths of Tyler scented air. She could feel the tension in his body, streams of electricity buzzing beneath his skin. But she'd been right to ask him to hold her. A violent shudder ran through him, his arms tightening as if he couldn't hold her close enough. After a while he rested his chin on her head and she felt his throat convulse.

'I'm sorry,' he said roughly, the impression it wasn't something he said very often making her heart twist.

'I know.' She turned a little and rested her cheek against his tie. 'It's okay. I forgive you.'

'You shouldn't. I can't forgive me.'

'Maybe you should start.' She took another breath before jumping in with both feet. 'What happened to make you so angry, Tyler?'

'How do you know you didn't just get a glimpse of the real me?'

'Because you're holding me right now and giving me what I need.' She snuggled closer to prove the point before confessing, 'And because I don't want to believe it was…'

When he moved his head she felt the whisper of his breath against her hair. 'You can't save me, if that's what you're thinking. I'm beyond saving.'

Leaning back to look up at his face, she discovered he was frowning; his gaze lowered so she couldn't look into his eyes. The arms holding her loosened as he took a half step back. Unwilling to let him retreat when they'd taken such a major leap forwards, Miranda freed up a hand and raised it to stroke her fingertips along his jaw, her thumb gliding to the edge of his mouth.

Heat resonated from him, seeping into her skin and removing the chill from her bones.

Watching her thumb as it traced his lower lip, she whispered, 'Kiss me.'

He stood rigidly still.

Moving her hand to wrap her fingers around the thick column of his neck, she pulled his head down to hers and rocked forwards onto her toes. She lifted her chin, closed the last of the distance between them and pressed her lips against his. He stiffened but didn't jerk away. Miranda took that as a good sign, even if she'd never kissed such an unresponsive partner. Launching a tentative exploration, she kissed a corner of his mouth, willing him to relax.

The thought of him remaining still while she explored every inch of his body was a heady enticement to continue. Emboldened, she traced the valley between his lips with the tip of her tongue. Then she wasn't in control any more.

Long fingers threaded into her hair, his palm cradling the back of her head and holding it still as he sampled her lips in softly sipping kisses that coaxed her into opening her mouth. When his tongue slipped inside Miranda moaned in appreciation, sensation pouring over her like a blanket of warm honey. Another large hand stroked over her shoulder blade as the kiss deepened, smoothing down her spine and dipping to the curve of her rear to draw her closer.

When her abdomen made contact with the evidence that he was as turned on as she was Miranda grabbed the lapels of his jacket between her fingers. He parted their lips and she dropped her head back, eyes closed, as he planted a trail of heated kisses along her neck. He pushed up the hem of her blouse, burrowing his hands underneath to touch the heated skin of her midriff. When she sucked in a breath the movement granted him access to her torso. He traced a finger along the band of her bra, knuckles skimming the lace-covered swell at the underside of her breasts.

'We shouldn't be doing this,' his deep voice rumbled against her neck.

'I'm not sure reminding us both it's forbidden will help,' she answered breathlessly, clinging to him as if he was the only thing holding her upright.

'I'm supposed to keep my distance.'

Her mouth curved into a decadent smile. 'That might sound more convincing if you weren't saying it while you have your hands on me.'

'You're the mayor's daughter,' he said as he kissed his way back up her neck.

'One day I'm hopeful people will think of me as more than that. Using my name would be a great place to start.'

He raised his head and looked down at her. 'I've used your name.'

'No, you haven't.'

'I can't have gone this long without saying it.'

She smiled again. 'Wanna bet?'

'There was that time when I was listing everything I knew about you…'

She shook her head. 'Doesn't count.'

He nudged the tip of her nose with his before lowering his voice. 'Miranda…'

The sound of her name said in the deep rumble of his voice sent a tingle across her sensitive skin.

He placed a light kiss on her lips. *'Miranda...'*

She sighed contentedly. It sounded both sexy and reverent when he said it that way. Angling his head, he scrambled her thoughts with a longer, heated kiss. She felt one of his hands move against her breast and then…

He lifted his head and took a step back, his hands dropping from her body.

When Miranda opened her eyes she blinked at the sight of a half smile curving his mouth as he held up the keys.

'Nice move,' she said with begrudging respect.

He clamped his fingers around the keys and lowered his arm. 'I have plenty more where that came from but right now you're going home before we both end up in trouble.'

When he took her hand and led her back to the SUV, her thoughts unscrambled for long enough to allow something she'd overheard in the alley to make its way through to the front of her mind. 'The guy you sent a message to—isn't there a chance he'll come looking for you when he gets it?'

'He won't try anything when I'm on duty.'

'How do you know that?'

'Not his MO. If he has the stones to come after a cop he'll do it in the shadows.' Long fingers flexed around hers. 'Despite evidence to the contrary I wouldn't do anything that could place you in danger.'

'It wasn't me I was worried about.'

The softly spoken words made Tyler stop dead in his tracks and turn towards her. 'I won't let anything happen to you.' His voice was suddenly deeper, richer and accompanied by what almost felt like déjà vu. 'You can trust me.'

The level of intensity seemed out of place, even for him. Miranda searched what she could see of his eyes. 'What aren't you telling me?'

He shook his head. 'Nothing.'

A sense of foreboding created an unfamiliar heaviness in her chest. 'Tyler—'

'I think we've covered enough ground for one night, don't you?'

He had a point. Suddenly she was exhausted in a way she'd

never been before, both physically and emotionally. What worried her was how badly she wanted to draw strength from him and how quickly she'd become reliant on him being there. It wasn't like her.

From the night they met she'd been following his lead. Even when she'd resisted she'd been caught in the undertow of a wave of attraction, unable to come up for air. At some point she knew she would have to—he wouldn't be there for ever. But until that day and while there was something that made it feel she should hold on to him, she wrapped a second hand around his and held on tight.

CHAPTER FIFTEEN

'I'M HEARING rumours on the streets there's a rogue cop gunning for Demietrov. Tell me it's not you.'

When Tyler silently took the fifth his partner swore in his ear. 'This isn't the Wild West where you can clean up the streets with a gun. Hang on.' He raised his voice to yell at someone who had obviously walked in on his end of the conversation. 'Anyone wants me I'll be in the porcelain reading room.' His voice lowered again. 'I haven't been keeping you in on the loop so you can turn vigilante on me. You can't take on every low life in the city. What difference do you think one man can make?'

'We think that way we've got no business being cops,' Tyler replied flatly. For him there was more to carrying a shield than family tradition. He'd signed up to make a difference; his lack of success over the years more than half his problem. A little never felt like enough. Textbook overachiever most likely, but the way he saw it there was no point doing something if it wasn't done right.

'Do what you're thinking about doing and you won't be a cop for much longer,' his partner replied. There was the sound of a creaking door being opened. 'You seem to be under the impression 'cos you're not married with kids it means no one will get hurt if something happens to you. How do you think your family would feel about that?'

Probably the same way they'd feel if they'd had ring seats when he'd treated Miranda the way he had. Like all good Irish boys he'd been raised to be respectful to women. Hadn't been much indication of that with her, had there? His mother would tear strips off his worthless hide if she knew what he'd done. But when it came to how his family would feel if he became part of the darkness he'd been fighting for so long, Tyler realized he'd convinced himself they would understand. Be disappointed in him—no doubt about that—but they'd get it. Miranda wouldn't.

Not so long ago what she thought hadn't mattered.

But it did now.

She'd been worried about him. No matter how hard he tried he couldn't wrap his head around that. Being offered forgiveness with soft, sweet kisses he found impossible to resist had been difficult enough for him to understand. But that she'd been *worried about him?*

'You listening to me?'

'I can hear you.'

'Not what I asked.'

Tyler watched the people going about their business with cell phones pressed to their ears, cups of coffee in their hands, briefcases as extensions of their arms or a combination of all the above. New Yorkers living busy lives and never worrying about crime until something happened to them. It was the way it should be but it took a thin blue line of defence to keep it that way.

He wondered when he'd first thought about crossing it and then questioned for the hundredth time why he'd made the exact same vow to Miranda he'd made to the woman who'd died when he couldn't live up to his word.

'Did it occur to you by calling him out he might come gunning for you?' his partner asked. 'What am I saying? Course it did. You think by painting a target on your back you'll force him out of hiding. I thought we had a *plan*.'

'We're barely making a dent in his operation. Every time we take his dealers off the streets he replaces them before we've had time to do the paperwork.'

'What if he puts a price on your head and the mayor's daughter gets caught in the crossfire?'

It was an unnecessary reminder of his thoughtlessness but in his defence it had been a while since he stopped to consider the effect his job could have on someone else. Once he did he realized his need to protect her had nothing to do with duty any more. It was personal. She made him wish the world were a better place, adding to the dissatisfaction he couldn't do more to make it that way.

Placing some distance between them was the only way he could focus clearly.

When she was around it had got to the point where every step he took and every thought he had was centred on the knowledge she was nearby. She clouded his judgment and weakened what was left of his resolve not to sleep with her. He couldn't seem to be near her without wanting to touch her. Wherever possible he found himself offering a hand to help her in or out of a vehicle, placing his palm on the inward curve of her spine to guide her in the right direction, handing bottles of water to her or taking them away when she didn't need them any more.

Her reaction to each stolen touch or heated glance made him forget all the reasons he couldn't have her. But he needed to remember them, for his sake as much as hers.

'…till you give me your word you won't do anything stupid,' his partner's voice said.

Tyler frowned. 'Didn't catch all of that.'

'The hell you didn't.'

He stopped in front of a storefront. 'I gotta go. I'll talk to you later.'

'Don't hang up on—'

Hitting the screen to end the call, he pushed through the door, walked to the nearest member of staff and flashed his shield. 'Detective Brannigan—I noticed the lion on your company logo and was wondering if I can take a look at some of your stationery.'

While the woman led the way he checked his watch. Two hours fourteen minutes and twenty-eight seconds until he saw Miranda again. Not that he was counting.

Under normal circumstances they would be locked on a heading he suspected neither of them wanted to change. But kissing her was one thing, taking advantage of their enforced proximity to scratch an itch was another and all it could be. Apart from keeping her safe and being there when she needed him, he had nothing to offer. There'd been a time he'd thought about settling down, getting married, having kids and moving up the ranks so his family could be proud of him. But even if she wanted a commitment from a guy like him, those days were gone.

His partner's concern wasn't misplaced. One way or another there would be a day of reckoning. It had been a long time coming and when it did Tyler wasn't convinced he would do the right thing.

Standing close to one of the windows he looked outside and saw a silent figure standing on the other side of the street, dull, lifeless eyes staring at him with accusation.

He wondered how Miranda would react if he mentioned he could see dead people.

CHAPTER SIXTEEN

SHE missed him when he wasn't around. That Tyler had become such a strong presence in her daily life concerned Miranda, but not enough to distract her focus from the increased frustration it added to the lack of privacy.

Detective Patty-Fingers was going to drive her insane if she couldn't get him on board with the idea of some quality alone time soon.

Adding the finishing touches to her make-up, she leaned back from the mirror and forced the ever-present thread of worry from her mind. Knowing the work he did allowed her imagination to run riot with dozens of horrific scenarios, all of which resulted in him getting hurt.

That no one would think she needed to know if he was didn't exactly help.

Reaching for an assortment of mismatched gold bangles to accompany the chunky squares dangling from her ears, she stood up, pushed her feet into a pair of waiting Jimmy Choo's and stepped over to the full-length mirror for a final inspection. The fashion police would be out in force on the red carpet but, for the first time since they'd started tearing apart everything she wore, she didn't care what they said. So long as the short shift of cap-sleeved emerald-green material overlaid with fine black lace got Tyler's attention nothing else mattered.

The flutter of tiny wings tickled the inside of her stomach with anticipation as she lifted her purse from the end of the bed and crossed the room. It wasn't a *date* they were going on but it felt like one.

He was effortlessly taking the stairs two at a time when she walked down the hall, his gaze lifting to tangle with hers. As always, her breath caught. Now it really did feel like a date. He wasn't wearing a suit. Instead his long legs were encased in black jeans and he'd layered the top half of his body with a dark sports jacket worn over a V-necked sweater with a white T-shirt underneath.

They met at the top of the stairs, his gaze slowly caressing her from head to toe before he quirked his brows and rewarded her efforts with, 'Wow.'

A smile blossomed on her lips. 'Exactly the response I was aiming for.' She angled her chin. 'Are both your suits at the dry cleaner's?'

'I heard bodyguards were supposed to blend in at these things. And for the record, I have more than two suits.'

'Are they all navy and black?' She resisted the urge to reach out and brush her fingertips over the lapels of his jacket while they were under the scrutiny of the security cameras. 'Now that I think about it, do you even have any colour in your wardrobe?'

To her delight he looked amused. 'You gonna start dressing me now?'

Au contraire; while he looked as mouth-wateringly good as he did, she was much more interested in *undressing* him.

When he read the message in her eyes he shook his head and inclined it towards the stairs. 'Let's go, princess.' They were halfway down before he lowered his voice to ask, 'You're wearing underwear under this one, right?'

'Only one way you're going to find out,' she replied in an equally intimate tone. 'And did I mention this is supposed to be kiss-proof lipstick? We might need to conduct a consumer test later.'

As they stepped onto the foyer the weight of a large hand on the inward curve of her spine drew a sharp breath through her lips. She could feel each long finger, her body aching in all the places she wanted him to touch. Then the door to the vestibule opened, her father appeared and Tyler's hand dropped a split second before he took a noticeable step back.

She hated that he had to do that.

'I thought you were speaking at a dinner this evening,' Miranda said to her father with a smile.

'Came back to get your mother,' her father replied. 'Where are you off to?'

'Movie premiere in Times Square. I'm afraid Detective Brannigan will have to suffer his way through a rom-com.'

Her father leaned in to place a kiss on her cheek. 'Have fun, sweetheart.'

'You, too.'

He nodded at Tyler. 'Detective.'

'Sir.' Tyler nodded in reply.

They continued across the foyer and into the vestibule as her father made his way upstairs. When Miranda used one of the tricks she'd learnt and slowed her pace so Tyler would touch her again the outer door opened and Lou Mitchell walked in.

'Miranda.' He smiled.

'Good evening, Lou. How's the family?'

'Great, thanks.' He looked at Tyler. 'How'd you get on this afternoon?'

'Might have something,' Tyler replied. 'I'll talk to you tomorrow.'

Miranda lowered her voice as they stepped outside. 'This place is like Grand Central.'

'Yeah, I'd noticed that. But at least we'll get some peace and quiet in Times Square.'

The combination of dry humour and the thought he might be as frustrated by the lack of privacy as she was made her smile. 'What were you doing this afternoon?'

'That's on a need-to-know basis.' He stopped at the front of the SUV. 'Where do you think you're going?'

'I want to sit up front.'

He shook his head. 'No.'

'Why not?'

'Have you ever sat in the jump seat?'

'No.'

'Then you're not starting now.' Raising a hand he beckoned her with a crooked forefinger. 'Round you come.'

Miranda stood her ground. 'I thought we were parking at the Hyatt.'

'We are.'

'Then it's not like I'm getting out where anyone can see me, is it?'

'That's not the point.'

'We'll be late if you don't open the door.'

Tyler nodded. 'Best come round here and get in, then, hadn't you?'

She rolled her eyes. 'I can't believe we're arguing about where I sit.'

'And I can't believe you're kicking up such a stink about it when you've never sat anywhere else.'

Miranda aimed a mock glare his way. 'Maybe it might be nice not to feel like I'm being chauffeured everywhere.'

'You *are* being chauffeured everywhere.'

'You could indulge me just this once,' she cajoled.

'Not paid to do that.'

She batted her lashes and pouted, 'Pretty please?'

Tyler sighed heavily before the finger he'd used to beckon her pointed in warning as he moved. 'No touching anything while I'm driving.'

Why did he think she wanted to sit in the front?

'I *mean* it.'

He was still a party pooper but, the way Miranda looked at it, the night was young.

When the locks clicked she opened the door and climbed inside, carefully arranging her dress so it wouldn't crease and then sliding the skirt a little higher so it revealed a couple more inches of leg. As they reached for their seat belts she glanced surreptitiously at Tyler to see if he'd noticed. Judging by the frown on his face as he turned the ignition key, he had.

She wondered if teasing him would ever get old. He had to know it was foreplay. There was nothing about him that suggested he didn't have skills in that area. When she thought about what he could teach her, she squirmed a little on the seat.

'Quit that,' he said in a rougher voice as the gate raised and they left the compound.

'I'm settling in.' She looked out of the windscreen and stifled a smile. 'It feels different sitting up here.'

'That's not what you're doing.' He checked for traffic before turning onto the street.

'Are you an expert on how a woman's mind works?'

He aimed another heated gaze her way. 'I know getting inside a woman's head can have spectacular results in the bedroom, if that's what you're asking.' When he focused on driving again, he frowned. 'Most cops learn to read body language. It comes in handy.'

Nice attempt at trying to change the subject.

Miranda turned towards him, much more interested in what was happening inside the SUV than she was in anything outside. 'How do you do that?'

'Read body language?'

'Get inside a woman's head.'

'You pay attention.'

'So what have you discovered about me?'

'You're not who I thought you were,' he replied with a hint of uncharacteristic reluctance. 'Not entirely.'

She took a deep breath. 'I'm not sure I'm going to like everything about the answer to this question, but here goes. What do you mean by "not entirely"?'

'You're high-maintenance.'

Miranda disagreed. 'Unless someone is supplying the necessary personal grooming must-haves of a mani-pedi or a fabulous haircut I manage my beauty regime the same way any other woman does.'

'That wasn't what I meant.' He checked the mirrors before changing lanes. 'You're hard work.'

She could see how that would be true from his point of view. 'Do I need to remind you that you weren't exactly Mr Friendly at the start? I might have been nicer to you if you'd been nicer to me.'

'You telling me you don't like getting your own way?'

'Most people do,' Miranda countered. 'Especially if it can mean the difference between surviving in an environment you find suffocating or drowning under the weight of a responsibility you never asked for in the first place.'

When she realized how much she'd revealed she fixed her gaze on the traffic in front of them. She couldn't expect him to understand how she felt. No one could until they'd walked a mile in her shoes.

'I already figured that part out,' his voice rumbled.

'It's not as easy a life as some people might think it is,' she confessed.

'I couldn't do it.'

'You wouldn't have let it continue for so long.'

'I'm surprised you have.'

'As crazy as they can make me, I love my family.' She shrugged a shoulder. 'They're the only one I've got.'

With the reminder she lifted her chin and sat taller. Young ladies didn't slouch; they had poise and composure, even when having a discussion that made them feel exposed and vulnerable to criticism.

'You don't have to do that when we're alone. Save it for the crowd.'

Miranda's startled gaze leapt to his profile.

As he straightened the wheel he glanced at her. 'You thought I didn't know?'

It was difficult to think anything when the sensation he really had stepped inside her head was so...*unsettling*...

'Everyone has a front,' he continued while she tried to find her voice. 'Work the streets for long enough you learn there's usually a reason for it.'

Having raised the topic, he had to know she would turn it around. 'What do you hide?'

The corner of his mouth lifted. 'If I answered that question it wouldn't be hidden any more, would it?'

'You've spent more than your fair share of time in an interrogation room, haven't you?'

'They're called interview rooms these days.'

When she wondered how much his job affected the rest of his life Miranda decided the easiest way to find out was to open the topic. 'It can't be easy not to bring your work home with you.'

'It's not.'

'So how do you strike a balance?'

A muscle in his jaw clenched. 'You accept the fact you made a vow and live up to it as best you can for as long as you can.'

She understood that better than he probably thought she did. What she didn't understand was how he dedicated so much of his life to his work without needing something for himself. Didn't he have things he enjoyed doing in his downtime—people he wanted to spend time with, places he wanted to see? She couldn't have survived if she didn't have those things, even if some of them were still part of her dreams for the future.

'You remind me a little of my father,' she reluctantly admitted. 'He has the same level of dedication to his job.'

'Public service takes a particular kind of person.'

'Self-sacrificing?' she enquired.

'Mule-headed,' he replied.

'Oh, yes.' She nodded. 'He can be that, too.'

'You ever have the kind of talk with him that you had with your mother?'

Miranda angled her chin. 'Exactly how long were you standing outside that door?'

'Long enough to get the general gist. You'd think the doors in a place that old would be thicker.'

'In fairness to the door my mother does have a knack for getting me to raise my voice.' She rolled her eyes. 'In the olden days she'd have been described as unflappable.'

'Useful trait for a politician's wife.'

'True, but there's nothing worse than someone who won't argue with you when you're itching for a fight.'

'Might help if you were more open with her…'

'Now you're starting to sound like my father,' she complained. 'This is *so* not the conversation I planned on having with you the next time we were alone.'

'And now you're annoyed because you're not getting your own way,' he stated without missing a beat. 'Like I said—*hard work.*'

Miranda scowled at his profile. 'Did no one ever tell you it's okay to have the thought but it's not always okay to say it out loud?'

'Not much call for tact in my line of work.'

She shook her head and looked out of the windscreen as he steered them through the narrower side streets that fed into the main artery leading to the heart of Times Square. Speaking her mind wasn't something she'd been encouraged to do, especially when every word she said or Tweeted could be held against her. She'd always struggled with that. But with Tyler she didn't have to fight against her nature. It made sense of several things once she thought about it.

'Do you think if you were given more freedom you'd feel the need to go looking for trouble?'

The question made her sigh. 'I don't go looking for trouble. It has a tendency to find me.'

'Like a drugs raid in a nightclub,' he said dryly.

'How was I supposed to know the place had a drugs problem when I'd never been there before?'

'If you'd had an advance check it out they'd have told you.' When they stopped for a crossing light he looked her in the eye. 'There's an army of people at your disposal twenty-four-seven—never occurred to you to take advantage of their skill set?'

'I'm not going to bother someone every time I get the impulse to go out for ice cream.'

'It's your security detail's job to protect you,' he pointed out as bluntly as she'd learned to expect. 'You go skipping out any time you feel like it or get caught in the middle of a raid it makes both them and the department look bad. Wouldn't look a whole heap better for your father if he let something happen to you, would it?'

She wasn't trying to make anyone look bad. How could he not know that by now?

When the light changed and the last of the pedestrians on the crossing parted to make space for them to move forwards he surmised, 'You didn't think of it that way.'

'I suppose that makes me selfish?'

He shook his head. 'I don't think it's selfish to want time to yourself—I get that's what you were doing now. What I don't get is the reason you've stuck it out for so long if you don't enjoy it.'

Not true. 'There are parts of it I enjoy—meeting people, going places, supporting worthwhile causes.'

'So why not find a job that involves those things without the same restrictions?'

'I intend to. But I made a promise to my brother.'

She blinked. Had she just said that out loud?

'What kind of promise?'

That would be a yes, then. Briefly hiding behind the hand pretending to brush her hair into place, she checked to see how she felt about telling him. On a gut level it didn't feel wrong but there was a limit to how much she could say without delving into her family history. 'After abandoning him five days a week while I was at NYU I said I'd make sure he didn't have to smile for the cameras until the next election—he's due home the week before to help with the run-in. Win or lose, the plan was we'd make a stand together when he finished college.'

'What changed?'

'I did,' she answered truthfully before lowering her chin. 'I've never told anyone that. About the promise to my brother, I mean.'

'What about Crystal?'

'She wouldn't get it.'

'So why tell me?'

'Because I think you do.' Miranda lifted her chin and looked into his eyes as the traffic slowed. 'Like I said not so long ago—no one speaks to me the way you do. Maybe I needed someone to be frank with me so I could learn how to do the same in return.'

'If brutal honesty is what you need you're never gonna have to worry you won't get it from me.'

As much as it ruffled her feathers—particularly when he said something she didn't want to hear—she liked that about him. It was refreshing. 'You're never gonna let me win an argument for the sake of keeping the peace either, are you?'

'Nope,' he answered succinctly as he focused on the road ahead. 'And don't ever take me on in a sport unless you plan on losing.'

It was too good an opportunity to miss. 'Is there anything you're *not* good at?'

'Wouldn't you like to know?' he drawled.

When he turned his head the smile he flashed was so completely unexpected it stunned Miranda into silence. Enraptured by the sight she stared at the immediate change it brought to his face. His eyes were suddenly dozens of different shades of blue, the lines at the corners of his dense lashes deepening to give the impression there'd been a time in his life when he'd laughed often and loud. Added to the flash of pearly whites beneath the adorably crooked line of his lips, he wasn't just handsome.

He was irresistible.

Miranda felt her body and heart sway towards him with the same impulse as a flower turning its petals to the sun. She was smiling back at him before she realized she was doing it, her chest expanding with warmth.

But like all good things the moment didn't last.

When the SUV moved forwards again she decided it was probably just as well. She couldn't get more attached to him than she already was. So long as everything they did was treated as nothing more than foreplay she'd be fine.

Until she'd lived a little, explored some and quelled the doubts she had about her capability to do something worthwhile with her life, she couldn't so much as *think* about making a commitment to someone else.

Tyler Brannigan was a commitment kind of guy; twelve years on the job would have told her that even if he hadn't made the comment about wearing a wedding ring. From that point of view she was glad there wasn't any chance *he* would get more attached to *her*.

She just wished she knew why it made her feel so sad.

CHAPTER SEVENTEEN

A LIFE that involved posing on a red carpet wasn't one Tyler could ever see himself living. Considering the number of flashing cameras, it was a miracle she hadn't gone blind.

Posting up a few feet away from the spotlight, he watched her at work with a newfound respect. She seemed to know exactly where each lens was pointed; how to stand to display her stunning figure to its best advantage—though in fairness some folks were probably looking at her clothes—and throughout the test of endurance her smile never faded.

She was a pro. If she ended up supporting worthwhile causes when she had her freedom, they would be lucky to have her. The thought of her putting as much passion into her work as she did when she kissed him…

Well, suffice to say the world had better watch out.

When they stepped inside the movie theatre to make way for the Hollywood stars she was equally adept at working the room. Some of the people she talked to he recognized, some he didn't, but she knew each and every one by name and managed to slip in several mayoral sound bites inside ten minutes. Since it was more than apparent he wasn't the only bodyguard present—some of them standing out like pro-wrestlers in a ballet class—he allowed her a little more space and stepped over to the counter nearby.

Her eyes sparkled when he returned. 'What is that?'

'Can't watch a movie without popcorn,' he reasoned.

'And a bucket of soda, apparently.' She smiled as they lined up to take their seats. 'You bought diet, right?'

'Not in this lifetime.'

Reaching out, she snagged a kernel of popcorn and popped it in her mouth.

'Did I say I'd bought it to share?'

She smiled brightly as she chewed.

It set the tone for the following hour and a handful of minutes. In the darkness of the auditorium, with numerous brushes of their fingertips in the search for popcorn, some of the tension seemed to ease from his body. He might have left the theatre feeling pretty relaxed if it hadn't been for the sex scene in the movie.

As the tension rose onscreen it seemed to coil around them. His senses became sharper and clearer. The seductive scent of her perfume, the contact of their elbows on the armrest between them, the saltiness on his lips he knew he would taste on hers when they kissed.

When his little finger brushed rhythmically into one of the groves between finer-boned fingers he glanced sideways and saw her press her knees together. His gaze lifted to the dark pools of her eyes; the thought her body was preparing for him immediately making his do the same in return. For a moment it felt as if they were the only people there. Then something was said onscreen that made the audience laugh, snapping him out of it and allowing him time to gather what was left of his senses before the credits rolled. But reminding himself of all the reasons he couldn't have her wasn't working. If anything it made the need for mutual release seem as vital as his next breath.

She tugged his sleeve to get his attention when they reached the foyer. 'Last time I was here, Mac thought it was quicker to use the side exit than wade through the mob out front.'

Tyler didn't argue, but when the door opened there were almost as many people in the side street as there had been out front. The barricades were human—a line of uniformed police officers, some of them with outstretched arms, some as interested in who came out of the door as the crowd.

When Miranda appeared people started calling her name.

'I don't like this,' Tyler said tightly.

'It's fine,' she reassured him before pinning a smile in place and stepping forwards. 'Hi, how are you? Yes, it was great, you should go see it.'

While she worked her way down the line every instinct Tyler possessed screamed at him to get her out of there. He glared at one of the uniforms, tempted to get his badge number and report him for not doing his damn job.

As the door opened and a well-known talk-show host stepped outside the crowd yelled louder and moved forwards in a rolling wave that could barely be contained. His gaze immediately darted to Miranda. She'd got a couple of steps ahead and had her back to him. As he moved closer he saw her elbow move in a way that suggested whoever was holding on to her hand wasn't keen to let go. The minute he saw who it was Tyler grabbed the man's arm.

'Back off,' he warned.

'It's okay,' Miranda's voice said. 'I've got this.'

'I said, *back off*.'

The dark-haired man grimaced behind his glasses but didn't let go. When he raised his other arm and tried to put it around her waist Tyler's most basic instincts kicked in. Nudging her to the side to make room, he grasped fistfuls of sweatshirt and shoved the guy away from her.

'What are you *doing?*' he heard her say a split second before one the Hollywood stars appeared.

Suddenly the crowd was screaming and surging forwards. The guy he was holding stumbled backwards—was torn from his grasp—and Tyler was surrounded. Whirling around, he searched frantically for Miranda while his muscles clenched with the adrenaline-fuelled need to protect her. When he got a glimpse of her hair a second before her head dropped out of sight the thought of her being crushed almost made him lose his mind.

'Get out of the way!' he roared, shoving bodies aside until he could see her on the ground trying to get to her feet. Dropping down onto his haunches, he placed a hand on her shoulder and squeezed. 'You okay?'

She looked up at him and nodded, her eyes glittering with fear. 'I'm fine,' she lied.

Tyler pressed his forehead against hers for a moment, relief surging through his body. 'Let's go.'

Helping her upright, he took one of her hands in a firm grasp, his pace not slowing until he'd dragged her across Times Square and into the underground parking of the Hyatt. When they got close to the Escalade he turned around and hauled her into his arms. But instead of holding on to him, she struggled free and took a step back.

'Have you lost your mind?'

Tyler frowned. 'He wouldn't let go of you.'

'I was handling it.'

'It didn't *look* like you were.'

'You're putting me more on edge than those stupid letters,' she said with exasperation. 'How am I supposed to act normally if every time we go somewhere you freak out like I'm about to be kidnapped?'

'I suppose I should just stand there and let you get sucked into the crowd or *crushed*.'

She frowned back at him. 'What you should do is what everyone else who has surrounded me for the last eight years never learned to do—*ask me* if I'm okay.'

For the first time since he'd realized who she was talking to in the crowd Tyler stopped to think. Telling her it was the same guy he'd seen outside the school wouldn't help. He couldn't confess how uncharacteristically scared he'd been when he thought she might be hurt or how relieved he was when she wasn't, either.

So where did that leave him?

'You're right,' he admitted flatly, partly because she was but mostly because he couldn't think of anything else to say.

The admission took the wind out of her sails. 'Thank you.' She searched his eyes. 'Now do you want to tell me what happened back there?' When he didn't reply she took a short breath. 'Tyler, I'm trying to make an effort to communicate with you but you're gonna have to help me out here. I can't do it alone.'

He popped his jaw and tried to meet her halfway. 'Maybe I'm having a problem with the crowds.'

'Why?'

'Too many people.'

'We live in New York—it comes with the territory.' Her expression softened, the warmth of understanding in her eyes making him feel about two feet tall. 'It's because everywhere you look you're seeing potential dangers, isn't it?' She smiled. 'You don't have to worry about me. I've survived this long, haven't I?'

Tyler ground his teeth together. He'd liked it better when they were arguing.

'When I'm not appearing at public engagements I barely merit a second look.'

He very much doubted that. The night they met he would have picked her out of the crowd without any difficulty.

Stepping forwards, she took his hands and tangled their fingers together. 'I'll prove it to you.'

'How exactly are you gonna do that?'

'You have to trust me.' She lifted their arms out to the sides and briefly rolled her gaze towards the concrete ceiling. 'And possibly veer off the schedule a little bit…'

He didn't like where the conversation was headed any better than he liked the sensation he was being managed. 'Where are we going?'

'For a walk,' she replied with the same impossibly soft smile he'd seen her use on a small child.

'Not in Times Square, we're not.'

'I was thinking more along the lines of Carl Schurz Park.' Rocking forwards, she lifted her chin, her voice taking on the liquid cadence he'd been able to resist not so long ago. 'Seems to me we could both use the break…'

'Why there?' he asked while weighing up the pros and cons in his mind to distract his body from accepting the invitation she'd issued to kiss and make up.

'Because I've never got to see much of it beyond the view from my bedroom window. You can help me change that…'

Tyler finished the sentence for her when he realized what

she was doing. 'And it's close enough to the mansion to set my mind at ease if you get mobbed.'

'I won't get mobbed,' she promised. 'You'll see.'

He'd been right; he *was* being managed. But while it was laced with thoughtfulness and a shared need to escape…

Flexing his fingers around hers, he lowered their arms to their sides and warned her, 'If I'm being played again, there'll be consequences.'

Just because it felt to him as if their relationship had changed didn't mean she felt the same way. He'd fallen into *that* trap before.

She fluttered her eyelashes. 'You promise?'

CHAPTER EIGHTEEN

AS THEY walked side by side along paths that twisted and turned through theatrical staircases Miranda tried to enjoy the surroundings. It probably looked like Narnia in the winter with a blanket of snow on the ground, especially when the paths were lit by old-fashioned lamp posts. But even with her hand held in a reassuringly strong grip as soon as they were out of sight of the mansion, she couldn't relax. The incident outside the movie theatre had shaken her more than she cared to admit.

It magnified the sensation she should hold on to him but when she questioned if it was more than the natural reaction to a second reminder of the frailty of her body in comparison to his strength, she wasn't certain she wanted to know the answer.

They eventually got to the boardwalk where even with the FDR driveway beneath their feet it was easy to forget they were in the city. In silent agreement they headed to the railing. Sharing a few quiet moments of nothing—something she suspected was a rarity for them both—she smiled at the view. The thousands of square and rectangular windows lit up on the buildings across the river, the stars and moon above, the draped twinkling lights of the Fifty-ninth Street Bridge reflected in the moving water below.

It was magical.

Closing her eyes, she breathed in and caught a hint of the sweet scent of pipe smoke coming from some of the old men sitting on a bench to watch the last boats go by. Then—as if someone felt the need to add another layer of fairy dust—a harmonica started playing.

Opening her eyes, she tugged on Tyler's hand to draw him away from the railing. 'Dance with me.'

He shook his head. 'I don't dance.'

'Didn't anyone ever tell you that everyone should dance a little every day?'

'I don't sing into a hairbrush in front of the mirror, either,' he replied dryly as he allowed her to pull him into the centre of the boardwalk.

'How about laughing—you ever try that one?'

As they stilled he looked into her eyes and confessed, 'It's been a while.'

The returning hint of hollowness to his voice made her heart ache. Whatever had happened to him—the thing that made him so angry—wasn't something she could fix. But she could make an attempt at helping him put it to the back of his mind for a while.

'One arm goes around my waist like this…' Stepping forwards she moved the hand she was holding behind her back and released it. 'You hold this hand… I place this one on your shoulder…and we sway…'

She could feel the resistance in his body as she started to move. 'Don't think about it. Listen to the music—let it wash over you—and move your weight from one foot to the other.' When she felt him start to move with her a smile blossomed on her lips. 'It's like the ebb and flow of the tide. You're just a leaf in the wind…' When he lifted his chin her smile grew. 'The leaf was too much, wasn't it?'

'You could enjoy this a little less…'

She chuckled softly. 'I don't think that's possible.'

As they slowly turned in a circle she revelled in the luxury of being close to him and openly studied his face. Despite the times it felt as if she knew him better than she possibly could in such a short space of time there were others—like now—when she found him impossible to read. What was he thinking? Did the closeness feel as good for him as it did for her? Did he want her as much as she wanted him?

While he looked at her in a way that made it feel as if he could see her soul and held her with a gentleness that belied his strength it didn't feel wrong to trust him with her body. But before she did she wanted *him* to trust *her* and she wasn't certain he did yet.

Swiping the tip of her tongue over her lips, she took a short breath and decided to broach what she suspected was a difficult subject. 'If I talk to you about something you have to promise you won't freak out.'

'Meaning it's something I'm not gonna like.'

She searched his eyes before continuing. 'I think you know you can't go around intimidating people.'

'Not much call for good guys in the world I inhabit.'

Meaning he thought he wasn't one or he'd had to change to survive? She could have pointed out bad guys didn't come to a girl's rescue, share popcorn at the movies or dance with her in the moonlight, but instead she said, 'I'd have thought there was even more call for them there. At times lowering to the level of the people you deal with probably seems like the only way you can make them understand you—it's dog-eat-dog, right?—but—'

'It's not how the people in your world behave.'

'You make it sound like we live on different planets.'

'To all intents and purposes we do.'

She shook her head. 'I can't begin to imagine some of the things you've seen.'

'You're not supposed to. It's why there are people like me doing the job we do. We're buffers.'

'Even soldiers in a war zone take the occasional break from the front line. When's the last time you did that?'

He frowned. 'That's been a while, too.'

Having spent more than enough time around people in high pressured jobs to recognize stress when she saw it, she'd thought it might be part of the problem.

'Taking time for yourself—spending it with the people you love and dancing every now and again—wouldn't that remind you of what you're fighting for?' When some of the tension returned to his body she sought a way to make him understand what she was doing stemmed from the fact she cared, even if it was more than she should. 'Haven't you ever had someone in your life you looked forwards to seeing—who made everything you did and all the sacrifices you make worthwhile? You can't have gone this long without meeting someone like that. Everyone has a one who got away, right?'

The fist of jealousy that gripped her stomach made her hope the answer was no.

'Yes,' he replied.

Not that she wanted to know details but, 'Was your job part of the problem?'

'We both worked long hours.'

'What happened?'

'She married someone else.'

The information made her look at him with new eyes. Had his heart been broken? She wondered what kind of woman he'd fallen for and came to the conclusion she must have been pretty amazing. It left her with the sensation she had a lot to live up to—something her insecurities would play on if she let them. But if the woman had been dumb enough to let him go she couldn't have been *that* great. 'Was that when your work started taking over your life?' she asked.

'We're back to the subject of finding a balance.'

'Yes.'

'It's not always easy.'

'You think I don't know that?'

When he stilled she realized the music had stopped and turned to smile at the musician as he saluted them with his harmonica before walking away.

Tyler removed his arm from her waist and lowered their hands. As he led her back into the park he took a long breath and exhaled before asking, 'How did you know?'

'About the discrepancy in your work-life balance?'

'That I wouldn't hurt you that night in the alley…'

Miranda answered honestly. 'I just did. It was a gut-instinct thing. When something feels right it feels right.'

'You place that kind of faith in everyone?'

She arched a brow at him. 'After spending a quarter of my life surrounded by people who are never themselves around me—who laugh even when my jokes aren't funny or pretend to be my friend just so they can say they know me?'

'I'll take that as a no.'

Miranda stopped and turned towards him. 'Wait a minute. Are you telling me you *didn't* know?'

'No one knows what they're capable of till they're pushed,' he said flatly.

'Something pushed you before me, didn't it?'

The shadows between arcs of lamplight illuminating the path seemed to close in around him. 'Yes.'

Despite the dark tone to his deep voice her feet took a step forwards, her hand reaching out to the tense line of his jaw. When a muscle clenched beneath her fingers she wanted to reassure him nothing he said would change how she saw him—that when a person had the kind of faith she had in him it wasn't just for a minute or a day. She wanted to tell him that she thought he was strong enough to carry the weight of the world on his shoulders but he didn't have to. Not alone. But when it came down to it all she could manage was his name. *'Tyler—'*

'Don't.' A large hand covered hers and removed it from his face. 'We can't do that here.'

The rejection stung but somehow Miranda managed to rise above it and seek a rational explanation when she knew he wasn't immune to her touch. 'Has there been a noticeable rush of people who have recognized me? Why do you think so many famous people choose to live in New York?'

'You've made your point,' he replied. 'And I'm open to the idea of allowing more off-schedule walks to let you take a break. But we're still not doing that here.'

Frowning a little at the intimation she still needed permission to do what she wanted, she laid her palm on his chest, sidled up to him and cut her inner siren loose. 'Then take me somewhere we can be alone…and *get naked...*'

From her perspective, the sooner they started playing out a few of her fantasies, the better she'd feel.

'Not gonna happen.' Suddenly he was standing taller and straighter, his voice edged with fierce determination. 'I'm not interested in helping you stick a middle finger at your parents before you leave the family business.'

It was the closest she'd ever been to experiencing a slap in the face.

CHAPTER NINETEEN

THE second the words left his mouth Tyler regretted them.

When Miranda flinched it wasn't outwardly visible but he could see it in her eyes.

'You're trying to push me away again, aren't you?' she said with a hint of uncertainty that almost broke his resolve. 'It's what you do when someone gets close to you.'

He had to stay strong. Encouraging her anger would be better for both of them. 'I'm on the couch now, am I? Okay. I'll take a seat.' He moved over to one of the benches at the edge of the path, sat down and stretched his arms along the back. 'Don't you need a pen and paper to take notes for the rest of this therapy session?'

Miranda shook her head in a way that suggested she was disappointed in him. 'All you had to do was say you weren't ready to talk about it.'

Reminding him how close he'd come to spilling his guts wasn't the best tactic. 'What makes you think I'd talk to you when you have no idea how the world works?'

'If there weren't so many people trying to protect me from it I might have a better idea.' She arched a brow. 'You think I can't handle whatever you tell me?'

Good question. He knew she had guts and bravado. She'd demonstrated she had compassion, warmth and understanding. When added to her sensuality and the way she could turn him on with just a glance, it made him realize she was exactly the kind of woman a less tainted guy might want to build something with if things went well.

But the truth was it didn't matter if she could handle it. Simple fact was she shouldn't have to try.

Clearly seeking an explanation for what had gone wrong when they'd been getting along better she came up with, 'I'm certain getting personally involved isn't something you're encouraged to do during working hours.'

'What makes you think I find it difficult to avoid?'

She sighed. 'No one is that detached.'

'It's my claim to fame. Kinda like yours is being your father's mouthpiece by day and a closet rebel at night. That's what this is—' he lifted an arm to wave a forefinger between them '—another rule for you to break.'

'Deflection—you invented that, right?'

'I'm sure the mayor would be overjoyed to discover you're doing the nasty with one of your bodyguards.'

'What a delightful way to put it.' She lifted her chin a defiant inch. 'But even if I was, what happens between us has nothing to do with my family. It's not like this could go anywhere. They won't have to size up your suitability for a future son-in-law.'

Just as well, wasn't it? He could imagine how great he'd fit in at fancy dinner parties and how happy he'd be to traipse out his firstborn for the cameras. He'd create more negative publicity inside a couple of appearances than she had in years. 'Which is another part of the attraction, isn't it?'

'Unlike *someone* I could mention I didn't know who I was kissing that night in the hall. So what's your excuse for breaking the rules?'

'I needed a way to get you out of there before you were identified. It was the first thing that came to mind.' If he'd known how it would feel he might have thought twice, but when he tried to regret it, he couldn't.

'You hate that you're attracted to me, don't you? I'm probably not even your type.' Her chin lifted another, more defensive inch. 'What was *she* like—your one who got away?'

When the thought she was jealous immediately made him

want to reassure her she had nothing to worry about on that score, Tyler frowned. 'Not going there.' He pushed to his feet. 'This is just another example of you getting mad at me because you're not getting your own way.'

'That's not why I'm— You know what? I'm not going to be goaded into an argument with you. Back on the boardwalk I thought...' She clamped her mouth shut and shook her head. 'Obviously not—my mistake. I get it now.'

Tyler bunched his hands into fists at his sides so he wouldn't reach out to her.

He couldn't tell her that she was the first woman he'd danced with or that while he did he'd experienced his first moments of peace in longer than he could remember. He couldn't tell her when she'd asked if he had someone in his life he looked forward to seeing the first person he'd thought of was her. The number of things he couldn't say increased with each passing day. But they'd known each other for *two weeks.* Even if they had a future he wouldn't be telling her how he felt after two measly weeks.

What was next—a marriage proposal inside a month, quickie ceremony at six weeks and divorce a couple of weeks later? He wasn't that kind of guy. If he ever got round to putting a ring on a woman's finger it would stay there.

She rolled her eyes. 'I mean, how silly of me. You're obviously totally oblivious to me in that way. I could strip naked right now and you wouldn't even notice.'

The hell he wouldn't.

'I could date a string of guys while you're forced to watch and you wouldn't care. Better still, I could spend the night at their apartment while you stand outside the door and listen to every sound.'

The *hell* she would.

'Not that it would matter to you if I slept with every guy in the city...'

Something savagely territorial twisted hard in Tyler's gut. He'd kill every one of them with his bare hands.

'I could take every sex fantasy I've had about you since the night we met and try them out with whoever feels like getting down and dirty—'

That did it.

A single stride took him to where she stood. Then his hands were on her face and his mouth was on hers. There was nothing hesitant about it: a brazen mating of lips and tongues that sent him up in flames. The pent-up frustration of the past week, knowing what it was like to touch her and being unable to do anything about it, was released in a flurry of kisses.

If they'd been within striking distance of a bed she wouldn't get to leave it until he'd shown her no other man would put as much effort into making her feel better than she'd ever felt before. He would find a way to brand her, bind her to him and make sure the world knew she was his, all the reasons he couldn't claim her forgotten in a red haze of desire.

'The things I said,' she mumbled against his lips. 'I would never do that to you.'

'I know,' he mumbled back.

The suggestion had been enough.

'I don't want you to think—'

'I don't.'

When he dropped his hands so he could wrap his arms around her waist and fit her soft curves to his body a moan vibrated in the base of her throat. 'You drive me crazy.'

Then they were even.

As he lifted his mouth to place worshipful kisses on her closed eyes and her forehead in an attempt to slow things down she sighed contentedly. 'Can we call the "who'll crack first?" competition a draw now and progress to the kissing marathon?'

Tyler brushed a waving lock of silky hair from her cheek, committing the softness of her skin to his memory. 'We don't have that luxury with your schedule.'

'We could try making time for it,' she suggested.

'How about we see how it goes for the next while?' Having stepped over every line he'd tried to draw between them bar one, it was the only concession he could make.

'I'm okay with that.' She rocked forwards onto her toes,

crushing her breasts tighter against his chest as she lifted her chin and demanded, *'More.'*

Tyler was happy to oblige, picking her up off her feet as he slanted his mouth over hers.

After several minutes of kiss-filled silence she mumbled, 'You think I don't know you're carrying me back to the house right now?'

'If you'd shut up I could distract you better.'

'You can't carry me the whole way there.'

'Says who?'

Carrying her he could do. Looking after her while they were together he could do. Touching her and kissing her he could *definitely* do—wasn't as if he'd managed to stop himself from doing either one. Making love to her—no matter how desperately he wanted to—he still had to avoid. She'd thank him in the long run, especially if the alternative was living with the fact she'd given herself to a man who became a cold-blooded murderer.

He could protect her from that.

Even if it was the last honourable thing he did.

CHAPTER TWENTY

EITHER Tyler was more in control of the risk-assessment aspect of her security than she'd given him credit for or he was better at escaping than she'd ever been. Not that it mattered after two of the happiest weeks of her life.

Every time there was so much as the smallest gap in her schedule he would take her somewhere she'd never been. An impromptu concert tour of some of the best musicians performing in subway stations; to partake of lunch from a street vendor and run back to the SUV through the rain when the heavens opened; people-watching in parks where they could pit his detective skills against her imagination in games of 'guess the profession.'

It was a bittersweet romance.

Each place he showed her made her fall deeper in love with the city she called home and broke her heart a little when she realized how much living she'd missed. Add stolen kisses, forbidden touches and lingering heated looks to the mix and her only complaint was he hadn't found a gap in her schedule for sex. It was something she planned on fixing if he wouldn't. A girl had to do what a girl had to do.

When the suggestion was made they spend time together on a rare day off from campaign duties she thought they were finally headed for an afternoon of debauchery. But when they pulled up outside a neatly kept house in Staten Island her rising anticipation was replaced by surprise.

'This is where you live?'

It looked more like a family home than a bachelor pad.

'It's where I grew up.' He switched off the engine and unbuckled his seat belt. 'Hope you're hungry. There's always enough food to feed an army at Sunday lunch.'

Miranda froze. 'Wait. *What?* I can't meet your family.'

'You can sit out here if you want but you're gonna be here awhile.'

She'd never felt more in need of an escape route. 'I can go for a walk or take a ferry ride. I've always wanted to do that. I'll meet you back here in a couple of hours.'

'In what universe do you think that's likely?'

'It's your *family.* I can't go in there.'

'You meet people every day. I'm not seeing the problem.' He leaned across and opened her door. *'Out.'*

'I can't.'

'Yes, you can.'

'Would it make a difference if I said please?'

'No,' but it earned an all-too-brief brush of his firm mouth across her submissive lips. 'I got a call last night to say there's some big family announcement I'm not to miss and, since I can't get out of it, you get to be here. We'll be an hour, two tops, and then—if you're a very good girl—we can take a ride on the big orange boat.'

When he added a push of encouragement to her shoulder, Miranda chose to get out of the car rather than fall face-first onto the street. She stared at the house as she walked to the sidewalk, anything resembling an appetite replaced by the kind of churning that made her pray she wouldn't throw up on one of his relatives.

'How are you going to introduce me?'

'I don't know how rich folks do it in Manhattan high society.' He reached for the latch on the gate. 'But here on Staten Island we tend to use names.'

'I can't believe you're doing this to me.'

'It's not that big a deal.'

Yes, it was. How could he not know that—did they have to have the relationship definition talk? Maybe she was overthinking it. Maybe he brought dozens of women home.

The thought made her frown.

'Think of them as potential voters if it helps,' he said as they got to the top of the porch steps. 'But I should probably warn you most of them like the look of the other guy.'

She sent him a withering look.

When they stepped into the hall he took her coat, hung it on a rack and called out, 'We've got company.'

Persuaded around the corner with a large palm on the inward curve of her spine, Miranda discovered four pairs of curious eyes studying her. Standing there stark naked couldn't have made her feel more exposed.

'This is Miranda,' Tyler announced.

A woman with long dark hair and soulful brown eyes was the first of them to step forwards and hold out a hand. 'I'm Jo. It's nice to meet you, Miranda.'

'And you.' She smiled apologetically. 'If I'd known where we were going I'd have brought something with me—I feel terribly empty-handed.'

'Soon fix that.' A tall man who was obviously one of Tyler's brothers stepped forwards and shook her hand the second Jo let go. His vivid blue eyes narrowed a little. 'You look familiar.'

'My husband, Danny,' Jo explained before nudging him in the ribs. 'She's the mayor's daughter, you idiot.'

'Nah, that's not where I know her from…' A slow smile spread across his mouth. 'How's your Southern accent?'

It took a second but when she made the connection Miranda's eyes widened. He'd been one of the police officers in the hallway; more specifically one of the officers who had caught her making out with Tyler while pinned against a wall. There was just never a giant hole in the ground when a girl needed one, was there?

Danny winked as he let go of her hand. 'Don't worry, your secret's safe with me. *You,* on the other hand—' he pointed at his brother '—are gonna have to buy my silence for at least the next decade.'

'You open your pie hole your lovely wife will end up wearing black,' Tyler warned.

Jo linked arms with her husband and patted his chest. 'You can tell me later, babe.'

'You already know.'

'How about you remind me?'

As they moved away Miranda dropped her chin and aimed an accusatory glare at Tyler. 'You didn't mention your brother was there that night.'

'Didn't I?'

'No.'

'Uncle Tyler!'

Her eyes widened as a small child launched herself at him and was swung into the air. 'You have a niece?'

'Indeed I do.' He smiled indulgently. 'Hey, Munchkin, who's the best-looking guy in the room?'

'Daddy,' the girl replied with conviction.

Tyler glanced briefly at Miranda. 'They can get a bit confused at four.' He bounced the child higher in his arms as he walked away. 'Remember we talked about this? Let's go over it again…'

The image provided such a contrast to the dangerous man she'd seen in an alley Miranda couldn't quite equate the two as she watched him disappear into what she assumed was the kitchen. But the reminder of how gentle he could be was a powerful aphrodisiac.

Why weren't they at his place having sex?

'Amy adores him,' Jo's voice said beside her. 'I think it's because at times they're the same mental age.'

Detective-Takes-The-World-Too-Seriously-To-Dance had a Peter Pan side to his personality? Miranda blinked. She *really* wanted to see that. 'Is she yours?'

'No, we've only been married a few months. She's Johnnie's daughter. He's the eldest. Then—in descending order—there's Reid, Tyler and Danny. Liv is the youngest.' She smiled when Miranda looked at her. 'I know. It can be a lot to take in on the first visit and I'm afraid they're not even all here yet. Liv and Blake are running a little late with their big announcement—my money's on baby news. Reid is undercover so we haven't seen him in a while—makes it twice as important for everyone to be here if it is baby news, y'know? Momma Brannigan is in the kitchen.' She leaned closer and lowered her voice to a conspiratorial whisper. 'But don't be scared. She's lovely.'

While she blinked at the overload of information Jo smiled and linked their arms at the elbows.

'Let's get the rest of the introductions out of the way. It's easier a few at a time.'

After meeting Johnnie and his wife Miranda swiped her palms over her hips and asked, 'Can I help with anything?'

'You can give me a hand setting the table if you tell me where you got those gorgeous shoes.'

A conversation about fashion and Jo's cheery chatter helped distract her until Tyler reappeared with an older woman. 'My mom,' he supplied as he set down a platter of food on the table.

'I guessed.' She stepped forwards and reached out a hand. 'It's a pleasure to meet you, Mrs Brannigan. Thank you for allowing me to visit your lovely home.'

Sky-blue eyes sparkled with humour as she looked up at her son. 'Is she always this polite?'

'No,' he said flatly.

'How do we get her to stop?'

'Couple of minutes in my company usually does it.'

'Then you'd best stay with her.' She patted his arm. 'With any luck some of it might rub off.'

Tyler nodded firmly. 'Knew that was coming…'

The interaction made Miranda smile. When he smiled crookedly in reply, her heartbeat stuttered and skipped a couple of beats. Dragging her gaze away, she reached out to straighten the cutlery on the place setting closest to her. The desire to ravish him and be ravished in return was at the very least wildly inappropriate in front of his family.

'We're here!' a woman's voice called from the hall.

Another round of introductions ensued and, despite some odd looks when Tyler placed her in the chair next to him for lunch within a short space of time Miranda fell a little in love with the rest of the Brannigans. They interacted like a single unit, at times talked over each other in a way that made it difficult to follow the flow of conversation, but what she found most fascinating was how different Tyler was with them.

She'd never seen him so relaxed, heard him express an educated opinion on so many subjects or realized how funny he could be when he set his mind to it. It gave her a glimpse of how he must have been before he saw too much. For the life of her Miranda couldn't imagine why the woman he loved had let him get away. To be loved by a man like him, to have children with him and spend her life standing by his side, being there when he needed her and knowing he would do the same in return...

A wave of longing overwhelmed her. Nothing had ever seemed more beautiful or more terrifying.

Understandably it made her more aware of the happy couples surrounding them as the meal finished and she helped with the clearing up. She looked at Jo and Danny as he tucked a strand of dark hair behind her ear. The intimacy of the touch and the heat in his eyes made it obvious Tyler's younger brother was very much in love with his wife. The feeling was just as obviously returned. They made it look as if there were no one else in the room but them. It was incredibly romantic but, since it also made her feel as if she was intruding on something private, Miranda tore her gaze away.

Inevitably it was drawn to where Tyler was leaning against the archway to the kitchen. She smiled as she ran a cloth somewhat aimlessly over the table. Even when sporting a basic blue-jeans-and-sweater combo he was devastatingly handsome. She watched as he cradled a mug of coffee in his hand, his expression pensive. When he blinked dense lashes she followed his gaze and discovered he was looking where she'd been looking. Jo laughed at something Danny said and as Miranda's gaze returned to Tyler the corner of his mouth lifted and his expression softened.

'What happened?' she'd asked.

'She married someone else,' he'd replied.

Miranda's heart twisted, a brief frown aimed at the woman she'd liked so much. How could she do that to him? Marrying his brother was bad enough, flaunting her happiness in front of him was unforgivable—and she'd seemed so *nice*.

Immediately crossing the room, she stood close enough to feel the heat radiating from his large body, her back to everyone else as if she could somehow shield him from pain. '*She's* your one who got away?' she whispered.

Tyler dropped his chin and frowned, his deep voice equally low. 'Don't make me regret bringing you here.'

'She's your brother's *wife*.'

'She wasn't always his wife. Leave it alone.'

'But how can you—?'

He shook his head and glanced around. 'Just this once do you think you could do what I tell you to do?'

When he looked into her eyes again what she thought she could read in the cobalt depths made Miranda want to march across the room and give his sister-in-law a piece of her mind. She understood how difficult it was for Tyler to be there even if no one else did. Had he brought her along as back-up or a smokescreen? She was a lot happier with the first option, would have volunteered if she'd known he needed support. Didn't he know that? She wanted to talk to him about it—hear the story from beginning to end in his words—but it was the archetypal wrong time, wrong place.

He lifted his mug and drained the contents. 'You want to take that ferry ride, we best say our goodbyes.'

Miranda acquiesced with a nod. A ferry ride would be the ideal place to talk. She just wished she didn't feel as nervous about hearing what he had to say as she'd been about meeting his family. Gathering herself together, she pinned one of her public-persona smiles in place and turned around. Even if it was more than likely she would never see them again she wanted his family to think well of her.

One by one the people she barely knew said their goodbyes with a hug, a kiss on the cheek or both. At first she felt awkward about hugging them back, her body stiff and unyielding; particularly with Jo. But by the time she got to the eighth person—his mother—she was holding on for a moment longer than strictly necessary, her throat clogged with emotion.

They made her feel so accepted it was all too easy to paint a picture of a fantasy future where she was part of their world. She would sit in the seat next to Tyler every Sunday, at Thanksgiving and Christmas, and be there just for him the way it felt he'd been for her.

She gave herself a mental talking-to as they left the house. If she wasn't careful before she knew it she'd be doodling Miranda Brannigan inside hearts on stationery. The man had been in love with another woman—still was for all she knew. Then there was the small matter of her freedom—she didn't want to trade one form of captivity for another.

Their relationship was about *sex* and, once they'd had a little chat on the ferry to ensure they were on the same page, they were going to his apartment to have lots of it.

CHAPTER TWENTY-ONE

IF PRESSURED Tyler might have admitted taking Miranda home to meet his family wasn't planned. But it would have taken extreme torture for him to confess the reason behind it was that it felt as if she had him on the ropes.

Truth was he doubted taking her to meet the family priest would keep them out of the bedroom for much longer.

As she walked beside him, unruly tresses of flame-red hair tossed by the wind, all he could think about was how it felt to have those silky soft strands sliding over his fingers. He wanted to strip her naked and keep her that way until he'd sated his hunger for her. He wanted to map her body with his mouth and his tongue, taking her close to the edge over and over again without allowing her release until she begged him to take her.

He'd used every trick he could think of to get it off his mind. He'd even summoned random pages of books from his memory and recited them word for word inside his head. When his talent for retaining information chose to remind him of the time he'd furtively flicked through a copy of *Lady Chatterley* during puberty, he'd stopped.

So much for *that* great idea…

But there was no point denying there was something else going on that had nothing to do with sex.

He'd watched from the sidelines as she smiled, talked and laughed with his family. She'd looked right there—as if she belonged—and Tyler realized on some level he'd known she would. What he *hadn't* realized was how much he would like having her there. He'd even looked at Jo and Danny and felt at peace with the past; as if things were the way they were supposed to be.

It felt as if a weight had been lifted.

Studying her from the corner of his eye, he tried to figure out what was different about her—the thing that allowed her to work such a miracle. But when she looked at him and flashed a small smile he was distracted by the sensation something was off.

'You okay?'

She avoided his gaze and nodded. 'I'm fine.'

'Did I ever mention one of my detective skills is the ability to spot a lie?' Tyler raised his hand and waggled a forefinger over his shoulder. 'Hairs on the back of my neck stand up.'

'They all hugged me.' She shrugged a shoulder, her tone deceptively dismissive. 'I'm not used to that.'

It made him want to sit her parents down for a little chat. Didn't they know their daughter *at all?* Would it be such a damn hardship for them to *get to know her?*

They obviously needed someone to tell them what they were missing.

Dropping her gaze to the ground for a moment, she took a short breath and asked, 'How long has it been since your father passed away?'

'Nine years. He had a heart attack.'

Her voice softened. 'I'm sorry.'

'It happens.' Tyler shrugged. 'Work hard, play hard—that was his motto. I doubt he had many regrets.'

They crossed the street to the boardwalk before she commented, 'You were different with them.'

'So were you.'

'I don't usually meet families.' She scrunched her nose a little. 'I mean, I do, but…'

'But?' he prompted.

'It was different this time.'

Tyler was about to ask why when he glanced ahead. 'Can you run in those shoes?'

'They're not exactly designed for running.'

'Try.' He took her hand. 'Ferry's in, we gotta move.'

They were the last people to board before it departed. Miranda looked up at him with sparkling eyes and flushed cheeks, so beautiful she was making it difficult for him to look anywhere else. When she laughed he smiled back at her. Every time she did that it made him want to be a funnier guy so he could coax the sound from her lips.

'Can we stand outside?' she asked breathlessly.

'You'll get cold.'

She shook her head. 'I don't care.'

Guiding them to what shelter he could find at the end of the deck, he watched her reaction to the new experience as she caught her breath from the run. He drank in her animated expression, the way her eyes sparkled with delight, and as always wondered how it felt to see the world through her eyes. The little adventures they'd taken might have been an attempt to keep them out of the bedroom but they'd done more than that. At least they had for him.

He saw the city with fresh perspective. It wasn't tarnished by cynicism or taken for granted the way he normally did. As a result he'd thought about the small part he played in the greater scheme of things and come to the conclusion a little was better than nothing. One less perp on the streets was one less crime—several in the case of repeat offenders. If it meant she was safe when she began to explore on her own he'd arrest each and every one of them in her name.

'They liked you,' he told her, in case she didn't know. 'That's why you were treated to the hug-fest.'

'I got the impression your family would make anyone you brought home feel welcome.' A soft smile came through in her voice. 'You're lucky to have them.'

'They're not bad,' he allowed. 'Probably a bit late to trade them in.'

'It can't have been easy for your mom with five little kids running around.' She waited until he looked into her eyes. 'You're all quite close in age, aren't you?'

'Arrived in an eight-year bonanza of adorability.'

'That kind of time frame would terrify me.'

'My great-grandmother had eleven.'

Her eyes widened. 'Seriously?'

'It's why the Irish never have to invade a country. We infiltrate.' The comment had the desired effect: she laughed. But Tyler shook his head when it was followed by an involuntary shudder. 'I said you'd be cold out here.'

'I don't want to go inside.' When the wind blew a lock of hair across her face, she raised her hand to brush it back and looked over the water again. 'This is amazing.'

Releasing her hand, Tyler took a step forwards, folded the edges of his jacket around her narrow shoulders and wrapped his arms around her body. 'Better?'

She settled in as if she'd always been there, her arms around his waist and her cheek against his chest. 'Much.'

He rested his chin on her head as they sailed past the Statue of Liberty.

'She's humongous.'

Tyler looked down at her with amusement. 'How can you *not* know that?'

'She looks smaller from farther away.'

Fair enough.

'Did you tell her how you felt?'

It didn't take a genius to work out they weren't talking about a national monument any more.

'I thought she knew.'

'She might not have married Danny if she knew.'

'No.' He'd accepted that long before he came to terms with it. 'Anyone who sees them together knows they're good for each other.'

'Can't be easy to watch.'

'Wasn't for a while…' A guy could come up with a lot of reasons not to attend Sunday lunch when he needed to, but that would change now, thanks to her.

'No one else figured it out?'

He sincerely hoped not—because that wouldn't be at all

awkward—but realistically all he knew for certain was, 'You're the first person to bring it up.'

There was a palpable moment of hesitation before she asked, 'Do you still love her?'

Not in that way. He wouldn't be standing there with her if he was in love with someone else. He wasn't wired that way. 'Part of me will always feel something for her. Just because it didn't work out the way I thought it would doesn't make it any less real.'

'Why didn't you tell her?'

And there it was: the million-dollar question.

When he didn't answer she leaned back and looked up at him. 'You don't know?'

'We were friends. I didn't think she was ready to hear it, but the fact is I never knew why until recently.'

'You don't want to tell me,' she surmised.

Considering some of it had to do with his attraction to the woman he was with, not so much.

'Do you regret it?'

He looked into her eyes. 'It's history.'

'You want to change the subject,' she said. 'Okay. What are we doing—you and me, Tyler and Miranda?'

'What do you think we're doing?'

'I thought it was foreplay,' she answered frankly. 'Neither one of us is interested in making a commitment, are we?' There was a beat before she added, 'We enjoy each other's company—most of the time—and you know I want you.'

He did. Even if he couldn't see it in her eyes, he could hear it in her voice. Her tone was liquid as she said the words, thick with sensuality and more potent than any drug. Resisting her was the equivalent of a slow, painful death, every muscle in his body straining towards her.

'I know *you* want *me*.' Her lips formed a decadently sinful smile. 'Some things are hard to hide…'

To prove the point she brushed her stomach across his abdomen in a deliberately provocative move. Tyler sucked in a sharp breath through clenched teeth, unable to stop his body from reacting. She had that effect on him even without trying. When she put effort into it he didn't stand a chance. He dropped his hands to her hips to hold her still.

'What do you want me to say?' he asked tightly.

'I don't want you to say anything. I want you to take me to your apartment, take me to bed and take me.'

He'd never wanted anything more. 'I can't.'

'Why not?'

'It's not that simple.'

'Yes, it is.'

He wished it were. 'You need to think this through.'

'You think I haven't?' Removing one of the arms around his waist, she snaked it between them and raised a hand to set fine-boned fingers against his jaw as she looked deep into his eyes. 'I haven't thought about anything else since the moment I laid eyes on you.'

Utilizing every microscopic fraction of resolve he had left, Tyler removed her fingers. 'We can't do this.'

'Look me in the eyes and tell me you don't want me.'

'I'm not gonna lie about that.' Not after she'd so ably demonstrated his weakness.

'Then what is the problem?' There was a brief flash of fire in her eyes. 'In case you hadn't noticed I'm throwing myself at you. That doesn't happen very often.'

Some of his frustration bubbled to the surface. 'Damn it, woman, I'm trying to do the right thing here.' He glanced over her head to see who was watching what they were doing, his fingers tangling with hers at their side. 'You're not making it any easier.'

'And I'm not going to until you can give me a rational explanation for why this can't happen when we both want it to,' she said on a note of exasperation.

'I won't take advantage of the situation.'

'Uh…*hello*...woman willing to be taken advantage of over here.' She lowered her voice. 'I want to have wild, uninhibited sex with you. I want to feel your hands on my body. I want…' she rocked forward and pressed her breasts against his chest '…you to make me *scream* your name…'

Tyler swore viciously beneath his breath. He'd said *he* was more trouble than *she* could handle? *Man* was he ever outclassed on that score. Every strand of knuckle-dragging caveman that remained in his DNA demanded he tame her and tie her down. But the part of him that had made the mistake of looking for something more meaningful in the wrong place wouldn't let him take her without it.

He wanted to strip her naked in more ways than one. He wanted to climb inside her mind and discover all her secrets. He wanted her to be more herself with him than she'd ever been with anyone else. He wanted sleeping together to mean something to her because he knew it would mean something to him. But he couldn't say any of those things without discussing a future he couldn't plan until after the day of reckoning.

From what she'd said it didn't even look as if she wanted a future with him. Then he remembered she'd *asked* about commitment. It hadn't been a statement of fact. The devil was in the detail. Where there was a loophole, there was a way in. He needed to know how she felt and in the absence of words he knew how to get to the truth.

Making the first connection with their eyes, he dropped his guard and allowed her to see how much he wanted her. It drew a low gasp from her lips, encouraging him to continue despite the glimpse of fear he got in return. Running his hand over her back in a soothing caress, he cradled her close, releasing her hand so he could brush the backs of his fingers over her cheek.

'What are you doing?' she whispered.

He angled his head and lowered his mouth to her lips. 'Don't speak, just feel.'

Moving his hand, he pushed her hair over her shoulder, changing the direction of his lips at the last possible second to place a kiss on the sensitive skin of her neck. He slid his mouth upwards, circled the shell of her ear with the tip of his tongue and felt a shiver run through her body.

'Tyler—'

'Shh...'

He kissed his way down her jaw and captured her mouth,

alternating between soft and hard, breathless and slow. While she responded in kind he could sense she was holding back, conflicted by the desire to have him take her hard and fast the way he knew she wanted him to and the warm, cherished feeling he was attempting to convey with tenderness. Then she was leaning into him. The kiss became deeper, richer, full-bodied and intoxicating, creating a haze around them that blocked out everything else.

Something he didn't recognize expanded in his chest. It pushed the air from his lungs and filled the cavity until it felt as if it would break his ribs and burst free. In seeking out the truth about how she felt he'd touched the edge of something so large within himself he couldn't see to the other side. But before he could figure out what it was, with no more warning than a low moan she wrenched her mouth free and took a sharp step backwards.

'Stop.'

When he looked at her Tyler discovered her eyes were wide with anguish. He frowned. What had he done wrong?

She sucked in a sharp breath and shook her head. 'This isn't what we're meant to be doing.'

'I thought you wanted to make love,' he said roughly, the after-effects of the best kiss of his damn life still rippling through his body.

'I want us to have *sex*.'

'Meaningless sex.' The empty, emotionless joining of bodies that led to a brief, unsatisfying climax held zero appeal for him. He didn't want that with her.

'No.' She frowned back at him. 'I mean, yes, but not *totally* meaningless…something somewhere in the middle… I don't know… I don't have much—that's not the point!'

A surge of affection lifted the corner of his mouth. 'Might need you to explain that a little better…'

'Don't look at me like that.'

Suddenly she was more scared than he'd ever seen her look before—even when she saw him roughing up a low life in an alley.

'Come here.' He took a step forwards and reached out to draw her back into his arms.

She took a step back and left her hands at her sides. 'We're not *dating,*' she said firmly. 'You don't have to spoon on the romance to get me into bed.'

'We're not having a quick roll between the sheets, either,' he replied with equal determination. 'If that's what you're looking for it's a deal-breaker. We do this, we do it my way.'

'Which is what, exactly?'

His reply got stuck in his throat, what he wanted to say suppressed by self-doubt. He'd known Jo for *years* before he thought he felt something more—had debated telling her for months and ultimately was glad he hadn't. If he was wrong again, if he'd misjudged, if the day of reckoning came and he was too far gone to haul himself back from the gates of hell—

'What kind of game are you playing?'

The tremor in her voice tore a hole in his gut.

'I'm not playing a game,' he replied flatly.

'I won't be your rebound.'

'You're not.'

She was clearly confused—and she had every right to be. Her gaze frantically searched the air above his head. Then it slammed into his, her tone heavy with suspicion. 'Are you doing this to control me and keep me in line?'

He flicked a brief glare her way. 'I'm gonna let that one slide 'cos I know you have trust issues.'

'You were given the talk, weren't you?'

Tyler frowned again. 'What talk?'

'The talk Lou Mitchell gives to all the new bodyguards at the mansion about boundaries. It never occurred to me before but now it makes sense…' Fire blazed in her eyes, incinerating her fear. 'What did he say to you?'

Tyler froze when he realized what she meant. He wouldn't lie to her but if it was taken out of context—

'What did he *say?*'

The rise in her voice drew the attention of some of the people at the other end of the deck.

'You need to calm down,' he said in a lower voice.

'I'll calm down when you tell me what he said.'

No, she wouldn't. Not if she didn't let him get it all out. Hauling in a deep breath, he took a run at it. 'He said to do whatever I had to do to—'

'Wow.'

'I'm not finished.'

She laughed sarcastically. 'Oh, you've said more than enough. Congratulations.' Her hands lifted in front of her body to reward him with a round of applause. *'Well played.'*

Tyler popped his jaw. 'Miranda—'

'How do I get off this damn boat?'

It might have been something that worked in his favour if they hadn't been so close to Manhattan. When she yanked open the door and headed inside, he followed her. 'We need to talk about this.'

'No, we don't.' Her gaze searched for exit signs as an announcement was made about their arrival.

'You haven't got the full picture.'

'Believe me, it's in high definition.' She spun on her heel and marched towards the other end of the boat. 'I won't be manipulated by you or anyone else.'

He reached for her elbow. 'I'm not manipulating—'

Yanking her arm out of his reach, she swung on him with enough ice to freeze boiling water. 'Don't. Touch. Me.'

Tyler was about two seconds away from losing it. 'We're gonna talk about this whether you like it or not. But not here.'

'We're done talking.' She angled her chin with blatant contempt. 'And don't worry—you won't have to give up any more of your precious time to amuse me as a reward for good behaviour. Just be thankful you didn't have to prostitute yourself to get the job done. But then you never intended to cross that line, did you? Everyone has their limits.'

'Step too far with that one, princess.'

'You're *fired*.'

'You can't do that.'

'I just did.' She smirked and turned away, using her hundred-watt smile to flirt her way through a group of tourists to the front of the line.

When the rest of the passengers moved forwards he had to push his way through, his gaze firmly fixed on a head of flame-red hair. 'Excuse me. Sorry. Coming through…' He had to jog a little in the terminal to catch up. 'Still trying to cut me loose?'

No reply but she picked up the pace.

Tyler simply lengthened his stride. 'Long walk back to the mansion from here.' He nodded when she lifted her chin. 'Okay. Silent treatment is fine with me.' He held open a glass door for her and followed her outside. 'I'll talk. You listen.'

'Go to hell.'

'That the best you've got?'

She stopped dead in her tracks, turned, took a step forwards and swung a palm at his face. He caught her wrist in midair, glared at her from the corner of his eye in warning and then loosened his grip when he saw the horror of what she'd almost done in her eyes. It was a strategic mistake because the second he did she twisted it free, shoved both hands into his chest and caught him off balance. His heels caught on the kerb behind him and the next thing he knew he was sitting on his ass in wet grass.

Planting her fists on her hips she angled her chin and snapped, 'Is *that* better?'

It caused the kind of life-changing epiphany Tyler hadn't seen coming. For a moment he simply stared at her in shock. Then a vibration started in his chest, moving upwards into the base of his throat. The sound was rusty from lack of use, but familiar.

'You choose *now* to laugh?' She shook her head in disbelief. 'You're a twisted individual.'

When she spun around and marched to the edge of the road to hail a cab Tyler scrambled to his feet and jogged after her to try a more persuasive tone. 'If you let me tell you the rest of the sentence we can clear this up.'

'I don't want to clear it up,' she retorted. 'I want you to stay away from me.'

'You don't want that any more than I do.'

The convulsion of her throat gave him an indication of how

hurt she was, instantly causing him pain in response. 'You don't care what I want.'

'You couldn't be more wrong about that.'

It made her glance sideways at him as a cab pulled up but she didn't look him in the eye. 'Don't follow me.'

He frowned. 'Where do you think you're going?'

'*Home.* Not that it's your problem any more.' She lifted her chin again. 'I have three weeks left to serve on my sentence. Once they're done I'm going to go out into the big wide world, find the first available guy who'll spend time with me because he wants to and not because he's being paid to do it, and I'll have meaningless sex with him until neither of us can stand up.'

'No, you won't,' he said with conviction while the words stirred another savage streak of territorialism. 'We've already had that talk.'

'Wind up a mechanized toy, you shouldn't be surprised when it keeps moving after you set it down.' She frowned when he placed a palm on the top of the door to stop it from opening. 'Let me go.'

'I'm going to,' he said reluctantly before taking a step closer. 'But only to give you long enough to calm down. When you're thinking clearly and have questions you know how to find me.' He gave her something to mull over. 'You might want to make one of them why I kissed you the way I did.'

Pushing against his palm, he stood tall, dropped his arm to his side and watched her get into the cab. As it left it felt as if part of him went with it, but he guessed he would have to get used to that.

When his phone rang he waited a few moments before answering it. 'Brannigan.'

'You wanna go on a stake-out?' his partner enquired.

Tyler's blood chilled. 'You found him?'

'Maybe…' There was a brief pause. 'Turns out your friend Jimmy has been worrying enough about being seen as a snitch to become one.'

'I'm on my way.'

CHAPTER TWENTY-TWO

THE club encompassed a city block with a dance floor, live DJ and a seating area for private parties at the back. Despite the fact it was a Sunday night and many of them had work in the morning, it was packed with a hip Manhattan crowd of twenty-to-thirty-somethings.

Miranda was at the bar with Crystal. She'd bought the first drink to sip while she tried to calm down. When it had the same medicinal effect associated with a stiff brandy she ordered another. The numbness that set in with her third was more welcome than any of the little umbrellas lined up side by side would ever know.

There were four of them now, not counting the one in her glass. They were pretty. She'd decided to see how many colours she could collect.

'You know what *really* bugs me?' she yelled over the music. 'By allowing me to throw myself at him like some kind of desperate woman he made me feel *needy*. I don't do *needy*. If I was *needy* I'd sleep with every guy who showed an interest in me.' She waved a limp-wristed hand in the general direction of the man hovering nearby. 'Like that guy over there. He's cute and he's been smiling at me for the last ten minutes.'

'He's the bartender and you've been tipping him the price of your drink every time you buy one,' Crystal said dryly while attempting to take the cocktail glass from her. 'I think that's enough alcohol for you, young lady. You never could hold your liquor.'

When Miranda moved the glass out of her reach some of the liquid splashed over her hand. 'If you weren't trying to take it off me, I wouldn't be spilling it.' She scowled. To solve the problem she downed the colourful contents. 'I love this song. Let's dance. I want to dance.'

'We should probably get you home—or to my place for coffee. Coffee would be good.'

'I don't want coffee and I'm not going home. I want to have *fun.*' When the screen of her cell phone flashed on the bar beside the empty glass she picked it up and squinted at the caller ID. '*Ugh,* he just can't take a hint, can he?'

'He won't be happy when he finds you like this.'

Miranda rejected the call with a flourish and set her phone down. 'I don't *care.*'

'Yes, you do. That's half the problem.'

'*He* doesn't care. He's only spending time with me because it's his *job.*'

'And there's the other half…'

She blinked. 'Is there something *wrong* with me?'

'Of course there's not,' Crystal said with conviction. 'You're a beautiful, sexy woman. Any guy would want you. Have a glass of water.'

'I thought he wanted me as much as I want him. I mean, when he kisses me—*wow*—and when he touches me—*boom!* Fireworks, y'know what I mean? He makes me. *So. Hot.* But does he follow through, even when he has permission to…' she made speech marks in the air with her fingers *'...do whatever he needs to do to keep me out of trouble?'* She rocked back and announced, 'He's a tease. I didn't think guys did that.'

'Who knew?' Her best friend nudged the glass a little closer. 'Take a sip, it's very refreshing.'

'It should *not* be this hard to get laid. Do you know I don't even know what an orgasm feels like with company?'

The comment earned a somewhat blurry-around-the-edges expression of interest. 'I did *not* know that. And it's a conversation we'll be having when you're sober. One little sip for Auntie Crystal, there's a good girl…'

'I bet when he gives a girl an orgasm it knocks her socks off. Not that I'm likely to find out any time soon. No toe-curling bliss on the horizon for me. Being the mayor's daughter is like wearing a *giant chastity belt.*'

'Would you prefer fizzy water?'

'And what the hell was he thinking taking me home to meet his family?' She swallowed the lump in her throat. 'They're wonderful. Did I tell you how wonderful they are?'

'About a half-dozen times…'

'Can I get you ladies another drink?' a voice said beside them.

Crystal smiled sweetly. 'I'll give you twenty bucks to shake your cute little cocktail shaker elsewhere.'

'They're exactly the kind of family I'd like to have some day,' Miranda continued. 'I love the whole meeting-up-for-Sunday-lunch thing.' She sat a little straighter. 'But we're not a *couple.* I don't want to *fall in love with him.*'

'Are you?'

'Am I what?'

'Falling in love with him…?'

'No!' she replied vehemently before taking a beat. 'Maybe… I don't know… I don't *want* to be.'

'How come?'

The tears she'd been battling since she left the ferry terminal threatened to break free, forcing her to take several deep breaths before she replied. 'Because then I'd belong to him and I'd really like him to belong to me for a little while.' She flicked her hair over her shoulder. 'I don't want to talk about this any more. It's depressing. If you love me, you'll dance with me.'

'I do and I would.' Crystal glanced over her shoulder. 'But I have a sneaking suspicion you're about to be carried out of here…'

Miranda twisted around, lifted her gaze and frowned. 'Go away, Tyler. I don't *like you.*'

His gaze shifted. 'How much has she had?'

'Too much,' Crystal replied. 'Not that it takes much to begin with—she's always been a cheap date that way. I've been trying to get her to go home for the last half hour.'

'I'll take it from here.'

'Go easy on her. She's hurting for a reason.'

'I know.'

Miranda shook her head in disbelief and regretted it the second the room began to spin. 'That's it—go right ahead and talk about me like I'm not here. Start making decisions for me and you'll both be like everyone else in my life who doesn't give a crap about how I feel.' She raised her arm high above her head and waggled her fingers. 'Hey, *cute guy,* drink me!'

'You've reached your limit,' Tyler said firmly as he lifted her cell phone and took her elbow. 'And you're gonna apologize to Crystal for that in the morning. Thanks for the heads up on her location.'

The last part made Miranda gasp. 'You sent for him? How *could you?*' Taught her not to leave her cell phone on the bar when she went to the restroom, didn't it?

At least Crystal had the decency to look apologetic. 'Because it's not me that you need to be talking to right now and you'd never forgive yourself if you made it into the papers this close to Election Day.'

'Up you get,' Tyler ordered.

'I'm not leaving.'

'Yes, you are.'

'Make me.'

'Okay.'

When he bent down and tossed her effortlessly over her shoulder, Miranda struggled. 'Put me down!'

'Bye, Crystal.'

'Bye, Tyler.'

'Stop him!' she yelled at the bouncer on the door before hiccupping. 'I'm being kidnapped!'

'No, she's not.' Tyler simply rearranged her weight to flash his shield. 'NYPD.'

'Isn't that the mayor's daughter?' the bouncer asked.

'She's one of those lookalikes,' Tyler said as he walked away. 'Been conning free drinks all over town…'

'Put me *down!*' Miranda repeated while she was carried down the sidewalk. 'Women *hate it* when guys do this.'

He muttered a reply that sounded as if it included the words 'worked for' and 'Brannigan' and 'when he did' before raising his voice to inform her, 'You're gonna have the hangover from hell in the morning.'

'Why should you care?' she asked his broad back.

'The thought I might scares the life out of you, doesn't it?'

She lifted her chin. 'What's that supposed to mean?'

'You're a flight risk. I knew that at the start. What I didn't know was why.'

'But you think you do *now?*'

His head nodded against her flank. 'This is what you do when things get too much—you run away to find solace in having fun. Up till now it's been the life you didn't want and how claustrophobic you felt. This time it's me.'

Miranda spluttered, 'Arrogant much?'

'This isn't you. You're more than this.'

'You don't *know me.*'

He took a deep breath she felt against her legs. 'You're an amazing woman with the potential to do equally amazing things with her life. Is this how you're gonna deal with your problems when you're forty? Whether you like it or not I do care so when you're ready to talk about what's bothering you let me know.'

'I already tried that,' she said in a smaller voice.

'No, you didn't. You ran away.'

The truth silenced her while he set her on her feet. Swaying a little she pushed her hair out of her eyes and looked up at him. Damn him for being so big and strong and bulletproof. She *hated* that he could make her feel so small and weak and vulnerable. She didn't want to fall for him.

It would be so much simpler if she wasn't.

When her lower lip trembled she bit down on it.

The pad of a thumb stilled the movement. 'Don't do that. You'll make it bleed.'

The husky edge to his voice twisted her heart into a tight little ball. She didn't want tenderness from him. Not if he was going to take it with him when he left. 'You're looking at me the way I don't like again,' she complained.

He shouldn't make promises with his eyes he wasn't prepared to keep. But what was worse was how it made her *feel.* At the beginning he excited her—he still did—but along the way he also surprised and challenged her, making her re-evaluate her life and what she wanted from it. She would do it—she would give up her freedom to be with him.

She would give up *everything.*

How had he made her feel that way in just a few weeks?

His thumb brushed across her cheek before he dropped his hand to his side. 'Let's get you home.'

Miranda allowed him to move her around so he could open the door and help her inside. She gazed at his profile as he leaned in to click her seat belt into place, saw him glance at her from the corner of his eye and wished she knew what to say. How was she supposed to tell him what she'd felt when he kissed her—lost and found, hopeful and hopeless, joyous and afraid? It was so many things at once.

It felt as if she belonged in his arms. But he'd had an opportunity to correct her when she said neither of them wanted to make a commitment and he hadn't. It wasn't his fault she'd discovered she wanted something more. The thought of her life without him in it *sucked.* When she'd thought he was only spending time with her because he had to the ground dropped out from under her feet.

It had hurt. *So. Much.*

She hauled in a ragged breath and blinked when her vision blurred. As she did long fingers closed around the hand in her lap and she lowered her chin, watching as she turned her palm into his. She loved holding his hand but if she had one wish it would be to hear him laugh again so she could take the time to appreciate the sound. She'd waited so long to hear it. What if it never happened again?

If they just had a little more time…

'Will you tell me the rest of the sentence?' she asked in the same small voice as before.

Tyler didn't need an explanation, the deep rumble of his voice washing over her in a soothing caress. 'He said to do whatever I had to do to keep you safe because you don't know how vulnerable you are in the spotlight.'

'That's not true.' She attempted to smile through her tears. 'I've always been vulnerable in the spotlight. I used to get stage fright. Threw up every time I had to appear in public—got reminded of it when we went to lunch today. I was scared people would find me lacking in any one of a dozen different ways. Not smart enough, funny enough, pretty enough or dressed well enough. It's why I took the part in the play during senior year in high school. I figured if I tackled my confidence issues head on…'

When her voice trailed off he squeezed her hand. 'People love you within minutes of meeting you. I've watched it happen.'

'They don't have to spend much time with me.'

'Well, there is *that*.'

Miranda chuckled, hiccupped and then sniffled before leaning back against the headrest. She didn't realize she'd fallen asleep until she was being carried up the stairs of the mansion in a much more romantic position. Snuggling closer to his neck, she took a long breath of Tyler-scented air and sighed contentedly. *This* she could definitely learn to live with. Being protected from the world wasn't so bad the way he did it. He even took her shoes off and tucked her into bed.

When he disappeared without saying anything she tried to lift her heavy head to see where he'd gone. Then the mattress dipped beside her, a fingertip brushed her hair off her forehead and he was leaning over her.

Looking deep into his eyes, she tried to remember what her life was like before he walked into it. Considering it hadn't been that long ago, it shouldn't have been difficult, but all she knew was how alone she'd felt without him, how overly defensive she'd been when she discovered he was her bodyguard, how much she'd loved their little adventures and that she owed him an apology for knocking him on his ass. She couldn't believe she'd been angry enough to hit him.

What must he think of her?

'Why do you put up with me?' she asked.

'You're cute when you're drunk.'

'I'm more trouble than I'm worth.'

'We'll debate that one another time.' He trailed his fingers along her cheek and watched the movement with one of his more intense gazes. 'Go back to sleep.'

'Stay with me?' she whispered. It was a loaded request but she couldn't stop herself making it.

'I can't. Even if we weren't in the mayor's house, I had to leave a stake-out to come rescue you.' He drew in a long, measured breath and slowly exhaled. 'I gotta go back. There's something I have to do. If it doesn't turn out so great…' He frowned before looking into her eyes. 'Just remember if I had a choice, things would be different.'

Miranda smiled sadly. It felt like a goodbye.

She didn't want him to go.

'Don't forget that,' he insisted.

'I won't,' she promised.

His gaze roamed over her face before he leaned down to press a kiss to her forehead. 'Go back to sleep.'

Miranda ran her palm up over his chest. 'I'll see you tomorrow, won't I?'

He smiled the crooked smile she loved so much. 'You fired me, remember?'

'You're rehired.'

'Go to sleep.'

Stretching upwards, she wound her arm around his neck and lifted her chin. 'I'm not sleepy any more.'

Tyler sighed heavily, his voice laced with regret. 'I was hoping you wouldn't say that.'

Something cold and metallic snapped around her wrist.

Miranda twisted her head on the pillow so she could see what he was doing. 'What is that?'

The restraint was unyielding as he closed a second loop around one of the iron rungs on her bedstead.

'If you'd fallen asleep I wouldn't have to do this.' He got to his feet. 'Water's beside you. I don't have any aspirin or I'd leave that, too. You're gonna need it when you wake up.' He bent over and lifted a washbowl off the floor to wave it at her. 'You can use this if you need to be sick or feel the call of nature.'

'It's an *antique*.'

'Then you better not break it.'

The outrage she felt was the equivalent of downing a dozen cups of espresso, the effects of the alcohol wearing off pretty damn fast as he walked away.

'You can't leave me like this.' She lowered her voice to snap, *'Tyler!'*

'I'll leave the key for Grace. She's usually in before everyone else.'

And then he was gone.

Flumping back onto the pillow, she lifted her chin to glare at the handcuffs and rattled stainless steel against iron. How was she supposed to explain *that* in the morning?

She was going to kill him the next time she saw him.

CHAPTER TWENTY-THREE

BY THE time Tyler returned to his partner and the rookie detective who'd been attempting to fill his shoes, the stake-out wasn't a stake-out any more. 'Can't believe you were gonna start the party without me…'

'ESU just got here. You haven't missed anything.' He frowned. 'Where's your vest?'

'In my locker,' Tyler replied. 'Tell me it's him.'

He wanted the day of reckoning out of the way so he knew if he had a future to plan.

'Arrived on the heels of a large shipment—we've got him this time. There's nowhere to go.'

As they silently approached the warehouse with their weapons drawn Tyler forced any thoughts of Miranda to the back of his mind. He knew she was safe, that had to be enough, even if he regretted not telling her how he felt when he had the chance. It was better he hadn't, he reasoned, especially now.

The raid was textbook, communication made with hand signals to place everyone in position before a countdown of fingers indicated when ESU would break down the door. Once they were inside it went equally smoothly—Tyler's voice joining the others to identify them as cops to the gang of men unpacking boxes. As they raised their hands in the air his gaze searched their faces and shifted in time to see a couple of men disappearing into the back.

Tyler ran after them, slowing his pace when the chase led into abandoned machinery and piles of empty crates.

His partner caught up to him. 'You see them?'

'Not yet.'

They split up, working as one to search high and low.

'One over there.' Tyler pointed when he heard a noise and saw a figure too short and stocky to be the man he was after. 'I've got the other one.'

'Don't do anything stupid.'

The warning fell on deaf ears, the dark side to his nature taking over as he stalked his prey. Tyler didn't fight it. He welcomed its arrival, embraced it and challenged it to do its worst. It was the only way he would know how far he could go. To fuel the need for revenge he summoned the image of a broken body to the front of his mind, saw the unnatural position of her limbs and thought about how much she'd suffered.

Then he rounded a corner into a narrow alley of crates and saw Demietrov standing a few feet away.

A slow, cold smile appeared on the man's face.

Tyler frowned, the gun wavering a little in front of him. Restlessly shifting his weight from one foot to the other, he locked his arms into place and looked down the barrel with determination. He could feel the weight of his finger resting on the trigger, but even when looking his nemesis straight in the eye he couldn't take the shot.

Something wouldn't let him.

When he spoke his voice rang around the empty space with the kind of conviction that came from doing the right thing. 'Andrei Demietrov, I'm placing you under arrest for the trafficking of illegal substances and the suspected murder of Candice James.' The darkness shrank within him, folding in on itself until it became the manageable part of his personality it had been before his life got so screwed up. 'You have the right to remain silent—'

As he stepped forwards the man reached out and tumbled the nearest pile of crates to the ground, creating a domino effect that forced Tyler to jump out of the way before he continued the chase. There was the sound of a door slamming shut. When he got to it and swung it open he discovered it was raining outside. He checked each side of an arch of security lighting and took a step forwards…

The impact knocked him backwards a second before he heard the shot and felt a searing heat blaze through his shoulder. There was another shot in quick succession—he felt a second burn in his upper arm—and then there was a hail of gunfire and a body slumped onto the ground. As he staggered backwards Tyler knew he hadn't fired his weapon. The ESU guys had done what he couldn't.

Sickly warmth soaked his shirt as his back hit the wall beside the door and his knees gave out.

He stared at the body as his partner appeared and swore succinctly while prying the gun from his hand. 'This is Detective Ramirez, we have an officer down—I repeat, officer down. I need a bus at—'

As he rhymed off the address—presumably over the phone—Tyler felt a sense of peace wash over him. When it came down to the wire he didn't have it in him to murder a man in cold blood. Maybe he wasn't as far gone as he'd thought. Maybe Miranda had pulled him back from the edge. He tried to focus past the pain while the warmth drained from his body. Getting shot hurt like a bitch. And he'd left Miranda handcuffed to her bed.

A rumble of laughter made him groan.

'You want to share the joke?' his partner asked as he took a look at the damage.

'The one time I don't wear a vest…' he mumbled back.

'Murphy's Law…you're Irish…work it out.'

Tyler swore when he added pressure to the wound on his shoulder. 'Don't think that'll help,' he gritted through clenched teeth as his vision blurred. 'I think that one went through.'

'Here's hoping. If it's gone through they won't have to dig it out. What about your arm?'

'That one they'll have to dig out.'

'Just as well you're right-handed, isn't it?'

Tyler frowned. A few feet back, to the side of the ESU's tactical guys as they checked the body lying on the ground, a silent figure stood in the pouring rain. Her face wasn't covered in blood any more and she was smiling at him. How could she be happy he'd failed her—wasn't the whole point of haunting him to keep him focused on avenging her death? 'I'm sorry.' It was the first time he'd told her that. 'I screwed up.'

'You've got nothing to apologize for,' his partner replied, obviously under the impression Tyler was talking to him. 'Can happen to the best of us.'

When he blinked the raindrops off his lashes Candice was replaced by another woman with long dark hair and while she was smiling, too, she was also shaking her head. Why was he seeing Jo? She wasn't dead. He blinked again, the movement taking more effort than it had before.

'Stay with me,' his partner's voice said.

A woman with tumbling tresses of flame-red hair appeared in Jo's place and even in the rain Tyler could see she was crying. His heart twisted. She should never have to cry because of him, even if part of it was alcohol related. He wanted to make her happy, hear her laugh every day and see the fire in her eyes when they argued. He didn't have to keep his foot on the brake any more. The obstacles standing in their way weren't insurmountable. If they were then he wouldn't feel the way he did.

Not that he had any control over it.

'Stay with me.'

She'd said that, too, and he'd never wanted anything more. If they'd been born in an earlier time he'd happily keep her barefoot and pregnant and protect what was his, keeping them safe from marauders. He'd have been good at that. All the touchy-feely modern-day stuff that said a guy was supposed to embrace his feminine side and emote, not so damn much. Tyler didn't have a feminine side. Karl Jung could take his theories on human psychology and—

'Ty, snap out of it.' A hand smacked his cheek a few times. 'You gotta stay awake.'

Damn, it was cold. He should have worn a jacket. Screw the jacket, he should have worn his damn vest and then he wouldn't be ruining a perfectly good sweater.

'Anyone on your team an EMT?' his partner yelled at the ESU guys. 'Get him over here!'

Excellent—someone else to fuss over him. Anyone would think he was the first person in the world to get shot.

'I'll call your family when we get to the emergency room,' his partner said in a lower voice.

'You do that I'll kick your ass.'

'Anyone you *do* want me to call?'

'No.' Since shaking his head took too much effort, he frowned again. 'Don't want to worry her.'

'We all need someone who does that.'

'You'd like her.' His voice slurred.

'Can't be that good a judge of character if she likes you…' His partner moved to make room for someone else. 'We need to stop the bleeding.'

'I'm on it,' a voice he didn't recognize said. 'Stay with us, brother.'

With his eyelids growing heavy Tyler used up some of his waning energy on what probably looked like a sappy smile. He didn't know what he'd done to deserve it but she did like him. Unless he was very much mistaken—and he prayed he wasn't—she liked him a whole heap. Way he saw it she was his—he just had to find a way to make her believe it, too. Jo hadn't been his one who got away. But if he was dumb enough to let Miranda go without putting up one hell of a fight she would be.

They just needed a little more time….

'Stay awake, Ty. Where the hell's that bus?'

It was the second time in less than twenty-four hours he found his ass on wet ground while he wondered when he'd fallen for her. The first had been the 'there you are' moment that identified her as the one he'd been waiting for all along. He'd even laughed with joy. She was the reason he'd been emotionally unavailable to other women. She was the reason he hadn't told Jo how he'd thought he felt. At times she drove him nuts but she was smart and funny and gutsy and sexy as hell. It shouldn't have been such a great surprise he wanted to hold on to her. Any guy would. But they could forget it. She was *his*.

'Tell her,' he mumbled.

'Tell her what?'

Somewhere along the way she'd got under his skin and crawled inside, filling him up until everything else was pushed out. It didn't matter if it was too soon or that there was still so much for him to learn about her. It was just there…like air… without it…

He couldn't breathe.

'Ty, come on, man, you gotta hold on.'

He hadn't known love could be so…*big.* He felt crushed under the weight of it. If he knew she could feel the same way it would lift him up higher than he'd ever been before. But until they got a chance to talk he just needed a little nap—he had to be at full strength to fight for her. Forty winks should do it.

With sirens sounding in the distance she was the last thought on his mind as he passed out.

CHAPTER TWENTY-FOUR

MIRANDA opened her eyes and groaned as she squinted at the bright light shining through a crack in the curtains. When she turned over to check the time on the alarm clock the handcuffs snagged her wrist.

'Damn it, Tyler.'

The three gentle knocks on her bedroom door echoed inside her head as if they'd been made with a demolition ball. 'Grace?' she asked tentatively.

The door opened a crack. 'Can I come in?'

'Yes.' Miranda fought embarrassment as the older woman crossed the room. 'Tell me there's a key in that envelope.'

'With a note which said to bring this…' she held out a bottle of aspirin '…and that you'd probably want a bucket of coffee…'

'You have *no idea.*' She took a deep breath while Grace negotiated the lock on the loop above her head. 'You're probably wondering what's going on.'

'I don't need an explanation.'

Miranda held up her arm when it was freed from the bed. 'You have a soft spot for him, don't you?'

'Well, he is handsome…'

'Yes, he is.'

'And you have been happier in the last few weeks…'

When the second loop opened she rubbed her wrist. 'Yes, I was.'

Grace studied her face with knowing eyes. 'I wouldn't give up on him yet. A man doesn't handcuff a woman to a bed to keep her safe if he doesn't care.' Setting the handcuffs on the bedside cabinet, she lowered her voice and smiled with a rare glimpse of mischievousness. 'Not that there aren't other things you could do with them…'

'Grace.' Miranda gasped. 'I'm shocked.'

'No, you're not.' She chuckled as she turned away. 'I'll have them bring breakfast to your room.'

'Wait.' Swinging her legs off the bed Miranda stood up to fold her in a grateful hug. 'You know I love you, right? I don't say it enough.'

Having been—what had he called it, treated to a hug-fest?—she wanted more hugs in her life. When Tyler was gone she would need them.

'You don't have to say it. You're the daughter I never had.' Grace leaned back and winked. 'Now make me proud and go give that handsome devil hell for what he did to you.'

'I will.'

The thought lifted her spirits a little and by the time she'd showered, had breakfast and was feeling more human she'd made a decision. There was no point dwelling over how little time they had left. If all they had was a few more weeks she was going to make the most of them. He did care—if she'd been thinking sensibly she'd have known that without him saying it. She had to accept that was enough, even if she struggled with it. But she didn't want a marriage proposal or a drawer at his apartment or even to keep a toothbrush in his bathroom. All she wanted was to continue seeing him. Maybe she should tell him that?

If it didn't feel like the biggest step she'd ever taken with the most massive gaping cavern for her to fall into if he didn't feel the same way, she might consider it.

She checked her watch and frowned. Grace was late with the itinerary. It wasn't like her. Lifting her things, she decided to meet her at her desk, the sight of someone she hadn't expected making her footsteps falter when she got there. 'Lewis. I didn't think you were working today.'

'I wasn't.'

Miranda's gaze shifted when Grace appeared from her father's office, the grim expression on her face creating a sense of foreboding. 'What's going on?'

'We don't know much yet,' she replied in a low voice. 'But it's all over the news. Apparently Detective Brannigan was on some kind of drugs raid last night and—'

'No.' The word parted her lips on a tortured whisper.

Grace reached out a hand and squeezed her arm. 'He's all right. Your father has asked me to find out what hospital he's in so we can send a gift.'

'What happened?'

It earned another squeeze—one that didn't loosen—which suggested she knew Miranda would need the support.

'He was shot.'

Grace had been right; she did need the support. Her body swayed, a wave of nausea rising in her throat. It was her worst nightmare. She couldn't bear the thought of him lying bleeding somewhere while she'd been sleeping. But falling apart wasn't going to help.

The only thing that would was seeing him.

Making a conscious effort to prick the bubble of shock surrounding her body, she summoned strength she didn't know she possessed and took charge. 'Lewis, bring the car to the door and use your connections in the department to find out what hospital he's in. You'll find out quicker than Grace.'

He nodded as he left.

'I need you to reorganize today's itinerary,' she told Grace. 'Most of the morning involves listening to speeches so they can do without me but there's a scheduled visit to a veterans' association before lunch. Give them a call and see if we can move it back a couple of hours. If we can't extend my apologies and see if we can reschedule for later in the week—tell them I'm sick if you need to.'

'I'll see to it. What do you want me to tell your father if he asks where you are?'

'Tell him the truth. If he has a problem he can discuss it with me later.'

'I'll call you with an update.'

Between several calls, a check on the internet for what little news there was and with Lewis driving with the lights flashing on the front grill of the SUV, they reached their destination in relatively good time.

Standing at a nurse's station, she announced, 'I'm looking for Detective Brannigan's room. I was told it's on the fifth floor.'

'Are you family?'

'He's my bodyguard.' She lifted her chin. 'I'm Miranda Kravitz. My father is the mayor.'

Meaning if the woman got in her way she would have a fight on her hands…

'Do you think you can get him to stay in bed?'

The question made her sag with relief. If they were having difficulty keeping him in bed it was a good sign. 'Point me in the right direction and I'll give it a try.'

'Third door on the left,' the woman replied. 'Good luck. You're going to need it.'

After pausing beside the open door to draw a deep breath of air into her lungs, Miranda crossed the threshold and took an inventory with her eyes. He was sitting on the end of the bed, frowning at a navy T-shirt as he tried to find a way of putting it on one-handed. Under normal circumstances her gaze would have snagged on his bare chest and marvelled at the sight of smooth skin stretched over taut muscle. Instead it was drawn to the squares of gauze taped to his upper arm and below his shoulder. If the second square had been a few inches lower the bullet would have punctured a lung.

She swallowed the jagged lump in her throat to ask, 'What do you think you're doing?'

His gaze lifted, a brief flash of surprise crossing his face before his voice rumbled, 'It's called escaping. You of all people should know that. How did you get here?'

'Lewis brought me. I didn't give him a choice.' She crossed the room and set her bag down on an empty chair. 'And you're not going anywhere. What did the doctor say?'

'That they dug out the bullet, replaced the blood I lost and stitched up the holes.'

'And that you should *rest,* right?'

'Look, I get what you're doing but if you want to do something useful you can get me the hell out of here before my family comes back. If I have to endure another candlelit vigil around this bed I'm gonna jump out that window. My mother is *this far away...*' he raised the hand holding the T-shirt to demonstrate the distance with a small gap between his thumb and finger '...from getting Father Mike to drop by and bless me.'

'They're worried about you,' Miranda argued in their defence, ignoring his obvious frustration.

Tyler lowered his hand, frowning at the T-shirt again as he held it at arm's length and tried to shake it straight. 'If it wasn't for one of Danny's ESU buddies flapping his jaw none of them would have known.'

'Well, it's nice to know I wasn't the only person you didn't think merited a phone call.'

His hand dropped onto his lap. *'Miranda—'*

'If the doctor says you're supposed to stay in bed—'

'I can do it at home.' He looked up into her eyes. 'I don't need anyone's approval to check out. They can put a note on the form to say it's against medical advice if they're worried about covering their asses.'

Her eyes narrowed. 'Why do I get the impression this isn't your first visit to a hospital?'

'Me and Father Mike go way back—broken leg when I was nine, first concussion when I was twelve...'

She arched a brow. '*First* concussion?'

'I read a lot. When I was a kid it made it feel like I had something to prove when it came to sports. Get me out of here and you can examine every inch of me for scars.'

'Promises, promises,' she muttered before accepting the inevitable. There was no way he was staying put, but if she couldn't stop him leaving she could make sure they took every possible precaution. 'You're not leaving until I've talked to your doctor and he's prescribed pain medication.'

Tyler stood up. 'I don't need any.'

Again with the something to prove, but the lines of strain at the corners of his eyes and the rigid set of his jaw suggested otherwise. She folded her arms. 'I have a vehicle and a driver who can take you straight home. Do you want help to escape or not?'

Surprisingly he took a moment to mull it over, his gaze searching the air before he lifted his hand. 'You can start with helping me put on a T-shirt. I've been swearing at this thing for the last five minutes.'

Miranda noted the way he avoided looking at her and got the sense he wasn't happy with her being there. It hurt that he wasn't—especially when she'd been so desperate to see him. But she wasn't there for totally selfish reasons—she wanted to be there *for him.* If he'd let her…

'In order for me to do that you have to sit back down…' She looked at the T-shirt as she took it from him, noticed something behind it and shook her head. 'Let me guess. You gave up swearing at the button on your jeans five minutes ago.'

Determined she could touch him impassively while he was injured, she stepped forwards and folded the T-shirt over her forearm to free up her hands. But it wasn't her reaction she should have worried about. The second her fingers folded around the waistband of his jeans—the backs of her fingers brushing against warm skin—he sucked in a sharp breath and tensed. Her gaze darted upwards and tangled with his, the mixture of heat and pain in his eyes making her grimace.

'Sorry,' she whispered.

'Don't be,' he gritted back before the heat in his eyes intensified to drown out the pain.

Miranda slipped the button into the loop and removed her hands. 'Sit.' She lifted the T-shirt. 'Bad arm first…'

The eye contact was broken to allow her to negotiate dressing him with as little discomfort as possible, but when the task was complete he forced her gaze back to his by capturing her wrist.

'I'm fine,' he said firmly.

'No, you're not.' Her voice trembled a little on the words. 'You got shot. With a *gun.*'

'Technically speaking I got shot with bullets *fired* from a gun.' A corner of his mouth tugged when she frowned. 'Still here, aren't I?'

A landslide of the emotions she'd been burying tumbled down on her, hammering her heart into a bruised ball of pulp. She'd known he would leave soon but if he'd *died*...

He was so much more than she was. While she'd slept off the alcohol she'd consumed in a bid to escape reality he'd been on the front line, protecting the city. He'd dedicated his life to making the world a safer place without seeking anything in return. How could a man like him ever love a woman like her? He deserved so much better.

Lifting her free hand, she ran trembling fingers over his short hair and down the back of his neck. He closed his eyes in response—what looked like agony crossing his face before he opened them. She wanted to take away his pain and soothe the tension from his body. She wanted to take care of him, listen to the things that troubled him and put his needs above her own. She wasn't any good at cooking or cleaning or doing laundry—doubted she would ever fill the role of domestic goddess—but she was willing to *try.* If there was anything she could do to make his life easier she would put her heart and soul into it. She just wished she thought she could be happy that way.

Even if she hadn't already planned to find something that could allow her to make a difference to people's lives, getting to know him would have inspired her. The irony was they could probably have teamed up. One of the charities on her shortlist dealt with victim support...

'You know this means I'm not your bodyguard any more.'

She stared at him. The thought hadn't occurred to her.

As her hand lowered to her side he explained, 'They'll make me take time off. If I'm lucky I'll get desk duty in a week but I won't be back on tour until after the election.'

Miranda felt the time that had meant so much to her slipping through her fingers. She twisted her wrist free and took a step back, turning away to pack what few things he had into the open sports bag on the bed beside him. His family must have brought what they thought he needed. They had the right to do that. She probably shouldn't even be there. Purposefully keeping her tone light, she told him, 'You'll heal quicker that way.'

'And you'll be busy with the campaign.'

'I will.' If he was trying to let her down easy there wasn't any need. She'd known a day would come when he wouldn't be there any more. She was just thankful he would be *somewhere*—could take comfort from that while spending the rest of her life trying to make him proud to say he'd known her. 'It can get hectic in the last few weeks.'

'When it's over you'll be free.'

'I'm looking forward to it. I've made a lot of plans—things I want to do, places I want to see.' Silently clearing her throat, she lifted her chin and informed him, 'I'm going to check in with your doctor. Lewis should be up in a minute. Then we'll take you home.'

She headed for the door.

'Miranda, *stop.*' The forceful edge to his rough voice froze her feet to the ground. 'Don't run away this time.'

Pinning a bright smile in place, she turned around to give the performance of a lifetime. 'If I was running away I'd take my bag. It's Gucci.'

Tyler frowned and angled his head a little to study her from the corner of his eye. 'Are you still mad at me for the handcuffs?'

'You did what you felt you had to do.' She shrugged. 'I'd probably have done the same thing in your shoes.'

He opened his mouth, sucked in a breath and hesitated. It wasn't like him but in the blink of an eye he recovered, his voice laced with determination. 'We need to talk.'

'Now?' she asked with as innocent an expression as she could muster. 'I thought you wanted to leave?'

'You rearranged your schedule to be here, right?'

'Grace did.'

'How much time did she get you?'

'I'm visiting veterans after lunch.'

'What about tonight?'

Since she wasn't convinced prolonging the agony would make it feel any better Miranda lied. 'I'm pretty solidly booked for the next few weeks. We could meet up for coffee after the election if you like. You have my number.'

'Still trying to cut me loose, aren't you?'

'You're not my bodyguard any more.'

'So that's it. There's nothing you want to say to me.'

'Of course there is.' She sighed, struggling to keep up the pretence. 'You've watched over me all this time, put up with *a lot* and I've enjoyed our time together. I can never begin to repay you for—'

Tyler shook his head. 'I shouldn't have left the keys with Grace. That was a mistake. Go find the damn doctor so I can blow this joint. But if you think we're done here you can forget it.' He pushed to his feet. 'Just be thankful I'm not in any shape to toss you over my shoulder again.'

She blinked. 'I don't get why you're angry.'

'Well, when you figure it out let me know.'

When he turned and started an argument with the zipper on the sports bag, Miranda took a step forwards. 'Tyler—'

He lifted the bag and marched past her. 'I'm going to sign the paperwork.'

The silence in the car on the journey to his apartment was deafening. He left with a curt 'thanks' and not so much as a sideways glance at her. It was awful. She'd never felt worse—empty and alone and facing an endlessly long Tyler-less future. It was over. He was gone.

Miranda would never know how she kept her facade in place for the rest of the scheduled itinerary. But at the end of an interminably long day it took its toll.

She dropped onto the edge of her bed, deflating like a balloon losing air. When the tears came she didn't stop them. There was nothing remotely dainty or feminine about it when the floodgates opened, either. When she lay down on the covers heaving sobs racked her body until her face was mottled and her eyes were red and swollen. Later, when she hauled herself upright and made it under a hot shower, she turned the water on to high and cried some more while its warmth did nothing to remove the chill from her body.

It was late when she was reduced to sniffling into her pillow. Staring into the darkness, she started to think things through. She thought about the first time he took her hand; how big a pain in the ass he'd been when he blocked her escape attempts; how he'd been the first person to be brutally honest with her; how the most dangerous man she'd ever met could make her feel safe and protected. Then she thought about the night in the alley, the shudder that ran through his body when he held her, how he resisted the kiss but wrestled control from her. From that point of view he'd always had the upper hand. When he kissed her nothing else mattered but kissing him back. At least it hadn't until her heart got involved.

Then something happened. Somewhere in the middle of her sentimental journey to revisit each landmark in their relationship a spark of hope ignited, the flame flickering defiantly in the midst of her doubt she could ever be enough for him.

'I want you to stay away from me,' she'd lied.

'You don't want that any more than I do,' he'd replied.

Her heart tripped and picked up speed.

Unless he was trying to push her away Tyler didn't say things he didn't mean. But what if he'd been saying more than she'd heard? What if she'd been so wrapped up in how she felt—*for a change*—she'd missed how he felt?

She hadn't gone looking for it until she needed it to be there, but once she did…

'I'm supposed to keep my distance,' he'd said. But he couldn't do that any more than she could.

Surely that meant something—what if he felt the same draw to her that she felt to him?

He'd said when she had questions, *'You might want to make one of them why I kissed you the way I did...'*

What if everything she'd felt in that kiss hadn't come from her? She'd felt lost but he'd found her. She'd been hopeful but he'd lost hope. He'd said he was beyond saving. Did he really believe that—what if he thought *she* couldn't love *him* the way *he was?* He'd told her if he had a choice things would be different. *'Don't forget that.'*

Why had she forgotten that?

Even with her confidence battered by waves of fear and self-doubt the flame of hope continued to burn. The truth was she was more frightened of losing him than taking a leap of faith for the man she believed in more than she believed in herself. She'd thought he couldn't love her but if one day he *could*...

'When you figure it out let me know.'

Heart pounding rapidly, she jumped off the bed, grabbed the essentials and ran downstairs. Nothing on earth would stop her from going to him. She couldn't spend the rest of her life wondering what might have happened if she'd taken a chance. If the freedom she'd been dreaming of for her entire adult life was all about choice, then she chose *him*.

All he had to do was choose her back.

CHAPTER TWENTY-FIVE

He *should* have kissed some sense into her. There was nothing wrong with his *mouth.*

But when Miranda was so nonchalant about never seeing him again it had knocked Tyler back. He couldn't even put on a damn T-shirt alone—how was he supposed to convince her that he would look after her for the rest of her life when he couldn't dress himself?

After a day spent fending off calls from his family, his partner, his captain, some moron from the press who wanted to paint him as a hero and a woman trying to sell him life insurance, Tyler paced the floor of his apartment like a caged animal. He reckoned Miranda had about twenty-four hours before he switched from the role of bodyguard to stalker. If he had to kidnap her and spend the next week demonstrating how much he wanted her then so be it. The physical pain he was experiencing from a couple of run-of-the-mill gunshot wounds was nothing compared to the agony he felt when he thought about losing her.

Now he'd risen from the ashes of his messed up life like the mythical phoenix of her code-name, he could plan a future. One he wanted to share with her.

But had he *told her that?*

He'd come to the sad conclusion he was a pathetic, cowardly weakling when there was a frantic knocking on the door of his apartment. At a little before midnight the last thing he expected on the other side was a breathless, wide-eyed Miranda. It was obviously raining again—the shoulders of her coat sparkling with silvery raindrops and her hair a shade darker. With her face flushed and devoid of make-up he thought she'd never looked more beautiful.

'Figured it out, did you?' he asked roughly.

Her brows wavered with uncertainty.

'Give it another minute.'

When she attempted to smile it wavered, too—her eyes shimmering with emotion as her breasts rose and fell with each rapid breath.

'Almost there…' The corner of his mouth lifted with the affection he didn't try to disguise.

Her smile was more convincing the second time, growing in direct relation to the dawning realization in her eyes.

Tyler nodded. 'Took you long enough.'

As she made a sound halfway between a laugh and a sob he reached for her hand to draw her inside and kicked the door shut with his foot.

'Coat off.' He led her into the kitchen and jerked his chin at the counter. 'Sit up there. I'll be right back.'

When he returned from the bathroom with as many towels as he could carry in one hand she'd done what she was told without putting up a fight. That was a first.

'Why didn't you say something?' she asked.

Tyler tossed the towels down, selected one and stepped in front of her. 'When you were playing the role of Little Miss Don't-Give-A-Damn? Close your eyes.'

As she did he dried her face, her eyes opening again when he progressed to her hair.

'I was going to let you go.' The words were said in the small, vulnerable voice that turned him inside out.

'Too bad. I told you a while back—I'm in your life now. Get used to it.'

She blinked. 'Are you telling me you knew *then?*'

'No. I knew when you knocked me on my ass.'

'I knew when you kissed me on the ferry.'

He nodded. 'That's why you got scared.'

'Yes.' She frowned and reached for the towel. 'You shouldn't be doing that. You're hurt. I should be taking care of you. Not the other way around.'

Tyler allowed her to take it and watched as she set it aside. 'If we're gonna make this work there has to be a little of both—not that I'll make it easy for you.' His mouth curved into a wry smile. 'In case you hadn't got it already, I'm not a very good patient. I like to think I'm better at taking care of other people, if they'll let me.'

'No one's ever been there just for me,' she confessed. 'Not the way it felt you were in the last few weeks...'

'And that's never gonna change.' Not when it felt as if he'd been born to be with her. He watched as she blinked a tear from her lower lashes and dashed it away with the back of her hand. 'Can you tell me why you were scared?'

'It was too much and not enough.' She searched for a way to explain it. 'What your eyes were saying—I didn't want to hear if you were planning on walking away, but if you're not—'

'I'm *not,*' he stated firmly. 'But there are a couple of things we need to get straight before we go any further. Starting with your father.'

Her expression questioned where he was going.

'I won't let him fast-track me up the food chain to make me more suitable for you,' Tyler continued. 'When I get my career back on track it won't be for him, it'll be for us. I passed the sergeants exam six years ago—can ace the lieutenant one the same way, but when the time comes to aim higher if I hear so much as a rumour of whispers in the right ears there'll be trouble.'

She listened intently while tears filled her eyes but, as hard as they were to see, he couldn't stop to do anything about them until he'd said his piece. 'I'm an expert on interfering families—did some interfering of my own in return—so I know how it works. Being in love with his daughter doesn't make me a soft target for manipulation. He ever tries it with you again we'll be having words on the subject. You've sacrificed enough for the family business. From here on in your needs come first. It's already been tempting to tell your parents that to their faces. If they knew you the way I've started to—why are you smiling?'

It was bright enough to compete with the sun.

'You're in love with me?'

'That's the only thing you got from all that?'

'It's the only thing that matters.'

If it was they would never run into any problems but… 'Being a cop's wife isn't easy.'

Her eyes widened. 'You're proposing now?'

'I like to think when I'm proposing you'll know I'm doing it.' Nudging her knees apart to make space to step closer, he laid a possessive palm on her hip. 'What I'm saying is we've got time—take as much of it as you need and talk to as many members of my family as you want. I can't change who I am for you or keep you in the lifestyle you've been accustomed to but—'

She shook her head. 'You don't have to. I have money. That's not an issue.'

'It is if you think we're living off a trust fund.'

'It's not a trust fund. Well, it is until I turn twenty-five, but my parents didn't set it up. It's an inheritance from my grandfather.'

Tyler's eyes narrowed at the offhand tone to her voice. 'Are you telling me you're rich?'

'I'm afraid so. You'll have to learn to live with it.'

The words left his mouth before he could stop them. 'Even if it begs the question of what I can offer you?'

She ignored the question. 'You're *in love* with me?'

'Are you listening to anything I'm saying?'

'Yes.' She blinked a couple of times. 'I just seem to be a little stuck on that one…'

'Why?'

'I didn't think… I mean I thought I'd have to…' The uncharacteristic lack of something to say removed the frown from his face as she took a short breath. 'I haven't done anything to deserve it. I was awful to you at the start and then I was difficult. You were right—I'm hard work.'

'And I'm not?'

When he searched her eyes he found wonder mixed with the vulnerability she kept hidden from everyone else. Added to the insight he'd gained when she'd talked about her fear of not being enough, it felt as if the final piece of the puzzle had slotted into place. The need to reassure her made him reach out so he could hold her while he admitted there had been plenty of times she was more than he could handle. But when the sharp pain in his shoulder made him grit his teeth to stifle a groan a second possessive palm on her other hip was as close as he got.

'I'm no angel and I don't want to end up married to a saint, either.' He leaned closer. 'So if you think you have to be anything more than you already are you're wrong. You pulled me back from the edge. No one else could have done that. Last night—' he cleared his throat '—I went there to kill him.'

As he stood tall and waited for her judgment Miranda frowned. What was he talking about? Then it clicked. 'He was the guy you sent a message to.'

'Yes.'

Not that she believed it for a second. 'Why were you going to kill him?'

'He made it personal.'

'How?'

His gaze lowered to one of her hands when she set them on his forearms. 'Her name was Candice.'

Miranda felt an immediate surge of jealousy.

'I busted her a few times when I was with Vice.'

She exhaled the breath she was holding.

'When she fed me some useful pieces of information I put her on the payroll—one of them led to a drugs bust that took me to Narcotics.' He took a long, controlled breath. 'A month before I got assigned to Municipal Security her dealer changed and she witnessed something that could have put a major player behind bars. I said I'd protect her if she agreed to give evidence in court but left her alone to chase the lead. By the time I got back she was dead.'

'What happened?'

'He beat her to death with a baseball bat.' The hand at the end of his good arm moved from her hip to tunnel underneath her sweater in a way that suggested he needed to feel the warmth of her skin. 'I recruited her. I ignored the danger she was in and it got her killed. To him it was business. To me it was personal.'

With the explanation, how seriously he'd taken *her* safety made perfect sense to Miranda. She ran a palm up his arm, across his shoulder and raised it to his jaw, waiting for him to look into her eyes before she spoke. 'I know you well enough to know if you thought something might happen to her you would never have left her alone. You'd have fought for her, Tyler—taken the beating for her if you could, died if it meant saving her life.'

While trying to bring her murderer to justice he almost had.

'I should have known the risk.'

'If you think worst-case scenario in every situation…' The realization it was exactly what he'd been doing twisted her heart. 'That's why you saw potential threats everywhere you looked when you became my bodyguard, isn't it?'

'Partly,' he admitted reluctantly, before pressing his mouth into a thin line. 'If I tell you something you have to promise not to freak out.'

Meaning she wasn't going to like it…

'The guy outside the movie theatre was the one I saw outside the school.' Long fingers flexed against her skin in reassurance. 'Lewis Rand was briefed but I need you to be careful until I track down the rest of the letter writers. There's only a couple more to go so—'

'Wait.' She interrupted. 'Are you talking about Paul?'

He frowned. 'Who the hell is Paul?'

'Dark hair, glasses, has a problem with the three-second handshake rule.'

'You *know him?*'

Miranda nodded. 'He's a self-professed superfan. Re-Tweets everything I say on Twitter and tries to see me in the real world as often as he can. He's quite sweet really. His mother died a few years ago and I think he's lonely.'

'Great,' Tyler said flatly. 'I threatened Bambi.'

'You can apologize the next time you see him. If we get married he'll probably be outside the church…'

'*If* we get married?'

'We'll get to that in a minute.' Sliding her hand from his jaw to the back of his neck, she wriggled closer to the edge of the counter and locked her legs around the backs of his knees. 'Tell me about last night.'

'I couldn't take the shot.'

'Because you're not a murderer,' she said firmly.

'I wasn't sure any more. Was starting to forget who I was until I met you…' A corner of his mouth lifted to form another wry smile. 'It was part of the reason I told myself I couldn't sleep with you. Believe me when I say it had squat to do with not wanting you.' As if to prove the point his hand moved, the tip of his thumb grazing the lace on the underside of her breast while his eyes darkened. 'I got hooked with dance moves—wanted to take you hard and fast in the hall that night. There isn't a single inch of your body I don't want to kiss.' When his smile changed the returning hint of predator sent a sizzle of heat through her veins. 'You're gonna be spending a lot of time naked.'

Miranda blinked, consumed by the hunger in his eyes. 'You're wounded…'

The protest sounded unconvincing, even to her.

'I'm not *that* wounded,' he replied with conviction. 'Where you are right now works for me—or you on top, that would work, too… I've had a mental image of that one for a while now.'

Not that it had ever taken much but in a heartbeat her body was ready for him, the squirming movement she made on the counter creating a knowing gleam in his eyes.

'And now you're picturing it, aren't you?'

'I have a lot of those mental images,' she confessed. 'But before we start swapping them, I should warn you being the husband of a politician's daughter won't be easy.'

'*If* we get married?' he repeated in a lower, rougher, unbelievably seductive voice.

'You haven't proposed yet,' she pointed out as she ran her fingertips over the short hair at the back of his neck. 'What I'm saying is we've got time for you to ease into it. Knowing my father, he'll run for governor in a few years and when he does we'll be asked to stand onstage with him to show our support.'

'You'll still do that?'

'Not full time.'

'Gonna have to vote for him, aren't I?' Tyler asked as he focused his intense gaze on her mouth and leaned closer.

The tip of her tongue flicked over her lips. 'I won't tell if you don't. I'm Team Tyler all the way.'

'No, you're not. We're Team Us.' He stilled and leaned back to look into her eyes. 'At least we would be if you'd ever get around to saying you love me back.'

She fluttered her eyelashes in response. 'You hadn't figured it out already?'

When he raised his hand from her hip the grimace of pain was impossible to hide.

'What are you doing?'

'I'm moving into position to kiss it out of you. It's just not gonna be with this hand.'

'When's the last time you took pain meds?'

Lowering his bad arm, he freed the hand beneath her sweater so he could push aside damp tendrils of hair and wrap long fingers around the nape of her neck. 'Kissing you will take my mind off it.'

Before he turned her brain to mush Miranda framed his face in her hands and looked deep into his eyes so he could hear her loud and clear. 'Of course I love you. How could I not? I believe in you more than I've ever believed in anyone. I may have questioned why but it never felt wrong. The only thing that did was fighting how I felt.'

Something endearingly close to relief crossed his eyes before they darkened to the colour of stormy seas. 'That guy you talked about finding when you have your freedom—the one who'll spend time with you because he wants to and not because he's paid to do it? *It's me.*'

The depth of emotion he projected with his eyes combined with the strength of conviction in his deep voice removed any lingering doubt she had left about being enough for him. He wouldn't love her that much, want her that badly or bare his soul to someone he considered unworthy.

'It feels like I belong here,' she said in a voice thick with the same depth of emotion. 'There's something about you that makes me want to hold on and never let go. When I thought this was over—'

'We're just getting started,' he argued. 'You can make me angrier than any woman I've ever known but I'd still rather fight with you than make love with anyone else.'

'Ooh…that was *good...*' She raised her brows. 'Do you have more of those?'

When he laughed it was the most glorious, uplifting sound she'd ever heard. 'You have no idea how much I wanted to hear that again. You have a great laugh. You should do it more often.'

'You know you're not going home tonight, right?'

'I *am* home.' She tore her gaze away to flick a brief glance over his shoulder. 'But you might need more closet space before I move in. Wow. You have a lot of books.'

A light kiss was placed on the corner of her mouth. 'I like to read.'

'You can't have read all of them.'

'Yes, I can, and you could sound less surprised.' He bestowed another kiss on her eager lips. 'What's more I remember them word for word. You can pick a page later.'

Miranda felt the heat coiling low in her abdomen. 'You have a photographic memory?'

'The term is didactic and I plan to rewrite the rules by filling my memory with images of you. The look on your face when I propose…' Kiss. 'How beautiful you are when you walk down the aisle…' Kiss. 'When you hold our first child…' Kiss. 'Wiping away your tears when we attend their graduation…' Kiss. 'We're gonna make a lifetime of memories and when it's my time I'll take every one of them with me and die a happy man.'

The demonstration of how much he'd been holding back created a swell of emotion it was impossible to contain, joy leaking from the corners of her closed eyes as she leaned her forehead against his. 'I love you *so much.*'

'And I love you. Don't ever doubt that.' He leaned back and waited for her to open her eyes before adding, 'Still questioning what I did to deserve you but I reckon I've got at least sixty years to figure it out.'

When he winked, Miranda grinned. He was all the fun she would ever need. As he went to work with remarkable one-handed dexterity on the buttons down the centre of her sweater she answered his question in a way that made perfect sense to a woman whose childhood belief in happily-ever-after had been renewed.

'That's the thing about rescuing the princess from her ivory tower.' She kissed his crooked smile. 'Once he does, the hero of the story is kinda stuck with her after that.'

* * * * *

COMING SOON!

We really hope you enjoyed reading this book. If you're looking for more romance, be sure to head to the shops when new books are available on

Thursday 25th July

To see which titles are coming soon, please visit

millsandboon.co.uk/nextmonth

For exclusive extracts, competitions and special offers, find us online:

facebook.com/millsandboon

@MillsandBoon

@MillsandBoonUK

Get in touch on 01413 063232

For all the latest titles coming soon, visit

millsandboon.co.uk/nextmonth